BURIED DREAMS

BURIED DREAMS

BRENDAN DuBOIS

THOMAS DUNNE BOOKS
ST. MARTIN'S MINOTAUR ✹ NEW YORK

MYSTERY

DuBois, Brendan.

Buried dreams

THOMAS DUNNE BOOKS.
An imprint of St. Martin's Press.

www.minotaurbooks.com

Library of Congress Cataloging-in-Publication Data

DuBois, Brendan.
    Buried dreams / Brendan DuBois.—1st ed.
        p. cm.
    ISBN 0-312-32731-5
    EAN 978-0312-32731-6
    1. Cole, Lewis (Fictitious character)—Fiction. 2. Hampton Beach
(N.H.)—Fiction. 3. New Hampshire—Fiction. 4. Journalists—Fiction.
I. Title.

PS3554.U2564B87 2004
—dc2'

                                                              2003069538

First Edition: July 2004

10 9 8 7 6 5 4 3 2 1

WITH THANKS TO THE AUTHORS
LARRY NIVEN AND DAVID GERROLD
WHO IN 1977 ONCE TOLD A YOUNG MAN
HE, TOO, COULD BE A WRITER SOME DAY

ACKNOWLEDGMENTS

The author wishes to express his thanks and appreciation to his wife, Mona Pinette, for her sure touch as an editor; to Bill Lautler for his technical support; to his St. Martin's Press editor, Ruth Cavin; and to his agent, Liza Dawson. And a special thanks to all those who love, cherish, and preserve the history of my home state.

BURIED DREAMS

CHAPTER ONE

The funeral service at Our Lady of the Miraculous Medal church in Tyler, New Hampshire, started right on time, ten a.m. on a rainy Saturday in October. I took the first pew to the left, just after escorting the casket down the center aisle of the church on a wheeled metal framework. Earlier I had helped five other men wrestle the heavy piece of wood and metal from the rear of the black coach—not a hearse, that word isn't used anymore—and up the granite steps through the open door, the steps slippery from the cold rain. The casket was draped with a white cloth with an embroidered gold cross that had been placed on it as it entered the church, temporarily replacing the American flag that denoted respect for a veteran.

Respect. What a concept. I spared a quick glance around the cool interior of the church, at the dozen or so people who had come here. The priest was before the altar, starting the service, and I looked at the faces of the people sitting in the hard wooden pews, recognizing a handful of Tyler residents who were active on town boards and organizations, plus a young couple, sitting by themselves, near the front. There were other faces as well: Detective Diane Woods, looking somber and sitting by herself, here in a variety of capacities, I'm sure, since she was leading the investigation of what had occurred that had led to this funeral. Sitting two rows behind her was Paula Quinn, reporter for the Tyler *Chronicle,* who gave me a quick smile as she saw my look, reporter's notebook held steady in her hands. She was here doing her job as well, recording what was happening for the benefit of the *Chronicle's* readers this coming Monday. And sitting by himself, nearly halfway to the rear of the church, as if being in a house of God was making him nervous, was Felix Tinios, a resident of North Tyler and a previous inhabitant of Boston's North End. Felix wasn't here in any kind of role that demanded his skills—dutifully noted each year on his IRS Form 1040 as a security consultant—but was here just for me, a gesture that I found quite moving, coming from a man such as Felix.

I turned around and looked at the young priest, going on about heaven and peace and mourning, and I glanced over at the casket— coffin was another forbidden word—and thought of the remains that were within that expensive piece of work: Jon Ericson, army veteran, retired accountant, amateur historian, and, for a brief time, my friend.

I folded my arms and stared straight ahead, past the priest to the stained glass window, wet from the continuing rain.

It had been a day late in May earlier that year when I had first met Jon, near my house on Tyler Beach. It had warmed up fairly well for a home right on the ocean, and I was on the rear deck, feet up on the railing, reading that day's Boston *Globe.* I was deciding whether to go to the editorial page or the comics section—each with its own partic- ular brand of amusement—when a voice from below nearly caused me to drop the damn thing. "Hello up there," came the male voice. "Any chance for a drink of water?"

I lowered the paper and looked over the railing. My house is one of the most isolated on the eighteen miles of New Hampshire coastline, an isolation I've always enjoyed. To the south were the wide and popular sands of the resort community Tyler Beach, blocked off by a jumble of boulders and rocks, and to the north was the Samson Point State Wildlife Preserve. Both directions usually meant a lack of visitors, which suits me just fine. This particular visitor was a guy about thirty years older than me, wearing knee-high rubber boots, dark green chino work pants and shirt, and with a small knapsack on his back and what looked to be a metal detector in his hands. I usually don't like unexpected visitors, but something about his expression made me smile. He looked like a guy who expected strangers to be friendly and open, and I wasn't in the mood to ruin his expectation.

"Sure," I said. "I'll be right down."

In a minute I was through the kitchen, filling up a glass of water, and went out the front door. My scraggly lawn rose up to a ridge of rocks that hid my home from the coastal road, Route 1-A, and I went around to the ocean side of the house, where my visitor was sitting on a large boulder, feet stretched out before him. His eyes were bright behind black horn-rimmed glasses, and he took off his Red Sox baseball cap to scratch at what was left of a fringe of light brown hair, circling around. The metal detector was at his side, like some old lance for a medieval knight, and cupped around his neck were the earphones for the apparatus. Standing next to him, I realized he looked vaguely familiar. He took the glass and swallowed about half of the water, and then held out his free hand.

"Jon Ericson," he said. "Thanks for the water."

I shook his hand. "Sure, and I'm—"

"Lewis Cole," he interrupted, smiling. "Resident of Tyler Beach and columnist for *Shoreline* magazine, out of Boston. Correct?"

Maybe I should have been paranoid, but he was smiling like he had just won a small prize, so I gave it to him. "Correct on both counts. We haven't met before, have we?"

He swallowed the remaining water. "No, we haven't met, but I've seen you at a few local functions. Occasional selectmen's meeting, planning board meeting, town meeting in March. I'm a rarity in this community, a native of Tyler. Born and raised here, spent thirty years in this man's army, going to Europe and parts of Asia, before coming back home where I belonged. I like to keep track of what's going on in my town. And who's living here. And you, Lewis? Your history?"

"Born here in the state, moved to Indiana when I was a kid. Came back here a few years ago when I decided I missed the place."

"So you have," he said, his voice the tone of someone who knew a lot about you and wasn't about to let on what he did know.

I took the empty glass back from him. "And what are you up to today? Treasure hunting?"

"You could say that."

"Why here, and not down at the beach?"

"Where all the tourists show up?" He shook his head. "Not likely. The sands down there get picked over before the sun goes down and the seagulls have finished eating food scraps. I like to go to isolated places."

"Like this one?"

He wiped at his bald scalp, put his frayed cap back on. "In a manner of speaking. There was a wild storm here two days ago, remember?"

"Sure," I said. "Left the doors open to my deck, wind blew in a lot of water to my living room floor."

"Well, Lewis, the wind can blow a lot of things around, with help from the waves. Stuff gets dumped from a shipwreck or something being blown overboard, it tends to sink and have dirt and debris build up on it. After a good storm, stuff gets uncovered, stirred up, so you can find things that have been hidden for hundreds of years. I like to go out after a nice big storm. You'd be surprised at what pops up."

I looked out to the constant movement of the waves, spotted a container ship, beating its way north to Porter, out by the horizon's edge. "Find anything today?"

"Nope," he said, standing up. "But I will. Guaranteed."

That made me smile. "Why guaranteed?"

"Because I know my history, that's why." His expression then changed a bit, as if he was transforming himself into a teacher, and he said, "That's something you should think about, the next time you take pen to paper. Or keyboard to computer screen, whatever it is you do, the next column you write for your magazine. Know your history, get it straight."

"Saying I got something wrong?" I asked.

A quick nod. "Yep. Two months ago. You did a column about the strange buildings and structures along the seacoast. Said something about those spotting towers, look like concrete lighthouses. Right?"

"Sure," I said. "Spotting towers for German U-boats."

A shake of the head, like a dad explaining the real truth about Santa Claus to a youngster. "Sorry. That's an old tale, one that gets passed around, years and years after the real story. Nope. Those towers were used for the old coast artillery emplacements, to spot targets out on the water. Not U-boats. Surface craft coming in to attack the

4

shipyard at Porter. Not as thrilling as hunting U-boats, but the truth, Lewis. The truth. Get your history right and everything follows."

Jon got up and said, "Time to get going. Thanks for the water."

"Thanks for the correction," I said, as he headed back down to the rocky shoreline, his back stooped over, his head lowered, looking for some kind of buried dream.

Inside the cool church, I shifted in my seat, looked around again, at the few faces, all looking up toward the priest performing his role. The priest caught my eye and nodded, and then I got out and went up the center aisle, to the lectern near the altar. I turned and pulled a folded piece of paper from my inside coat pocket. I had wanted to write something about Jon and his life and his work, his love of history and dedication to the town, but the priest had gently persuaded me to go with a traditional Bible verse. This was a church sacrament, not a memorial to one man's life, and I didn't feel like fighting, so I stood there at the lectern, reading the words written by some poor hungry soul thousands of years ago in some faraway desert.

The word were designed to provide comfort, provide some sort of understanding that in any time of trouble, life was wonderful and life went on, and we all went to our great reward.

But then and now, they were just words.

I next saw Jon Ericson a week later, about four miles away from my house, at the Meetinghouse Green, near the regional high school. Paula Quinn had called me in a panic, saying that her 35mm camera had quit on her, that the paper's full-time photographer was out on vacation, and could I please come up there with my own camera and save her perky little butt? And I had said of course I would, even though some other man in town currently got to see her perky little butt in more pleasurable moments. The Meetinghouse Green had a couple of dozen children racing around, trying to fly kites in the slight breeze, and it was a joy to see those eager and serious young faces, attempting to drag their little kites up in the air by running back and forth. Paula took my Canon 35mm with a quick kiss on my cheek and went to work. I stood back, seeing a familiar man behind a folding table, dispensing little paper cups of lemonade and chocolate chip cookies to the budding aeronautical engineers.

Jon Ericson looked up at me—dressed exactly the same as last time, except for no knee-length boots—and said, "Things so tough as a columnist, you're looking for free food?"

"Nope," I said. "And you know what? Those spotting towers, in addition to looking for warships, also kept an eye out for U-boats during the big one back in the forties. So I wasn't totally wrong."

He handed out another cup of lemonade. "That's the problem with history nowadays. There are no longer facts. It's always interpretation, looking at things from one point of view or another. There's gay history, feminist history, oppressed people's history. Bah. History is history. It shouldn't be used as a tool to advance somebody or some group's agenda."

"And what's your agenda today? Enjoying the sight of the youth of Tyler?"

"Sure," he said, smiling. "And I get to pick up and clean up when it's done. Want to help?"

And I think I surprised both of us when I said yes. An hour later, the kite-flying competition, sponsored by the Tyler Recreation Department, ended and Paula give me back my camera, sans film, and left me with Jon and some fold-up chairs and about six or seven garbage bags full of cups, napkins, and half-chewed cookies. We brought everything into the rear of a one-story wood building that was the Tyler Town Museum, and I was embarrassed to note that this was the first time I had ever set foot into the place. Jon gave me a look and said, "Want the grand tour?" and I said sure.

It wasn't grand, and wasn't much of a tour. The museum was small, and as Jon explained, existed on the charity of the few visitors, a trust fund set up a half century ago, and the generosity each year of those Tyler citizens who went to town meeting every March and approved a small appropriation. There were two rows of locked glass cases on wooden legs, and some framed certificates and old prints up on the cracked plaster walls, along with a couple of Civil War–era swords. The artifacts in the glass cases ranged from the Native Americans—bits of broken pottery and stone fishhooks and arrowheads—to the first settlers—an old musket and a stitched sampler—all the way up to memories of the Greatest Generation—ration books and captured Japanese flags—who had marched out of Tyler more than a half century ago.

Jon said, "Not much, but it's treasure, still the same, and should be guarded as such." I followed him out the rear door and said, "Do you run the museum?"

That brought a laugh. "Sort of. Just a volunteer and sometime tour guide and curator, when I don't piss off the board of directors."

"Anything you find out on the shoreline end up here yet?"

His mood then suddenly changed, and his voice was more quiet. "No, not yet. But it will. One of these days. Look, can I trust you?"

"In what way?"

Jon said, "Trust that whatever I tell you won't end up in your column. And I don't mean that I think you'll make something off what I have to say in some big scoop or something. I just don't want to be embarrassed by some snide and snotty column down the road about the local lunatic in Tyler. Okay?"

"Fine," I said. "You can trust me then."

We walked around to the other side of the museum, where a large stone was set up with a dark plaque commemorating the Tyler men who had fought and died in the Civil War. Farther away from this stone was a round structure of bricks, about knee-high, that looked to be the top of a well. We reached it and I looked down, past a grillwork of metal bars. In the dirt below the bars was a boulder, flat on top, with grooves or scratches on top. A plaque nearby identified it as THORVALD'S ROCK.

"Who was Thorvald?" I asked.

"Ah, there you go," he said. "My chance to be the tour guide for one more time. Thorvald was supposedly the younger brother of Leif Eriksson, who left Iceland to raise a settlement at Greenland around the year 1000 A.D. or thereabouts. From Greenland, Leif and his brethren went further west, and eventually met up with the Canadian coastline, where they discovered a land covered with vines and grapes that they called Vinland."

"Newfoundland," I said, recalling a newspaper article I had read years ago. "Someplace in Newfoundland, they formed a settlement. Something meadows, am I right?"

"Very good," he said. "It's nice to run into someone who actually reads and retains knowledge, Lewis. For a number of years they had a settlement at a remote village in Newfoundland that's now called L'Anse aux Meadows. In this town there were old mounds near the coastline that no one quite knew where they came from, until they were excavated in the 1960s through the work of a Norwegian writer named Helge Ingstad. At first nobody believed that this was a Viking site, but excavation proved it. There were artifacts—tools, wool spinner, a blacksmith's anvil—that weren't Indian and were dated back to the tenth century."

"Eriksson," I said. "Your family name, perhaps?"

A smile. "Guilty as charged. I've always been proud of what my ancestors did back then, sailing out from Norway and Sweden on these wooden boats. Vikings sailed and traveled and traded with Rome and Moscow and Baghdad. They were great explorers, and I'm proud to have been descended from them."

"Including Thorvald?" I asked.

"Who knows?"

I looked down again at the rock with the scratches on it. "So why does this rock belong to Thorvald?"

"Another little history lesson, I'm afraid. You see, all the great Viking sagas mentioned Leif Eriksson discovering a new world, the place he called Vinland, where he established a settlement. But there's a problem with that site up in Newfoundland, even though it is a legitimate Viking settlement. You see, wild grapes never grew that far north. Vinland has to be farther south. Not Newfoundland."

Again, I looked at the rock. Some of the scratches looked like letters. "A Viking rock? This?"

"In a way, that's what the old histories of the town state. Supposedly this was found near Weymouth's Point, south of where you live. Thorvald was supposedly killed while exploring Vinland, and his body was buried where he fell."

"Who killed him? The Indians?"

"The same. Though the Vikings called them *skraelings*, an insulting term meaning wretch or something. So about a hundred years ago, this rock was found near Weymouth's Point, and those scratches on top of the rock are supposedly Viking runes, marking the burial spot of Thorvald, here, at Tyler Beach."

Out on the fields, some kids were still playing with their kites. "Some story," I said.

He laughed. "Yeah. Some story. And it's all crap. If those are runes, then I'm the pope. Best I can figure it, some land developer in the late 1800s came up with the tale, to help move some beachfront property. That's the story of the rock, though the town museum is too polite to say anything about it."

I thought about the first time I had met him. "So if the Vikings never came here, why are you out searching? Looking for something else?"

He looked at me and there was something in his eyes, something haunting, like a man seeing a dream from a very great distance, a distance he wasn't sure he'd be able to cross. "I never said the Vikings didn't come here, Lewis. I'm sure they did. And I'm going to find the evidence. Just you wait and see."

Back in my spot in the pew, I folded my arms as the priest continued the funeral mass. Rain continued to spatter against the stained glass. I found that my eyes kept on turning to the casket, not more than a handful of feet away. In that box and on the cushions were the remains of a man who had traveled the world, and loved and laughed and had lost, and through all of his days, had always fought to reach his dream.

Always.

An inadvertent encounter at the center of town one day, after I picked up at my mail at the post office, led to lunch at the Common Grill & Grill. After lobster rolls and chips for the both of us, I said, "Okay. Vikings. Why do you think they came here?"

He took a swallow from a Diet Coke. "They had to come somewhere south, didn't they?"

"Sure. But why New England? And why New Hampshire? We've got the shortest coastline in America. It seems the odds would be against it."

"I agree," he said. "Lewis, look. When I joined the army, they found out I had an aptitude for numbers. So I crunched numbers for the army, all thirty years that I was in their service. And when I came out of the service, I came back home to Tyler, crunched numbers again as an accountant. Had my own little firm. Me and the wife. More numbers, more crunching. Pretty dull, don't you think?"

"Seeing how terrified I am every April 15, I can see how it wouldn't be that dull."

He smiled, reached back, and pulled out his wallet. "But all those times, I had a dream I was following, a dream I had when I was a little kid. Look." From his wallet he retrieved a folded-over piece of white paper, which he handed over. I pulled it apart and saw a blurred photocopy of what looked to be a coin.

"All right," I said. "A coin. What about it?"

He put a finger on the paper. "That's a coin that was found up in Brooklin, Maine, in an excavation of an Indian camp near Blue Hill Bay. It's a Viking coin, minted between 1067 and 1093 A.D. Get that? About sixty-five years after the Viking settlement up in Newfoundland, a Viking coin found its way down to Maine."

"Maybe it got there through trade," I said. "Doesn't mean that it fell out of a Viking pouch on the Maine coastline."

"True," Jon admitted. "Except for one other thing. You see, I've seen another coin, just like that."

"Where?"

"On Tyler Beach. Right after a storm."

I looked in his eyes, to see if he was joking, but there was nothing humorous in that gaze. "All right. When?"

"When I was kid. Thirteen years old. Even back then I was interested in history, and I did a lot of beachcombing, especially after big storms. This one was some unnamed nor'easter that came through, and I dug around and looked around, and found this same kind of coin. Right here in Tyler Beach."

I folded up the piece of paper, handed it back to him. "Where is it now?"

He shook his head. "Blame it on greed, blame it on stupidity, blame it on a younger brother. I brought it home and my parents didn't think anything about it, but my younger brother, Ray, he said I should sell it. To a coin collector, down in Newburyport. And whatever money I got, I could buy some model airplanes or some damn foolish thing. You see, Lewis, money was always tight when I was growing up. And maybe that's why I was good at numbers, keeping track of every spare penny or nickel. But we didn't have an allowance, didn't have much of anything. So we rode our bikes down to Newburyport and got a whopping ten dollars for that coin. I thought it was wonderful, and even back then, Ray was a sharp one. Demanded two bucks for a finder's fee or something."

"Did you know it was a Viking coin when you sold it?"

"Hell, no," he said, his voice loud enough to cause the other patrons to look around at us. "It was only years later, when I saw a story about the Maine coin, that I realized what I had found. But by then it was too late. The coin dealer had died, his store closed up, his records gone who knows where. Still blame Ray, years later." A furtive smile. "Even now, he's a wheeler-dealer. Runs an antique store up in Porter, manages to sell some things from me that I do find in my searches, old English and American coins, mostly. But I had that evidence, right in my hand, Lewis. Right in my little hands, and I know that they came here."

"You're going to need more than just a coin," I said.

He nodded slyly. "Oh, I've got a couple of leads. Just you wait. A couple of things I'm checking out."

"But where—"

He interrupted me, saying, "And speaking of checking things out, I think you should spring for the check. Don't you have an expense account or something?"

I picked up the check. "I certainly do."

Now the service was winding down, and I looked again at the sparse congregation, searching for that particular face of Ray Ericson, whom I had met exactly once, and who was the sole surviving relative of Jon Ericson.

And who wasn't here. At his brother's funeral.

I turned around, faced the front, where the priest was making the sign of the cross over the mortal remains of one Jon Ericson.

Perhaps feeling guilt over having stuck me with the check, or just feeling lonely, Jon invited me to a bachelor's dinner at his small home in Tyler. It was a traditional Cape Cod, set off one of the side streets that came out of High Street, one of the main avenues from the small downtown to the shores of the Atlantic Ocean. Inside it was neater than I expected for a bachelor—my own home sometimes has piles of newspapers, magazines, and books on the floor that involve a lot of tricky footwork, going from one room to a next—but when I pointed that out, Jon just laughed and said, "Army training. Always have to be neat."

Dinner was steaks on an outdoor grill, mashed potatoes—"my own secret recipe," he said, "sprinkle some grated Parmesan cheese through it"—and a salad, and for dessert he took me into his office.

There the neatness was cluttered up by homemade shelves along the walls, the shelves clustered with bits of stone, old coins, and barnacle-encrusted brasswork. "My collection," he said, motioning to it before sitting behind a wide oak desk. "Such as it is. Stuff that either I didn't want to give to my brother for sale, or stuff he thought wouldn't move."

I looked along the shelves, picking up some of the coins, rubbing the smooth metal, wondering what it must have been like to have the coins safely in one's pocket or luggage and then to fall desperately into the cold waters of the Atlantic, off the coast of Tyler, drowning within sight of safety. The coins felt old, the compasses and brasswork felt old, the whole damn room felt old. There was a smell to the room, as well, of dust and salt and things kept underwater for a very long time before being brought up to the surface. At his desk, Jon switched on a green-shaded lamp and reached behind him, to a crowded bookcase. He took an old volume out, the leather binding cracked and worn, and opened it up to what looked to be a familiar page for him.

"Come here, let me show you something," he said. I came around to his side of the desk and looked down at the book, which was opened to a woodcut illustration, showing an open field, with raised mounds, with men using teams of horses and plows to break through the mounds.

"Viking ruins? Like the ones up in Newfoundland?"

"That's what I'm thinking," he said, a thick finger tracing the old illustration. "This is a history of Wentworth County, written in 1850. There's this drawing and a two-paragraph reference, talking about a farm in Tyler that had these odd mounds on top of it, and how they were plowed under so that the farmer could expand his fields. Thing is, the Indians in this part of the world never had any structures like these. And this illustration looks exactly like the mounds up in Newfoundland."

"And who was the farmer back then?"

He sighed. "Damned if I know. I've gone through old newspapers, journals, microfilms, books, deeds, and about anything else with a written word on it. Not one of them ever mentions a farm in Tyler and old mounds on them that were plowed under. Not a single one." He tapped the illustration with his finger. "But there it is. The problem is, where's the location? There were scores of farms in Tyler at about that time, and you know what the development around here has been like. Chances are, that old farmland is under a parking lot or an office complex or the Interstate, for all I know. Still . . . those mounds and that coin, Lewis, are the best evidence I have about the Viking settlement here."

I kept quiet. Jon quickly broke the silence. "I know what you're thinking. Some evidence. One illustration in an old book, and the memory of a young boy that he in fact found a Viking coin, nearly a half century ago. But that's what I have." He closed the book and then looked out to the dark corners of the office, where the table lamp didn't illuminate. "That's what I have. A brother who I can hardly stand, and an ex-wife who got tired of traveling and tired of my tales, and who's living in Oregon. And a dream I won't give up on. Not ever. Not ever."

So I joined the procession, flanking the casket as we went back down the center aisle. The organist was playing some sort of recessional tune, and the sparse congregation stood up as we made our way to the open double doors. Again I looked around to see if Jon's younger brother had snuck in during the service, though I knew the chances of that happening were quite slim indeed.

Just before going outside, the church cloth was removed from the smooth metal top of the casket, replaced by the American flag. The men from the funeral home worked in the quick, spare movements of those who deal with the dead and the grieving week after week. I grasped one of the metal handles as we lifted the casket up, the metal cart underneath pulled away and folded up. We stepped out onto the wet steps, and I looked out to the parking lot, knowing that no, I would not see Jon's younger brother out there, for now Ray Ericson was more than just a brother, he was a suspect.

For three nights ago, I had gotten an excited phone call from Jon Ericson, saying he had finally found it, the evidence that Vikings had lived in our town of Tyler, and it seemed that soon after that, Ray had gone to Jon's house, where two shots from a 9mm pistol were fired into the back of Jon's head as he sat at his old desk in his old room.

The rain was cold on my face, as we wrestled the casket into the rear of the coach.

CHAPTER TWO

The first and only time I met Ray Ericson I went to see Jon after borrowing a book of his about the old lifeboat stations that were sprinkled up and down this stretch of the New England coastline, one of which eventually became the building that's my home.

There was a car parked in the driveway that wasn't Jon's—a small blue Dodge Colt with dented rear bumper—and when I went up to the door, I could make out shouting from inside. Just as I reached the cement steps leading into the front door, the door flew open and a short man tumbled out, built like a fireplug. He made it to the lawn, standing and swaying, and then fixed a bleary gaze in my direction. His bald head was wide and built close to his shoulders, his face was covered with stubble, and he wore a short-sleeve lime-green polo shirt that exposed his arms and the elaborate tattoos on both limbs.

"What the hell are you looking at?" he demanded.

"I haven't the foggiest idea," I said.

This answer seemed to irritate him, for he reared back and tossed a punch my way. I moved quick but not quick enough, and the punch grazed my shoulder and right ear. I stepped back and swerved, and when he came at me again, I got around his punch, stuck out a foot, and pulled him past me. He fell to the front lawn with a satisfying thump. I was deciding my options when Jon was next to me, looking down at the man, who was breathing hard, face very red, as he rolled over on his back.

"Ray," Jon said in a soft voice. "That's enough. You get along, right now, or I cut you off totally."

"The hell with you," he said.

"No, the hell with you," Jon said, arms folded. "I know you want more coins, more artifacts. But I'm doing what's important for me. Whatever I find extra goes to you. But I won't make a change in the way I work."

Now Ray's mood changed, as he sat up, dirt and a couple of strands of grass stuck to his back. "Jon, c'mon, you know your stuff moves really well, and you know you've got the nose for finding good stuff, really good stuff that can set the both of us up. And what do you waste your time on? Norsemen! Here, in Tyler Beach!"

Jon said, "The discussion is over, or I stop giving you anything. All right? Now, get up, apologize to my friend Lewis, and please leave."

Well, two out of three ain't bad. He did get up and he did leave, but not one more word was said to either of us. He got into the Colt, the back of his neck quite red, and slammed the door shut. As he backed out of the driveway, slammed the brakes, and then sped off, I said, "Nice guy."

"Nope. My brother. Definitely not a nice guy."

"Well, nice tattoos. I especially liked the flaming skull."

Jon sighed. "One of the many things he picked up in prison. Come on, let's go in."

Which is what we did.

I followed the short funeral procession from the church to the High Street Cemetery, driving behind a black Lincoln Town Car that was right behind the coach, or the hearse, if one wanted to be more traditional. The Town Car contained the workers from the Tyler Funeral Home, and I could not imagine what was being said in that dark car as we made our way to the burial ground. The rain was lightening up and my headlights were on. The little parade went up Lafayette Road, where a police officer in an orange raincoat stood at the intersection of Lafayette and High Street, holding up traffic for a moment, and we turned right, heading to Jon's final resting place.

The night after meeting his brother, I sat with Jon in his office, as he pulled out a photocopy of an old town map of the beach. He pointed to a little square on the map and said, "Recognize it?"

"Nope."

"You should," he said. "It's where you're living."

"Oh."

He looked around his office and said, with a touch of dismay in his voice, "My house was built in 1953 by the Hanratty Construction Company. It was first sold to Tom Hanratty, the son of Greg Hanratty, the owner of the company. Three other families have owned it since then besides me: the Glynns, the O'Hallorans, and the Peaces. That's the history of this place. Not much, but I know who built it and I know who's lived in it. And you . . . you've lived in one of the most historical sites in Tyler, and you don't know squat."

"I know it was a lifeboat station," I said, a little defensiveness creeping into my voice. "And I know it was officers' quarters when Samson Point was a coastal artillery site."

"Really? Did you know that over time, that lifeboat station was responsible for saving more than two hundred lives from shipwrecks up and down the New Hampshire seacoast? Did you know that one of the officers who resided in your home as an artillery officer became a general in World War I? And did you know that for a while, your house was going to be razed for a bomb shelter, during the cold war, when Samson Point was a radar station looking for Soviet bombers?"

"No, teacher," I said, trying to keep my voice soft. "I didn't know."

He took a breath, seemed to relax. "Sorry, I do go on, I know. I get passionate about history, and its mysteries." Then his head tilted some and said, "Speaking of mysteries . . . When Samson Point was shut down, back in 1963, your house had been used as a record storage area. Then it was transferred to the Department of Interior, and there it sat, year after year, boarded up and dusty. Until you came along."

"Unh-hunh." Since I had been retired from the Department of Defense (officially, for medical reasons, unofficially, for being the sole survivor of a particularly nasty and illegal training disaster), the question of how I actually got to live in this particular building occasionally came up with friends and acquaintances I've made during my time at Tyler Beach. And I have yet to have come up with a satisfactory reply for any of them. Like tonight.

"Not much of an answer," he said.

"Sorry, didn't hear a question there."

"All right," Jon said, a hesitant smile on his face. "I've always wondered how a house that belonged to the government came to be in your possession."

"Just one of those things."

"Really?"

"Yep."

Jon said, "Before you came here, you used to work at the Department of Defense. Then you left your job abruptly, and came to Tyler Beach, moving into a house with lots of history and which belonged to the government. How did that happen, Lewis?"

I waited, knowing my palms were moist. "I'm afraid that when I left government service, Jon, I had to sign a nondisclosure form about my service and reasons for leaving. Sorry."

He went back to the map. "Must have been a hell of a thing, then."

"Yeah," I said, not wanting to remember. "It was a hell of a thing."

At the High Street Cemetery, our little procession came to a halt as the rain decided to return with a vengeance, making the tombstones look old and worn. My shoes splashed through puddles and sank into the wet grass and soil as we proceeded to an area that was marked by a light green artificial rug, a mound of dirt, and some sort of contraption with canvas webbing and metal tubing that we placed the casket on. Since there were no close relatives, the flag was folded up by the funeral home personnel, and they moved back in a little group to join the rest of us, which included a handful from the church service, including Detective Diane Woods, Paula Quinn from the *Chronicle*, and Felix Tinios, and the young couple. The woman had red hair, and her companion was bearded. I nodded in appreciation at all of them, and then turned to the casket, the rain beading up on the wood and dribbling down the sides.

As someone held an umbrella over the priest, I looked at the mound of dirt, thinking about the events that had brought me here, events I had kept secret from Jon and everyone else in Tyler Beach. Once upon a time, as so many stories begin, I had been a research analyst at the Department of Defense, working in an obscure and secretive group that read and analyzed information. One day this little group—which included some dear friends and a woman I was madly in love with—went on a training mission to the high desert of Nevada, where disaster fell upon us. I was the sole survivor, and in exchange for keeping my mouth shut about what I had seen and what happened to us—a secret biowarfare experiment gone awry—I was pensioned off, given a job as a magazine columnist, and was also given the old house that Jon Ericson had been so interested in.

Looking at the casket, I wished I had opened my damn mouth when he had been asking so many questions.

It had been my turn for a barbecue, and when a late summer thunderstorm came racing through, we retreated to the interior of my house. We ate cheeseburgers and potato chips and carrot sticks and drank Sam Adams beer, listened to the Red Sox lose another one, and when they were finished, I asked, "How goes the Viking hunt?"

"It goes."

I got him another beer. "And where is it taking you?"

"Ah, well, that's a trade secret. But I'll pass it along to you, if you promise it won't end up in your next column."

"My next column is about fishing restrictions on George's Banks, so I think you're clear."

"All right." He hunched over the beer bottle, like he was protecting it or something, and he said, "I've decided to risk ridicule and everything that goes with it by telling other people what I've been up to. So that's what I've done, talking to folks."

"Like who?"

"Like an anthropology professor up at UNH. Like the head of

an Indian awareness group, over in Porter. Like the retired curator of the Tyler Town Museum, living up in Conway."

"Why those three?"

He took a careful sip from his beer. "Way I figure it, if the Vikings came here when I think they did, and if somewhere on a plot of land there were Viking remains, then somebody else might know about it. Thing is, they might have evidence and not know what they have. Like the Indians. Maybe there were old tales, old legends that they've kept to themselves. Or a strange artifact that doesn't make sense. Same thing with the anthropology prof, and the old curator. Maybe they have something that doesn't make sense to them, but would make a hell of a lot of sense to me."

"And what have you been able to find out?"

"Hmmm," he said. "Let's just say I've got a nice lead I'm following, and leave it at that."

"Really?"

"Really," he said. And like he did so often when he didn't want to go any further, he changed the subject. He swiveled on the stool at the countertop where we were eating. From the small kitchen, the view gave to the sliding glass doors out to the rear deck, my living room and stone fireplace with brick chimney heading up through the ceiling. "Hard to believe that this was actually officers' quarters, back when the artillery units were up and running. Man, there sure was a lot of reconstruction work since then, though. I doubt if much of the original woodwork is here. What's the basement look like?"

"Small, and dirt. Why? Want to take a look?"

He grinned. "Thought you'd never ask."

The door to the cellar was underneath the second-floor stairway, and we made our way down the steep steps, not going far before we reached the cool soil. I had a flashlight in my hand, for the basement light consists of a solitary sixty-watt bulb hanging from a cord. Before us, on concrete blocks, was my oil furnace, and further beyond was the oil tank. That was about it. But Jon wasn't interested in my heating system; he was interested in something else. He looked up and sighed and ran his fingers across the beams holding up the first floor. They were rough-hewn, pockmarked with worm holes, and didn't look like they had arrived here from a local lumberyard.

"There you go," he said. "Nice, original wood. When these

20

timbers were felled, my friend, we were still a nation half slave and half free. Imagine that."

I did, and it made me shiver, made me think of just how old my house was. Jon then knelt down and let his fingers trace through the cold dirt. "Ever find anything in here?"

"Like what? Viking rune stones?"

He shook his head. "No. Old bones. Broken bits of pottery. Coins."

"No, I haven't, but then again, I really haven't dug around my house."

He brushed the dirt off his fingers. "You should. You might be amazed at what you find."

"Shouldn't I let somebody else do it?"

Jon stood up, being careful not to knock his head against the beams. "Like who? A professional? Look, Lewis, the state of archaeology being what it is here in New Hampshire, I doubt anybody has any particular interest in what's around your house, except for you. The students and the state are looking at bigger, more important sites, especially places where a highway's going through or there's other work that's going to permanently change the landscape. Like a gas pipeline or something. So don't be afraid of history, especially when it's on your land. It belongs to you just as much as anybody else. Remember, the first settlers came here in the 1620s. Think of that. Almost four centuries ago. There's a lot of history buried out there, and if you want to poke around in what's on your grounds, go right head."

"And if I find a Viking coin?"

"Oh, by all means, let me know," he said.

"Deal. But only if you let me in on it when you find what you've been looking for."

He seemed to think for a moment, and then stuck out his hand. I shook it.

"Deal," he said.

And that was the last time I ever saw him alive, standing there, a smile on his face, in the tiny basement of my old house.

Now the ceremony was over and my throat got thick, as the priest turned away and so did the funeral crew. Standing under an old maple tree, its fall leaves of orange and red and yellow still hanging on, were two men in work clothes and yellow rain slickers, ready to do their work. I took a breath, felt it catch, rubbed at my eyes. That was it. Done. And very shortly Jon was to be returned to the soil that he had such delight in exploring.

I rubbed at my eyes again, rainwater now dripping down the back of my neck.

And so it happened, on a late afternoon when I decided to catch a movie at the Tyler Cinema, a four-screen theater near the center of town. One of the many advantages of being a magazine columnist—besides working out of the home and having a very liberal monthly deadline—was the ability to have a schedule that let me do pretty much anything I wanted to do, day in and day out. On this particular day, one of the screens of the Tyler Cinema was being dedicated to a rerelease of a great old science fiction film from 1950, *Destination Moon*. I sat by myself in the middle of the theater, sharing it with about a half-dozen other moviegoers scattered around, and cheerfully munched on popcorn and drank a Coke and admired the half-century-old special effects, which still held up pretty well.

After the movie let out, I joined a copy of that day's *New York Times* with a light dinner at the Mooring Line, a fine old restaurant right next door to the movie theater. Dinner was a crock of French onion soup, a salad, and three jumbo shrimp, a glass of merlot, and a healthy dose of attitude from the *Times*'s editorial page. And then I left for home, and when I got there, about fifteen minutes later, I spotted the blinking green light on my answering machine, and the solitary numeral one. I punched the play button and after a long *whir-whir-whir,* from the tape, Jon's voice came up from the tiny speaker:

"Hey, Lewis . . . It's about five o'clock . . . Hey, you're not going to believe it, but I found it! I've got the evidence!"

He laughed on the tape and I looked down at the little speaker, hearing the syllables come pouring out, listening to the excited and happy tone in his voice, as he went on and on: "All these long years . . . man, I've got it in my hands, Lewis. No doubt about it . . . Two carvings, an ax blade, a spinning stone . . . real, live Viking artifacts, found right here. Jesus!"

Another bout of laughter. "Look, call me when you can. I'm gonna put 'em in a safe place and give somebody else the news . . . time to show somebody I knew what I was doing. Call me . . . Jesus! Can you believe it? I finally found it!"

With each sentence that he threw out, the hair was rising on the back of my neck. By God, he had done it. Jon had actually done it. I checked the clock in the kitchen, saw that it was 7:30 p.m. I picked up the phone and dialed Jon's number, and got a busy signal.

Another busy signal at 7:35 p.m.

And more at 7:40 and 7:45 p.m.

Viking artifacts. Here in my hometown. And my friend had just proved it.

I decided life was too short to spend on busy signals, so I got in my Ford Explorer and drove up the bumpy driveway, out to the parking lot of the Lafayette House, and within about ten minutes, I got to the neighborhood of Jon Ericson's house.

A whole lot of people had gotten there before me.

I pulled over and got out and just felt like I couldn't move, could not move a single limb. Yellow police evidence tape was stretched out all around his house, there were four Tyler police cruisers and the unmarked Ford LTD cruiser that belonged to the department's sole detective, Diane Woods. There was an ambulance there as well from the fire department, the blue-uniformed firefighters resting on the rear bumper, waiting. It was a horrible sight, seeing their relaxed casualness. Neighbors of Jon were clustered in tiny little groups around the perimeter of the yellow tape, talking to each other, pointing, wondering, discussing.

I found myself by the tape barrier, facing a Tyler police officer. His name tag said STYLES and he nodded at me like we were old friends, but for the life of me, I could not even remember anything about him. "Hey, Lewis," he said.

"Hey, yourself," I said, knowing how weak my voice sounded. "What's going on?"

He shook his head. "Crime scene. That's all I can say."

"What kind of crime?"

Another head shake. "Sorry. Can't say."

"Diane Woods. I need to speak to her."

"You know she's busy in there."

"I know," I said. "But I've got information about what might have happened."

Styles looked at me suspiciously. "You're not shitting me, are you?"

"No."

"Because if you are . . ."

"It's the truth. Tell Diane that I'm out here, that I have some information."

He seemed to ponder that for a moment, and I kept looking at the house, hoping that maybe it was just a burglary, maybe a theft or simple assault or something, anything other than what I knew exactly had happened. Styles stepped away and spoke into his radio's microphone, "Unit twenty to D-one."

I heard the crackle of static. Nothing else. He tried again. "Unit twenty to D-one."

Then Diane's voice came out. "D-one, go ahead."

"Have a witness here to speak to you. Says he has information."

"I'll be right out."

"Okay," Styles said, returning to the crime scene tape. "Now we wait."

We didn't have to wait long. Diane came out of the front door, clipboard under her arm, wearing rubber gloves. Her brown hair was longer now, tied back in a simple ponytail, and she had on black sneakers, jeans, and a blue windbreaker with the Tyler Police Department insignia on the side. When she saw me she didn't look happy, and the short scar on her chin—from a drunk who fought with her once long ago in the station's booking room when she was a patrol officer—was blazing white, always a danger sign.

I beat her to it when she got close enough. "This is legit," I said. "I'm not spoofing you."

"Good," she said, her brown eyes glaring at me. "Because I'm not in the mood. What's going on?"

"Please," I said. "Jon, is he . . ."

Then the look in her eyes faded away and she said, "A buddy of yours, wasn't he? Yeah, I'm afraid so. Shot, Lewis."

"Shit," I said.

She opened up the metal lid on her clipboard. "Lewis, the investigation is just starting, so if you've got something, let's get to it."

"He was alive at five p.m."

She started scribbling on the clipboard. "How do you know that?"

"He called and left a message on my answering machine. He said it was five p.m. I'm sure phone records will back that up."

"Unh-hunh, okay, that's good," she said. "What kind of message did he leave you?"

A secret, he once said. Can you keep a secret?

But the time for secrets was gone. "Okay, this is going to sound crazy, but Jon's a treasure hunter. He's been looking for artifacts for all these years, looking for Vikings."

She looked up from the clipboard. "What?"

"Vikings. I know it sounds crazy, but he was convinced that Vikings had settled here, almost a thousand years ago. He's been looking for those artifacts, ever since he got out of the army."

"Still not spoofing me?" she asked.

"Still not spoofing you. And that's what the message said. That he finally found the artifacts, after a decade of looking."

Diane looked up from her clipboard and said, "Hell of a thing, to find something you've been looking for, all these years, and get murdered right afterward."

"Yeah, it's a hell of a thing, and I think I know who you might want to talk to."

"Who?"

"His brother, Ray Ericson. Runs an antique store up in Porter, ex-con. Not very friendly and the two of them have had words before."

"What kind of words?"

"While looking for Vikings, Jon also manages to find other things. Like coins, old nautical artifacts, stuff like that. What he didn't like or didn't want to keep, he passed on to his brother to sell. But his brother thought the whole Viking thing was a waste of time."

"Unh-hunh," she said, scribbling some more in her clipboard. "I'm going to need to talk to you later, Lewis. After we clear the scene and figure out where we're headed."

"Look, can I come in and—"

Diane took a hand from the clipboard and gently touched my shoulder. "My friend, there's nothing you can do in there for him. It's

25

my job now. Please let me do it. You've already done enough, giving me that phone information. Just let me be and we'll talk later, okay?"

I nodded, finding it hard to talk.

Diane turned and went back into Jon's house. I stood on the street, hands in my coat pockets, and waited in the growing darkness, waited until my feet hurt and my stomach growled, waited until my throat hurt from being thirsty, waited until there was some movement from the firefighters and they went into the house with a collapsible gurney and came out a few minutes later with a shrouded shape on the wheeled stretcher that had once been my friend.

Then I left.

I started walking past the grass and Paula Quinn came up to me, smiling and then giving me a quick kiss on the cheek. "You okay?"

"Not particularly."

She motioned with her reporter's notebook. "I'll do a good write-up on him, don't you worry. It'll be in Monday's paper. Do you have anything you want me to put in the story?"

Something sharp started making its way around my tongue and lips, and then I forced myself to stop. Paula was just doing her job, was doing what she did best, and I smiled and said, "No, not really. I'll trust your good judgment."

Paula said, "All right, but if you change your mind, call me before ten a.m. on Monday, before deadline. Okay?"

"Fine," I said, and then Diane Woods made her way over and said, "Tough day."

"You got that," I said.

"I'd like to have a couple of words with you, if you don't mind."

"For you, detective, name the place and time."

She said, "All right. How about in an hour, at Jon's house?"

"For real?"

"Yes, for real. I've got a couple of more questions for you. And something else."

"Like what?"

Diane looked over at a man standing by himself under an oak tree. "Let's just say we need to come to an understanding. All right?"

"Sure."

Diane went over to her unmarked police cruiser, and I went over and joined the solitary man, Felix Tinios, wearing a long black cloth raincoat, a tweed driving cap, and some kind of boots that looked like they cost about as much as my monthly food budget. Felix shrugged as I got closer and said, "Tough thing, going through a funeral like this. Practically alone."

I stood next to him and watched as the workers did their job, tossing dirt into the open hole. I flinched as I heard the wet slapping sound of the dirt hitting the wooden surface of the casket.

"Some were here," I said.

"But not much. Back home in the North End, a guy this old, a funeral would last all afternoon, and the line of cars would be going out the gate and out to the street."

"Yeah."

I noticed Felix staring straight ahead, and then he shifted his weight from one foot to another. "You looking for help?"

"I am. How much?"

"Please. This one is gratis. What do you need?"

"I need to find his younger brother. It looks like he's the one who did it."

"Okay," Felix said. "What are you going to do once I find him for you?"

"Let nature take its course," I said.

Felix looked over at me, the stubble on his face blue-black against the dark skin. "You mean, give him a fair trial and then kill him?"

"Sounds good to me."

Felix turned back to the open grave, slowly being filled. "No argument from me."

"Thanks," I said.

"Don't mention it," Felix said.

CHAPTER THREE

I went home quickly after the burial and got changed into dry clothes, and then drove back over to Jon's house. Diane's unmarked cruiser was in the driveway and I felt a bit irritated, as if it didn't belong there. I pulled in on the street, got out, and walked up to the house. Every other house in this stretch of suburbia had its lawn cleared of leaves, save this one, and that bothered me as well. I would have to take care of it. I looked at the house and saw that the shades were drawn, and it struck me as appropriate. A house where someone lived and breathed and was then murdered should always hide its insides from the shame.

Diane met me at the door, held it open for me as I went in. The door frame was dirty, covered with the dark gray dust of fingerprint powder. The living room was lit up, but everything looked wrong for me, out of place, and I figured it out in just a moment. The furniture had all been moved around by Diane and her fellow officers, and the pieces had not been put back in their proper places. She sat down on a couch and I took a chair, and she said, "This has been tough for you. I'm sorry."

"Thanks," I said.

"Now, I'm going to say something, and you're not going to like it."

"Okay."

"Leave it be."

"Excuse me?"

She managed a smile. "We've known each other for a long while, my friend, and I know what drives you. You're the one who gets wound up over friends of yours who get hurt or get cheated or who are otherwise harmed. That's one of your many charms."

"If that's true, then my charm hasn't worked well with you."

"Then blame genetics," she said. "And I'm going to have to blame your genetic makeup as well. You have this drive for justice. So do I. And you and I both have the same goals, and that's to bring the shooter in. Okay? And if the shooter is going to be appropriately punished, it's going to happen because the case I have against him is rock solid, with a long string of good evidence, none of it tainted by a vengeful magazine writer whose history and background will be so much raw meat for any half-wit defense attorney. Have I made myself clear?"

"Perfectly."

"Good," she said.

"Have you found the brother yet?"

She shook her head. "No, but we're running him down."

"Is he the lead suspect?"

Diane crossed her legs. "Look, you're getting right into it, all right? Let's say this. He's someone we want to talk to, very badly."

"You got anything besides what I've told you about their history together?"

She moved one leg back and forth. "Last answer from me. Okay?"

"Fine."

"Next-door neighbor saw the brother come to the house the day of the shooting."

"What time?"

"Just after five p.m."

I nodded. "Right after Jon called me."

"Exactly."

I looked around the living room, recalled the times I had spent here with him, talking and drinking and discussing town gossip or the latest news, but always, always, the conversation would veer back to history, the history of the town, the state, the country. And, of course, once we started talking history, we would always end up discussing his obsession, the evidence that his Norse ancestors had walked the same soil that he did. Just last month, each of us drinking a Molson Golden Ale, he clenched his fist and tapped it on the couch's armrest: "I'm close, Lewis. God, I am so close. And when I get that evidence, a lot of people are going to eat crow, and I'm going to be right there to serve it."

"The Vikings," I said.

"Yeah, the Vikings," Diane said. "You know, the few homicides I've investigated in Tyler have all revolved around the big two: love and money, and of those, I prefer money. Usually the love is an obsessive love, like some creep boyfriend who can't take no for an answer. Money is so straightforward. Somebody has something valuable that somebody else wants to take, and wouldn't mind killing to do it."

Then she uncrossed her legs and stood up. "But I've never had a homicide that might have something to do with thousand-year-old visitors to Tyler Beach. Look, can you do me a favor?"

"Sure."

"You've been here before," she said. "Can you tell me if anything's missing, anything out of the ordinary that we might have overlooked?"

The inside of my mouth was starting to feel pasty. "I guess that means going into his office."

Diane came over to me. "You up to it?"

"Yeah," I said. "I am."

"Okay," she said. "Let's do it."

The walk was short but my heart rate went up about ten percent with each step that took me closer to Jon's office. The lights were on and I tried to ignore the desk in the center of the room, which was about as easy as ignoring the proverbial elephant in the living room. Oh, what the hell, Jon would have laughed at seeing how queasy I had become—"most of history is written in blood and violence, no way to get around it"—and so I stared at the desk. The bloodstains had turned to a crusty red, and there was spatter on the hood of the nearby lamp. The chair had been moved back, and there was a fresh stain in the leather, and the sadness of it all just struck me there, that poor Jon had soiled himself after being killed, after the sphincter muscles let loose.

"How do you think it happened?"

Diane said, "Best guess is that he knew the shooter. His body was found in his chair, his head and shoulders were on the desk. Looked like the shooter got him with two shots to the back of the head. A nine-millimeter round, it looks like. No spent cartridge casings on the floor, so our shooter was careful."

"And nobody heard the shot?"

"That's right."

I found that I was breathing pretty fast, so I forced myself to slow down and then look at the shelves, on both sides of the desk, remembering why Diane had brought me in here. I went up one shelf and down the other, seeing all the old things, all the old things that had been handled and owned by dead people, and I had another flash of realization, that the circle had come right back again. These possessions once owned by people dead and gone were now once again owned by the deceased. I looked to Diane and said, "I'm not a hundred percent positive, but it looks like everything's here. The coins, the brasswork . . . it doesn't look like anything's been taken."

Diane had been standing there, arms crossed. "True. Everything does look like it hasn't been moved—there's dust in and around the shelves that hasn't been disturbed—but there's one thing missing from this house."

Oh, Jon, I thought. Taken away from you so soon.

"The Viking artifacts," I said. "He told me on the phone message that he was going to put them in a safe place."

Diane nodded. "Maybe he did, but Lewis, we've gone through everything in this house, in his car, and out in the yard. If the artifacts were here, they're gone."

"Then the shooter has them," I said.

"Sounds reasonable, doesn't it?"

"Yeah," I said.

As we went back out to the living room, Diane said to me, "Besides the brother, is there anything else you can offer me?"

I stopped, thinking about just that question, and I said, "No, I can't. His brother has done time, up in Concord. I saw the two of them have a violent disagreement over Jon's artifacts, and his hunt for the Vikings. Besides that . . . Just find him, Diane, all right? Just find him."

Then there was a flash of steel behind those calm brown eyes, and I didn't envy the next few weeks of Ray Ericson's life. "You can bet the house on that, Lewis. You surely can."

Outside a wind had come up, but at least the rain had stopped. I walked Diane over to her cruiser and I said, "How's Kara?"

"Kara is fine," she said, opening the door.

"You two moving in any time soon?"

She laughed. "Nice to know you're so concerned about my love life. How about you?"

"Excuse me?"

"The lovely Miss Quinn of the *Chronicle*. You still going to let the town lawyer have full dibs on her?"

"Mister Mark Spencer? I don't think I have a say in it. It's Paula's choice."

Diane sat down behind the steering wheel. "If you say so. But I think it's your decision as well, and by not doing anything, well, you've already made your choice. Correct?"

I gently closed the door on her, my last words: "Forget my love life and go find a killer."

I'm not sure if she heard me, but at least she was smiling as she drove away. Then she halted in the street, backed up, and lowered her window. "One more thing."

"Yes?"

"Remember what I said. Leave it be."

I nodded. "I remember."

"Good."

And when the cruiser was out of sight, I said in a low voice, "I remember, but I didn't promise anything, Diane. Not a damn thing."

I was heading back to my Explorer when I saw the two boys in the front yard of a house just two down from Jon's place. They were working on the lawn, moving about rakes that were about as tall as they were. They looked up at me and I saw that they were brothers, maybe a couple of years apart, wearing baggy jeans and thin down vests. The smaller of the two had a runny nose.

"Hey, there," I said.

"Unh-hunh," the older one said.

"You guys good with those rakes?"

The older one kept quiet but his brother said, "Dad says we spend more time playin' with the leaves then rakin' 'em."

"Tell you what," I said, taking my wallet out. "You know Mister Ericson's house, up there?"

Now it was the older brother's turn. "The guy who got killed."

"Right, the guy who got killed," I said. "How much to rake his yard?"

The younger one said, "You mean, in money?"

"That's right."

The two brothers looked at each other and not wanting Mom or Dad to come out and give me hell about talking to their boys without permission, I took out two ten-dollar bills. I passed one to each of them. "Here," I said. "Do a good job, okay?"

They both looked surprised and didn't say anything, but I was glad when I got to my Explorer; They were both racing up the sidewalk, dragging their rakes behind them, as they went to Jon's yard.

At home I made a fire in the fireplace—a strange phrase, I know, since it's the only place one should really make a fire—and checked the phone messages. Nothing new. I hesitated for a moment, thinking it would be nice to hear Jon's voice again, coming out of the speaker, but I thought that was just a bit too ghoulish. I was tired and achy and hungry, and made a ham and cheese and mushroom omelette for lunch, and ate it while sitting on the couch, balancing the plate on my knees, while I spent a quiet afternoon watching a documentary on the History Channel about Allied bombing tactics during World War II. The History Channel has been one of my great joys and frustrations for television viewing, for it's a great place to escape the mindless chatter on the bulk of my other cable channels, but it's also a great place to lose chunks of valuable time.

But today, losing time was a good thing, for it allowed me not to think about how I had dealt with Diane, my oldest friend in Tyler. For when she had asked me if I had anything more to offer, I knew I should have said something about what Jon had mentioned weeks ago. Three people. Jon had gone to three people, looking for more information on that farm site in Tyler that supposedly had contained a Viking settlement before being plowed under. I didn't know their names, but I knew their occupations—anthropology professor, American Indian activist, and retired Tyler museum curator—and I also knew one other thing. After having talked to one of these three people, Jon had soon found the artifacts, and had soon been murdered.

A hell of a coincidence.

And as I got over to the kitchen to wash the dishes after hours of television viewing, the coincidences just kept on piling up, for when the phone rang it was Felix, and he was just the man I wanted to see.

A half hour after he called, Felix was at my house, bearing gifts. He had brought a fettucine dish and a salad and garlic bread, which he heated up in my kitchen. The formal dress he had at the funeral was gone, replaced by stonewashed jeans and a black turtleneck sweater. We both ate at the small table and had a bottle of Australian merlot, and when it came to the coffee and cannoli stage, Felix got right to it.

"I've done some preliminary work on your man's brother," he said.

"What do you have?"

Felix said, "Guy's been in trouble since he could pee standing up. Lots of juvie stuff that's sealed away, of course, and a short stint in the navy, followed by a dishonorable discharge for brawling. Then, a bunch of muscle jobs here and there, construction and landscaping work, broken up by jail time."

"What for?"

"Robbery, assault, burglary, some drunk drivings."

"Any homicide, or attempted homicide?"

"Nothing I could find out," Felix said. "But it's early yet. This guy really spent most of his time here and in Maine. Didn't spend too much of his exciting life down in Massachusetts. Current residence is in Porter."

"Still, I appreciate it."

Felix nodded, used a fork to slice off a piece of cannoli. "All right," he said. "Now that you have his record, anything strike you strange about it?"

"One big thing," I said.

"Which is . . ."

"Which is how did a guy who spent most of his life either doing grunt work or being in the county or state lockup, how did a guy like that end up running an antique store?"

"Nicely done," he said. "Glad to see that you're as sharp as ever."

"Spare me the compliments. There's more to running an antique store than just renting a storefront and putting some old furniture in there. You've got to know what you're selling, know the history and the provenance, and you got to have rock-solid reputations with the other dealers. It's a very close, clannish bunch, and everybody knows what everybody else is up to. You have a record, you do some things that aren't on the straight and narrow . . . well, your business won't last long."

"Sounds right to me."

"What do you know about his business?"

Another bite of the cannoli. "Not much. Except I know where it's located, and where he lives, which is in the same place. Small building outside of the harbor district. His living quarters are right above the store."

I got up and poured us another cup of coffee. "And his neighbors?"

"An adult bookstore and a gas station. Not a very upscale neighborhood. Quick talk with people at both establishments came up with nothing."

I sat down and passed the cup over to Felix. He put in some sugar and half-and-half and said, "I have a suggestion."

"Go ahead."

"You're serious about finding this character before the cops, right?"

"That's been the general idea."

"Well, one approach might be to visit his building. See what can be found."

"The cops have probably already been through it, once or twice."

"True," Felix said. "But there might be something there they might ignore, something I can use."

"Through your usual contacts?"

35

He took a sip from his coffee cup. "Don't make fun of my contacts, Lewis. They often know a hell of a lot more than the cops."

"No fun intended," I said. "Okay. A visit to the house and store it is. When do we go?"

"What do mean we, young man?"

"I mean the two of us would be going in, not just you. That's the fair thing to do."

He shook his head. "Nope. That'd be the dumb thing to do. Look, if I go in, I'm going in and doing something I'm familiar with, all right? And one man going in and one man going out is a hell of a lot easier to manage than two men. Plus, if I get caught . . . well, I've got the background and ability to either talk my way out of it, or have a lawyer friend take care of me. But you? Your record is somewhat clean, Lewis. Why not keep it that way?"

"Because I need to do this, that's why."

"Not a good answer."

"Best I can do for right now," I said.

Well, that conversation went around in circles for a while, until we both got tired of it and Felix retrieved his coat and I walked him to the front door. As he put the coat on, he looked at me and said, "Why not let Diane take care of it? She's a fairly competent detective for this state."

"Yeah, but she hasn't managed to catch you for anything."

That brought a smile. "Not for lack of trying. Seriously, though, why not let the professionals do their job?"

I realized I had been holding my breath, and I let it out. "Something you would understand, I'm sure. This time, it's personal."

Felix looked at me with an odd look on his face, and then tapped the side of my shoulder. "You should really let Diane and the cops handle it. We're going into my world, now, and it'd be for the best if I work alone."

"What do you mean, your world?"

"You know," he said. "The world of grudges, revenge, blood feuds, arguments settled with two bullets in the hat or a ride out in a boat. That's my place in the universe. Not yours."

"You mean, the North End way?"

"You could say that."

"Well, don't forget my Irish background," I said. "We know a few things about feuds and such."

Another smile. "Yeah, I guess you're right."

"Okay, now that we've gotten our family backgrounds out of the way, when do we go visit Ray Ericson's place?"

Felix checked his watch. "Let's say . . . three a.m.?"

I tried to hide my enthusiasm. "Sounds great."

"No, it's an awful time, but a good time to get things done. Look, I'll come pick you up, about two-fifteen. Get some sleep, all right?"

"I'll try."

"Good," he said, and he walked out my door into the cold October night.

I washed the dishes, dried them, and put them away, and I knew I should have gone upstairs, at least to lie down and rest. I would have to be up and about at two a.m., and that time of the morning was going to come damn quick.

But the dinner and the coffee and the events of the day made me restless, made my legs jumpy, and I knew a night of reading or surfing the Internet or seeing what was on the History Channel wasn't going to work. I had to do something different, something physical, and then I went back into the kitchen, and in the back of one of the drawers, I pulled out an old serving spoon. From underneath the sink I found a wire-mesh colander, and with tools in hand, I went to the door to the cellar, and went downstairs.

The single light was on and I had grabbed a flashlight as well. I turned on the flashlight and illuminated the small cellar, remembering the time I had been down here with Jon, talking about history, talking about my home. I reached up and touched the old timbers, almost imagined I could feel the strength of the wood, and the patience in the years that the wood had served here, holding up my home. I shone the light around in the corners of the cellar, at the old stonework, remembering again what Jon had said about the history of one's place. This was now my home, and the history here belonged to me.

I knelt down on the cold dirt, placed the wire colander at my side, and started digging.

CHAPTER FOUR

Two a.m. can come pretty early and pretty damn cold, and I was standing outside, shivering slightly, waiting for Felix to pick me up. I was at the parking lot for the Lafayette House, which is across the street from the hotel. Most of the lights at the hotel had been dimmed, and from where I stood in the lot, I couldn't see my house, which suited me fine. About fifty or so feet from the parking lot was a rocky stretch of shoreline, and the incessant waves of the Atlantic, performing their million-year-old show. I put my hands in the pocket of my jacket, shivered again, and looked up, hoping to see some of the winter constellations, announcing their early arrival. But there were no overhead lights to be seen, just a flat, black surface that told me it was overcast and that more rain was no doubt in the offing.

At what must have been 2:15 a.m., give or take a nanosecond, a car slowed down on Route 1-A—also known as Atlantic Avenue—and a black Lexus with Maine plates purred up next to me. I opened the door, slipped thankfully into the warm interior, and looked around.

"Very nice," I said.

"Thanks," Felix replied.

"Mercedes in the shop?"

"Nope," he said. "Job like this, I like to use rentals. Cops and AGs have funny rules nowadays, and one of the funniest concerns seizing vehicles used in crimes. I like my Mercedes too much to give it over to the state of New Hampshire if something gets screwed up tonight."

"Sounds reasonable to me. But a Lexus? Pretty high-priced."

"Cops see a car that doesn't belong, they get suspicious if it's just run-of-the-mill. A parked Lexus means money, means rich people, and why would rich people be breaking into an antique store at the ungodly hour of three in the morning?"

We were now on Route 1-A, accelerating gently into the night. Felix said, "Thermos bottle under your seat. Some coffee if you'd like."

I bent over and retrieved the bottle, and in the dashboard lights noted Felix's appearance. I knew I looked and felt like the truth, which was a lousy night trying to get to sleep, preceded by a lousy couple of hours digging through my cellar and finding nothing except a few rocks and pebbles. But Felix looked freshly showered and cleanly dressed, like he could operate on three hours of sleep and an oil change every three thousand miles.

"Felix?"

"Yeah?"

"Don't you ever look . . . tired? Or disheveled?"

He laughed. "Don't got time for that crap."

We reached Porter about a half hour later, and as Felix had said, Ray's antique store—Seacoast Antiques, such a well-thought-out name—was in a part of Porter that didn't get mentioned in that city's chamber of commerce mailings. We were on a stretch of Route 1-A that boomed its way over the Piscassic River bridge on the way to Maine. On one side of the store was an all-night service station, and on the other was an adult bookstore. The gas station was well lit and the lights were all off at the adult bookstore, like the owners were embarrassed at what they offered behind its darkened door. Seacoast Antiques was a two-story brick building, unlit, with two storefront windows. Up above, on the second story, were smaller windows, also darkened. Felix pulled into the store lot and drove out back, where a tall fence separated the property from a set of homes. Felix backed in next to a dumpster and switched off the engine and waited.

I yawned. About fifty yards away, traffic streamed east and west, going in and out of New Hampshire, and the bulk of the traffic was semitrailers, secretly bringing food, drink, and fuel to the demanding stores of the region. Felix said, "Looks quiet."

"Unh-hunh."

"Thought we'd wait for a bit, see if anything's going on."

"Like the cops, for example? Keeping surveillance?"

Felix said, "Got a contact with the city. She tells me that the cops are busy elsewhere. Don't know where, but she does know there's no surveillance on the place."

"Sounds like a good contact."

I could just make out his smile. "Oh, she's got a couple of contacts herself that can brighten up one's day."

I yawned again, managed this time to raise a hand to my face. "Any idea of what you might be looking for once we get in?"

Felix said, "If I do, I'll let you know."

More traffic went by and I thought about getting another cup of coffee, decided not to. I didn't want to be in the store with a desperate need to release water, and fumble around, looking for a restroom. Felix shifted in his seat and said, "Okay, let's go."

I got out with him and he said, "Don't bother locking the door."

"I know," I said. "If we need to get going in a hurry."

We walked across the cracked pavement of the parking lot, the humming noise of the traffic growing louder. Felix made a motion with his hands in his coat pocket and then passed over a pair of latex gloves, which I snapped on. We reached the rear door, and he said in a low voice, "Another reason this place seems so off to me. Came by earlier today, no alarm system."

I didn't say anything. The whole past few days had seemed off. Felix lit off a tiny flashlight, handed it over to me, and I flashed the beam on the doorknob of the rear door. Back into his coat pocket he went, and then started working with a set of tools. He whispered something to himself in Italian, and then reached up and spun the doorknob. It clicked open with a satisfying noise, and then we were in, having just committed the crime of breaking and entering.

I felt pretty good.

We were in a cluttered hallway, Felix keeping the light low to the ground. Cardboard boxes were piled on either side, and we had to walk sideways to make our way to the main store. Felix switched off the light and we came out into a display area. Curtains had been closed on the windows and the front door, but there was enough light from the streetlights out on the highway to illuminate the interior. Felix stood next to me and I could sense his quiet gaze, as he looked around the store.

"A mess," he said.

"You got it," I said. My hands were warm and moist inside the latex gloves, but I tried not to pay it any mind. Small price to pay for leaving no fingerprints behind.

There were shelves against the walls and low tables in the center of the room, and even in the dim light, I could see there was no reason, no sense of order to the old belongings here. Piles of books were stacked next to some vases, next to clear plastic bags of silverware, to more books and little statuettes, to more glassware and some cutting knives. There was a smell of damp decay, of old things not kept well over the years. I had been in a number of antique stores in New England over the years, searching for old books, magazines, and small souvenirs, but I had never been in a store that seemed so distressed. Felix gently grasped my arm and said, "There's a set of stairways over there, by the store counter. Why don't you look about the countertop, see if you can find an address book, ledger book. I'll take a run upstairs to the apartment."

"Why don't we both run up to the apartment?" I asked.

"Time, my friend," he said. "We're burning it up, and we can't waste anymore."

Good point. "All right, go to it."

He went up the stairs and I swear, he moved like a cat for I heard not a sound. I went over to a waist-high counter with a silent cash register, and not much else. There was a shelf behind the counter with stacks of newspapers, which I flipped through and found nothing of interest. It was tight quarters back there and I was surprised at what wasn't there: any kind of ledger, any kind of filing cabinets, anything at all that marked a business. Just the cash register and some old newspapers. I went back out to the store interior, looked around again. A thought was forming in my mind of what had been going on here, what Jon's younger brother had been up to, and why the store seemed so wrong. The thought was coming together when I heard footsteps on the stairs behind me, turned, and was going to ask Felix what he had learned, when somebody came forward and knocked me down with a blow to the chest.

I fell back against one of the tables, things falling off and clattering. There was a whispered exclamation from my assailant and I could feel a boot barely brush my left ear as it hammered into a desk leg. I rolled and my hand went against a burst plastic bag, felt something sharp, grabbed a knife, and rolled again back toward my assailant, stabbed upward. There was a gasp of pain and then there was another noise, the sound of feet coming down the stairs, and then the guy I had just stabbed in the leg picked up a chair and threw it through the front window.

It made a loud and satisfying smash and Felix was there, grabbing me up under my arms, saying, "You okay?" just as the shape leapt through the window, through the curtains, out to the front, and then went out of sight.

"Yeah." It was all I could say through the dense sensation in my chest, which felt like wet cement was suddenly surrounding my heart. Felix grabbed an arm and said, "Come on, let's get the hell out of here."

We went back the way we came, through the rear corridor and outside into the cold air. Felix made a point of glancing around the empty lot, to make sure my assailant wasn't out there, waiting for us. In a matter of moments we were back in the Lexus, and Felix started it up and drove slowly out of the parking lot, and I took a breath and it hurt, and was going to tell Felix to step on it, to punch out that accelerator, but I left him to his business. He knew what he was doing, and then, so did I. A vehicle slowly moving away from a parking lot meant nothing. A vehicle moving quickly, laying down rubber with a loud screech, garnered attention. And attention was something we desperately wanted to avoid.

About fifteen minutes later we were at an International House of Pancakes in Lewington, a town right next to the city of Porter, and home to heavy traffic, two large malls, a number of chain stores, a variety of shipping terminals, and the McIntosh Air Force Base. The residents of Lewington enjoy one of the lowest property taxes in the state in exchange for putting up with the heavy traffic and the possibility that the air force base may be a target one of these days, and most seemed happy with the exchange.

I made do with a glass of orange juice and two scrambled eggs, my chest aching something fierce and hard, while Felix dug into eggs Benedict, home fries, and toast. Most of the customers in the IHOP were either truck drivers or the young, out for a night of partying and Ecstasy-taking, and I think the hostess took one look at Felix and me and didn't know what the hell to make of us, so she sat us in a far corner in case we started speaking in tongues or something.

Felix said, "Sorry about that."

"Sorry about what?"

He shook his head. "I was a bit sloppy. Didn't think anybody was in the building when we got there. Somehow, the guy who tried to whack you one was hiding in the upstairs bathroom. I was in Ray's bedroom when the door opened up and I heard him thundering his way downstairs."

I ate some of the eggs, which were better than I expected. "No apologies necessary. I'm thinking, maybe that was Ray, coming back to the homestead to pick up something."

"Nope," Felix said.

"Well, you could at least give me the courtesy of pretending that I might be right."

"No point to it," he said. "First of all, it doesn't make sense for a guy to come back to his home turf. Too many chances of the cops keeping an eye on the place, of witnesses seeing him go in, of getting caught."

"All right," I said. "You said 'first.' Can I guess that there's a second to your theory?"

"Not a theory. Plain fact. You said this Ray character is bald, correct?"

"That's right."

Felix made a slicing motion into his eggs Benedict with a fork. "Streetlight illuminated the back of our hero's head, just as he was bailing out of the broken window. Short but thick hair. It wasn't Ray."

I said, "You could have told me that first, instead of giving me that minilecture on criminals returning to their homes."

A smile. "I always enjoy teaching you something, Lewis. It makes my whole existence worthwhile. And I see you gave somebody something as well."

"I don't see what you mean."

He took his knife and touched the edge of my shirtsleeve, and I looked down and saw the brown stain there. A bit of the flesh on my wrist was flecked with brown as well. Felix said, his voice quieter, "That's somebody's blood, and I'm pretty sure it's not yours. What happened?"

I suppose I should have spat out the eggs I was eating, but instead I swallowed calmly and said, "I think I stabbed him. In the leg."

Felix raised an eyebrow, which for him is about one step below yelling. "Really?"

"Truly and honestly."

"With what?"

"When I got hammered in my chest, I fell over a table, knocking everything off. Part of the everything was a bag of silverware. I grabbed a dinner knife, and I'm glad it wasn't a butter knife, and poked him in the leg."

Felix said not a word. I looked at him and said, "Look, he plowed me over, was trying to kick my head in. Least I could do was return the favor."

His lips moved some, and it looked like he was trying to hold in either a smile or some laughter. He said, "Excuse me."

"Yes?"

"Who the hell are you, and what have you done with my friend, Lewis?"

It was my turn to smile. "Surprised?"

"Very. I know you and how you think. Times like those, your biggest problem is that you analyze too much, try to think through all of the options and repercussions. That was part of your innocent charm. Now, I don't know what the hell to think. Somebody attacks you and instead of engaging them in a thoughtful discussion of why they're being mean to you, you stab them. Maybe I've been a bad influence on you."

"Probably."

We ate some more and I said, "I was thinking of something back there, before that tire iron or baseball bat or whatever went sailing into my chest."

"What's that?"

"The whole store . . . it didn't seem like a store at all. There were no records I could find, no sense of any kind of record keeping at all. It was like everything in that place was for show."

"Go on," Felix said.

"For lack of a better phrase, I think that place is a front for something. I don't know what for. But whatever is going on there, it doesn't involve selling antiques."

"Yeah. Which leads me to what I found upstairs, taped to the refrigerator, before our hidden friend bolted from the bathroom."

"And what's that?"

He reached into an inside pocket of his coat, pulled out a thin stack of postcards. He fanned them across the countertop and I gave them a look. There were six of them and all of them were advertising Florida. They were that hokey type that showed a rear shot of an attractive woman in a skimpy thong bikini at the beach, with the phrase, "Getting behind in our vacation!" That sort of thing. After I had given them a quick glance, Felix—acting like a conjurer—flipped them over. All were addressed to Ray Ericson at Seagrant Antiques, Route 1-A, Porter, NH 03801, and I noted three interesting things: The postmark was from St. Petersburg, the dates on the postmark were about two weeks apart, and the message side of each card was blank.

"Well?" Felix asked.

"A code," I said.

"Go on."

"Ray getting this postcard meant he was supposed to do something. Pick somebody up at the airport, go on a trip somewhere, rob a bank, scratch his left buttock, I don't know. But that's what this tells me. A code."

"Very good. Your Pentagon training has served you well."

I didn't take the bait, which I think disappointed Felix some. He has always pressed me on my prior service at the Department of Defense, and I've never given in. He said, "Anybody or anything you know down in St. Petersburg?"

"Just that they have a hell of a nice newspaper, that's about it. You?"

"A little more. Let's just say that St. Pete is a favorite for retirees from a variety of different occupations."

45

"Let's see, loansharking, knee breaking, bookmaking . . . Leave anything out?"

"Cooking schools, of course," he said dryly. "What I mean is that I can make a few calls, see what I can find."

"Thanks."

We finished up our meal, which seemed too late for dinner and still too early for breakfast. While we were waiting for the check, Felix said, "All right, truth-telling time."

"Okay."

"What the hell is going on with you?"

Felix was now sitting, arms folded across his chest, and I shrugged. "Just trying to find out who killed my friend."

Felix said, "Oh, you're doing much more than that, and we both know it. My question is, what's driving you? I know you said it's personal but please, Lewis. The man was not family. He was just a friend. And no offense, but from what I can tell, he hasn't been a friend of yours for that long. Am I right?"

"Maybe."

"So. What's going on?"

I looked at Felix and recalled the times we had shared, the blood we had seen spilt during some unusual circumstances, and saw his quiet eyes, knew the usual evasiveness on my part wouldn't work. The sensation in my chest was still there, like heavy cement, slowing everything down.

"It's hard to explain."

"Try me," Felix said.

"He's just . . . well, he was older and we had the same interests . . . and . . . Look, he wanted to do something in his life, accomplish one goal. That's all. One goal. And when that had been reached, somebody killed him . . . Right after reaching his dream, he's dead . . . And . . . I just can't let that stand."

Felix leaned over the table. "Lewis."

"Yeah."

"Time for a personal question, so here we go. Something you've never talked about, something I've never asked, figuring you could use the privacy. But here we go. Your parents. Are they alive?"

The sudden memory made my eyes blink, and for a while I was

a college student again, at Indiana University, wondering why the phone in my dorm was ringing at such an ungodly hour. "No."

"When did they die?"

"You mean, when were they killed?"

A nod. "All right, when were they killed?"

"When I was a senior in college. They were . . . um, it was wintertime, and they were taking a commuter flight to Indianapolis, to visit some family. It was raining. The wings on the aircraft didn't have the proper deicing equipment, and they were delayed getting in and were told to fly in big circles around the sky. Which they did, until the ice on the wings caused the plane to flip over and bore a hole into an Indiana cornfield. My parents and nineteen others."

"Jesus," Felix breathed.

"If you say so."

"You're an only child, correct?"

"Correct."

Felix nodded and he unfolded his arms and moved his hands some across the table. "Explains a lot, then."

"You don't seem to be the kind to psychoanalyze, Felix."

"No, but I am the kind to see things, and what I see is this guy being a father figure to you. Older gent, retired, taking an interest in you and your home and having things in common. Makes some sense, especially after he's been murdered."

I started to say something and he raised his hand and said, "Look, let's just leave it at that, okay? That's all I needed to know, and that's fine. No more pushing on my part. I now have my answer."

The waitress came by, put the check down, and Felix moved quicker than me and said, "And now I have the check. Let's get out of here."

I made a suggestion and Felix thought I had really gone around the bend, but I managed to say that it wouldn't be that bad, so we headed down to the Porter traffic circle, flipped around, and found ourselves back on Route 1-A again, heading into Maine. Felix swore as he saw the flashing blue lights up ahead and tapped his fingers on the steering wheel and said, "If somebody recognizes this car and we get hauled in, you can get your own damn lawyer to bail you out. Okay?"

"Sure," I said. "A small price to pay to satisfy my curiosity."

Felix moved us over into the left lane, to leave plenty of room for the little sideshow that was taking place at Seacoast Antiques. There were two Porter police cruisers parked there, with an unmarked vehicle that had flashing lights in the grill. What little traffic out here at this hour had slowed down some, taking in the show, and I saw two uniformed cops, talking to each other, while a plainclothes cop—the detective, no doubt—was working around the edge of the broken window. The chair was still in the paved area out front, on its side, as well as a shower of broken glass. The detective looked up and I quickly sank down into the seat.

"Problem?" Felix asked.

"Yeah. I know the detective."

Felix swore and said, "Did he see you?"

"I don't think so."

The traffic moved ahead some, and then I raised my head and said, "You and the contact in the police department still on speaking terms?"

"You could say that."

"Well, find out if there was a blood trail they found at the store. Maybe my stabbing victim ended up at a hospital or something."

"Unh-hunh," Felix said. "And what are you going to do in the meantime?"

I yawned, sat back in the seat. "Get the Sunday newspapers and crawl into bed, that's what."

We were silent for the next twenty minutes as Felix drove us south, back to Tyler Beach. By the time we reached Atlantic Avenue the sun was rising out there, above the cold and wide waters of the Atlantic Ocean. I kept watch of the changing patterns of pink and red and blue, as the sun rose up over the ocean, thankful that at least the damn rain clouds had moved on. Felix pulled into the parking lot of the Lafayette House and said, "I'd drive you to the door, but I'm afraid I'd lose the transmission on some of the rocks in your yard."

"Fair enough," I said. "Thanks for your help. And for breakfast."

"No problem," he said. "We'll talk."

"I'm sure we will."

I got out into the cold morning air, but before closing the door, I leaned back in and said, "Felix."

"Yeah?"

"What about your family? Your own parents. What about them?"

Felix smiled. "You've never asked me."

I nodded. "That's right. I never have."

He said, "It's cold out there. Get on into bed with your newspapers, all right?"

"Sure," I said, and I slammed the door shut. He backed his way out of the parking lot and then was back on Route 1-A, heading north, driving safe and sure, like he always did, like he knew exactly who he was and what he was doing, a trait of his that I've always envied.

I stood for a moment, watched the sunrise, and then trudged across the street to the Lafayette House, as promised, to get the Sunday newspapers.

CHAPTER FIVE

On Monday the storm clouds had returned to the New Hampshire seacoast, and the bruise on my chest was turning an impressive green and blue. Getting dressed took some time, as moving my arms caused my chest to throb and tighten up, and I spent a few minutes before the mirror, trying to decipher what in hell I had been struck with the previous night, back in Porter, whether it was a tire iron or golf club or cricket bat. By the time I buttoned up my shirt, I had given up on my quest. I was just glad that whatever had hit me hadn't gone into the back of my skull.

I was also happy about another thing, my morning ritual, in checking my skin for any unusual bumps or swellings. There are four scars of various sizes and lengths over my body, where noncancerous tumors have been cut away over the years, a recurring souvenir of my time in government service.

Satisfied that my body had gone through another day without betraying me, I went out into the bracing morning air and went looking for the second-best writer in Tyler.

I found Paula Quinn of the Tyler *Chronicle* not in her office, but at a small home on Lafayette Road, also known as Route 1. That's the problem with lots of roads around this part of New Hampshire; they end up having two or three different names, sometimes changing names in midstream, which goes a long way toward confusing visitors and out-of-towners. Not that confusing visitors is always a bad thing; it just means precious time wasted sometimes, giving directions to people who want to know how come the Tyler Road suddenly became the Exonia Road, and why couldn't somebody do something about it?

The home was set away some distance from the constant traffic of Route 1, which is a two-lane highway with a middle turning lane that runs from Falconer in the south, by the Massachusetts border, all the way up to Porter, just before the Maine border. I had seen photos of the highway at the end of the nineteenth century: narrow two-lane, with lots of homes, white picket fences, and large elm trees, overarching everything. But the elms are dead, the road is wide and busy, the fences are gone, and so are most of the homes. This house was an aberration, and I couldn't figure out why Paula was there.

She was sitting on the hood of her car, a new red Toyota Camry, and waved at me as I approached. It was another brisk day for October, the wind kicking up some, the chill in the air predicting a heavy and hearty winter. The home was brick and dark wood, with small windows, a narrow pitched roof, and it seemed out of place. It looked like it had been picked up from some English village with a name like Burberry-on-Kent or something, and dropped here intact. Maple and oak trees surrounded it, and the lawn was tiny but well kept. There were hedges marking the yard, and the home's immediate neighbors were a branch of Coastal Savings Bank, a car wash, and a condominium. And smack-dab in the middle of the door was a red and black sign: NO TRESPASSING.

"Hey," Paula said. She had on tight jeans, small black boots, and a short black leather coat.

"Hey, yourself," I said, sitting next to her on the Camry. "Are we both lawbreakers, young lady?"

She laughed. "You talking about the No Trespassing sign?"

"It certainly caught my attention."

She tapped me gently on my hand. "Not to worry, my friend. This lovely homestead is now considered property of the town of Tyler, and I have permission from the town counsel to visit it as much as I want."

"Knowing how the town counsel feels about you, I'm surprised he didn't give you permission to move in and take the place over. What's the deal? Tax lien?"

Paula said, "Among other things. Look, do you know who built this place? And who lived here?"

"No, but I'm sure I'm about to find out."

"You certainly are," she said. "Donald F. Burnett. Retired newspaperman and a poet, lived here right after the Civil War. Was in love with all things English, and had this home built to certain specifications. He said he wanted to live like a lord in Elizabethan times, which is what he did. Lived here and wrote some great poetry, and had a comfortable life, corresponding with authors like Mark Twain and Nathaniel Hawthorne and Walt Whitman. A minor celebrity here in Tyler, bit of an eccentric. Achieved a small part of fame before he died, peacefully in his sleep, just before the dawn of the twentieth century."

"Sounds like you're keeping his flame alive."

"Doing my best," she said. "And right now, I'm trying to keep his house alive." She nodded in the direction of the home. "The inside of the place is a dump, Lewis. Past owners really haven't taken care of it and the last owner was evicted back in the spring. The wiring, the plumbing, the insulation . . . all about twenty years out of date. The building inspector has said it could cost thousands to rehab the place into anything approaching livable, and even if you do that, who wants to move in next to a highway and car wash? The thing is, what's valuable here isn't the building. It's this nice high-priced lot, right in the middle of a commercial zoning district."

I said, "This is where I'm supposed to say, you have a plan, correct?"

She kept her view of the house, like she was waiting for the ghost of the old New Hampshire poet to quietly appear. "You're right about that. See, the thing is, the owner of the car wash, one Sy Hartmann, from down Lawrence way, he wants to purchase the land and take the house down and build what Route 1 desperately needs: another convenience store to sell beer, slurpies, and artery-clogging snacks. But for once in their life, the Tyler selectmen have decided to put the brakes on destroying a piece of the town's history, and have told Sy that yes, he can pay off the tax lien and secure the property, but he has to give somebody a chance to save the house. So that's the deal. See this pretty house in front of us?"

"Can't miss it," I said.

"Care to figure the asking price?"

Having gotten my own home for free from the United States government, and not one for keeping up with the real estate market— all I know is that the prices are obscene—I gave it my best guess. "Oh, maybe two hundred thousand. Maybe more."

She gently nudged my ribs with her elbow. "Not hardly. Lewis, this wonderful and unique piece of Tyler history is for sale for the magnificent sum of one dollar."

"A dollar?"

"One hundred pennies. And this is when you're supposed to ask me, 'What's the catch?'"

"Must be a pretty damn big catch," I said.

"Yeah. A catch the size of a blue whale. The purchaser has to agree to move the house off the property. Which means that the aspiring buyer needs to come up with a moving company, not to mention a piece of land to drop the house on once it gets picked up. I mean, most of these storage areas you see up and down Route 1 don't really have a locker big enough to hold a house."

"You really going through with this?"

"Like you said, I have a plan." She turned and smiled at me, her ears poking again through her long blond hair. "I love this house, Lewis, I love it to death. And I'm meeting with the Tyler Cooperative this afternoon, try to set up the financing. I'm tired of apartment living, of dealing with landlords and neighbors next door with loud stereos and neighbors upstairs with overflowing tubs. This is my one chance, and I'm going to grab it."

I clasped her hand, let it go. "Good for you."

She moved a bit on the hood of her car. "Here I am, blathering to you the moment you showed up. You did good at Jon's funeral on Saturday."

"Thanks."

"Story will be out this afternoon," she said. "Anything going on I should know about?"

Silently, I thanked her for that little phrase, 'I should know about.' Aloud I said, "I'm going to try to meet up with Diane Woods this afternoon, see if I can get an update, but I'm not holding my breath."

"From Diane the detective, I can see why. Need anything from me?"

"How about a picture of you in your favorite bathing suit?"

A nice smile and another nudge in the ribs. "No, not today, I'm afraid."

"Okay," I said. "Guess I don't need the town counsel checking on my property tax status. Look, I'm thinking of doing something about Jon and what he did in the town for the magazine. Do you know who the past curator of the Tyler Town Museum was, before Jon?"

"That I do," she said. "Brian Mulligan. Practically set the place up himself, back in the seventies."

"Still alive, I hope?"

"That he is, but he doesn't live in Tyler anymore. There was some political feud a couple of years before you showed up, and he moved up north, to Conway. Guess he developed a hate for the ocean and wanted to be up in the mountains. Why do you want to talk to him?"

"Jon had mentioned that he had talked to Brian about . . . well, about something Jon was looking for."

"The mysterious Vikings, am I right?" she asked.

So much for Jon's deep dark secret. "I didn't realize you knew."

She crossed her legs, a maple leaf stuck to the sole of her boot. "Oh, I've known for a while. You see, every now and then, Jon would come in and go through the bound back issues of the *Chronicle*. We really prefer people go to the library to do research work like that, but for Jon, we made an exception. A sweet older guy with an obsession, and you know what? God bless him. Better he was out looking for Vikings than writing letters to the newspapers about conspiracies and UN black helicopters and the Zionists. The thing is, I can't believe what happened to him. Apparently murdered the same day he found the artifacts." She shook her head. "One of these days I want to write a novel, and something like that makes me feel like the day I get a book contract, a tree will fall on my head."

"Did he say anything about what he was looking for, or where he might be going?"

"Well, can I give you a name?"

54

"Another name? Sure."

"Olivia Hendricks."

"Nice name," I said. "What about her?"

"About a month ago, Jon was in my office, trooping around, carrying these big binders of old newspapers, and he spotted my UNH coffee mug on my desk. We got to talking and he wanted to know if I had any contacts up there, and I mentioned a friend of mine that worked in the alumni affairs office. Seemed like Jon wanted to talk to someone about old New Hampshire, a professor of anthropology, and a few phone calls later on my part, Olivia Hendricks is the name that came up. She's an associate or assistant professor of anthropology up at UNH, specializing in precolonial New England."

"Did Jon say anything about talking to an Indian activist from the area?"

"Nope, not at all," she said, glancing at her wristwatch.

Two out of three, I thought. God bless you, Paula, you've given me two out of the three people that Jon had said he was going to talk to. "Late for something?"

"Late for an early lunch," she said. "How does that sound?"

"Sounds reasonable," I said. "Thanks, thanks for everything. You've helped a lot."

She dug car keys out of her coat pocket. "I sense another Lewis Cole column coming up for *Shoreline* magazine, a column that will never appear in print. Am I correct?"

"You do know my methods," I said.

"True, but be careful. All right?"

"Sure," I said, and just for the hell of it, I leaned over and kissed her. I think I surprised us both, and her eyes got shiny and she said, "Get going, before your tax bills get audited."

"All right, but one more thing."

"I can hardly wait."

I took out my wallet and removed a single dollar bill, which I placed in her hand. "I've just paid for your house, Paula. And if the Tyler Cooperative isn't helpful, give me a call. Maybe I can help you out."

Her small hand squeezed the dollar bill tight. "Thanks for the dollar, and your vote of confidence."

"You're welcome," I said, and I headed back to my vehicle, leaving behind the young woman with the big dreams and the old house.

About twenty minutes later I was in the parking lot of the Tyler police station, which is about a hundred yards away from the sands of Tyler Beach. If the police chief and the voters of Tyler reached agreement next spring, during town meeting, this was probably the last winter for the police station, which is built of cement blocks and looks like a storage facility for nerve gas or some damn thing. It was too warm in the summer, too cold in the winter, and instead of being just right in the fall, heavy rains and wind from the ocean often meant flooding in the dispatch area.

Diane was back in her office, the cement blocks now painted a pale yellow. Her desk was clean and neat, unlike the desk next to hers, which is used in the summer by a patrol officer temporarily assigned to her to assist in the heavy upswing of felony cases. That desk was piled high with file folders, newspaper clippings, and packets of photos. During those months that don't fall between Memorial Day and Labor Day, she is the entire detective force for the town of Tyler.

I sat down across from her and said, "That desk looks like it could use a clean-up."

She smiled at me, the scar on her chin faded, a good sign. "Tell you a secret?"

"Secrets from cops are the best ones. Sure, go ahead."

She was leaning back in her office chair, hands folded against her slim waist. "That mess over there, that all belongs to me. This desk is just fake. All those files are cases I'm working on."

"Then why are you sitting here, and not there?"

"You know how depressing it is, to walk into an office first thing in the morning and look at a mess? Thing is, you come and sit at a clean desk, you start the day in a good mood. Sets the whole tone."

"Sounds too weird to work," I said.

"Well, it does," she said. "Guess you're here looking for an update on your friend Jon."

"I am."

"The investigation continues," she said.

I waited. There was one window in the office, heavily barred and screened, that overlooked the rear parking lot of the police station, the marshland beyond that, and a couple of miles away, the impressive bulk of the Falconer nuclear power plant. Diane sat there, silent, and I said to her, "You know, I haven't changed jobs."

"You haven't?"

"Nope. I don't work for the Porter *Herald* or Tyler *Chronicle* or even the Boston *Globe*. It's still me and my monthly column for *Shoreline*."

"I didn't think you've changed jobs," she said. "So why bring it up?"

"Because that crappy answer you gave to me back there, about the investigation continuing, is the kind of answer you'd give to anybody else. But not for me. What's going on?"

She slowly unfolded her hands and said, "What's going on is the investigation, Lewis. And you and I have the same goals—to find the asshole who murdered your friend, and to put him away. But this case is an important one, and it's not one that I'm going to look the other way while you do your poking and prodding, pretending to be doing a story for *Shoreline*."

"It's not stopped you before."

"Times have changed."

"How?"

Then her face shifted, like some memories back there that she had kept quiet were suddenly coming to the foreground. "Two things, my friend, two things have changed. One personal and the other public. Guess it's time to hear some more secrets, eh?"

"I guess."

She looked over at the door and I got the signal, and got up and gently closed it. I sat back down and she said, "Okay, friend to friend. This is what's going on, and I'm sorry I wasn't upfront with you the other day, at Jon's house. First and foremost. Kara."

"Is she all right?"

A nod. "Yes, she's doing fine. The occasional nightmare but she's recovered well from last winter. But something's up. You've been reading the newspapers?"

"Every day."

"Sure, but have you been reading the business news?"

Oh. "Her job."

Another nod. "She was laid off from what's left of Compaq, about two months ago."

"I'm sorry, I didn't know."

Diane said, "It didn't seem to be a problem at the time. Kara is very good, she's very talented, and we were both convinced that she'd find another job in a matter of days. Well, those days have slipped by, and nobody's hiring. Now she's trying to make a go of it as a consultant, but the woods are thick with ex-computer analysts, trying to start up a consulting business. In a few days, my friend, she's moving out of her apartment in Newburyport and is moving in with me."

"Oh. Congratulations, I guess."

Outside a Tyler police cruiser, painted green and white, pulled up to the rear entrance. Diane sighed and said, "That's a good one. 'Congratulations, I guess.' I've always pushed her to move in with me, and she's always resisted. The usual tale about keeping one's space. Fine, I could handle that. But having her move in now . . . Well, it's tough. I always wanted her to live with me because of our love and our relationship. Having her move in with me because her bank account is draining away isn't quite the romantic fantasy I've always had."

"I see."

"Very good," she said. "Now, it's time for the public secret. And please do keep this a secret, especially from your girl toy Paula." Diane swiveled some in her chair and opened the center drawer to her desk, pulled out a triangular-shaped patch, green and black. She turned it over and I recognized the three chevrons of a sergeant rank.

"Really?" I asked, delight in my voice, and that seemed to please her. She smiled and twirled the patch in her fingers.

"Really and truly," she said. "In a few days time, if I keep my nose clean and keep my work up, this well-dressed and muscular woman sitting across from you will be known as Detective Sergeant Diane Woods, not just plain old Detective Woods. Even though it's a one-man detective bureau, Lewis. It's a very big deal."

I nodded and said, "Okay. Both secrets received, loud and clear. No time for loose cannon, no time for jeopardizing anything."

"You've got it, my friend," she said. "I've wanted this promotion for a long time, Lewis, and with it, comes extra money and a few more bennies. Stuff that I can really use with Kara now living with me. And truly, don't take offense when I say this."

"Okay, I won't.

A smile. "A sign of a true friend, saying yes before I say a damn thing. What I'm saying is that my first loyalty and first priority is to the woman in my life, and I'm not going to do anything to threaten that. And you may be number two and try harder, Lewis, but still, when you ask me about the Jon Ericson case, you're going to get the very basics. I can't afford to do anything else."

I got up from the chair, knowing what she said made sense, still not enjoying hearing it. "I understand, Diane. I really do."

She folded her hands back together. "I knew you would. But still . . . if you do hear anything that might help me, please call, all right?"

My chest ached—maybe it was guilt, maybe it was a memory of where Felix and I had been the other morning—and I said, "Let me get this straight. You're not going to tell me anything, but if I hear something, I'm supposed to pass the information over to you."

"That's right."

"Sure doesn't sound fair." Which made my not saying anything about our little break in at Seacoast Antiques seem just fine.

She leaned farther back in her chair. "Welcome to the realities of police work."

Outside, the wind had died down some, but cigarette butts and fast food wrappers and even fine grains of beach sand blew across the cracked pavement of the parking lot. Diane had just told me her priorities, about taking care of her life and her first priority, which made sense. No argument there.

The only argument I had was that she didn't ask me about my life, about my priority, and that was something I was going to take care of, no matter the realities of police work. I reached into my coat, rubbed at the sore spot on my chest. It still hurt.

I got into my Explorer and went home.

Before getting busy, the phone rang, and it was Felix, who got right to the point. "Talked to my Porter police contact, about a little event at Seacoast Antiques the other night."

"And?"

"Nothing to report. No evidence of who was in the building, how many people were in the building, and also—I'm sorry to say—no blood trail from whoever was in there that ran into a, um, knife."

"Thanks for the update."

"Not a problem. Now it's time to work the phones and talk to some guys in St. Pete. You feel like a Florida trip anytime soon?"

"Could we get to Cape Canaveral?"

"That's on the other damn coastline."

"So it is. So I guess I won't," I said. "Besides, I've got things here to do while you're reconnecting with your godfather or whomever."

He laughed. "I'm sure you do. Talk to you later."

After hanging up the phone, back into the cellar I went, after a late afternoon lunch of a grilled tuna fish and cheese sandwich. I was excavating one part of the cellar, recalling what Jon had told me. It had seemed simple, but I quickly saw how hard the work was, staying on one's knees, digging gently not to break any possible objects, and then sifting the dirt through the old colander, the rain of dirt making a whisperlike noise as it fell back to the cellar floor. When I had started the other day, it had seemed magical, peeling away the layers of dirt that represented months, years, and decades of history. But after a while of moving dirt, boredom started setting in. I always had the imaginative thought of what being an archaeologist was all about, of digging for a few days and finding treasure or the Holy Grail or a shinbone from a T. rex, but face-to-face with the fantasy, reality was settling in for a long stay. Each little spoonful of dirt, which earlier seemed to represent something magical, with lots of potential, eventually ended up being just another spoonful of dirt. Soon my wrists felt stiff, and then they started to ache, matching the ache in my chest.

I dug for about an hour, slowly moving across one side of the cellar, and when the old lightbulb hanging up by the furnace flickered, flared, and died, I took it as a sign from some greater power. I dropped the colander and spoon and, with some difficulty, tapped my feet free of dirt, and started up the stairs. It was now dark out and cooler, and I guess I should have thought about dinner, but I wasn't particularly hungry. The first floor of my house was unlit, and I moved quietly through the kitchen and out the sliding glass doors to the rear deck.

I went out without a coat, which was fine, for I didn't want to spend too much time out there. It was just past seven p.m. and night had already fallen. Part of me felt that little twist of melancholy, knowing that in a few days' time, when the clocks changed from Daylight Savings Time, this dark part of the night would be six p.m., and soon enough, it would be pitch black at four-thirty.

I leaned against the railing, looked out at the lighthouse on White Island, at the Isles of Shoals, out there on the Atlantic, and noted the lights up and down the coastline, from here in Tyler, down to Falconer, and up to North Tyler and Wallis and Porter. A few ships' lights were apparent as well, out on the dark ocean, and up in the night sky was the sound of a whisper-jet and its red and green running lights. I squeezed the railing tight, wondering what it must have been like, about a thousand years ago, to be out here in the ocean, far away from home, in a longboat with sails and oars, exploring a forbidding coastline, looking for treasure, for wood, for furs, knowing you were part of a brave tribe, the Norsemen of history and sagas, and out here, there would be no lights, no signs of home and hearth. Just the darkness, just the woods, and maybe, just maybe, the quiet glances from the inhabitants of this rough coastline, looking on with maybe awe and a bit of hate for the strangers in their midst.

It must have been something, to have been here a thousand years ago, but unless I was quite skilled and quite lucky, the evidence to prove they had actually been here, the evidence that my friend Jon had found, would remain lost for another ten centuries.

CHAPTER SIX

The University of New Hampshire is in a small town called Durham, about ten miles up from Tyler, inland and near the Oyster River. Starting out in the middle 1800s as a typical state agricultural school—it still has barns and horse stalls and dairy equipment at one end of the campus—it has grown, through luck and the good fortune of having influential friends in Washington, into a respectable university. It dominates the center of Durham, with old brick buildings and some newer construction, and a moving mass of students who clog the sidewalks and the wide lawns of the campus between classes. Paula Quinn had gotten her degree at UNH and said to me once, "I can't even recognize the place anymore. Every time I go back there, either they're building something up or tearing something down."

With its growth meant an apparent disappearance of parking spaces, and I had to leave my Explorer at a small shopping plaza almost a half mile from my appointment. I had to walk quickly to make my way to the anthropology department, which was located in a cube of a building called the Horton Social Science Center. The tile floors were worn from thousands of feet over the years, and bulletin boards flanking the glass doors were festooned with multicolored flyers offering everything from guitar lessons to memberships in the vegan food cooperative. Up on the fourth floor, near the east corner, was a series of offices, each with a black metal door. The one I sought was half open, with a little plate on the outside that said O. HENDRICKS. Below the nameplate was a sign-up sheet for student conferences, each conference lasting fifteen minutes.

I rapped on the door and said, "Professor Hendricks?" and a woman's voice came right back with, "Come on in."

The office may have been good size at one time, but now it was packed and cluttered. Walls on the left and right were filled with overflowing bookshelves, and before me were two wooden chairs, a large wooden desk, also cluttered with books and papers, and behind the desk, a woman in her midfifties, with short brown hair, wearing a light green sweater. She stood up, smiling, and I figured I would have enjoyed being a student in one of her classes. She had horn-rimmed glasses and simple gold-hoop earrings, and I held out my hand and she gave it a quick shake.

"Mister Cole, from *Shoreline* magazine, am I right?"

"Yes," I said, sitting down across from her. "Sorry I'm late. Parking here is—"

She laughed. "Years ago, believe it or not, I was a student here, and I worked for a while at the student newspaper. I won't tell you how long ago, but let's just say our president had just announced he wasn't a crook. One day, just for the hell of it, I went through the previous twenty years of the bound newspaper, just poking around, and you know what? One constant story, year after year, was parking, or the lack thereof. The great thread linking years of history here at UNH. Where in hell can we park our cars?"

I smiled at her in return as she sat down, and I saw that behind her was a built-in radiator and picture window, overlooking a small wooden ravine. On one side of the radiator was a small coffee machine, and on the other side was a black and white cat, sitting on a tan pillow and curled up in a ball, who stared at me with an equal mix of curiosity and disdain. She noticed with some amusement that I was looking at her cat, and she said, "My muse and boon companion, Oreo. Named for a certain black and white cookie."

"People mind having a cat in your office?"

She shrugged, folded her hands across her stomach. "If they do, they keep quiet. It's part of the image, I suppose. Eccentric professor and all that. Besides, he's nice to have around. Quiet, well-groomed, not too demanding. Lots of other faculty have done worse. It also helps relax some of my students. Makes me seem less fearful. So. Enough of my choice in companions. What can I do for you, Mister Cole?"

I took a breath, thinking again of how many times I had gone down this path, trying to elicit bits and pieces of information from different people, all by letting them think that they were doing me a favor. Not a pleasant task but one I had done before, and would no doubt do again, but at least this time, it was different. The spirit of Jon was back behind me somewhere, watching me as I worked, and I had to do what was right.

"I write a column for *Shoreline,* called 'Granite Shores.'"

A nod. "I know. I've seen it."

I guess there was shock on my face, for she laughed and said, "You look quite surprised."

"Well, it's not often that I meet people who've even heard of my magazine. Not to mention my column."

"Well, I like to keep up with the history of the region, Mr. Cole. That's my speciality. And I remember reading something you did last fall, about the start of shipbuilding in New Hampshire. Not bad."

"Thanks."

"So. Your column this time?"

"About an acquaintance of mine, an amateur historian, who died last week."

"Oh. I'm sorry. And how can I help?"

I took another breath. "It seems you met him a couple of weeks ago, before his death."

"Ah." She unfolded her hands, leaned forward, moved some papers around and then revealed a desk calendar. "Here it is. Jon Ericson. From Tyler. Am I right?"

"Yes, you're right."

"Sure, I remember him. Vikings." She shook her head. "Sorry to hear he's dead. What happened?"

"He was murdered."

"Oh." She sat back in her chair. "Oh. That's horrible. I mean, well, I just talked to him, less than a month ago. Oh, how awful. And you're doing a story about—"

I made a point of taking out my reporter's notebook. "About his life, about his quest. You see, he was convinced that—"

"Yes, I know. Convinced that Vikings had set up residence here in New Hampshire, hundreds of years ago." She shook her head again. "Brrr. To be murdered. What a nice man . . . not your typical barefoot doctor."

"Excuse me? Barefoot?"

She flashed me an embarrassed smile. "Sorry. An academic secret. Please do me the favor of not spreading it around."

"All right, I won't."

"There. You've made progress all ready. All right. Barefoot doctors. You know anything about history, Mr. Cole?"

"Some." The phrase she had mentioned was now bouncing around in my memory, and when she said, "The Great Cultural Revolution in China, back in the Sixties, when Mao sent people into the countryside, and—"

"Barefoot doctors," I said. "Trained peasants in basic medical care, went into the villages. Am I right?"

She gave me her best professor smile, and I was surprised that it made me feel good, like a student. Perhaps it was an old professor's trick, handed down from generation to generation. "Yes, that's right. Barefoot doctors. A noble idea, like so many of the sixties ideas, that absolutely failed in in its execution. You see, there was a shortage of trained medical professionals in China at the time. So it was thought that one way to address the problem was to give rudimentary medical training to particularly bright peasants and send them on their way to remote villages. Like I said, a good idea that failed."

"And why did it fail?"

She shrugged. "The barefoot doctors thought they were graduates of Johns Hopkins, that's why. Instead of doing the basic treatments they were trained to do, they overreached. Thought they could do surgeries, cancer treatments, and so on and so bloody forth."

"Barefoot doctors," I said. "And how was Jon a barefoot doctor?"

Hendricks reached over and scratched Oreo's head. "Not in a pejorative sense, you understand. It's just that most professors here have had run-ins with amateurs—bright, enthusiastic amateurs—who believe they may have something to contribute to our fields of learning. For our math professors, it's amateurs who are convinced that either they've successfully found the answer to a problem theorem that's centuries old, or they've created an entirely new system of mathematics. For our physicists, it's the dump attendant from Lee who's figured out the unified field theory. And for anthropology professors, well . . ."

I made a note in my notebook. "Crazy tales about Vikings."

She smiled. "No, not entirely. In fact, I'd say Mr. Ericson was probably the most polite and well read of the barefoot doctors that I've ever met. I've had people in here with proof that the Druids inhabited New England for hundreds of years, chased out of the British Isles by the Romans, or proof that the missing tribes of Israel were the actual predecessors of the Algonquin and the Passaconaway tribes. Then, of course, I've had people in here, arguing with me that I was part of some great cabal or plot, keeping the truth away from the rest of society."

"And you said Jon was polite?"

Her hand was now gently rubbing the back of the cat's head. "Oh, yes, quite polite. He started off by saying that he knew that from the start, I would pooh-pooh his theories, but he was still looking for information on pre-1500 visits from Europeans to New England."

"Did he specifically mention Vikings?"

She kept on stroking Oreo's head. "Not at first, but after I started asking him some rather pointed questions, he told me what he was after. He said he was confident that Vikings had made it down here to New Hampshire from Newfoundland and had set up a settlement for further exploration. Of course, he didn't have any proof, but that didn't stop his interest."

"What did you tell him?"

She shrugged. "What I've told others who have some specific group or person who they think got here before the English. That in many, many years of archaeological digs and research—almost ten thousand excavations—not once have we ever found one piece of evidence suggesting a pre-1500 visit. Not once. Oh, Basque fishermen probably ended up here occasionally in the 1400s, but there was nothing permanent. The first permanent European settlement happened here in 1623. Of course, there are pieces of evidence out there, from carved stones from a Scottish knight to a supposed Viking storehouse in Rhode Island, but that's all later been proven to be fake or otherwise misinterpreted."

"How did Jon handle what you told him?"

"Oh, I think he handled it pretty well, but my last comment . . . well," and with that, she pulled her hand free from Oreo and folded her hands again. "Just before he left, I told him that I didn't think it made any difference whether the Vikings got here or not. Mr. Ericson was quite displeased by what I said, though he was still quite polite about it."

Another note in my notebook. "What do you mean, it wouldn't make any difference?"

"That's what I meant," she said, and her cheery professor de meanor got a bit chilly. "It doesn't make any difference. Look, the native Americans here in New England had a wonderful, vibrant culture that existed within its means for thousands of years. It had adapted to the environment, was doing quite well right up to the point when strange large canoes appeared on their shores. That's what matters. What happened to the natives. I don't particularly care if a Viking or two or Druid or a member of the lost tribes of Israel was out here, traipsing around the wilderness. They didn't make an impact. The Europeans of the 1500s and 1600s did. That's what the history is all about, that's what counts. And he didn't want to hear it."

"But even with the evidence he had . . ."

"What evidence? An old coin he may have found as a youngster, and a tale of mysterious mounds in a farm field somewhere in Tyler. That's it. Plus the pride in his Nordic ancestors. I'm sorry, Mr. Cole, but barefoot doctor or no, that doesn't cut it in my world. Look. You're a writer, correct?"

"Of sorts," I said.

"How many times have you encountered men and women, nice and polite and well mannered, who say that one of these days they want to write as well? Or that they want to know your secret to getting published? Or say that they have a great idea for a novel, and if they gave you that idea and you wrote the novel, you'd split any profits, fifty-fifty?"

I shifted in my seat. "Okay. A few times."

"And did you try to reason with them, after the third or fourth time? Try to tell them about the apprenticeship and years of work that went into your skills? Or did you give up after a while, just smile and change the topic?"

I nodded. She went on, warming up to the subject. "I do that now, smile and change the topic. But earlier, I would go into great detail about the training I went through, telling about the years at college and graduate school, and the months abroad on a doctoral project, in Tunisia, and all that work led up to where I am now. I was especially fond of describing my time in Tunisia, warding off sand fleas and amorous suitors who thought American women would spread open their legs at a smile. I talked about all the weeks and months and years of hard work to get where I am today. And then I'd have someone come in off the street, who thinks that I'm part of some grand conspiracy to hide the, quote, truth with a capital T, unquote, from the people. Well, that can be irritating."

"You seem to be handling it well."

That caused her to laugh, and she reminded me of a friendly elder aunt who would feed you tea and cookies and explain to you how she lost her virginity during the World's Fair of 1938. "Very good, Mr. Cole. Let's just say that after years in academia, you can develop a fairly thick skin. Kissinger, that charming old war criminal, he had it right, you know."

Back into the memory bin I went. "The fights in academia are so vicious because the stakes are so low."

"Exactly. So instead of going into great detail of why I think Druids did not in fact set up camp in New Hampshire, I try to change the subject. But with your friend . . . well, he was so eager and well prepared, it almost hurt me to see that look in his eyes."

"What exactly was he asking you about?" I asked.

"Oh, the usual. If I had any knowledge of any digs in the state that uncovered artifacts that didn't belong or that were questionable in their origin. He knew what kind of questions to ask, about what kind of artifacts wouldn't belong at a pre-European dig. But I was afraid I didn't have any information for him."

"In his talk with you, did he ever mention his brother?"

She shook her head. "No, not a word. I didn't know anything personal about him, siblings or whatnot."

"Did he tell you who else he might be seeing in looking for information about the Vikings?"

She scratched at her chin and said, "I recall him saying he was heading up to Conway, to see somebody from Tyler. I asked if it was an old friend, and he laughed and said, only if the poor bastard has Alzheimer's and has forgotten all about me. Oh, one other thing. He was off to see Billy Bear."

"Excuse me?"

"Oh, Billy Bear. A frequent visitor, unfortunately, to this campus and this office. His full name is William Bear Gagnon. He runs an organization over in Porter, called the First People's Civil Rights Council."

"An Indian?"

"Don't call him that if you intend to have a conversation lasting more than a minute. And don't try Native American, either. He says that's a slave name, given to him and his ancestors by the slave owners back in the 1600s and 1700s. No, he goes by First People, which sounds perfectly reasonable. Which, sad to say, is about the only reasonable thing about him."

I carefully wrote down his name. "You say he's been in your office. Not to discuss Vikings, I imagine."

She smiled. "That's right. Not to discuss Vikings. No, William is on a quest, a quest like your friend Jon. But this quest is to gain justice for him and his ancestors, to set the historical record straight, and to make sure that my department and this university aren't hiding native remains or artifacts. Which, no matter how many times I tell him we are not, he refuses to believe. And when he's done with that little bit of talk, he slides into the curriculum here in the department, and my work incidentally, when it comes to the tribes that were here before the Europeans."

"Sounds like a lot of fun for you," I said.

The professor went over to touch Oreo's head again, and Oreo moved, as if not wanting the extra attention. "The funny part is, I sort of do enjoy his rants, though on a limited basis. For he does have a point, about what happened to his people, so many years ago. The problem for Billy, according to me, of course, and entirely off the record, is that I believe he and his movement are a fraud."

"A fraud?"

"Of course. You see, our first really heated discussion occurred when I made an innocent inquiry as to his ethnic background. This is going to sound extraordinarily racist and un-PC, Mr. Cole, but the sad truth is that there are not very many full-blooded Native Americans still residing in New England. Hundreds of years ago, after the wars and diseases, whatever survivors who didn't trek north to Canada stayed here and intermarried with the victors. That was my first mistake in dealing with William, in questioning his background, trying to determine what tribe he might belong to. But my biggest mistake came later, when I started to question his motives."

"You mean, besides justice for him and his ancestors?"

"I guess it depends on your definition of justice. You see, I learned something interesting about his council. Whatever funds he has managed to raise through donations or fundraisers, the bulk has gone to hiring a lobbying firm in Washington, D.C."

The cat yawned, the room was warm, and something suddenly made sense. "I'd think a lobbyist in Washington would work in your favor for only one thing."

The professor's smile was directed, it seemed, to a particularly bright student. "Go on."

"It would seem that Mr. Gagnon would want a lobbyist to help his tribe—whatever it might be—to be recognized by the federal government, leading toward—"

"Toward increased recognition, increased funding, and oh, by the way, a piece of land to call your own that can be turned into a multibillion-dollar casino. Exactly right, Mr. Cole."

"And what did you say to him about that?"

"Not much. Just raised the subject, he got angry, left, and I never raised it again. It's a losing proposition. Look at me, a privileged white woman with bad eyesight and thick hips, with a comfortable and secure life, whose only concern is securing tenure. Compare that with the shattered remains of a Native American tribe, trying to live through the new century. Besides, one can be in sympathy for what he's trying to do, as misguided as his approach might be."

"Really?" I asked.

"Of course. The Native American tribes out in the West are larger, more cohesive, and have land, as poorly placed as those reservations might be. The Native Americans still alive here in New England, they don't have much. And if convincing the descendants of the federal agents who killed and dispersed your ancestors to supply you with billions of dollars . . . Well, it's a rough sort of justice, isn't it? All they're trying to do is regain their history."

"Sort of like Jon Ericson."

"Perhaps," she said, nodding. "Though I have to say that William Bear Gagnon has a better claim on his ancestor's deeds than Mr. Ericson. Poor soul. Murdered, correct?"

"I'm afraid so. Just a few days ago."

"Well, I—"

There was knock at the door, and a young man with an impressive set of shoulders and a head that appeared to sit there with no neck, was looking in, wearing jeans and a UNH sweatshirt. "Uh, Professor Hendricks?"

"Yes, Stan."

"It's uh, well, my appointment is right now."

She looked at me. "If you don't mind."

"No, I appreciate the time you've already given me."

She raised her voice a bit. "Stan, give me a moment, will you?"

The young man exited and Professor Hendricks lowered her voice and said, "Pleasant young man. Here on a football scholarship and with hardly any ability to express any random thoughts of his own. But he's sweet and would do almost anything to get a passing grade, and I do try to help them as much as I can. Well, Mr. Cole, I've enjoyed our little chat."

I got the signal and didn't mind. I had gotten enough from this pleasant little visit, and I stood up and shook her extended hand. "Thanks, professor. I do appreciate your time."

"Not a problem. Do call me if you have any more questions. Especially after visiting Billy Bear. That might prove to be sticky, if you know what I mean."

"I can figure it out."

"Good," she said, smiling, and then like she was remembering it again, her face changed expression. "Jon Ericson. Murdered. Hard to believe, isn't it, that someone whom you've just met, who sat in that very chair you were just in, is now no longer breathing. Brrr. It does give one a chill, doesn't it? Random violence."

"There was nothing random about it," I said. "Somebody wanted him dead."

She reached over for another pat on the cat's head, who in turned moved away, as if accusing her of exceeding her daily allowance of affection displays. "Somebody who was a friend of yours, am I right?"

"That obvious?"

"The way you phrased your questions, the way your eyes looked as you asked them. I'm sorry. I wish you luck with your article."

I started for the door. "And I wish you luck with your students."

I took my time exiting the building, for some reason enjoying myself as I glanced into the open doors of the professors and associate professors and assistant professors as I made my way to the main staircase. The offices were almost always cluttered with books, papers, and artwork and artifacts. There was something about the seriousness of their work that suddenly appealed to me, of being in a university, working toward a greater knowledge of mankind's past and future, and passing along this knowledge to later generations. I knew there was pettiness and political correctness and oh-so-polite-bitchy-conversation at faculty parties and whatnot, but I enjoyed the feeling of people here being paid for learning. Not a bad feeling. I wondered if Jon had felt the same when he had left this campus.

Before heading back to my Explorer, I took a few minutes out and went to a coffee shop in the same shopping plaza where I was parked. The interior was warm and crowded, but I managed to get a cup of coffee and a cinnamon danish from a young girl with long brown hair and a charming smile, and in a corner table, I ate this midmorning meal while reading a copy of *USA Today* that some student or professor had thoughtfully left behind. There was a constant flow of students in and out of the coffee shop, most lugging knapsacks that looked like they were heavy enough to be used by Special Forces troops. A lot of the students were clustered around in little groups, talking earnestly about something, and I fooled myself into thinking that they were discussing medieval art history or the latest discovery in physics, rather than who got drunk at the latest TKE fraternity kegger.

When I left the coffee shop, more clouds were rolling in, and I was thinking about my next couple of trips. Jon had seen three people before being murdered. I had just completed interview number one, and I was wondering where interviews number two and number three would take me.

In my Ford Explorer, I started her up and left the parking lot, and joined a line of traffic heading out to Main Street, and in a few minutes, I was on Route 4, a busy two-lane country road that had taken me to Durham from I-95 and from Tyler Beach. I figured if the traffic was light, me and my Explorer should be back home in about a half hour.

But in the next few minutes, that would certainly not happen.

CHAPTER SEVEN

It started as a vibration in the steering wheel, a vibration that made me think, damn, was it time for an alignment again, so soon after the last one, and while I was trying to remember which month the Explorer had gone in for a checkup, the trembling in the steering wheel escalated into a major shaking, like the damn thing was tearing itself apart. My hands popped off and I slammed on the brakes, and the next few seconds were a confusing mix of screeching brakes, the harsh sound of metal on pavement, and a topsy-turvy feeling in my stomach as I realized I had lost control of the Ford, and it was going where it wanted to go.

Which was across the oncoming lane of traffic.

I think I closed my eyes, as the horns blared and other brakes screeched. The Explorer slewed to the left, hit the down slope of the dirt embankment, and like it was in some damn special effect for an action movie, did a magnificent one-and-a-half roll, my head bouncing off the roof, just as the air bag exploded and punched me in the face.

Somehow I got out, and then I was sitting on dirt and grass, as people gathered around me, asking the same questions, over and over again, sometimes asking them in a loud voice, like I had gone deaf back there. Are you okay? Are you hurt? What happened? Are you okay? Are you hurt? What happened?

And to each series of questions, I said the same thing: yep, nope, I have no idea.

Before me the Explorer was on its side, the driver's side door yawning open, and even from here, I could see the deflated air bag, which had caused a spectacular nosebleed down my face and the front of my jacket. The dirt around the front end of the Explorer was torn up, like a tank had rolled through, which made a bit of sense, for when I had clambered out and went around my wounded vehicle, I counted three tires, not four.

The right front tire was missing.

The police and the Durham Fire Department and the volunteer Durham ambulance corps made their arrival shortly. The fire department hosed down whatever gasoline had been spilled during my Explorer's imitation of a figure skater going down hard. A man and woman EMT fussed over me for a few minutes, asking me the usual questions, flashing a tiny light into my eyes, checking me over for anything broken. With an icepack at the bridge of my nose, the bleeding stopped pretty quickly, and the young lady—who told me she was a nursing student at UNH—gently wiped down my face with a moist towel. They offered to take me to Wentworth-Douglas Hospital in Dover for a checkup, but I refused. I was stiff and I knew I would be sore in the morning, but I was also slightly embarrassed, with all the rubberneckers slowing down on Route 4, watching the free show taking place just yards away from their own safe and functional vehicles. I felt like somebody going to a Broadway play and then being pulled from the audience moments before the curtain rises to play the leading role. The EMTs went back to their equipment, and then a Durham police officer strolled over, face clean-shaven save for a tidy black mustache. His nameplate said SCOTT, and he had a clipboard with him and said, "You doing all right, Mr. Cole?"

"I've had better mornings," I said.

"That I can see. Care to sit for a bit in the cruiser, tell me what happened?"

"Sure." I stood up and the ground seemed to sway under my feet for a moment, and I was hoping that the two EMTs hadn't spotted me. I had plenty of things to do, and spending the rest of the day in an emergency room up in Dover wasn't one of them. Inside, the cushioned seat of the cruiser seemed like the softest pillow in the world after the ground I had been sitting on, and I politely answered Officer Scott's questions as he started with my name, address, date of birth, social security number, occupation, and right up to what had just happened about twenty minutes ago.

"So," he said. "You were heading east, getting ready to get back on the Interstate and head south. Right after your interview with Professor Hendricks."

"That's correct."

"And then the steering wheel started vibrating?"

"Yes, it did."

"Did you hit anything before the vibration? Any debris in the road? A pothole, anything to cause damage to your front wheel?"

"Nope."

"Hmmm," he said. "Okay. What then?"

"The vibration got worse, so much that I couldn't hold on to the steering wheel. I punched the brakes and we went into a spin, and then into this field."

He turned the accident report over and I helped him sketch out what had occurred, and he looked over at me and said, "You're a lucky guy."

"Tell me about it."

"Okay, I will. After you lost the right front tire, Mister Cole, you went across an oncoming lane of traffic. You were probably about a few seconds away from a head-on collision. And another minute or two of driving, you would have been near a bay off the Oyster River. You got out pretty good on dry land. I don't know if you would have been so lucky, trying to get out while you're in a dozen feet or so of water."

I nodded, my hands clasped firmly in my lap, for I was certain that if I let them go, they would start shaking, and I didn't want this young cop to see that. He made another notation on the report and said, "Anybody you'd like to call?"

"Yes, but I don't have a cell phone."

From the center console he opened a tiny drawer, pulled out an even tinier cell phone. "Here. I'm feeling generous today. Maybe some of your luck will rub off on me. You make your call and I'm going outside, take a few pictures."

"Thanks."

With the cell phone, I lucked out again, for I managed to catch Felix Tinios at home, and when I told him what happened and where it had happened, he interrupted me and said, "You going to the hospital?"

"Nope."

"You with a cop?"

"Yeah."

"Okay, I'm on my way. You sit tight and in public. Don't take any rides from any Good Samaritans, all right? You just sit there and wait."

"Thanks," I said, but I think I said it to empty air, for Felix had already disconnected his end of the conversation and like he said, he was on his way.

I liked the way that sounded.

After a few minutes more of sitting, Officer Scott came over and rapped on the window, and I stepped out. "You have any preferred tow company in the area?"

"No, I don't."

"All right, we'll just work down our call list," and he turned his head and keyed a microphone clipped to a shirt lapel and asked dispatch to send along a tow truck. When that was done, he looked at me strangely and said, "Come with me for a moment, will you?"

"Sure."

We walked back down Route 4 for a short distance, the air crisp and cold, the traffic still moving along slowly. We didn't have far to go, for I noticed a gouge in the asphalt, where the exposed wheel drum of the Explorer had struck hard. Nearby, resting by itself in the short grass, was the offending right front tire. Officer Scott bent down and picked up the tire and said in a slightly amusing tone, "I'm no detective, Mister Cole, but I imagine that the accident happened right about here. What do you think?"

"I agree."

He let the tire flop to the ground, and then his mood changed a bit. "But this is when I want to be a detective, Mr. Cole. You want to know why?"

"I sure do."

Officer Scott reached into his pants pocket, pulled out a small piece of metal, and held it out for my inspection. A lug nut.

"Now here's the problem, Mr. Cole. I've gone up and down a good stretch of this roadway, and this is the only lug nut I could find. There should be six. And this one is in good shape, which means it didn't break or shatter. No, it means that it fell off, and that the other five are probably on the side of the road from here to the center of town. Are you following me, Mr. Cole?"

"That I am," I said, my feet getting cold again. "This was no accident. The lug nuts were loosened on purpose."

For a moment he juggled the lug nut in his hand, before putting it back into his pocket. "That's right. You have any enemies, Mr. Cole?"

"Some people who aren't particularly friendly toward me, but no, nobody who comes to mind that would do something like this. Maybe somebody mistook my Ford for somebody else's. A college prank, maybe?"

"Like a fraternity prank, something from a sorority house?"

"That's what I was thinking."

"Unh-hunh," he said. "Problem is, Mr. Cole, we are intimately familiar with college pranks on our force, as you can imagine. Pledges stealing college trophies, pledges being dumped on the football field, naked and painted blue and white. That kind of stuff we're used to. But this mess . . . No, this is way beyond a prank. This was someone trying to cause you intentional harm. And going about it in a particularly nasty way. Do you hear what I'm saying?"

"I do."

"And you still don't think there's anybody out there who would cause you such harm?"

A quick memory, of Ray Ericson, drunk and pissed off on Jon's front lawn, tossing a punch my way, and I pushed the memory aside. "No, officer. I truly don't."

He slowly nodded, like he knew I was lying, and that the both of us knew what was going on, but he let it go. He handed over his business card and said, "Well, I'm going to write this up and give it to one of our detectives. It's serious business, and we don't intend to let it slide on by. You understand?"

"Perfectly."

"Good."

"All right, let's head back."

When a flatbed tow truck from Circle H towing arrived and I worked through the paperwork of showing my AAA card and filling out yet more forms, I took a break and sat against an old stone wall, positioning myself so that I had some mid-October sun in my face. Officer Scott had left, and it was just me and an enthusiastic young man from the tow company, who wanted to show me how this latest rig worked, with its computerized system and intricate hydraulics. Instead, I begged off and sat down and thought for a while. Orange and red leaves from a nearby maple tree blew across the dying grass while I watched the tow truck operator do his thing. For a moment I wished I smoked, for it would have been nice to have something to do, something to calm me down. Ray Ericson. Missing, and the prime suspect in the murder of his brother. I had a feeling that he wasn't much missing, but was in the area. Mainly, my area. I rubbed my hands and watched as the young man worked some cables about the framework of my wounded Explorer. Traffic was still slowing down some, and I was eagerly awaiting the chance to stop being the latest tourist attraction on Route 4.

I rubbed my cold hands together and looked off to the left, where traffic would be coming down from the Interstate, and there I spotted some stones in a row, by the wall. I got up and went over and looked at them. Tombstones, most of them canted to one side or the other, grass thick around their base. All of the stones had the same last name: N U T E. And the latest date I could spot was 1898. There were about ten of them, a family plot no doubt, and I looked around the stone walls and imagined what had once been here before, a large farm, struggling to make a go of it, until the males left the farm and went to find work in the mills in Manchester and Lawrence. The passage of time. Flesh and bones to dust, barns and homes to rotten wood, and the trees and brush taking back the plowed land.

There was a sharp *bang* that made me flinch, and I quickly

turned around, to see the Explorer was now up on its four wheels, sagging to the right where the tire was missing. The tow truck operator waved at me and I waved back, and then he went back to the truck, where the flatbed was now raised up. A low-pitched whining noise started up, and I looked back at the tombstones and said to them, "I hope you don't mind that I don't plan to join you for a long, long while."

A car horn honked. I looked over to the road, suddenly felt better. Felix had arrived, his Mercedes Benz convertible parked to the side. He got out of his car and started coming toward me, wearing blue jeans and a long leather coat. In his right hand he held a small paper bag, and as he got closer he looked over at me and said, "Your nose okay?"

I touched it reflexively. "Still sore, but doing better than it was an hour ago."

A crisp nod, as he looked around, and I felt that little sense of electricity coming from him, like the quiet hum from a power station. Felix was on the job, on alert, and I was glad he was on my side. "Cops come and do the usual?"

"That they did."

"What happened? Besides the front tire of your car flying off."

I took a breath. "Looks like somebody undid the lug nuts. On purpose."

"Okay. That answers that."

"Excuse me?" I asked.

"Here." He handed over the bag. "This is yours, am I right?"

I opened up the paper bag, looked inside. My 9mm Beretta semi-automatic pistol, in its leather holster. "I'm pretty sure I locked the front door before I left this morning."

"Yeah, you did. But I thought you might want this. So I was a little creative, like I was at Seacoast Antiques the other night. Hope you don't mind."

I minded a hell of a lot, but coming from Felix, this was about as thoughtful and affectionate a gesture as one could expect. The paper bag seemed to grow heavier in my grasp. I knew what that Italian piece of metalwork represented, but I still didn't like it.

"Thanks, Felix. I appreciate it."

I took my coat off and he held it for me, as I quickly slipped on

80

the shoulder holster, the pistol bumping against my left side. Felix had no expression on his face as he handed my coat back, and I said, "Okay. I guess we know what this means."

"Yeah. Somebody's after you."

I slid the coat back on, feeling it tight against my left side, where the pistol hung. A heavy feeling, in more ways than one.

"I figured that out after the airbag punched me in the face."

The whining noise from the tow truck stopped, and the young guy came over and said, "It'll be at our garage in Durham. Storage fee is twenty bucks a day, but tell you what, you might be able to drive it off with the spare if you'd like after I check the rim. It's not a real tire but it can get you home, or to a tire store."

The Explorer looked exposed and vulnerable, up on the flatbed of the tow truck, its side stained with dirt and grass. "Not today. Maybe tomorrow."

"Okay," he said, passing over a yellow sheet of paper. "Here's your receipt."

Felix said, "Hey, it's nice to be standing out here and passing the time of day, but I really think we need to get going."

With the tow truck operator climbing into the cab of his truck, I said, "Worried about snipers in the woods?"

He grasped my arm, started walking me back to his parked car. "You should learn to be as worried as I am, my friend."

Inside the Mercedes, I stretched out and then the shakes started, little quivers in the lower part of my legs. That had been a close one, and I had a thought again of being upside down in the Explorer, seat belt secure across my waist, as water from the Oyster River flooded in through a broken window. I shivered again. Felix looked over at me and then pulled out into the road, where the traffic was thin and moving, since the show was now gone.

"You okay?" Felix asked.

"Doing better, that's for sure."

"Yeah, breathing well after somebody tries to whack you one, there's nothing like it in the world."

Felix pulled into a driveway, backed out, and then we were heading east, toward the coast. I said, "I've been doing some thinking."

"I certainly hope so."

"Why me?"

"Well, why not you?" Felix replied.

"There has to be a reason."

"And you think you've got the reason?"

We sped over the Scammel Bridge, heading into Dover, the Bellamy River on our left, the expanse of Great Bay off to the right. "Yeah, I do. The relics."

"The Viking relics?"

"The same," I said.

"What about them?"

I looked at Felix. "The killer didn't get them at Jon's house. They weren't there. He thinks I have him. That's what I think."

"Good going," Felix said. "That's what I thought, too, about one minute after you called me for a ride."

"Which begs another question," I said.

"Our friend at the antique store?"

"Yep. That guy had hair, you remember. Which Ray doesn't. If it wasn't Ray, then who was it?"

"An accomplice," Felix said. "A rival. Who knows. What's more important is keeping you breathing until things get straightened out. And first things first, getting back to your house as soon as we can."

"And that's because . . . oh. Now I get it."

We were now in Lewington, on Route 16, the main north-south highway in this part of the state, which fed into I-95 in Porter. On one side of the road were the two main shopping malls of Lewington, and on the other side of the road was McIntosh Air Force Base. Guns and butter, separated by four lanes of asphalt.

Felix said, "You do get it, then? Explain it to me, if you don't mind."

"The little exercise with the front tire. Designed one way or the other to disable me, until someone could go through my house."

Felix gently tapped the side of the steering wheel. "Very good, Lewis. Stick with me and who knows what else you'll learn about the dark sides of people's souls. Yeah, that makes sense. Delay or disable you to allow somebody a clean time with your house."

Little quivers returned to my legs. "Can I go out on a limb here?"

"Climb out as far as you'd like."

"I'm hoping that you had this little brainstorm before you

82

headed north, and that you made some sort of arrangement before you left."

"Ah, Watson, you know my methods all too well," Felix said, in a fake British accent that made my ears ache. "By the time I got out of there with your Beretta, a couple of guys who've done freelance for me in the past had set up, both in the Lafayette House across the street and in a plumbing and heating van parked in the lot near your house. You shouldn't have any unwanted visitors, anytime soon."

The quivers in my legs stopped. My house is old and is creaky and the sand from the nearby beaches can blow into cracks in the woodwork and get into everything, but damn it, the house is mine. I didn't like the thought of strangers trooping through, upending drawers and going through my belongings. Once again, Felix had pulled through.

"Thanks," I said. "I owe you big-time."

"Friend, the things you owe me are beginning to get as big as Jupiter. And it's just started. I've been doing some talking to some old associates in Florida and I think I might have something to check out in the St. Petersburg area. Only thing is, the guy I want to talk to got burned years ago, talking over the telephone. Spent ten years as a guest of Uncle Sam out in Illinois. Will only agree to a face-to-face."

"What might be down there, waiting for you?"

"Don't know. No details, only something worth my while to check out. So off I go, and if it doesn't work out, Florida in October can be fun. But I'll make sure to let you know in either case."

"Fun," I said. "A nice word."

We sped south now, not much traffic heading toward the border with Massachusetts. Felix reached over and switched on the CD player, and Sarah McClachlan's voice started soothing its way into the interior. I tried to show some sort of surprise on my face, which Felix noted.

"Yes?"

"Nothing. Just wondering why you're not listening to something more—"

"More operatic? Please. Another cliché, in such a long series of them. I like Canada, and I like her voice. And that's why."

"Okay."

We slowed some, as traffic began to approach the tollbooths to

Tyler. We took the exit that led us to Route 101, which eventually would return the both of us to Tyler Beach. But before that would happen, we would have to pass through a tollbooth.

Felix said, "Feel like repaying part of your debt to me?"

"Sure."

"Then come up with two quarters, will you?"

"Coming right up."

I dug two quarters out of my pants pocket, handed them over to Felix, who slowed down at the gate to about twenty miles per hour or thereabouts, and tossed them in. He sped ahead and we turned right, going to Tyler Beach.

"Debt to you still the size of Jupiter?"

"Yeah."

"Okay," I said. "I can live with that."

"Good."

Before us was an open road, lots of unanswered questions, and the sands and rocks of Tyler Beach.

CHAPTER EIGHT

True to Felix's promise, as we went through the parking lot of the Lafayette House I spotted a black van at the near corner, right by my dirt driveway. A well-painted sign on the side said SAM'S PLUMBING AND HEATING, with a Falconer phone number and address. Felix gave a little wave as he pulled up, and self-consciously, I waved as well. A young man in the front seat wearing a baseball cap the correct way—with bill pointing forward, thank you—waved back. Felix stopped and said, "Don't want to risk the undercarriage, so off you go."

"All right. When's your flight leave?"

"Tomorrow. I'll snoop around in St. Pete, talk to my contact. Should be back with something worthwhile by the end of the week."

"Great." I turned in my seat, looked back at the van. "How long will they stay here?"

Felix grunted. "They're cousins, and so far I've managed to channel their larcenous ways into some activities safer and more profitable. So they'll stay here as long as I want them to. That okay?"

"That's great."

"Fine. What have you got planned next, young man?"

"The fun thing would be to sit on the couch and watch some afternoon talk shows with a pistol on my chest, but I've got work to do."

"Don't we all. What do you have going on?"

"Just before he got killed, Jon saw and spoke to three different people about his quest. And right after he talked to those people, he found the artifacts. And was killed. I've talked to the first person on the list, a UNH professor. I've got two more interviews to set up."

"Sounds like a full day. Now, get out of here, will you? I've got some packing to do."

I climbed out of the Mercedes, and was going to turn around and once again express my thanks, but Felix, as he does so well, was already on the move.

Inside my house, I locked the door, and checked the windows, making sure they were all locked. I took out the Beretta, made sure there was a round in the chamber, and did a leisurely search of the cellar, the first floor, and the upstairs. Save for a top drawer in an oak bureau that was partially open—which a few hours ago was holding the very same pistol that was in my hand—everything else looked fine. Someone had been in here earlier, but since that someone had been Felix, I was fine with that. From outside two men were keeping an eye on the place, and that made me feel pretty good, all things considered.

I got out of my dirty and bloodstained clothes and then looked in the mirror, at the purple-green bruise that was still pretty visible across my chest, from where it had been struck the other night at Ray's antique store. I touched my sore nose, which had spurted blood so copiously after being struck by the airbag. It felt better, but not much.

I attempted to make a tough-guy look in the mirror, and failed. All I saw was a tired guy who had just been beaten up twice in the past few days and was getting tired of it.

I went out into my bedroom and got dressed.

After a lunch of tomato soup and a hunk of French bread, I started working the phones, making calls to three different people and organizations. The first call ended up with an answering machine picking up, the second phone call got a man who seemed both curious and a bit miffed at my call, and the third was to a rental car agency that promised to "come to your house and pick you up."

Which they eventually did.

I was now back outside, waiting for the rental car company rep to arrive, and I carried a small paper bag. I went up to SAM'S PLUMBING AND HEATING, and before I could knock on the driver's side door, the window rolled down. The young guy inside looked out at me, his face a bit red, maybe from the cold, and he said, "Hey."

"Hey, yourself," I said. I handed the bag up to him. "Inside's some coffee, a ham and cheese sandwich, a couple of other things."

He grinned. "I'm doing okay, really. My cousin Tom is across the way, and we get to switch off every few hours or so."

"Still, suppose he gets seduced by room service menu and doesn't want to leave?"

He nodded, still smiling. "Yeah, that's a thought. Thanks."

I handed the bag over and he took it, and then I held my hand out and he looked surprised, but shook it, nonetheless. "Name's Lewis Cole."

"Frank Duffy."

"Thanks for what you're doing."

He went into the bag, took out the cup of coffee. "Hey, for what we're getting paid, doing guard work on a house like yours is pretty simple stuff. Beats having to . . . Well, Felix always told us, not to mention stuff like that, so I guess I won't."

"That's wise."

A silver GM car came into the driveway, one of those models that has a name you forget within ten seconds of noticing it, with a rental car logo on the side. I raised my arm to the young lady driving the car, and said to Frank, "My ride's here. Thanks again."

"Don't thank me, thank Felix."

"I've already tried."

An hour later, after filling out more paperwork at the rental car agency in Porter, I was heading north again, not to Durham or the University of New Hampshire, but to North Conway, driving another hunk of anonymous GMC metal. I was back on Route 16 and went through two more sets of tolls, before the highway folded into a two-lane roadway in Rochester. Despite being one of the fastest growing states in the country, there's still a lot of open space and trees in New Hampshire, and the drive north proved that again to me. Some areas were still holding on to the fall foliage, and as I sped through the towns of Wakefield and Ossipee and Tamworth and Chocorua, I found myself relaxing some. As I passed through towns that still had downtowns that would practically be recognizable to a time traveler from the 1700s or 1800s, I had a pang of regret, that Jon and I had never really talked much about the rest of this state, of how it had been settled, and how little some parts had changed.

There were the usual fast-food joints, convenience stores, and gas stations, but the outskirts of the White Mountains were becoming visible, as the time passed, and I thought of the particular bravery or drive or insanity that had caused simple farmers and shopkeepers to leave their quiet villages in Europe and try to make a living here. I have a healthy respect for the mountains and how cold and treacherous it can get up here in the winter, and I think if I had landed on these shores hundreds of years ago, I would have stuck close by the water.

About two hours had passed when I went through Albany, and then the traffic started backing up as I made it into Conway, a charming little village that is unfortunately right on the outer boundary of several miles of roadway and strip malls that look like they had been airlifted from southern California and dropped into this valley. From Conway I kept on Route 16, and soon enough the traffic slowed to a crawl as I got into North Conway, the two-lane road now boasting a center turning lane, and the sides of the road had outlet shops of everything from the Gap to Polo to L.L. Bean, and the impressive mountains were barely visible past the signs and motels and restaurants.

I checked the time, saw that if I was lucky and could find a parking place, I just might make my appointment on schedule. I guess luck was with me, for when I got into the center of North Conway, there was an open space by a park, and I got into it before a gentleman driving a Lincoln Town Car with New York plates coming at it from the other direction. The New York gentleman congratulated me on my driving prowess with a honk of the horn and a cheerful one-finger wave, but I did my best to ignore him as I walked across the busy street to a restaurant, to meet with an old man who had been Jon Ericson's predecessor.

The restaurant was called Horsefeathers, and it was cozy and crowded, with a low ceiling and lots of exposed brass and woodwork. A man dressed in blue jeans, a red flannel shirt, and a tan down vest stood up from a rear table and motioned me over. I went over and shrugged off my coat, doing my best to keep my holstered Beretta from popping out from underneath a buttoned-down sweater. He held out a hand and said, "Lewis Cole, am I right?"

"And you must be Brian Mulligan."

"The same. Have a seat."

Which I did. He seemed to be some years older than Jon, with thin white and gray hair slicked back on his skull, and a prominent nose that made me think that he was like an old greyhound, tired from so many years of fruitlessly chasing a mechanical rabbit around a track. He took off his vest, hung it over the back of his chair, and passed over a menu. "Okay, since you said you're writing a story about Jon and his life, I imagine this is going to be a business dinner, right?"

"Sounds fine to me."

He grinned, "Good. Then I can count on you to pick up the tab."

I opened the menu and said, "Sure. That sounds fair, considering you took the time to see me so quickly."

"Hah," he said. "Got plenty of time to do with what I please, and if you want to talk about that silly guy, then that's fine."

I think he noticed the expression on my face when he then said, "I take it you were fond of him."

"You could say that."

"Look, I'm sorry to hear he got killed and all, but I don't think you know everything you need to know about Jon and his life."

"Maybe so."

"Huuh. Well, did he ever tell you the story about how he became curator of the museum, and how I got replaced?"

"No, he never did talk about that."

Brian flipped through the menu. "Then that's Jon for you. He'd talk for hours about artifacts and where was the exact spot where the Reverend Bonus Tyler settled on Tyler Beach in 1623, but he wouldn't give you five minutes on how he took great delight in stabbing you in the back."

A waiter came by and Brian looked over at me and ordered one of the more expensive items on the menu, a lobster pie, and I looked right back at him, matched his lobster pie, and raised it by a bottle of merlot. As the waiter left, I looked around the place and saw a good mix of locals and tourists up here to look at the last of the foliage and drop a few hundred dollars at the local outlets. Right by my elbow was another table, and a guy with an outdoors type of face, full head of hair, talking about a real estate deal over a cell phone, while his attractive blond wife was talking low to her son, a boy of about eleven or so with a blond crew cut who wore a CRANMORE SKI TEAM sweatshirt.

When the waiter left, I said, "All right, I gather there was bad blood between you."

"An understatement."

I took out my reporter's notebook, flipped it open to a clean page. "Then tell me about it."

Brian looked astonished. "You mean you'll put that in your magazine, what really happened to the two of us?"

Time to put on my poker face, such as it is. "I mean I'll write it up, and my editor will then decide what happens to it. But even then, I want to know the background of Jon and his time at the museum."

Brian seemed to ponder that for a moment, and then shrugged. "Oh, what the hell. It's been years and the poor guy's dead, and most everyone else involved is dead, too. Look. It's a real simple story, okay? Back in the sixties, I had this little firm, out in the Tyler Business Complex, near the Interstate. Extruding plastic into specialized forms. Pretty boring, hunh? But I found a way of doing it faster and cheaper, and by the time I was forty-two, I had a major plastics company buy me out. So there I was, single and practically middle-aged, and with lots of money, lots of money that I could do with it whatever I wanted to do. Some of my buddies at the chamber of commerce, they said I should pack up and go to Florida or Tahiti and just get drunk and play golf the rest of my life, but no, my parents didn't raise me to be a drone like that. So I got involved in the town, that's what I did."

I made a point of writing a few notes, which seemed to please him, for Brian kept on talking. "Started off simple. Got on the zoning board, then the planning board. Thought for a while about becoming a selectman, decided it was too much work, too much political crap, too much ass kissing. Then we had the national bicentennial come through, and I decided to see what I could do with my energy and my money to help Tyler celebrate its history. And what I found horrified me, Mr. Cole. Care to guess why?"

"Sure. Here's my guess. Things were in disarray."

"My God," he said. "Disarray. Now there's a word. We had parchment documents from the late 1600s, rolled up and kept together by rubber bands, on wooden shelves in the town hall basement. The *Boston Post* cane, to be given to the oldest resident in the town, was in the town clerk's office, in an umbrella stand. And town reports from the 1700s and 1800s were dumped in a pile in the attic, right below a leaky roof. I tell you, Mr. Cole, it was a damn crime, it was."

I looked over and saw our waiter approach, carrying a tray, but he was delayed for a moment, talking to a guy I took to be the owner, a tall fellow with a white goatee, who laughed and slapped him on the shoulder after a moment. The fellow with the goatee went by the entranceway and talked to a tall slim woman with auburn hair, who had her arms around a young boy and a young girl. The boy was trying to squirm away from his mother's attention, but the daughter seemed comforted by having her mother's arm around her.

"And let me give another guess," I said, as the waiter started laying down the dishes and the bottle of merlot. "You decided to do something about it."

"Damn straight," he said. "The town had an old building that was being used for storage of landscaping equipment, by the town common. I started a fund-raising campaign to change that place into a museum for the town. Nothing fancy, nothing that would draw lots of tourists or get written up in the *Globe* or *Yankee* magazine or even your magazine. It was just going to be a place to preserve history, to show later generations what it took to build Tyler and keep it whole. That's all."

I took a spoon, dug into the lobster pie, which was in a bread shell and was made with lots of sherry and lobster meat. It was delicious, even considering that we were more than a hundred miles from the ocean. We ate in silence for a few minutes, and then I looked to my notebook and said, "How did the fund-raising campaign go?"

He wiped at his chin with a blue cloth napkin. "The truth?"

"Sure. That'll do."

"Truth is, it went lousy. People can be funny, and it was during a recession when I was trying to do this. Lots of screaming about taxes and such. Most people in town were concerned that if the damn thing got built, then the town would be responsible for its upkeep and for any staff, which would mean added expenses and increased taxes. Pretty soon, as a year went by, the only way the proposal had enough money was because of a last-minute, anonymous donor with a hefty checkbook."

I eyed him. "Your middle name wouldn't be anonymous, would it?"

He smiled, dug into his lobster pie again. "It sure was, that month. Okay, enough of that ancient story. Let's just say that it was a good feeling, seeing it all come together, seeing the building get re-done, seeing some of the townspeople get caught up in the spirit of the place. First year it was open, we would have people in there every weekend, bringing in something from their attic or their basement that they thought belonged in the museum. Ah, it was great."

I scribbled in my notebook. "When did Jon show up?"

"Oh, he had been there all along, doing his part, helping catalog and store the artifacts. He was a history buff, just like me. Hell, in some ways, he was my assistant in getting the museum off the ground. But once the place was finished, was practically running itself, he started going weird on me."

"Define going weird."

Brian put his spoon down. "Okay. Here's weird. We have a per-fectly respectable and interesting history of the town of Tyler, all in one building. It tells the story of how a community that was founded by Church of England dissidents became a farming and fishing town, and then evolved into a place that has a hi-tech industrial park in one end of town and a popular beach resort in the other. My God, I could have filled a building alone with all the artifacts we had about fishing, boatbuilding, and the shipwrecks and rescues that occurred off Tyler Beach. But that wasn't enough for Jon. No, he wanted to go out into unknown mystery land."

"Vikings," I said.

"Yeah, his damn mysterious Norsemen. Look, I didn't have any problem with storing Thorvald's gravestone in the backyard of the museum. It was a hoot. It was something funny to point out how gullible some people were, and how—even almost a hundred years earlier—people in town were trying to figure out ways to bring in tourists and investors. A piece of history. A strange one, but still a piece of history."

"But Jon didn't want to just rely on the Thorvald stone, did he."

Brian shook his head. "No, he didn't. He had this . . . oh, Christ, I don't know. It was like he was on this holy mission to prove that Vikings had camped out in the woods of Tyler a thousand years ago, and by God, he was going to try to prove it. I guess when he was a kid he thought he found a Viking coin on the beach, and that he never got over the fact that he had sold the coin. So he wanted to come up with a plan to attract more tourists, more attention to the town by setting up a display that was a lot of what-ifs. You know, what if the Vikings from Newfoundland came down the coast, what if they stayed here, what if maybe the Thorvald rock isn't a hoax after all."

I dropped the pen, picked up a spoon, stirred my lobster pie some. "And you probably said something to the effect that you wanted to stick with the real history of the town, and not flights of fancy."

He wiped his hands on the napkin. "God, I guess you are a writer after all. Flights of fancy. Like that phrase. Yeah. By then the museum belonged to the town and there were five directors on the board overseeing things, and Jon didn't like the fact that I dumped all over his idea. Though I didn't say flight of fancy. I think I said something like crazy bullshit, and Jon didn't like that at all. So he went before the board of directors with this plan to highlight the Vikings, bring attention to the Thorvald rock, and maybe bring more tourists to the town. Jesus."

"And what did you do?" I asked.

"When it was my turn—and it was during the same meeting—I said any sane person looking at the traffic coming in and out of Tyler most weekends definitely wouldn't want more tourists coming in. And if they were going to come to this museum, by God, it would be a real museum. Not some circus freak sideshow. I told the board of directors that if they wanted to do that happy crap, they'd have to get a new curator. Which is what happened. Bing, bang, boom. I was out, Jon was in, and as far as I was concerned, the museum lost all of its credibility that day."

Something didn't seem right, and I thought about it while the two of us finished our dinner, and when we went into dessert, some sort of toffee thing that was so sweet it made my teeth ache. When the check arrived I finally figured it out.

"But it didn't happen."

"Excuse me?"

"The Viking displays, the emphasis on the Thorvald rock. It didn't happen."

Another wipe of the napkin on Brian's face, but not quick enough to hide a smile. "Yeah. Funny about that, hunh?"

I took out my credit card. "What did you do?"

"Who? Me?"

"Yes, you. Or did Mister Anonymous ride again?"

"Yeah. That's nice. Mister Anonymous did ride again, and punched a big ol' hole in their plans. You see, I had a niece working for the Boston *Herald*. She told me that a reporter was doing a story for the Sunday paper, about popular historical hoaxes in New England. I called him up and asked him if was planning to do anything about the Thorvald stone in Tyler. He hadn't been, but he was interested just the same. Two weeks later, boom. Nice story, with a photo, poking fun at the rubes in Tyler who had once tried to fool people to come into town. End of story. End of trying to redesign a new approach for the museum. Once that article appeared, the board of directors got cold feet."

"But their feet weren't cold enough to hire you back, right?"

A smile. "Since when does any board of directors like to admit its mistakes? Nope. Jon stayed there and I stayed alone in Tyler, at least for a while. Then I got out and ended up here."

"Why?"

"What do you mean, why?"

The waiter came by, picked up my credit card. I flipped to a blank sheet in my notebook. "You're a native of Tyler. You volunteer to help the town out. You seem to have a commitment to the place. And after one setback, you head out. That's why I asked why."

The smile faded, like moonlight being obscured by a passing cloud. "I burned some bridges, Mr. Cole. I . . . I took it quite personally, and I'm ashamed to admit that. It was like everything I had worked for, everything I had volunteered and given money to, was taken away by some guy with a nutty story. I mean . . . Look, Mr. Cole. You're a writer. Correct?"

"That's what I get paid for." Not a full lie, but pretty close.

"All right. Let's say you do a column that gets national attention. Let's say you write a column about . . . oh, I don't know what. Let's say you have information about the pirate, Captain Kidd, burying treasure on one of the Isles of Shoals. You put your heart and soul into the story, you have the documentation, you get some attention . . . and boom, it's gone. Somebody else has taken your work and said, hey, that looks okay, but you know what? It wasn't Captain Kidd who buried that treasure. It was a group of lost Aztecs, sailing north from Central America. And no matter how loony that idea sounds, people grab onto that idea. And your work is ignored. See what I mean?"

"Yes, I do."

He nodded, like he was pleased by my response. "So I got angry. I got bitter. And I left Tyler a few years ago and headed up here, and I've never looked back. Oh, I miss the ocean, but the mountains and the lakes and skiing are a pretty good substitute. After a while, I began to stop brooding about what had happened. I started enjoying my new home. Not a bad place as places go, Mr. Cole."

The door to the restaurant opened and a group of people trooped in, including a man and woman, both wearing brightly colored hand-knit sweaters, with a springer spaniel on a leash between them. The man had a gray beard, the woman had a bright smile, and the dog was sniffing around the entrance like he owned the place. Outside traffic seemed to be backed up in both directions.

"But why here?"

"Excuse me?"

I said, "You said back in Tyler, that you hated tourists, hated backed-up traffic. Seems like you have plenty of that around here. So why North Conway?"

He took a swallow of water. "I still have money, still have drive. There's a lot of things wrong up here, with all the construction and sprawl and open space being gobbled up, but somebody like me can make a difference. I'm a Red Sox fan, so I'm a believer in lost causes. Which is why I'm here."

The waiter came back with my credit card and slip, which I signed and carefully kept the receipt. "And when did you last hear from Jon?"

"Last week. Right here, if you believe it. He called and said he was in the neighborhood, wanted to go over old times. What crap."

95

"I take it he wanted to talk about Vikings."

"Of course he did. What did you think he'd talk about, the weather, or apologizing for screwing me? Nope. Vikings. One more time."

"What did he want to know?"

"Pretty simple stuff. He wanted to know if I remembered anything unusual from the time when the museum was being put together."

"Unusual in what way?"

"Well, remember what I said earlier, about when the museum was starting up? We had people coming in from all parts of the town, offering us stuff from their basement and their attics. Usually it was junk, but sometimes there were a few bits of treasure. Some letters from the early 1800s. A Civil War uniform. Or a pilot's license from 1919, signed by Orville Wright. But no, that wasn't good enough for Jon. He wanted to know if I had spotted anything that might have Viking origin. An axe head. A spindle wheel. A coin or piece of sculpture."

Brian looked at me, sighed, and drummed his fingers on the table. "If only he had come up here just to talk for a while, and then get into the Viking crap, maybe things would have been different. But no, he had to go right into it. So I listened for a while and got up and told him to stuff it, and walked on out. And that was it, until I saw the story in the *Union-Leader* about him being murdered, and his brother being a possible suspect."

"Did you know Ray?"

"Met him once, when I was running the museum. Wanted to know if he could leave his antique store's business cards at the front counter, to publicize his store. I said no."

"Did he make a fuss?"

"Nope. Just said something like, can't fault me for trying, and then left."

I closed my notebook and said, "And if things had gone differently when Jon came up to see you, what would you have said?"

"Hunh?"

"His original question, about artifacts from the residents. Did you remember anything, anything at all?"

Brian looked bemused. "This is beginning to sound more like an apology piece than a magazine article. You must have really been taken in by him."

"Maybe I was, maybe I wasn't. But still . . . Did you have anything to tell him?"

He looked right at me. "Not a thing. And I'm sorry, I've got to get going."

I grabbed my coat and he his down vest, and we made our way outside. I felt warm and full and slightly blue. I had no illusion that Jon walked on water during his spare time, but still, I didn't like having his faults laid out so starkly by someone who knew him longer and better than I had.

Brian stood next to me on the crowded sidewalk, zipping up his vest. He looked at me and said, "Go ahead. Ask the question."

"What question is that?"

"The standard one. I knew the man who was murdered, he wasn't my best friend, could I account for my whereabouts on the day he got killed."

Out in the early dusk his eyes took on a strange shine. I took the bait. "All right, where were you, on the day in question?"

"Here. In town. During an afternoon planning board meeting, attended by a couple of dozen people. And if that doesn't cut it, the local cable access channel here—Valley Vision—actually tapes the program and you can see me sitting in the audience. Good enough for you?"

"Very good," I said.

He laughed, slapped my shoulder. "Say it like you meant it. Mr. Cole, the dinner and the conversation were delightful. Good luck in your article, or whatever it is that you're doing."

We shook hands and then he headed down the sidewalk, where the moving mass of people quickly swallowed him up.

CHAPTER NINE

With the full meal and some wine in me, and with the darkening sky before me, I didn't feel like driving the two-plus hours back to Tyler Beach. Having not thought forward enough to pack anything, I needed to get a few essentials if I was going to spend the night. I drove south a few score yards until I reached White Birch Books, a bookstore built in an old Victorian house. I browsed there for a while and left with a copy of John Keegan's latest and then made a short walk to a combo gas station–convenience store, where I bought a toothbrush, toothpaste, and razor. Thus prepared, I drove south again to the outskirts of North Conway, to the Moose Point Lodge, a two-story motel with a swimming pool out front that was covered with a blue tarp and decorated with fallen leaves.

And within a half hour of seeing Brian Mulligan, teeth nicely brushed, I crawled into a strange bed and pulled the blankets up, and started reading once again about our last, best war. I read for a long time, until my fingers found the book too heavy to hold, and my eyelids found themselves too heavy to stay open.

Lights off, trying to get to sleep, listening to the drone of traffic nearby, going by on Route 16, after a while I decided that I should have gone to a drugstore as well, to pick up some earplugs, for no matter how hard I tried, I couldn't convince my mind that the traffic sounds were in fact the soft roar of the ocean.

I stretched out on my back, replayed the conversation again that I had just had with Brian Mulligan. There was an old saying that the truth hurt, and that was certainly the case tonight. Again, I had no illusions that Jon had been a perfect man. Far from it. But I had liked the way he talked, his passion for history, and his drive to prove his age-old dream, that Norsemen from his ancestral land had gotten to his neighborhood about a thousand years before he did. A nice little picture of someone, a picture that didn't include letting his passion become an obsession, an obsession that had led to a feud with another old-timer, one with a similar passion for history, but a passion that was grounded in reality.

I rolled over, the traffic sounds still haunting me. Reality. Jon had taken over Brian's dream, had run roughshod over it, had taken Brian's singular accomplishment of setting up the Tyler Town Museum, and for what? To try to prove something that was unprovable. That's what. And in the process, had also exiled Brian about a hundred miles north from the seacoast.

Did he tell you, Brian had said. Did he tell you how he had screwed me over?

No, he hadn't, I thought.

And what else hadn't he mentioned, in all the conversations that had been shared, at his house or my house, or even in the cellar, digging for—

I stopped listening to the traffic.

Started listening to something else.

The doorknob to my room, moving back and forth.

I sat up, reached for the light, instantly thought better of it. No need to advertise that I was awake. Back and forth, back and forth, the doorknob moved, making a slight clicking noise. I got up and padded across the carpeting, my heart now thumping right along, and automatically, my hand brushed against the old, still tender bruise on my chest. I stood there in my underwear, listening to a murmur of voices. Two, then. Not just one. I leaned in, not letting my body get in front of the door, trying to get closer.

A male voice: ". . . not much time . . ."

". . . don't worry, we'll do it . . ."

I stepped back, went to the nightstand, where my Beretta lay, snug in its leather holster. I slipped the 9mm pistol free and went back to the door and slowly undid the chain, letting it dangle free without touching anything. The voices on the other side of the door were still quiet but were more insistent, like they were on a deadline or were screwing up, or that they had to hurry up before they lost their nerve.

All right, I thought, nerve it is.

One hand with the pistol, I grabbed the doorknob with the other, spun it open and slammed the door open, bringing it in. I brought the pistol up to the first young guy I saw, aimed it right at his forehead, maybe two inches away from the skin, and said in a voice that was calm, even for me: "Help you gentlemen with something?"

There was a thud, as one of three guys in front of my room dropped a case of beer on the hallway floor. The guy who had the pistol at his forehead said, "Oh, shit," and then his face reddened, as I heard a trickling noise and he wet himself. The third guy was standing a bit off to one side, a couple of brown grocery bags in his arms, and there was a crunching noise, as he squeezed the bags tight, like he was trying to mold them into a bulletproof vest. My eyes flicked around to all three of them, smelled them and their breath, and saw the baggy jeans, sweatshirts, ill-groomed facial hair, and decided that, in all probability, they weren't assassins prowling in the October night to eliminate one inquisitive Lewis Cole.

I lowered the pistol, took a breath. "You guys lost?"

The guy with the grocery bags nodded real quick, like an eager student in class, wanting to show the teacher how smart he was. "You bet, mister. We're looking for Sammy Sinclair, he's in room twelve-fourteen. Supposed to be waiting for us, start a party."

"Right room number, wrong person," I said. "I'm not Sammy, and I don't know where he is."

The guy who had wet himself swallowed. "Sorry. Didn't mean to bother you."

I shook my head. "My apologies, guys. You startled me. Let's call it a night, okay?"

Lots of happy nods all around, and I got back into the room, closed the door, and walked back into the darkness to put my pistol away. Great. Just great. Talk about passion sliding into obsession. Hear a noise out there and you don't think it's a bunch of college kids, looking for a party. Nope. It's the trained killer, the one who whacked your chest and who sabotaged your Explorer, all the way up to the White Mountains to finish the job.

Idiot, I thought. You'll be lucky if the kids don't call the cops about the lunatic who just threatened to kill them all, over a wrong room number.

I slid back into bed and turned on the light, and resumed my reading, trying to relax, trying to get my mind back in shape to fall asleep, but I read all through the night and the gray morning light was coming in the window, before I was tired enough to roll over and sleep, which I did, for a couple of hours, until housekeeping pounded on my door with a sledgehammer or something, wanting to know if the room was ready to be made up.

Nearly three hours later, I parked my rental in the Lafayette House parking lot, next to the van with SAM'S PLUMBING AND HEATING on the side. The guy inside had a reddish beard and looked me over as I approached him. He lowered the window and I said, "Tom Duffy, right?"

"Yep. And you're Mr. Cole."

"The same. Things okay?"

"Things are fine."

"Where's your cousin Frank?"

Tom coughed. "About five minutes away from seriously ticking me off. We've been switching off from the Lafayette House, the guy in the van watching the driveway, the guy in the room watching the coastline near the house. He's supposed to have an early lunch and shower and come back here, and he ain't showed up yet."

"Can I get you anything?"

Tom shook his head, folded his arms across his chest. "Nope. The only thing I need to get done, I got a plastic tonic bottle in here I filled with piss 'bout an hour ago. When my cousin finally strolls across this here lot, I'm gonna toss it at his head."

"Sounds like a plan."

"Best one I could come up with."

I thanked him for his time, walked down the dirt driveway, and again felt that nice sense of serenity and calm, seeing my home sitting there, undisturbed and peaceful. I went in the front door, boosted up the heat some, and checked my phone messages. Just one, from Detective Diane Woods, which I returned. She suggested a lunch date and I quickly agreed, and then I changed clothes and checked the time. About an hour to kill. I went back downstairs, where my old oil furnace chugged along, and I got down on my knees. About half of the cellar had been searched, and I picked up the spoon and old colander, and started digging again. The dirt was cold and damp, and I imagined what little secrets might be in there, what might be hidden, as I dug, sifted, and dug again. Looking for bits of information, looking for clues, looking to find out what in hell had gone on before me, but the hour slipped by, and more of the cellar was searched, and I had not found a damn thing.

We met for lunch at the Whale's Fin, a small restaurant at the Tyler Beach Palace, right in the center of the Strip at Tyler Beach. Large windows looked out over the sidewalk, where during the summer you couldn't see the sands of the beach because of the crowds. But since most of the tourists were at home or were working or were doing whatever they do when they're not here, the view was clear out to the ocean and the Isles of Shoals. We sat in a booth by the windows, and after we ordered, Diane looked at my hands and said, "Your fingernails are dirty."

"Thanks, mom."

She smiled. She had on a black turtleneck and a light pink sweater and black slacks, and said, "The only way I'm going to get called mom is through divine intervention or some change in my lifestyle down the road, so don't hold your breath."

"I won't."

"So. What have you been up to, to get such dirty fingernails?"

"Digging in my cellar."

"And what are you looking for?"

Lots of possible answers to that one, from chasing another man's dream to wasting my time and making a mess, but I answered by saying, "All this talk about Jon and archaeology got me thinking of what might be in the basement of my house?"

"What have you found so far? Any buried treasure?"

"Just buried rocks, that's it."

Diane looked toward the kitchen and said, "You see how many people are here for lunch?"

"Lucky for me it's not in double digits, or I'd have to take my shoes off to count that high."

"Ha, ha," she said, with not much mirth in her voice. "Thing is, I can't figure out why service is slower here than it would be in August."

"Maybe they want us to enjoy our time together."

"Could be." She clasped her hands together on the table and said, "There're a few things we need to clear the air about, before lunch arrives. Okay? So when the food comes we can enjoy it and have some fun conversation, and not ruin our digestion. Deal?"

"It's a deal, detective."

"Good." She seemed to take a breath and said, "Why haven't you called?"

"Excuse me?"

"Today is Thursday. I haven't talked to you since we were in my office, back on Monday."

"Gee, mom, I guess I should have."

The scar on her chin seemed to whiten some. "Mom reference was funny the first time, not funny the second. You know what I mean. I'm working a murder investigation involving a friend of yours, and you haven't asked me for an update since Monday. Which begs the question why. First reason, of course, is that you don't care about what happened to Jon and my investigation. Which is bullshit."

"True. I do care. So tell me. How goes the case?"

"The investigation continues. End of statement."

"All right, maybe I didn't call because I knew that was what I was going to receive for an answer."

"I doubt that would have stopped you. So you didn't call on a case that you care very deeply about. Which means that either you're pissed at me, or you're off doing something on your own."

"I'm not pissed at you," I said. "You're doing your job, and

I know that with the two secrets we discussed . . . well, I'm not angry, Diane."

She squeezed her hands some. "All right, for what that's worth. Let me tell you two other things, my friend. The first is that I heard from a buddy of mine with the Porter police, that somebody broke into Seacoast Antiques over the weekend. Not sure if anything was missing, but since it was the residence and business of a prime suspect in your friend's murder, that sure raised my interest."

I stayed silent, wishing that the damn waiter would show up with our lunch, or a tidal wave would suddenly come through the front door, or something equally distracting. Diane went on. "Another thing. The chief's secretary, she loves to read newspapers through her lunch. Reads about five or six every day. She passed over a little clipping from the Durham paper, about a Tyler resident who was involved in a car accident on Tuesday. Sound familiar?"

I still didn't want to say anything, so I just nodded. "Okay," Diane said, "I'm going to let you in on another little secret. I don't know what you're up to, and I don't want to know, all right? The break-in at Ray Ericson's place, your traffic accident, whatever. Here and now, Lewis, we're coming to an understanding, an agreement. You're not going to ask me anything about the investigation. In fact, it would probably be healthy for the both of us, if this is our last gabfest for the foreseeable future. Because when your buddy's killer is caught—and one of these days, he will be—some scum defense lawyer is going to go overtime trying to find a weakness in the state's case. And that weakness is not going to be our relationship, as dear as it is. Understood?"

This time, I spoke. "Understood."

"Good. And while I'll miss you dearly over these next few weeks, I am going to count on you to pass along anything you find to me, through an anonymous phone call or tip or something. Because we both want the killer caught. Right?"

I said, "You're right. We both want justice done."

She cocked her head at that one and said, "Okay, I'll let that one slide, because I really don't want to know any more than that. Just don't screw up my case, okay?"

I nodded. "Okay."

"Because I've already told you why this one is personal to me, friend. With Kara and my promotion."

Finally, the waiter approached, carrying a tray. "It's personal to me as well, Diane."

She undid her hands, offered me a smile as the waiter came up to us. "All right, friend. It's official. Topic A is now off the table."

"What's Topic B going to be?" I asked, as I took a cloth napkin and spread it over my lap.

"How about your love life?"

"Going to be a damn short topic," I said, and both she and the waiter laughed.

Lunch was fried clams for her, fried shrimp for me, and Diane wiped her fingers and looked out the window, to the nearly empty sands. There were tiny moving figures out there, people who wanted to be near the cold ocean and cold sands on this windy day. She leaned back against the padded seat and said, "I know I've said it before, but I'll say it again. This and winter are my favorite times of the year. The workload gets down to a manageable level, only the diehards show up at selectmen's meetings to complain about the police department, and all of the tourists stay away. Not healthy for the chamber of commerce, but healthy for me."

"You mean you don't like working on your tan during the summer?"

She smiled. "Not much time for that. You know, it's days like this when you can really appreciate the history of this place. You just try to unfocus everything around you and look at the beach and the ocean, and you think, this is what it was like, hundreds of years ago. Before the English showed up and ruined everything."

"As someone of Irish descent, I appreciate your opinion of the English."

Another smile. "Another reason not to like most of the tourists. They come here and they think it's a big playground, a big Disneyland put here for their amusement. They don't realize this is a community of people, living here year round, and they certainly don't appreciate the history, the blood and sweat that had been poured out to give them a place to get sunburnt and drunk."

"When people are having picnics at Gettysburg, you know they don't know their history."

"True . . . and it's not like I'm thinking they should pay homage or not come here. They should just show some respect for the past. Some appreciation. My God, listen to me. The longer I live here, the crustier I get. Pretty soon I'll be listed in the damn tourist brochures, the police detective with an attitude."

When the check came, I paid for it, and Diane said not a word, which was fine. I looked to her and said, "Jon had an appreciation of history."

"That he did."

"But his history didn't follow the usual path. He had his pet theory, about Vikings."

"So far, you're telling me things I already know. Got a point there, Lewis?"

"And I'm beginning to wonder if his way of looking at things got somebody angry. Somebody who didn't appreciate the thought of the history of this place being turned around to mention Vikings."

She raised a finger to her lips, looked at me. "Not one word more, my friend. Remember our agreement."

I reached over and got my coat. "Okay. I'll remember."

"And remember the other part, too. You find anything I should know about, you let me know. Quietly."

"With such a crusty personality, how could I forget?"

And for that, she punched me in the shoulder. But lightly, since we were friends.

Outside, the breeze was whipping from the ocean, causing our open jackets to flap in the breeze, and Diane leaned into me and said, "Thanks for lunch."

"You're welcome."

"A question?"

"Go ahead."

"How long have you been carrying?"

I didn't insult her by asking her to be more specific. "For a couple of days now."

She turned her head, and the wind was blowing hair into her eyes. She pulled it back and said, "Ever since the car accident?"

"Yes."

"You have reason to be scared, then."

I zipped up my coat. "I believe I have reason to be cautious, Diane. That's all."

She nodded. "You feel all right then? You going to be okay?"

I brushed some of the hair out of her eyes. "I will be fine. Honest."

"Good," she said, her voice suddenly sharp. "Because one homicide investigation is plenty. Take care, Lewis."

"You, too."

I kept an eye on her, as she headed to her Volkswagen Jetta, thinking about what must be going through her mind. Juggling a homicide investigation, trying to keep things clear for her upcoming promotion, worried about the love of her life moving in with her. And li'l ol' me, the male friend in her life. I put my hands in my coat pockets. On Diane's ladder scale of priorities, I knew I wasn't near the top, not at all. And that, combined with her sharp words, bothered me.

I waited. Diane got in the car, started it up, and backed out onto Atlantic Avenue. She drove by, and then there was a honk from the horn, a cheery wave and a big smile, and I waved back, suddenly feeling much better.

Silly, I know, but there it was.

In the late afternoon, I was back in the cellar, breathing hard, leaning up against the cold and old metal of my oil furnace. My fingers were caked with dirt, and there was a smear of blood on the back of my right hand where I had scraped it against an old piece of brick. The jagged chunk of brick was the only manmade object I had found in my hours and days of digging, and now, at whatever hour it was, I was finished. I had gone from one end of the basement to the other, a foot or so deep, without finding a damn thing. About the only place left was the dirt that was under the brick and concrete mat that held up the oil furnace and tank, and I wasn't about to disturb that. Not yet, anyway. The seductive scent of being on the verge of making some important discovery certainly hadn't come along. The only thing that was here was a tired man with blue jeans almost worn through at the knees, an aching back, and dirty hands.

Upstairs the phone rang. It rang and rang and rang, and I looked up at the floorboards above me and said, "Leave me the hell alone, why don't you?"

My words must have worked magic, for when the answering machine clicked on, there was silence. Nobody had left a message.

It was silent again. I shifted my weight, tried to get comfortable, decided sitting in dirt and resting against an oil furnace were never going to be comfortable, any time soon, but I was too tired to move.

"Was this how it was?" I said to the empty cellar. "Hunh, Jon? Lots of long hours, hard work, and nothing to show for it? Was it like this?"

Nothing. Wood creaked as something in the house settled. I bestirred myself and collected my pathetic amateur archaeological tools—bucket, spoon, and old colander—and clumped my way upstairs. If I had been a neatnik, I would have washed the spoon, washed the colander, and rinsed out the bucket and returned it to the shed that served as a garage. Instead, I dumped the entire mess on the floor and went into the kitchen, where I did battle with hot water and a chunk of Lava soap, trying to get the worst of the grime off. After a quarter hour of effort, I declared a truce and dried off my hands with a clump of paper towels and made my way to the living room.

A neatnick would also have spread newspaper or a blanket or something on the couch to protect the fabric from the three or four pounds of dirt my jeans were carrying, but I just dumped myself there, and spent a couple of minutes deciding whether I had the strength to pick up the remote. When I decided a few more minutes of inactivity were called for, another challenge approached me when the phone rang again.

I guess I should have ignored it again, but the noise was making my head ache, so I picked it up and grunted something, and Felix replied, "Man, you sound like you just woke up."

That made me yawn. I said, "Mentioning sleep isn't a good idea now, Felix. I've been busting my butt the past couple of hours and I could drop right off. What's up?"

"Oh, what's up is that I'm sitting poolside at my nice little hotel in St. Pete, and there are two sisters looking over my way, one in a pink bikini, the other in a green, and it's a heavy burden to carry, but I think they're about to get into a serious fight over me."

"Things are tough all over," I said. "What else is going on?"

"Not to get spookland on you, but I've made my contact, and I'm meeting him tomorrow. At first he didn't want to talk to me, but lucky for the both of us, I was able to bribe him."

"With what? Cash? Girls? Coupons for the early-bird specials?"

He laughed and I could make out a young lady laughing, somewhere in the background. Felix said, "Your last answer's pretty close. I got him through food-related means."

"Which means what?"

"Which means is that before I headed into Logan, I went over to the North End and picked up some specialty items that are hard to get in St. Pete. Certain sauces, spices, cheeses, and meats. When I told him what I had . . . well, he practically rolled over and started panting on the phone. So it's a go."

"Good." I shifted some in the couch, decided enough energy was coming back that I could start thinking about dinner. "Sorry I missed your earlier call."

"What earlier call?"

"About ten minutes ago, the phone rang. It wasn't you?"

"Nope. Ten minutes ago I was helping a young lady get her back oiled up. So it wasn't me. You okay up there?"

"Yeah."

"Those two cousins, they doing all right?"

"Still on the job, as far as I could tell." I yawned.

"Hey, sorry I'm keeping you up. What the hell have you been doing to get you so tired?"

"I was digging in my cellar."

"Your cellar?" Felix asked. "Your cellar's dirt?"

"It surely is."

"Then stop digging and put in some concrete or something. Jesus. What are you doing tomorrow?"

"Tomorrow," I said, "I'm going back in time."

"Oh. Care to explain?"

"Not yet," I said.

"All right, go back in time," Felix said. "But still watch your ass then, okay?"

"I most certainly will."

"Good. See you soon."

After he hung up, I put the phone down and decided to rest my eyes for a moment. I stretched out my legs and folded my arms and rested my eyes, and when I opened them next, an hour had passed. Diane had her Kara and Paula her lawyer friend, and Felix was making do with two sisters.

But I had to make do for myself, so I got off the couch and tried to determine what I was going to have for dinner in the short walk I made from the living room to the kitchen.

CHAPTER TEN

For thirty years or so, the downtown of Porter, the state's only port, has seen an amazing change. In talking to some old-timers and reading books about the area, I learned some fun facts about the neighborhoods around the harbor, especially the places that have high store rents and which feature expensive hand-blown glassware, jewelry, or pieces of sculpture whose cost could feed a family of four for a year. All the tourists trooping through the little shops with their underdressed and overpretentious help, none of them would have lasted five minutes in the area if they could magically be transported back in time about forty years. For the dirty little secret of the most high-priced area of Porter is that nearly a half century ago, it was a dark warren of alleyways, bars with sawdust on the floor, and brick boardinghouses where rooms rented for an hour, and where the occasional sailor or marine from the shipyard or one of the ships in port would end up dumped in a dark corner, bleeding and with broken bones.

It was a rough piece of work, where the Porter police only entered in pairs after dark, and attempts by the city—okay, halfhearted attempts, since so much of the money from the bars and whorehouses ended up in the right pockets—to clean it up always failed. The only thing that killed the harbor district's reputation was when the shipyard started laying off folks in the sixties, the naval prison at the shipyard closed, and military ships stopped calling on a regular basis at Porter. Customers dropped off, bars closed, and the boarding-houses were boarded up, all because of Department of Defense cut-backs. With land and buildings cheap, it was primed for a boom, which is what happened some years later. Call it military gentrifica-tion, if you like.

But if one looked hard enough, there were a few out-of-the-way places where the money hadn't changed the neighborhood, where the drinks were cheap, and if there were no boardinghouses around, late at night the right questions and the right amount of money could rent you some physical entertainment.

One of those places was Stark Street, where I was the day after I came home from my trek up north. It's near a tidal basin which stinks up twice a day during low tide, and since real estate developers haven't yet determined a way of eliminating odors from mudflats, it's still kept its rough-and-ready nature. Right next to the Muddy Bottom Pub was an old storefront that still had Marelli's Grocery in faded let-ters over the glass windows, but which said First People's Civil Rights Council on a cardboard sign in the window. I went into the small storefront, and there were a number of high school kids working the phones, stuffing envelopes. There were four desks—none of them matched—and a longer table on one side that held a photocopier, piles of papers, and other office stuff. One of the young ladies, with a light blue tinge to her hair and a ring through each eyebrow, looked up at me cheerfully and said, "Can I help you?"

"Sure," I said. "I'm looking for William Bear Gagnon. I have an—"

Just then a voice came from the rear of the storefront, "If that's you, Cole, come on back."

Which is what I did, maneuvering my way across the soiled green carpeting, held together by gray duct tape. On each of the walls was a variety of posters, which could have come from a Smithsonian Institution display on sixties-era protests, with the customary and usual slogans: War Is Bad for Children and Other Living Things, Visu-alize World Peace, and Think Globally, Act Locally. The door to the rear office was flanked by two dented four-drawer metal filing cabinets, and in the office was a large man, standing behind a desk. He looked to be in his midthirties, wearing a denim shirt and blue jeans. Around his neck and on both wrists were elaborate pieces of silver and turquoise jewelry. His dark hair was pulled back in a ponytail, and his eyes seemed black. He nodded crisply at me as I came in and briefly shook hands, and I was glad it was brief, for if he was in the mood to break my hand with his grip, I'm sure he could have done it with no difficulty.

In his office the posters were of a more direct bent. There were a couple demanding freedom for Leonard Peltier, one showing what looked to be Geronimo, another of Sitting Bull, and a last one showing a Native American woman squeezing an American flag. This last poster said: AMERICA, LOVE HER OR GIVE HER BACK.

"Mr. Cole," he said.

"Mr. Gagnon," I said. "Thanks for giving me some of your time."

"Not a problem," he said, leaning back, the chair squeaking ominously. "I'll only ask you one thing."

"All right."

Gagnon said, "I'll talk to you about when Jon Ericson came by, all right? I'll tell you everything you want to know. I'm sorry he's dead. He seemed like a nice old guy, even though I didn't think he knew what he was talking about. But I want you to promise me that you'll do a column about the council, in a few months. Deal?"

I said carefully, "That's fine. I promise I'll write and submit a column about the council."

"And see it gets published," Gagnon said. "Just so we're clear."

I shook my head. "I'm sorry. I can't guarantee that. I write columns all the time that my editor turns down. I can't promise you that."

"Then I'm afraid this interview is at an end," he said.

"If you say so," I said, and I got up and started out of the office, when he said, "Okay, wait a minute."

I turned and he was grinning. "Can't fault me for trying now, can you."

"Depends on what you're trying to do, I guess."

He opened his arms wide. "What do you think? I'm trying to do the best for my people, and that includes publicity from magazines like yours."

I motioned to the front of the store. "Looks like you've got some awareness going on out there."

Another grin as he folded his arms across his chest. "Oh, that. Yeah. I did a class at Porter High School last week. History seminar. Opened up their little middle-class white minds into what really happened on this soil, nearly four hundred years ago, when the Europeans came and killed off most of us and stole our land. Spread a little guilt around. Guilt can be good and can be used, Mr. Cole, and these kids have plenty of it. So a bunch of them volunteered and I intend to use them until they feel guilty about nuclear power or whales or whatever, and then I guess it'll be time to do another seminar."

Despite the cheerful cynicism he was displaying, I was enjoying hearing him talk. "So the kids out there are part of a plan."

"Sure. The plan is to get organized, raise awareness, and get what's owed us." He turned around and pointed to an old, small plaque on the wall, just above a lamp. "See that? Commemorates the founding of the New England Indian Council, back in 1923. And the motto they chose back then is telling, Mr. Cole: I still live. Get it? The first people of New England are still alive, are still here, though history tells us otherwise. You know, even before the Pilgrims set foot in Massachusetts, many of the New England tribes had been nearly wiped out by disease, from Europeans. Around the time of Columbus—and this is still a history that isn't taught in schools—Basque fishermen would take up station off our coastline, fishing for cod. They could give a shit about stealing land; all they cared about were the fish. But that was even too much for the local tribes, because the Basques brought a whole set of nasty things along with them when they traded with the First People: measles, chicken pox, smallpox."

He took a breath, unfolded his arms. "Even when the Pilgrims came here, we still lived. Lived through the wars, through the massacres, through the times when our people were driven north to Canada or were sold south to be slaves in the Caribbean. Lived when our land was taken, the forests cleared, the animals slaughtered. Lived even when the anthropologists and the history professors called us extinct, said that the New England Indians had perished from the scene. We still live, and will continue living."

I took a few notes and said, "Sounds like you have a hell of a job then."

"Don't you know it," he said, moving the chair back and forth a bit. "I've met with my brothers in New York and out West, and in spite of all that we share, I must admit a sense of envy. They have reservations, land that they can call their own, and they have their history. You see, when the white man rolled in here back during the 1600s, this was when they perfected their approach to the First People. At first, they would befriend them, learn how to live in the environment, how to fish, how to eat certain plants. They would trade with them, and then steal their land through treaties or bribes. And when the tribes resisted, well, they were nonwhite and nonbelievers, and they had to be slaughtered. And the survivors were then driven out. Eventually this system was perfected, all the way from here to the Mohawks in New York, to the Delawares and Cherokees and the Seminoles down south."

Some phones rang and he ignored the noise, as he continued with his little minilecture, one I'm sure he had practiced many times before. "So the farther west they went, the white man just kept on doing what he did best. But by the late 1800s, the First People had learned, had resisted, so at least they were able to squeeze some bits of survival, some ways of keeping their tribes intact. But here, in New England? The Micmacs and Passaconaways and the Abenaki, they were like shattered clay pots, scattered across the countryside, and we descendants centuries later, are doing our best to bring the pieces together."

"And what piece of the pot do you think you belong to?" The moment those words left my mouth, I regretted them, for I recalled how Professor Hendricks said that Gagnon hated having his past questioned.

But maybe I had caught him in a good mood, for he smiled and said, "Yeah, eventually that question comes up. Who are you? Who are you? It's like if we don't have a label on the back of our necks, ready to whip out at a moment's notice, then we don't count. We don't exist. Okay, let's flip the question for a moment. Where did your ancestors come from, Mr. Cole?"

"Ireland."

"Both sides of your family?"

"Yes," I said, getting a feeling of where this was going.

"Okay. Prove it."

"Excuse me?"

A brief laugh. "There you go. How do you know you have Irish ancestry? It could be French, could be German. Unless you've done extensive genealogical research, Mr. Cole, I doubt you have any evidence of your Irish background. You're depending on what was told to you by your parents and your grandparents. Now, then, you're still at an advantage over me and my brothers and sisters, since you have records to rely on. Passenger lists on ships. Immigration records. Other records from church parishes and towns in your native Ireland. If you had the desire and the time, you could probably do a fair job in tracing your ancestry back. But me? Like you, I depend on what was told to me, by my mother and father and grandfather. I know I'm not pure First People—so few of us are. But I know what I am. And to finally answer your question, a branch of the Abenaki. And my job now is to make sure we keep on living."

"By doing what?"

The sound of voices out in the storefront seemed to peak for a bit, as somebody told a joke and there was laughter. Gagnon said, "Two goals, right away. Raise awareness and raise funds. The first part starts with the schools, the media, the historical societies in all these quaint little New Hampshire towns. Most of those towns have historians who believe the damn land was empty when their ancestors rolled in and started up their farms. Once you get your story out, once you get people understanding that the First People lived and continue to live around them, then you need funds. To preserve old documents, old artifacts. To get some of our land back. Perhaps a cultural center, someplace to celebrate our history."

I flipped a page in my notebook. "And to pay for a Washington lobbyist?"

Whoops. His mood suddenly changed, like a switch back there had been flipped, and I could feel those dark eyes of his boring right into my skull. "You've done your research."

"Some."

"I thought you were interested in Jon Ericson."

"I am," I said. "I'm just trying to get some background information, about what's going on here and what Jon's part of it was. Among the facts I learned was that lobbyist. No intent to offend."

He thought about that for a moment, and then the smile reappeared. "Hold on. I'm not the only person you're talking to about Jon Ericson, right?"

"That's right."

"Then you must have talked to Professor Hendricks, over at UNH, before you came here. Jon told me that he had just come from seeing her, before he made his appointment with me. That explains it."

"Explains what?"

"Explains why you know about the lobbyist. You see, Professor Hendricks has a thing about us noble Native Americans. She loves to study our history, our traditions, the way we led our lives. She's participated in digs around the state, looking for fire pits, artifacts, old bones, arrowheads. She's done research on our migration and trading patterns, and how the tribes reacted to the first settlers. Oh, she certainly has a thing about the noble savage, but do you see a pattern in her interest?"

I did. I said, "It looks like she's just interested in what you've done, what you were once."

"Exactly," he said, the look on his face now showing no irritation over my lobbyist question. "You see, she loves everything about us. So long as we're dead and part of the past. She has no interest in our survival, in how we're living, in what we're doing to keep our people alive. Which is why she gets all righteous and mighty over the fact that we've spent some money on a lobbyist in Washington. Tell me, Mr. Cole, if you had to navigate the treachery down there, in going through the different departments, in trying to determine what requirements they needed for federal tribal recognition, and what kind of treaty obligations might exist, wouldn't you want somebody who knew the lay of the land?"

"Makes sense to me," I said, deciding not to raise the question of a possible casino. I still hadn't gotten what I needed yet, and if that meant being on the receiving end of a lengthy lecture, so be it.

"Man," he said, shaking his head. "She's almost as bad as the dreamcatcher thieves."

"The what?"

"Ah," he said, opening up a drawer to his desk, which he had to yank pretty hard to open. A hand went into the drawer and came out with a wooden object, that he tossed on the desk. "Seen these?"

I had, hanging from rearview mirrors of vehicles, in storefronts, and in a few offices I've visited over the months. It was a circular piece of wood, with bits of rawhide woven in the center, and a couple of feathers and other objects hanging from another piece of rawhide. I picked it up and said, "Dreamcatcher. Okay, now I get it. This is an object that's supposed to catch bad dreams, am I right?"

He picked it up and tossed it back in his drawer, slammed the drawer shut. "A simple explanation, but yes, that's what a dream-catcher is supposed to do. It's a sacred object, prepared by a mother and father, with the aid of a medicine worker. It's supposed to hang over the bed of an infant, to protect him or her from bad dreams. The dreamcatcher catches the bad dreams, the bad spirits, and protects the infant as he or she grows older. That's what a dreamcatcher is. The problem is, well, the problem is that a certain segment of the population, having now exhausted channeling and healing crystals and mag-net therapy, has stolen our dreamcatchers."

"Oh," I said. "I understand."

"No," Gagnon said sharply. "No, I'm sorry, you don't under-stand. Look, you said you were Irish. I'm going to make a leap of faith here and say you were raised Roman Catholic."

"Yes, I was."

"All right," Gagnon said. "Not knowing much about Catholi-cism, I do know that you folks believe that during the ceremony, whaddya call it, the Eucharist, you believe that the bread and wine that's consumed is the actual flesh and blood of Christ. Right? That somehow, during the Mass, because the priest says certain words and phrases, that the bread and wine are mysteriously transformed into the actual flesh and blood of Christ. Correct?"

I took a breath, feeling uncomfortable under the spotlight. "Look, I'm no Catholic theologian, but I'd say—"

He interrupted. "Okay, I understand. But I got the rough con-cept right, okay?"

"Okay, you've got the rough concept."

"Good. Now, let's say you're a practicing Catholic, go to church every Sunday, think the pope's a good guy, got his act together. All right? How would you, the good Catholic that you are, react if all of a sudden you saw non-Catholics yukking it up and drinking wine and eating bread, who thought they were receiving communion, getting in touch with an ancient religion, and that through their actions and their actions alone, they were getting what you thought was a holy sacrament? Do you see now?"

"I do."

"Ay, ay, ay," he said, suddenly rubbing his eyes. "No offense, but typical white people. You destroy us and kill us and steal our land, and you think you honor us by naming mountains or lakes after us, or sports teams, or by stealing our religion. Damn white people even make money off our holy relics."

Lecture or no, I was tired of the indirect approach, so I said, "And Jon, was he like a dreamcatcher thief?"

"In a way, yes."

"Why?"

Gagnon sighed, folded his arms back against his chest. "Look. We get all kinds in here, okay? Most of the time, it's simple curiosity, simple respect. Like those kids out there. For the first time in their lives, somebody's opened up their little eyes to the real history of this part of the world, that years ago another people and another culture called this home. Those are the kind of visitors I respect."

"And you didn't respect Jon?"

"No, I didn't say that," he said. "He was polite, he was nice, but it was his ideas I didn't respect. Forgive me, Mr. Cole, for being rude here but I could give a shit which white man stumbled onto our land first. Jon Ericson wasn't the first to come here and try to ask me questions, and I'm sure he won't be the last. I've had an old lady in here, convinced that the First People were the actual descendants of the missing tribes of Israel, and she wanted to take skull and bone measurements of friends of mine, and then fly to Israel and compare them with the population there. Jesus, old lady or not, I tossed her out on her ass. And then, last summer, I had some crazed writer from Ireland show up, who had a theory that some Irish monk, some St. Something-or-another, came here before Columbus, before the Vikings, even, and preached the Gospel to the First People. He wanted to know if we had any oral traditions about strange men in boats made of cowhide showing up."

"And what did you tell him?"

Gagnon laughed, and spoke in an awful brogue: "I said, begorra and sure we did, if me name wasn't William Bear O'Gagnon." I had to laugh with him and then Gagnon dropped the accent and said, "Yeah, so he got pissed and left pretty quick."

"The monk."

"What monk?"

"Do you remember the name of the Irish saint who got here first?"

Gagnon shook his head. "I forget. Some strange name. Whatever."

"All right," I said. "And how did your visit go with Jon Ericson?"

"Polite, like I said. He made an appointment and asked all the right questions, knew the names of the tribes in the area, what kind of lives they lived. Most of them were migratory in some way, living for a while at the seacoast, collecting shellfish and such, and then moving into the forests at different times of the year. Then, after going round and round for a while, he came right out and told me his theory, that some Vikings had ended up at Tyler Beach, and had established a settlement there."

"What did you say to that?" I asked.

"Hah. He didn't like the answer. I said something like, so? What's your point? He got kind of flustered and said he was looking for information about his ancestors, his ancestors from Scandinavia, and he hoped that I could appreciate where he was coming from. I felt like telling him about how at least his ancestors were still respected and feared, but I let that go. I told him to go on, and he said that he had bits of evidence that a crew of Vikings had made it this far south from a settlement in Newfoundland. I asked him what kind of evidence? He said a Viking coin, found at the beach—and now conveniently missing—and an old illustration that showed what appeared to be Viking mounds, on somebody's land in Tyler. That's it."

Same story, I thought. Jon was telling the same story to three different people. So where had it taken him?

"And he came here to see you because . . ."

"Because he wanted to know, just like that crazy Irish writer, if the tribes here had any legends, any stories, about white men in long canoes—man, I hate that phrase, long canoes—and what might those legends have said. Or, failing that, were there any artifacts we might have, squirreled away someplace, that showed evidence of Viking origin. I sat here and waited until he finished his spiel, and then . . . well, I didn't think he liked what I said in return."

I said, "Meaning, you weren't nearly as polite as he had been?"

No emotion in his voice. "I didn't have to be polite. I just had to be true to my people. I told him that no, we didn't have any legends of white trespassers coming here, hundreds of years ago in long boats, to invade us and kill us. And as far as artifacts went, I didn't think any of the people I know, or the collections they have, contained any strange, European artifacts. Then he got a bit flustered and asked whether or not I'd ask around. I said no, I wouldn't."

"I take it things deteriorated from there," I said.

"Oh, yeah, that's a nice term. Deterioration. He started blathering on about history and getting to the bottom of things, and why would I stand in the way of finding out the historical truth. I told him something I just told you, that I didn't give a great crap which thieving white man stumbled on these shores first, and I didn't think it mattered one bit. I also said something like even if we had a Viking longboat, hidden on the shores of Lake Winnepesaukee, I wouldn't tell you, because all you'd want to do with it is use it to steal our birthright, our history. We were here first, we were here first for thousands of years, and we still wish you hadn't come."

"And what did Jon say to that?"

Now Gagnon's face had darkened and his breathing had quickened, like he was reliving the argument he had had with Jon. "He got even more angry, started talking about respecting history, no matter where it takes us. I said, history, you want to talk about history? The Vikings up in Newfoundland, they called the people there *skraelings*. A term that means disgusting cannibals. Cannibals, that's what they thought about us back then. He said he knew that, and I interrupted him and said, look, you want to know some more history? Here's a part of history I'm real fucking proud of. That those dirty skraelings, my brothers and sisters up north, they were able to kill enough of your Vikings to kick them out of North America, and to give the First Peoples another four hundred years of peace. And I wish that their ancestors up there and their ancestors down here were more on the ball the next time round when Europeans showed up, so they could kick them out as well. That's the history I knew, that I was proud of."

I stopped writing, looking at the anger in his eyes, hearing the anger in Gagnon's voice. At first I thought it was a damn silly thing, for I was of Irish ancestry, as he had so correctly noted. And I didn't lay awake nights or brood through the days, thinking about how the British had essentially starved my ancestors back in the 1800s, how their own land was stolen, and how millions of them were forced to flee their country to settle elsewhere. But by the time I had gone through this, I knew it was a false analogy. If I wanted to, I could move back to my nation of origin and, save for a few counties in the north, could live in reasonable peace and prosperity. It wasn't like the land of my ancestors was still dominated, ruled, and lorded over by the British, and I couldn't imagine what it must be like to travel across this land, see the buildings, hear the foreign languages being spoken, and say to oneself, over and over again: This was once ours, this was once ours, this was once ours.

"I take it the meeting ended around then," I said.

"You got it. He got all huffed up, and now, I can't blame him, and he left, and he said that he was going to prove his Viking theory, with or without my help, or anybody else's help. And he left, and I sat here, and then I went out to lunch. End of story."

I looked at my notebook, looked back up at him. "Anything else I should know?"

"About Jon? Nope. First and last time I ever met him. Never knew him until that day he stopped by."

"All right," I said. "I appreciate your time, talking to me."

He smiled. "Not a problem. Now, it's time for a couple of questions from me."

"Sure."

"This guy a friend of yours?"

"You could say that."

He tapped his fingers on his desk. "Yeah, I could tell. You see, I've been interviewed by reporters a few times before, and usually they come in with their questions, and it's pretty rote, and once they've got what they need, they're looking for an excuse to get the hell out. But not you. You stuck with it."

"Thanks, I guess."

"A dead friend. I can see why you took the time. The cops getting close to nailing whoever killed him?"

"If they are, they haven't told me."

He got up and so did I, and we shook hands, and he said, "Okay. Next question."

"A couple of weeks."

"Excuse me?" he asked.

I picked up my coat. "Give me time to finish this column, and then I'll be ready to come back for another interview." And I really meant it. The research and questions I was doing about Jon were all about one thing only: finding his killer and taking care of business. But I would need a real column to send south to *Shoreline* in a little while, and the story of a Native American activist from Porter would do just fine.

That brought another smile from him. "Fair enough, then. A couple of weeks it is. Walk you to the door?"

"No, I'm good," I said, which was not really a lie. I headed out into the storefront, where one could sense the cageiness from the teenage boys and girls working there, and I envied their youth and their energy, and their utmost confidence in themselves that they were making a difference. Outside, a cold and smelly breeze was coming in off the harbor, and as I went through my coat pockets, I couldn't find the keys to my rental car. I always carry a spare key to my Ford in my wallet, but since the Ford was in the process of being fixed up over in Durham, that wasn't going to be any help.

I went back to the storefront, to see if I had dropped them on the floor, when I found them, nestled in my pants pocket. Idiot, I thought. Next thing you'll be needing is a notebook to tell you how to get through the day.

At the entrance, I looked in through the glass windows, saw William Bear Gagnon standing among the worshipful group of high school students, volunteering their time and energies to helping him out. And from where I was standing, it looked like Gagnon was repaying them by having a temper tantrum. I could barely make out the raised voice, but I could see his eyes bulging out, veins standing out on the side of his neck. In one clenched fist he had a bunch of envelopes, and it just seemed like somebody had misfiled something or misprinted something, for there were a lot of downcast faces in there, as Gagnon yelled and looked at each and every one of them, and then ripped the envelopes in half.

I turned and headed to my rental, no longer envious of those students.

CHAPTER ELEVEN

A half hour later I was back home, the trip being uneventful, save for the cheery wave I gave one of the cousins, guarding the driveway to my home, and a clumsy incident as I was trying to get into my house. I had my keys out and for some reason missed the doorknob and dropped them to the ground. I was just thankful it wasn't January or February; having to root around for keys in the snow was never any fun. Once inside the house I called Paula Quinn and lucked out when I found her in the office, and I said, "Can I dive into the favor jar and pull out a couple?"

She laughed and said, "What do I get in return?"

"A late lunch, place and price of your choosing," I said.

"My, that's the best offer I've had all morning. Okay, go ahead."

So I asked her and she said "mmmm" a few times, and said, "Well, second favor will be more of a problem than the first, but I think it won't be a problem."

"You're the best," I said.

"Lewis, do me a favor and spread that around, will you?" And she laughed again.

"Sure. So. Name the price and place."

Which she did. Which caused me to laugh this time, and when I hung up the phone, I saw that I had a couple of hours to kill.

The house was warm, the house was comfortable, and the house was full of distractions, from books to magazines to the television. I didn't want any distractions. I wanted something else. So I went back into the cool cellar, sat on the bottom step, and tried to think for a while, wondering if I was doing the right thing by asking Paula to check up on something. I had met with the three people that Jon had said he was going to talk to, right before his murder. None of them said they offered him something to go on, a lead that would end up with him having his hands on the artifacts, just a few days later. The professor knew William Bear Gagnon. Brian Mulligan knew Jon's brother Ray. And Gagnon had the most confrontational meeting with Jon.

What, then?

Who gains, was the question that kept me coming around, poking and prodding. Who would gain from Jon's death and the disappearance of the artifacts? His brother Ray, a suspect and on the run? A man with a criminal past?

Maybe.

But one of the three I had just talked to, well, if somebody was hiding something . . .

Who gains?

I got up from the steps and decided it was time to get to work.

But where next?

And then I thought about my keys, and went upstairs. There, I picked up my spoon and bucket and colander, and got dressed again, and went outside. For a moment I thought about my faithful watchers, and what they might think about what I was going to do, and I decided I didn't care. Let the two cousins gossip. It didn't matter. I sat down on the stone steps and looked at the old door frame to my house. I had just dropped my keys here, something I had done at least a half-dozen times over the years. Now imagine decades upon decades, stretching out to the mid-1800s, when this house was first built for the lifesaving service. Imagine all the men—and perhaps a few women as well—coming into the house. Dozens, hundreds, maybe even thousands, walking in and out over the years, as the lifeboat crews changed, as the house was taken over for officers' quarters when the Samson Point coast artillery station was set up, and when the house was finally boarded up, a few decades ago.

Imagine all those people, all those people, coming in and out of the doorway.

And what they might have dropped in the meantime.

I got up and knelt on the cold, hard ground, and started digging. And kept on thinking.

Paula looked over at my hands and said, "All right, tell me again why you were playing in dirt this morning?"

Even in the warm interior of her new Camry, my fingers would shake now and again from the cold. I had just barely made it here in time for lunch with Paula, and I hadn't done a very good job in cleaning up when I saw how late it had gotten. Between dropping off the rental and getting a ride back from the pleasant woman from the agency, the rest of the day had melted away. But the digging had gotten away from me, as the amount of dirt piled up to equal the frustration I had been feeling. Nothing. Not a thing, and I wondered how archaeologists could even stand their profession with so much daily disappointment.

"I was looking for something," I said.

"Okay. What?"

"Artifacts," I said. "From when my house was first built, and thereafter."

"Lewis, that sounds pretty—"

"Paula, isn't your lunch getting cold?"

She laughed. "Fine. A nice way of changing the subject. Yeah, let's eat. I'm starving."

We were parked in front of her dream house, which still looked lonely and unoccupied. Unraked leaves littered the front yard, and I kept the engine running and the heater going, while the car was filled with the smells of food. For some reason Paula had insisted on me driving, which was fine. We both had big bowls of lobster stew and packaged salads, and as I was opening up my salad, I saw that Paula had gone straight to the stew.

"I thought the salad was supposed to be eaten first," I said.

"Who says that?" she murmured, bringing up another spoonful of cream and lobster meat.

"Well, the etiquette for—"

"Screw the etiquette," she said. "If I eat the salad first, I might not have enough appetite to eat the lobster stew. So there."

I put my salad aside, decided she made sense, and started eating the stew as well. And as we ate, Paula brought me up to date with her housing quest. "Believe it or not," she said, "the Tyler Cooperative didn't actually toss me out of their office when I stopped by. They promised a fair and thorough review of my finances."

"Any leads on land?"

"A couple, out on the other side of the county. What I'm trying to do now is to work with a moving crew to get the house up and out of there, and my friend, there aren't that many in the area to work with. With the cost of the land and the moving . . . well, it's a pricey proposition."

I gently nudged her with my elbow. "At least the house is paid for."

"Mmmm," she said, swallowing. "Yeah, thanks for taking that worry away. Now, if I can keep the town happy . . ."

I looked over at her. "I thought having the town counsel on your side would be helpful."

She grimaced. "Lewis, be real. This is Tyler. A wonderful place to live and work, but a sometimes a small place with small minds. The gossips here are already having the time of their lives with me dating the lawyer for the town. If there's any hint that Mark's doing any favors for me, especially when it comes to something like a house, they'll have him fired and out of here within a week. I don't want that and neither does Mark."

"So what's the deal with the town?"

She sighed. "I've got a week to come to the town with a plan. Or the tax lien gets paid and the wrecking crew comes in here."

"Is a week doable?"

She looked at me and wiggled her nose. "My dear boy, if I'm very lucky, I'll have this project wrapped up in three days. So yes. It's quite doable."

I reached over and squeezed her hand. "Good for you."

We finished our lunch and had room for the salads, and even room enough for dessert—a slice of chocolate layer cake for her and a piece of key lime pie for me—and we settled back in the seats of her

Camry and she said, "Luck must be with you this morning, because I got lucky."

"Define lucky."

"Well, for you luck is that I have a buddy on the staff of the Porter *Herald*, Connie Slater. Luck is also the fact that she was in this morning, and more luck is that she knows a lot about your friend William Bear Gagnon."

"He's not my friend," I said.

"Hah," she said. "Well, if you do anything with this information, then he's really not going to be your friend."

"What's the deal?"

"The deal is," she said, wiping her delicate fingers with a fistful of paper napkins, "is that he has a couple of things going on. One is trying to nail a piece of land that belongs to the city of Porter, an island in the harbor. Peavey Island."

"What's there now?"

"A one-lane bridge connecting to the mainland, scrub grass, park benches, some playground equipment, and the usual weekend arrests for drunkenness, public lewdity, and other assorted acts that come from tiny minds and big thirsts. It's belonged to the city for years, but your activist friend—all right, acquaintance—wants it."

"Does he now?" I said. "Something to do with an old treaty signed by the state and an Indian tribe, many years ago?"

"Good guess," she said. "That's exactly what's going on, and the hilarious thing is, this character might actually have a case. There really was a treaty signed, way back when, that gave this tribe—an offshoot of the Abenakis—certain rights to this island, and this treaty was not signed when New Hampshire was a crown colony. It was signed when New Hampshire was a state."

I wiped down my own fingers with napkins and adjusted the heat some. I was finally warming up. "Which makes a big difference?" I asked.

"Of course it does. Somebody could make an argument that a treaty between an Indian tribe and the British government has no standing, hundreds of years later. Harder to make that argument when it took place when New Hampshire was a state, even a young one."

"And William Bear Gagnon is arguing that it's time to enforce the treaty, and that he's a descendant of that original tribe."

"Bingo. Trouble is, the federal government has certain rules over what constitutes a tribe, but Gagnon might be able to do it, if he can prove that a number of tribe members still live in the area, and that they could arguably be called a tribe. And if that happens, well, Connie tells me that there's a provision in the treaty that allows the tribe to buy the island back, any time in the future. Of course, Connie and about half the city government in Porter knows exactly what's going on with Mister Gagnon's sudden interest in his ancestors and tribe."

"Casino," I said.

"Correct again," Paula said. "My, you are sharp today, especially for somebody who's been playing in the dirt. And the humor quotient keeps on getting better, because while some in the city are horrified at the thought of a casino going up in their neighborhood, with no real oversight since it's owned and operated by Native Americans, a whole other contingent are drooling at all the money that can be made over the increased tourists, increased bus traffic, so forth and so on."

I looked over at the house, tried to think of the work that would go into excavating and lifting that structure up, and decided it was too much to think about. Instead I said, "What happens next?"

Paula giggled as she started putting some of the trash away in the plastic bags that earlier had held our lunch. "I haven't told the real funny part yet."

"I can hardly wait."

"Oh, it's worth waiting for. You see, and this hasn't come out and God knows if it ever will, but it's doubtful that William Bear Gagnon is who he says he is."

"A member of that Abenaki tribe?"

"No, silly, an Indian. Native American, or whatever term is being used this year."

The car was beginning to feel a bit stuffy. "You're kidding."

"Tsk, tsk, not when it comes to hilarious stories like this do I kid. Look, my bud Connie is a bulldog when it comes to checking things out. You know the old journalism classroom joke?"

"No, I can't say that I do."

"If your mom tells you she loves you, check it out. Connie got suspicious when this character rolled in, claiming to be a Native American, of a little-known tribe. She's done some background research on him, finding out where he's from and such. Truth is, his name is Billy Gagnon, and he got his middle name, Bear, after spending some time up in Warren, Maine. Do you know what's in Warren, or do I have to spell it out, Lewis?"

I knew very well what was up there. "The Maine State Prison."

"Yep. Did some time for aggravated assault, attempted rape. Charming fellow. And his ethnicity is French-Canadian. Oh, there may be a great-great-grandaunt or two that had Indian blood, but I believe Connie when she says that he's nothing more than a fraud."

Now the car interior seemed too warm. "What's Connie going to do with this great information?"

"Well, that's when the hilarious factor gets taken over by the pathetic factor, because the paper probably won't do a damn thing."

"Why? Seems like a hell of a story."

"Sure it does. But Connie tells me— and this is all on deep background—that the conglomerate that owns the Porter *Herald* would not look on too unkindly if Billy Gagnon gets his wish and a casino is built in Peavey Island. And she's also getting some pushback from her editors. You see, the *Herald* has always prided itself on sticking up for the underdog, for pushing unpopular causes, for going after the people in power. How do you think their readership would respond if they decided to take down a charismatic and increasingly influential Indian leader in the seacoast? Hmmm?"

"Probably be brought up on charges of hate crimes, I'd imagine."

"Or something like that. So the story of William Bear Gagnon, who discovered his true roots after spending time in prison, will remain deep in Connie's notes or computer files for the foreseeable future. Hey, you ready to leave?"

"You still okay for the first favor?"

"Sure," she said, shoving the bags of trash into the rear of the car. "Have I ever said no to you before?"

"Plenty of times," I said, which earned me a jab in the ribs.

About thirty minutes later we were in Durham, at a small stretch of roadway outside of the campus that Paula told me was called Gasoline Alley, for the number of gas stations lined up on both sides of the narrow road. Paula shook her head at all the traffic rolling in and out of Durham, to the place where she had gone to school, and she said, "Damn place was so crowded when I was here, I probably couldn't stand it now."

At the Circle H service station, I paid the usual and customary bills, got a lecture on how the dents and dings should get looked at before they started to rust, and Paula joined me as we walked out and stopped by my Ford Explorer, parked forlornly at the end of the lot, near a line of other cars and trucks, most of which were missing chunks of fenders, bumpers, and windows. My own set of wheels had scrapes and dents on both sides, and a brand-new tire that looked out of place with the other three.

"Well," I said, reaching over to pull out a clump of grass from a broken sideview mirror. "At least it's the best-looking in the bunch."

Paula slipped her hand into mine. "Lewis, tell me again what happened."

"Wheel fell off."

"I know that. How did it fall off?"

"The lug nuts holding it together came off, that's how."

She squeezed my hand. "Lug nuts don't come off by themselves, do they."

"Not hardly."

"What's going on?"

I thought about that for a second, and I squeezed her hand back. "What's going on is that I'm grateful for the ride over here, and you should go back to Tyler and keep on getting your house together, and spending time with your town counsel. That's what's going on, Paula."

Her hand felt warm and soft in mine. She said, "We could have had something, the two of us. I think about that, every now and then."

"We did have something special," I said. "It was right for the moment, it was special, but . . . we both knew it wasn't going to last. Couldn't, not the way I am, and because of what you need. What you've got now is good, Paula. Don't worry about me."

She squeezed my hand and said, "You're welcome for the favor. And don't be sure you know just how good I have it."

I watched her as she got into her Camry, responded to her own wave, and then got into my wounded Explorer and headed home as well.

At home a light rain was starting to fall, which discouraged me from resuming my failed archaeological project, which didn't upset me that much. I spent some time in the kitchen sink again, trying to get the dirt off of my hands, and when that was finished, I gave Diane Woods a call at the Tyler police station. She was out and I was surprised at how comfortable that made me feel. I had a question to ask her, and with her not available, it allowed me to find out the information on my own.

But how?

I went up to my office and spent a few minutes on-line, until I found the phone number I was looking for, and I sat back in my chair, looked at the phone, ran some options and possibilities through my mind. There was a number of ways I could get this question answered, and some years ago it would have been just a matter of picking a particular fib that would work. But no longer. Technology had pretty much dumped the option of using the favorite method of private detectives, con artists, and snoopy journalists: the pretext call, phoning someone and pretending to be a loan officer, lottery official, or a phone company rep, all in the attempt to get information. With caller ID and the method of calling back and verifying a number, the pretext call was getting too hard to pull off.

Which just left one option.

The truth.

"The truth," I said aloud. "What a concept."

And with one hand, I picked up the phone, and with the other, I picked up a legal pad and pen, and started calling.

After the initial call north, I was transferred one way and then another, until a pleasant-sounding young man named Jeff Simpson took pity on me. He was a press officer with the state of Maine's Department of Corrections, and he said, "Run that by me again, please?"

So I told him who I was and explained what I was doing and

what I was looking for, and he said "hmmm," a lot, and I guess I got him in a good mood or government workers in Maine by nature are always in a good mood, for Jeff Simpson said he would get back to me in a while with the information I was looking for. I said that was fine and hung up the phone and decided to stay in my office instead of rooting around out in the front yard any more.

And I was also under no illusions. The polite young man was no doubt at this moment on the phone calling *Shoreline* magazine to check on my bona fides. He wanted to make sure I was who I said I was, and not some nut or freelance or somebody out to do something. So the checkup would go on, a call to Boston to the offices of *Shoreline* would take place, and I would just sit here and wait until the young man up in Augusta—about a three-hour drive from where I sat—was satisfied that he could talk to me.

So what to do then?

Not much. I looked fondly on a small black rock that was sitting on top of my computer and briefly recalled how that bit of American history ended up in my home, when I had a strange encounter with a female representative of the federal government some months ago. Then I turned my chair around, ready to pull something down from the nearby bookshelf to read, when the phone rang. I took a breath, picked up the receiver, said hello.

"Mr. Cole?"

"That's right."

"Jeff Simpson, returning your call."

"Thanks."

Over the receiver, I could make out the sound of paper being moved around. "I've made the necessary phone calls, and I can confirm your question. But any other additional information would require a Freedom of Information Act request. Do you understand?"

"I do."

"All right," he said. "William Gagnon. I can confirm that he was in fact an inmate at the Maine State Correctional Facility in Warren. He was released just over a year ago, on September first."

"Okay. And the other name?" The phone suddenly felt slippery in my grasp, like it was ready to be propelled across the room.

"Oh. Yes. The other name you mentioned. I can confirm that as well."

"Sorry?"

"The man you asked about. Ray Ericson. He was an inmate at Warren, and he and Mr. Gagnon were at the facility at the same time for approximately seven months."

I didn't bother writing anything down. I didn't have to. I hung up the phone and stared at the nearest bookshelf for a moment, and then got up and got going.

CHAPTER TWELVE

So back to Porter I went in my Ford Explorer, back to Stark Street. I drove by the still-lit storefront twice and saw a pickup truck near the front. It was a dark blue Ford with rusty wheelwells and FREE TIBET and FREE LEONARD PELTIER stickers on the rear bumper. I then found a place to park in a dirt driveway that belonged to a small white house that had its windows covered by plywood and decorated with a number of NO TRESPASSING stickers. The house was on the other side of the street, two buildings down from the storefront. Backing in, I shut off the engine and waited. The storefront didn't seem as crowded as before. Through the windows I could tell there was movement back there. I sat and waited, hands folded in my lap. On the passenger's seat next to me was a copy of today's *New York Times*, a bottle of water, and underneath the *Times*, my 9mm Beretta and a pair of 7×50 binoculars.

I squeezed my hands tighter. Earlier Billy Gagnon had said he had never heard of Jon Ericson, had only met him that one time. Perhaps. But he had been at Warren with Jon's brother, the one who had been on the run since Jon's murder. A coincidence, maybe, but I hated coincidences.

I waited. Over the years, I had read lots of detective novels in which the hero went out and conducted surveillance on somebody.

Interesting tales, but one thing authors usually left out was the sheer boredom of sitting on one's behind, keeping watch on a building or a doorway. The seconds and minutes dragged by, like staring at a shadow on the ground and keeping track of its travel as the sun moved overhead, and distractions like a radio or music couldn't be risked.

So there I sat. Waiting. Alone with my thoughts and the sound of traffic. I moved my hands up to the steering wheel, kept an eye on the movements inside the lit storefront. A door opened up and I saw two high school students—both young girls—head out and start walking away. I picked up the binoculars but the view inside the building was terrible. I could only make out movements, shapes. The Mormon Tabernacle Choir could have been in there giving a free concert for the cause, and while I might have heard them, I certainly could not have seen them.

I kept waiting. It was getting darker. Before racing up here from home I had spent a few unsatisfactory minutes, going on-line and flipping through a couple of local phone books, and if William Bear Gagnon had an address or phone number in his name that was local, then he was doing a pretty fair job of hiding it.

And why was I here? Because I wanted to see what he was like outside of his storefront, outside of his little office. I wanted to see where he went, what he did, and where he slept at night.

Something happened. The lights went off at the storefront. I turned the key and got the Explorer's engine running, just as a tractor trailer truck grumbled by, obscuring my view. I was too keyed up even to curse properly, but when the truck finally gave way, the pickup truck was on the move. I eased out onto Stark Street and was right behind the pickup truck. It came to a stop sign, made a very legal and complete stop, and then made a left turn. I followed, noticing that there were two people in the truck. I could see that Gagnon was driving, and his passenger appeared to be female.

Well, whaddya know.

The truck went slowly through downtown Porter, and I managed to keep pace with him. He headed east, toward Maine, but then made a right from Congress Street, to the oldest section of Porter, Strawbery Banke, where the first settlers came here in 1623. I had a brief thought that perhaps Gagnon was here to burn down some of the historic homes, in some way righting a historic wrong, but he didn't slow as he drove through the narrow streets, lined with homes that are older than most nations in the world.

Then, another left. Past a sign that said PEAVEY ISLAND CITY PARK CLOSED AT DUSK.

It was way past dusk, but in the charming way that New Hampshire communities sometimes run their parks and government, there was no gate or chain blocking the entrance. I followed them into the park, being careful to stay a few car lengths behind. The roadway entered onto a narrow causeway, spanning Porter Harbor. Off to the right were the lights of Foss Island, a larger island and town to the south of Porter, and to the left, were the buildings and cranes and bright illumination of the Porter Naval Shipyard. On the small island the road curved to the left, and then to a dirt parking lot. There were swing sets and picnic tables and benches off beyond the dirt lot, but Gagnon pulled his vehicle over, to the farthest side of the lot.

I switched off the lights to the Explorer and rolled in past him, and then parked where I got a good view. I kept the engine running, looked about. There were just two other cars in the lot, which made sense. No doubt the serious visitors and partyers came in as the night grew longer.

I looked over at Gagnon's pickup truck, picked up my binoculars. The lights from the shipyard illuminated the interior of his truck cabin fairly well. He seemed to be talking to his female companion, who was nodding a lot. Maybe he was explaining the centuries of oppression that had led the New England Indian tribes to their current fate. Maybe he was explaining how Peavey Island rightly belonged to his people. And maybe he was explaining what was going to be eventually built on this piece of property, from a casino to a museum to a cultural center.

Or maybe not.

He was over her, kissing her it seemed, and that went on for a while, until he leaned back on the driver's door and the young lady's head dropped from view. Gagnon seemed to rest his head back, and even though the light was poor and the viewing through the rear of the truck cabin wasn't the greatest, I could detect the smile on his face, as the high school girl performed upon him.

I put the binoculars back on the passenger's seat, waited.

A convicted felon and a high school girl. Though I'm not that familiar with the laws of the state of New Hampshire, I'm sure there was a crime going on over there in that pickup truck.

I kept on waiting. Then the brake lights came on as the truck roared into life, backing up and then speeding out toward the causeway. I left the lot as well, followed them out back to Strawbery Banke, where Gagnon headed back into the downtown, and as I was catching up to him on Congress Street, he blew through a red light.

I almost skidded to a halt, as traffic from the cross street went its way, one vehicle blowing its horn at Gagnon's departing truck.

Damn.

I waited through the light cycle, wondering if Gagnon was in a hurry to get his young charge home to wherever she lived, or if he had noticed me following him and was in a hurry to get away.

Either way, my goal for the evening, to see where Gagnon rested his head at night, had been blown.

It was time to go home.

Back to Tyler Beach I went, for the second time that evening, and as I went into the Lafayette House parking lot, I saw a man standing by the plumbing and heating van. I slowed down and saw that it was my two guardians, the two cousins. Tom and Frank Duffy. Tom, the younger of the two, was standing outside and ambled his way over to me.

"Everything all right, Mr. Cole?" he asked.

"Things are fine. How are you two doing?"

"Getting ready for shift change. Frank's giving me grief about being ten minutes late. He's looking forward to some room service food and an adult movie on the pay-per-view."

"Sounds like a good night to me."

"Yeah, well, he's gonna have to get his ass back here in four hours anyway."

I nodded and said, "You hear anything from Felix?"

He shook his head. "Not a word. You expecting anything?"

"Something, sometime, but I didn't know if he had contacted you at all."

Another shake of the head. "Mr. Cole, Felix just put us here and told us what to do, and how to do it, and we're supposed to stay here until he comes back and tells us to our face that it's done and we can go home."

"Yeah, that sounds like Felix," I said.

"Don't it. Now, if you excuse me, I've got to get back and get my ass in the van, 'fore Frank has a freakin' heart attack or something."

I drove the Explorer down the rough dirt road, parked her in the open garage and walked over to the front door. I had left a couple of the lights on inside and I could make out the spot where I had been digging earlier in the day. Nothing. Not a damn thing. It was hard to believe that generations of people trooping in and out of my house wouldn't have dropped anything in the process, but either they had sticky fingers in this home's earlier life, or somebody with better luck than I had gone through here earlier, digging on his or her own.

Inside, I dropped my coat and pistol and binoculars and unread newspaper in a chair, and went to the answering machine, which had a little red numeral that said 4. Four new messages. I hit the play button as I got a pen and small pad of paper, but I was just wasting time, for the message was the same, each and every one.

A hiss of static, and a hang-up.

That's it. Four hang-up calls.

Solicitors, upset that I hadn't been home?

Or who else?

I lifted the phone and did what those little phone company ads always push, for those who can't live without thinking of who might have been behind that missed phone call, so I pressed the star key and then the numerals six-nine, and got a polite recorded message that the incoming number had been blocked. Well, how about that. If this had been any other time, I might have called up Diane Woods and asked her to perform some kind of police magic, but this wasn't one of those times. I had heard her earlier message—about keeping away for a while—loud and clear.

And no doubt Diane was with Kara at this very moment, adjusting to their new lives together. As I put the phone receiver back down, a bleak little thought traipsed through my mind. The two cousins up at the parking lot, arguing and talking with each other. Diane with Kara this cold October evening, and Paula Quinn was well, with her lawyer friend, Mark Spencer. Felix down south, vying for the attention of two bikini-clad sisters.

And me?

I went out to the small living room, turned on the television set quite loud, and went into the kitchen to find something to do, something to make for dinner.

About four hours after dinner the ringing phone in my bedroom shot me up like somebody had just drilled a load of adrenaline into my spine.

I fumbled in the darkness and the voice on the other end said, "Mr. Cole? Don't turn on any lights."

"Don't turn on—who the hell is this?"

"It's me, Tom Duffy. I'm in the hotel across the street. Don't turn on your lights. We got movement on the north side of your house. Frank's going over to check it out."

I rolled out of bed and in the darkness grabbed my 9mm Beretta from the nightstand. I shivered in the cool air, threw on a terry-cloth bathrobe that had been tossed on the bed. I kept the phone to my ear as I moved through the bedroom in the darkness.

"What time is it?" I asked.

"Two a.m."

"What kind of movement?"

"One person, out by the rocks. Moving slow, heading your way. I spotted it about ten minutes ago. We're both on night-vision scopes, old Russian stuff that's still pretty good."

I was on the stairway, moving slowly downstairs, the hand holding the pistol gently tracing the wall for guidance. At the bottom of the stairs I went over, made sure the front door was locked.

"What's he doing?"

"Who? Frank or the guy?"

"Frank."

"Frank's coming down your driveway."

"And the guy?"

"Looks like he stopped for a second. Okay. I think he's checking things out with a pair of binoculars. Hold on."

The phone was put down on a table or something, and I could hear a murmur of voices. Tom came back on the line and said, "Okay, Mr. Cole. You stay put. It's gonna be busy here for a sec. Where are you?"

"Right by the front door."

"All right," Tom said. "I'll make sure Frank doesn't come into your house. Anybody coming into your house, he's a bad guy, all right?"

I sat on the bottom of the stairs, pistol in hand. "Sure. Anybody comes through the front door, I'll blow his ass away."

Tom chuckled. "That's a good attitude. You stay on the line, all right? I'm gonna lead Frank right in on the target, but you be careful. There might be other guys out there."

The phone went down again, and I put my own receiver between my ear and my shoulder. The murmur of voices in the background continued. I took a series of deep breaths, trying to ease the jackhammer in my chest that was threatening to punch a hole into my aorta. There was something strange and terrifying and even comforting, being in my warm and locked-down house, pistol in hand, while two strangers outside on my land danced and moved toward each other. The murmur of the voices was a little drone inside my head, as I imagined Frank out there, with earphone and throat mike, perhaps, being told by his cousin where to go and what to do.

And the guy out there, with the binoculars? Ray Ericson, maybe? Here to check things out for his buddy William Gagnon? Or somebody else connected with Jon's murder and the disappearance of the Viking artifacts? I strained to hear anything from outside, like somebody walking or coughing or talking, but there was nothing. Just the constant murmur of the waves. At least that sound would give Frank some cover, as he crept up on my trespasser.

The voice from the phone made me jump for the second time that night. "Mister Cole?"

"Yeah?"

"Okay, the guy's gone."

I let a breath out. "Where did he go?"

Tom said, "I don't know if he got spooked or something, but when Frank got to your house, he just turned around and started climbing back up the rocks, up to Atlantic Avenue. He moved slow and Frank did his best to follow him up, but by the time he got to the road, there was nobody. Just some taillights, heading north."

I let the pistol drop into my lap, shifted the phone to another hand. "Did the car have one or more in it?"

"Hold on." More murmuring and then Tom came back and said, "Sorry. Frank just saw taillights. Nothing else. Couldn't even tell what vehicle it was."

"Oh. Well, tell him thanks for me."

"Sure will. Look, you all set?"

"For now," I said. "How about you two?"

"Frank's gonna do a little walk up and down the road, just to make sure your visitor's gone. I'll ride shotgun with him from the hotel room. We'll call you if anything comes up. All right?"

"That sounds fine," I said, standing up. "I think I'll go back to bed."

Tom said, "Sounds like a good idea. Get some sleep. Sorry to have woken you up."

"Nothing to apologize for," I said, and I hung up and walked back upstairs. I put the pistol back on the nightstand—not in its holster, so I could get at it quickly if necessary—and after dumping the robe on the bed, crawled back into the still warm sheets. My hands and feet were cold and the jackhammering in my chest had slowed down to a steady thumping, and I stretched out and stared up into the darkness. I thought about what had just happened and I guess I should have been wired or concerned and certainly sleepless, but the thought of Felix's two men out there, keeping a safe watch over me, actually calmed me down such that the next thing I knew, the morning sun was glaring into my bedroom, and it was time to start a new day.

It was a warm day for October, and I spent most of it around the house, waiting for Felix to call from Florida, waiting for the two cousins to report anything new, and mostly just waiting. I caught up on a bunch of old newspapers—let two days' worth of *New York Times*es accumulate unread and you've already kissed away an hour of your time—and spent another couple of hours doing mindless work around the house, stuff that always needed to be done and which never got done because so many attractive excuses could be rustled up. So as the day wore on and I kept the television set tuned to an all-news cable station, I cleaned the stove, emptied the refrigerator of mummified and dehydrated food stuffs, and tried to keep as busy as possible.

Lunch was soup and chunks of cheddar cheese and fistfuls of saltine crackers, and as the sun warmed up the front yard, I went out again, dirt-encrusted spoon in hand, to dig on the other side of the door, sifting the dirt as before, and, as before, finding nothing.

Following some of the digging, I rested for a while on the granite steps, thinking about the past few days, about the grip of history. Jon and his love of the Vikings, trying to prove his ancestors had come here. William Bear Gagnon, with love of his own ancestors—as murky as that might be—trying just as hard to keep the memory of his forebears alive. Professor Hendricks, trying to measure and record history, the same as Brian Mulligan up north, in self-imposed exile because his view of history wasn't respected.

And me?

Just trying to find things out.

Part of the curse, perhaps, or the blessing, to living in a part of the nation where the history was hundreds of years old, and the history sometimes had a habit of rushing in and grabbing you by the neck.

Back to work I went, digging again in the hard soil, the sun warm on my back. I dug around the foundation, sifting the soil, finding pebbles, rocks, and, once, a piece of seashell. As the afternoon dragged on, I found that instead of being bored, I was actually enjoying the monotony of the work, the digging, the sifting, and the piling up of the dirt. Maybe because the work took my mind off other things. Maybe because I was getting my hands on my own little piece of history. Who knows.

What I do know is that the afternoon went along quite well, even though as I worked, something metallic and unyielding dug into my back. My 9mm Beretta, just in case something or somebody got through the Duffy cousins. I dug until the sun had moved, my back was now getting cold, and my fingers were cramped and soiled. I got up, my knees yelling at me for having been in one position for so long, and so I limped into my house, wondering if archeologists had football player knees after years out in the field. Upstairs I dumped my dirty clothes into the laundry basket and went into the bathroom, turning on the shower nice and hard and hot.

I stayed until the hot water started turning lukewarm, and I got out, grabbing a nice thick towel. Fresh out of the shower, I checked my skin for bumps and swellings, thinking again of history. My medical history, of course, where there was always a little ticking bomb inside of my bloodstream, from when I had been in the employ of the government. The shower ritual was one that would last me until the day I died, and the cold thought that came on some days—usually in the middle of a dark winter—that who knew how many days away that might be.

Freshly dressed and back downstairs, there was a blinking numeral 1 on the answering machine. The call must have come in when I was in the shower. I touched the replay switch and the *whir-whir-whir* of the tape went on for a bit, letting me think that I didn't have a hang-up call this time.

And I was right.

The comfortable voice of Felix came out of the tiny speaker: "Hey, Lewis. You know who this is. Well. It's been a productive trip but I'm sure as hell am not going to leave you a message about it. My flight heads out in about . . . a half hour. I'll give you a ring tomorrow. I know how much you value a good night's sleep." He laughed at his own little joke and then hung up.

"Thanks," I said to the answering machine, and then I went out in the living room, saw it was near dusk. What now? Wait for Felix or do something?

It didn't take long for me to make up my mind. Sitting on my butt over the next few hours, at least on this couch, wasn't going to happen. I got up and got my low-rent surveillance gear together and headed out into the fading light. Something about William Bear Gagnon didn't seem right, and I thought it would be a nice night for a get-together.

In Porter I lucked out twice right from the start. The first bit of luck was that Gagnon's pickup truck was parked in the same place as before, and the second was that the driveway I had used the night before was still empty. I backed in and switched off the engine and waited.

Lights were still on at the storefront, and again I could make out movement back there, behind the glass. I rubbed at my jaw and thought over the message Felix had left me. A productive trip. In the manner and way of how Felix talked, it meant some good things had come out of his Florida travels, and I didn't mean any erotic encounter with two bikini-clad sisters. Maybe I should have stayed home this evening, waiting for him to show up. Maybe. But I still felt right, sitting here, keeping watch on things.

Movement, across the street. Three students heading out, laughing and talking among themselves. I had a feeling that one of them had performed an oral service on William Gagnon the night before, and for the life of me, I could not figure out why she would be laughing. I rubbed my hands together, kept my eyes on the storefront.

Lights off.

I started up the Ford.

Movement. I wasted a few seconds, getting the binoculars up and focused. There. William Bear Gagnon, in his pickup truck, and alone this time, heading out onto the street. I pulled out and followed him a block, and then switched on the headlights.

There. Hunter and the hunted. And this night, I wasn't going to let him get loose.

We made a pretty direct route through this part of Porter, getting onto Harborview Road, and then made a right onto an exit that lifted us up onto I-95, heading north. We went over the Kittery Memorial Bridge, and we were in Maine. Traffic was light and keeping track of his truck was fairly simple. Maybe because it was his criminal record or maybe it was just the way he drove, but he kept it straight and narrow, not speeding, not doing any lane changes as we headed into Maine. He took an exit just before the famed outlet malls at Kittery, and in a matter of minutes we were heading west through the towns of Kittery and Eliot. The road was now two-lane and busy, with service stations and stores and garages on either side, but not too many homes. A few minutes later, he took another right, on a rural road that didn't even have a street sign to announce its location.

I was getting thirsty, but I didn't dare try to reach for the water. I didn't want to fumble around and lose track of the truck and the taillights up ahead, moving into this fairly empty stretch of Maine. I tried to keep my speed down, so that it wasn't so obvious that I was following him, and a few times, I lost track of him on a particularly sharp corner or bend of the road.

All right. Brake lights up ahead, and he made a right, going down a steep dirt driveway. I gave it a quick glance as I went ahead, again not slowing down that much, but I did see that there was a house trailer down there, and a woodpile. I drove a number of yards, saw another dirt driveway with a sign that said NO TURNING. I turned in and thought, well, it's more like backing in and out than turning, and then, lights off, I slowly went back down to Gagnon's driveway.

Lucky again. Brush and leaves had fallen away with the onset of fall, giving me a somewhat cluttered yet clear view of Gagnon emerging from his pickup truck. He walked up to the front of the trailer, carrying a bag or something under his arm. He walked slowly, limping as he went up to—

Limping.

Gagnon was limping.

And it came storming back to me, that night at Ray Ericson's store with Felix, when I had turned around, thinking Felix was coming over to me, and that hammer blow to the chest, me falling to the ground, avoiding a boot to my head, flailing around, finding an antique knife, raising it up and stabbing the assailant in the leg.

Gagnon, really favoring a leg now, was at the front door of the trailer. It looked like he was fumbling around with the key, and then he unlocked the door and was inside, slamming it shut behind him.

My chest ached. I tried to ease my breathing. It didn't work. I put the Ford in park, switched off the engine, and reached over and under the newspaper and grabbed my pistol.

It was time for a talk.

CHAPTER THIRTEEN

There were no streetlights about and the light from the trailer wasn't much, so I took my time, walking down the steep dirt driveway, thankful that it wasn't the middle of winter. I wanted my hands free in case I stumbled, so I put the pistol in my rear waistband, wincing at the cold metal against my skin. I also had the flashlight in a coat pocket, just in case. I kept to the side as much as possible, thinking that the overhanging tree branches would provide some sort of cover. At the bottom of the driveway, at a cleared area where the pickup truck was parked, I went behind the rear of the truck, watching.

The trailer had seen better days. Around the base somebody earlier had installed a white picket-type fence, but now most of the wooden slats were broken or had rotted way. Parts of the trailer were rusting, and it sagged at one end, like one of those old Soviet submarines slowly sinking at dockside. Utility wires ran from the top of the trailer and followed three poles up to the top of the driveway.

It was quiet inside the trailer. I waited some more, and then tensed up as the door flew open and Gagnon limped out. He was whistling something and had on a down vest, and he went to the rear of the trailer. I kept my hands together, to keep them from shaking. Only a few seconds passed and then Gagnon came back, whistling still, carrying two chunks of firewood in his arms. Back up and inside he went, and after a few minutes more, I made out the comforting scent of woodsmoke.

I got up, my knees creaking from all the abuse I had given them these past days, and I went around to the front of the trailer, thinking things through. Gagnon was limping, and some sort of sense was coming together. Obviously he knew Ray Ericson in prison. Ray was on the run. So, Gagnon was at Ray's store the night Felix and I visited. What was he doing there then? Casing the place? Grabbing some records? Or maybe he had been hiding—or even trying to retrieve—the missing Viking artifacts and panicked when Felix and I had shown up.

I moved out past the side of the trailer, where I spotted a chimney pipe. It looked homemade. I shuddered. Though they were metal, house trailers like this one could go up in flames and be a charred shell in a matter of minutes, and it was either extreme stupidity or carelessness or—more likely than not—extreme poverty that had Gagnon living like this, heating a trailer with wood. I tried to see through the windows, to spot where he might be, but my angle wasn't right, and I didn't want to risk going out further into the woods to see through the windows, and raise a lot of noise in the process.

Up ahead was a woodpile, covered by a blue plastic tarp.

And it was by the woodpile, as I was circling around to come back toward the front of the trailer, that one hand softly grabbed my shoulder, and another hand, holding a knife it seemed, was brought to my throat.

I froze.

A quiet, calm voice. "Just so we have an understanding here, you're trespassing."

"That I am."

A chuckle. "Damn, it is you, Cole. What the hell are you doing out here?"

"Interested in a magazine subscription?"

I could sense his breathing. "Not fucking particularly. What I am interested in knowing is why you're out here, peeking in my windows, looking into my business. You a voyeur, a freak?"

"Nope, just a writer. Looking for some information."

A gentle jab of the knife into my throat. "Information? You're looking for information, out here in my yard? Not even a phone call, a visit?"

"You're not in the book."

"The fuck right I'm not in the book."

I said, "Look, let's calm down, all right? My apologies for trespassing. I'm just trying to find out—"

"No, you calm down. You fuck. You think you can just come here, hunh? Just like that? Come into my turf? Man, I should just cut your throat and dump your body out here. Nobody would miss you, right?"

Well, maybe a few people would miss me, but I was getting tired of this. "William, look, why can't we—"

Another jab from the knife, harder than before. "No. No more talking on your part. You know what? I think I'm going to cut you, just for the fun of it. What do you think about that?"

I fell forward, right past the woodpile, the knife blade scraping against my cheek. As I fell, I grabbed a length of wood and rolled over, and as Gagnon came to me, I popped him one across the nearest knee. He yelped but kept coming at me, as I moved around to the front of the trailer, where there was more light from the windows, and Gagnon came at me, face mottled with anger, knife out in a classic knife-fighting pose—no TV nonsense of overhanded blows with the knife, the correct way was holding it out and extended, with fingers relaxed, other hand held high to distract you—and he said, "Man, I was just going to cut you once, but you're going to get it bad."

I stepped backward quickly, my hand reaching underneath my coat, grabbing onto the blessed Italian metal of my Beretta, and I pulled it out, extending it toward him in the approved combat stance, pulling back the hammer so there was no confusion about there being a round in the chamber.

He stopped moving. I took a series of breaths. I said, "Ever hear the joke about coming to a gunfight with a knife?"

"Yeah."

He didn't say anything more. I took another breath and said, "Put the knife away, and I'll put the pistol away, and we can talk."

Gagnon grinned. "Maybe I'll come right at you. Maybe I'll cut you anyway. What are you going to do, shoot me?"

"The thought's entered my mind."

"Yeah, you fuck. And what will you tell the cops then? Huh?"

"I'd say I came over for a friendly talk, and this ex-con with a violent record lost it and came after me. Who do you think they'll believe? An ex-con with a bullet in him, or a writer with no criminal history?"

The grin faded. "What do you mean, ex-con?"

"I mean the time you served up in Warren, that's what I mean."

Now the grin was gone. "You fuck."

"You seem to like that phrase a lot, William," I said. "Don't you know any others?"

His tone become defiant, but I noticed the knife was lowering. "I know a lot, that's what. I know what it's like to be born poor in potato country, up in Aroostook County. I know what it's like, being bounced around, foster home to foster home, learning to do everything on my own. That's what I know. And I know that when I did things on my own, I screwed up a couple of times. I admit it. And I know how I got my act together, after Warren, and started doing good, trying to help out the shattered remains of my people. And damn you, you're still trespassing."

"That's right," I said. "And if you answer me two questions, I'll leave and that will be that."

"Not a chance."

"Oh. Really?"

"Yeah, really."

"Okay," I said. "Then how's this. You don't answer my questions, and I talk to a police detective acquaintance of mine in Porter. Detective Joe Stevens. I think he'd love to know about your background, what you've been doing, especially when it concerns sexual relations with a high school student. How do you think that will impact your fund-raising, William? Especially if some of the local papers—like the Porter *Herald*—decide to dig into your background and find out just how legitimate a Native American leader you really are? Do you think any plans for a casino or museum on Peavey Island will progress after that?"

He started to say something—I think it was going to start with "you" and end with an obscenity—but he said instead, "All right. Two questions. Then get the hell out."

Gagnon made a show of returning his knife to a leather scabbard on his belt, obscured by his gray sweatshirt, and I made a show of lowering the Beretta. "First question. Ray Ericson."

151

"Who?"

"Ray Ericson. Ran an antique store in Porter. Brother of Jon Ericson, the guy I was interviewing you about. Now considered a suspect in his death. He's disappeared since his brother's body been found. Where is he?"

"How the hell should I know?"

"Because you know him, that's why."

"Who?"

"Ray Ericson."

Gagnon shook his head. "Nope. Never heard of him."

"He served time with you, up in Warren. You telling me you never ran into him, never had any dealings with him, didn't know him at all?"

He folded his arms, smiled. "Man, you ever serve time?"

"So far, I've been lucky to miss that particular life experience."

"Then here's an education. You're in a concrete and steel hell with a couple of hundred other guys. All right? And there's county time and there's state time, and state time—which is Warren—is a hell of a lot harder and dicier than county time. And when you're doing state time, you're concerned about one thing, and one thing only. Survival. You case out your cellmate, your corridor, your wing. You see who's running the show, who's doing things, and you form alliances, agreements. And once that's done, you coast. You do your time, keep your head down, and keep things cool with other guys in your alliance. Doesn't matter what they are. Drug dealers, Aryans, bikers . . . whatever . . . and you're doing that, your whole fucking universe is about twenty or thirty guys. Everybody else don't matter. So sure, maybe this Ray character was doing time the same time I was, but that doesn't mean shit."

"How come I don't believe you?"

"How come I don't care?"

I shifted weight from one foot to the other, thought about what he was saying. Hard to prove a negative. Maybe if I was lucky and talked to the guy from the Maine Department of Corrections again, maybe a little more digging could show that Gagnon was lying and that in fact he did know—

"Hey."

I snapped back. "Hey, yourself."

"Two questions. I took care of the first one. What's the other?"

"Oh. This one's easy. Lift up your left pants leg?"

"Say what?"

"Your left pants leg. Lift it up."

"Why the hell should I do that?"

I said, "Because I'm concerned about your limping, that's why."

Gagnon said, "It's an old scar."

"Then show me and I'll be on my way."

I wondered what I was going to do if he told me to stick it in my car, but I was pleasantly surprised when he muttered something and bent down, and lifted up the pants leg, exposing his lower leg, all the way up to the knee.

With one hand I kept holding onto the pistol, with the other, I took out my flashlight, clicked it on, and played the beam over Gagnon's lower leg.

And there it was.

An old, purple and pink, round scar.

"Satisfied?" he said.

"Unfortunately, yes," I said.

He dropped the pants leg and I switched off the light and said, "Sorry."

"Hah. Not as sorry as I was when I got it."

"What happened?"

"A little lesson on being careful when taking your first shower in prison, when someone performs a public display of affection upon you. I punched him in the nose, he fell, and he nailed me with a shank made from a shaved toothbrush handle. Had it concealed in his other hand. Anything else you want to see? My naked and hairy ass, for example?"

"Nope, that'll do," I said.

We stood there for a moment, and then I took a step back and put the Beretta away in the rear waistband. "Guess it's time for me to head on out."

"A good friggin' guess," he said, heading toward the trailer. "You got any more questions, submit them in writing or something. You stay the hell away from my home."

"Good suggestion. And you should stay away from high school girls."

"Hah. I'll think about it. If they're near or over eighteen, they know what they're getting into."

As I started going back up the driveway, and he made his way to the front door, I turned and said, "Oh. One more thing."

"What? Another question?"

"No," I said. "It's just that I'll be calling you in a couple of weeks, that's why."

There was a look of confusion on his face, and it was funny how much that amused me. "Why in hell would you do that?"

"Because I said the other day that I'd do a column about you and your council, that's why."

"You mean . . . you're still going to do it?"

I shrugged. "I made a promise to you, William. I intend to keep it."

"Man, you are some friggin' piece of work."

"So I've been told."

He went into the trailer and then I went up the steep driveway, stumbling a bit on a rough patch. I thought about taking out my flashlight and lighting the way, but for some irrational reason, I didn't want Gagnon to see me do that. Even after everything that had just happened, I didn't want him to think I was weak.

Strange, but there it was.

While going home I swung by the Weathervane Restaurant in Kittery, which is directly across the street from the Kittery Trading Post, one of the largest firearms retailers in this part of the seacoast. Yet another example of guns and butter, separated by a few lanes of asphalt. I ordered a take-out meal of a lobster pie—the meat of two lobsters with stuffing and drawn butter, a meal guaranteed to make a vegan faint on sight—and it sat next to me on the long drive south. The drive wasn't long due to its length, but because of what was rattling around in my mind. I had struck out, and even the delicious smells of the dinner sitting next to me couldn't take that away.

For I had staked everything on William Bear Gagnon and his possible relationship with Jon's brother, and the fact he and Jon had exchanged words during their sole meeting. Plus, I could see how it could have happened: Jon finds the artifacts and decides to brag it to

Gagnon, pointing out that, see, his ancestors had been here a thousand years ago. And Gagnon, upset that his plans for a casino, a center for his people, would be overshadowed by the story of the Vikings, well, maybe he had lost his temper.

And the artifacts? Somehow, in Ray Ericson's hands. A debt paid from some prison experience. Maybe.

But that was done. Maybe I would dig more into Gagnon's past, see if in fact he had been telling the truth about his lack of connection with Ray Ericson. I could try to scam that nice young fellow from the Maine Department of Corrections. But I still felt that taste of disappointment, at seeing Gagnon roll up his pants leg and expose that old scar. I had been so certain that I would see a fresh wound there, a wound I had caused, and that hadn't happened.

What now, then?

Home and dinner, that's all.

Home and dinner.

I pulled into the Lafayette House parking lot, flashed my headlights in appreciation at the Duffy cousin keeping guard on me, and drove the last few yards to my home.

Maybe I had been sleeping in. I don't know. All I do know is that I was woken up by banging on the front door of my house, and the red numerals on the clock radio told me it was 7:30 in the morning. I rolled over and grabbed my Beretta, and then put on a robe as the banging continued. I kept the pistol concealed behind me as I went down the stairs, figuring that whoever was out there had to have been cleared by one of the Duffy cousins before coming down to my house, and that if someone really wanted to cause me harm, he wouldn't be announcing himself so openly.

I unlocked the door and opened it up, and there he was, looking fresh and clean and full of energy, carrying a plastic bag in one strong hand.

"Well, good morning to you, Felix," I said.

"Ah, bonjour, mon enfant," he said, smiling widely. "C'est temps pour aller, n'est-ce pas?"

"Is that French?"

"It sure is," he said.

155

"I thought you'd be speaking Italian, if anything."

"Well, I'm learning all sorts of new talents. Hey, I'm freezing my tail off here. Are you going to let me in or not?"

I stepped back as he walked in, wearing khaki pants, black turtleneck sweater, and long leather coat. He took the coat off, tossed it on a nearby chair, and I said, "When did your flight come in?"

"About ten last night. Got home by eleven, decided not to ring you up."

"Thanks. I appreciate it."

"You're welcome. And I'd appreciate it if you'd put that pistol away. Loaded firearms in somebody's hand tends to kill my appetite for breakfast."

I put the pistol down on the same chair he had flung his coat on, and I said, "Where in hell did you learn to speak French?"

He went into the kitchen and I followed. He dropped the plastic bag on the counter. "Just the other day, back in St. Pete," he said. "Remember the two sisters I was telling you about?"

"The ones with the orange and green bikinis?"

"The same," he said, pulling two containers of coffee from the bag. "Well, they both come from Quebec City, and instead of competing against each other for my attention, let's just say that they decided to cooperate. I taught them the joys of . . . well, let's say I taught them some joys. And I got a language lesson in return. Plus a cooking lesson and . . . well, let's leave it at that."

"I can see. What did you say to me when you came in?"

He started going through my refrigerator, and then my cabinets, shaking his head now and then, I guess, at the paucity of materials there. Besides his real work, Felix prides himself on his skills in the kitchen, skills I've never once called into question.

"Oh, I said good morning, my child, it's time to get moving," he said, his head in the open refrigerator. "You got eggs around here?"

"In the back of the first shelf. What else did they teach you?"

"*Ah, monsieur, tu es bien servi en faisant l'amour.*"

"And what does that mean?"

He came out of my refrigerator, expertly juggling a single egg. "Sorry, Lewis, that's a bit personal, even for you. I believe it's a compliment on my prowess, and I don't mean on the firing range."

I got up on one of the kitchen stools and said, "All right, besides the French lessons, what in hell did you accomplish down there?"

"Two more things, as you will shortly see," he said, taking down a container of flour from one of the cabinets, and then a mixing bowl. "One is a wonderful recipe for crêpes, which we will shortly be having for breakfast. Bacon. Got any bacon?"

"Some in the freezer."

He made a face. "Fresh would be better. Oh well."

Felix opened up the freezer compartment to the refrigerator, moved some items around, and came out with a plastic-wrapped package, which he tossed in my direction. "See if you can't defrost this and get it cooking. Least you could do is be helpful in the kitchen."

"And the second thing?"

"Hmmm?"

I was beginning to wonder if I was going to have to get my pistol and wave it under his nose, to get his attention, when he looked up at me, eyes twinkling. "Ah, you are so demanding. Not like Quebec City, from what I understand. Or so Nicole and Monique would have me believe. They say it's like Paris up there, slow and peaceful, and . . . you're about five seconds away from beating my head in with this frozen bacon, am I right?"

"Correct."

"Very understandable. All right, my friend, the second thing I learned down in St. Pete is where your buddy Ray Ericson is residing, right at this very moment, and after you and I are fortified by some French crêpes and some bacon—that is, if you get off your ass and start cooking it—we'll go for a nice drive and pay him a pleasant visit. That sound all right?"

I nodded. "That sounds fine. Why in hell didn't you say that when you first came in?"

Felix started measuring out flour into the mixing bowl and his voice took on a hurt tone. "And not let me have any fun? That's not very nice, Lewis."

"You're right," I said, finally smiling. "It's not very nice."

"There you go. Oh. How about a quick favor, first?"

"Name it."

He looked at me and then ran some water from the sink. "Go on upstairs and get dressed, will you? I don't mind half-naked breakfast guests. But I do mind half-naked male breakfast guests. No offense."

I got up. "None taken. But you'll have to start the bacon on your own."

"That I can certainly do," Felix said.

A half hour later, the kitchen was still filled with the scents of bacon frying and crêpes expertly cooked by Felix on my stove. He washed the few dishes and said, "I can't see how you can survive with a frying pan like that. Ugh."

"You have a better idea?"

"Yep," he said, drying a bowl. "Nice steel crêpe pan. Makes the best crêpes you've ever had. Nicole and Monique brought theirs down on vacation. Used it at their rental place."

"These were pretty good," I said.

"Thanks."

He wiped his hands dry, and I said, "Your information as good as your crêpes?"

"Oh, you know it," he said, opening up my refrigerator again, pouring the two of us fresh glasses of orange juice. "Here's the story. I go down to St. Pete, I run into Old Pete Tringali. Old Pete's been retired for a bunch of years, but like most with that background, he likes to keep his fingers in a few pies. Keep him sharp, you know? Besides dying in a federal prison somewhere, most of these guys are afraid of getting old and senile, spend their time playing bingo and planning their days around the early-bird specials. Even if they don't need the money or attention, they like to keep active."

"Sounds fair to me."

"Oh, you know it. And seeing Old Pete was a real break for me, Lewis, like you wouldn't believe."

"Tell me, then."

Felix took a swallow of his orange juice. "All right. When I was a young pup, learning my way around, Old Pete was in charge of a portion of Providence."

"Rhode Island? Really?"

"Oh, Christ, yes. Some parts of Rhode Island are more mobbed up than New Jersey. I was near Providence, feeling my way around, when something bad happened to Old Pete's daughter, Krista."

"How bad?"

He gently put the glass down on the counter. "Pretty bad. Was at some party at Brown University, a couple of guys slipped something in her drink. Date-rape drug, you know? Three of them were involved. Took her to an off-campus apartment and took turns with her, later dumped her in a restaurant parking lot. Old Pete heard about it and there was a row, 'cause at that time, Old Pete knew he was under some serious Fed surveillance, and the Feds, my, they thought they were going to get a break. Have Old Pete on some surveillance tape, ordering hits against these three characters. Old Pete didn't care, I remember him saying. He'd do whatever it took to get his family honor back, to avenge his daughter. But some of the guys in his organization, they wanted him to take his time, do it right. They didn't want him to chance getting nailed by the Feds."

I took a sip from my orange juice. It was cold and tart and cut nicely through the aftertaste of the maple syrup. I take it you offered your services."

"In a way. You see, I was new to the area. Feds and cops didn't know me, didn't know anything about me, and they didn't care. So I found out who these three characters were, their names, and where they were living. And I took care of it, over a weekend. End of story."

I shook my head. "Nope, that's the start of a story, Felix. What happened?"

"They left town. Were never seen again. Got it?"

I looked at that calm face, the brown eyes, the strong arms, wondering again what went on in that mind of his. "I guess . . . I guess there's no statute of limitations on some . . . matters, right?"

He offered me a thin smile. "Very good. On some matters, there is no statute of limitations. Which brings me back to Old Pete Tringali, who has no statute of limitations on gratitude. I looked him up, paid him my respects, he asked me what he could do for me, and I told him. Took him a couple of days, but your man Ray Ericson is living up in Sanford, Maine. In a little house at the end of a certain dirt road. And he's right there, right now, and will be there all day."

"How the hell do you know that?"

Felix leaned over the counter. "Because Old Pete has pull with the group that Ray was working for. Ray knows he's being hunted, knows he's the suspect in his brother's death. And he's been hiding out at this house ever since then, and his boss just talked to him last night, told him to stay put. That a couple of young fellows were going to arrive there today to pick him up, and bring him to a safe house somewhere in New York."

"I don't feel that young," I said.

"Too bad."

"Why in hell did we just have breakfast, then?" I asked.

He took the dish towel off his shoulder, tossed it at my head, and it just barely missed. "Because it's the most important meal of the day, fool. You feel like a ride?"

"Absolutely."

"Then let's make tracks."

Which is what we did.

CHAPTER FOURTEEN

On I-95 we made our way north, and I thought ruefully of the many times I had gone up and down this stretch of roadway these past few days, all as part of this damn great quest. Felix was driving another anonymous rental car, and in the rear seat were a number of black duffel bags containing a fair number, I was certain, of firearms and other means of coercion and destruction. My own firearm and means of coercion was in a shoulder holster under my coat.

I looked over at him as we approached Porter, and I said, "You said Ray was working for a group down in Florida."

"That's right."

I said, "The postcards you found at Ray's antique store. From Florida."

"What about them?"

"A signal, right?"

"You are correct, sir."

I thought for a moment, and then said, "They were indicating something was going to happen on a schedule, right?"

"Right again. Care to guess what?"

"Something to do with antiques?"

"Let you in on a little secret, Lewis. It has everything to do with antiques."

I pondered that as we passed around Porter and headed over the Memorial Bridge, spanning the fast-moving Piscassic River, which separates the state of New Hampshire from the state of Maine. I looked quickly to my right, saw the beached memorial of the USS *Albacore* submarine, and shivered for a moment at the memories.

"A shipment," I said. "The postcards were letting him know about a shipment."

"So far you're doing well, grasshopper. Continue."

"A shipment of stolen antiques, from . . . wait."

Felix waited. I thought some more and said, "You said Ray was working with a group from St. Pete?"

"Yep."

"This group active up here?"

"Not particularly."

We were over the bridge and were officially in Maine, passing a sign that said MAINE, THE WAY LIFE OUGHT TO BE, and I said, "Hold on. I was looking at this wrong. The stolen antiques . . . they weren't being shipped from New Hampshire to Florida. They were being shipped from Florida to New Hampshire. Ray was working a scam. Like money laundering. But this was antiques laundering. Right?"

"You should get on a game show or something one of these days. Yeah. That's the case. Look, who goes to live in Florida?"

"Retirees."

"Right. Retirees from New England who are sick of the snow and ice. They pack up and move south, and what do they do when they pack up and move south?"

"They take their antiques, their heirlooms, with them."

"Bingo."

"And they live there for a while and pass away and . . . Oh."

"There you go. People go to Florida from up here, they want to take things with them that mean a lot. Old mementos, antiques, heirlooms, stuff that will help ease the big move. Because it is a big move. Read a study somewhere, that the most depressed part of the elder population down there are people who've moved there recently. They're away from old friends, family members, the local newspaper. They're cut loose and they have to adjust. And it's comforting for them to have their old things with them. So, Lewis, when they do pass away, what happens then?"

"Their stuff gets stolen during the funeral. Or somebody comes in and pays almost nothing for stuff that's worth tens of thousands of dollars. Or more. And then it gets shipped up north—"

Felix passed a lumbering tractor trailer as he said, "Yep, back up north, where antiques are still high priced, are still valuable. Best I found out was that old Ray was a central distribution center. Stuff comes in—mostly stolen—sits there for a while, and then gets laundered out to legitimate dealers throughout the whole region. Not a bad scam as scams go. You said Ray had dealings with his brother?"

"Yes," I said, watching the bare branches of the maples and oaks whiz past us as we headed north. "Besides his hunt for Viking artifacts, Jon also found other items as well. Old coins. Nautical artifacts. Stuff like that."

Felix said, "Ray would probably want some real local stuff from your buddy Jon to sprinkle in with the stolen stuff. Help make it legitimate. And then when Jon found the Viking artifacts, well, I bet Ray wanted in on the deal. Maybe he wanted to sell them, make a fortune, through his contacts, and maybe Jon wanted to keep them for a museum or something. What do you think?"

It was a good guess, but it nagged at me. Something about it didn't seem right, and it took another couple of miles driving before I figured it out.

"No," I said. "A good guess, but I don't think so."

If Felix was upset at being contradicted, he sure hid it well. "Okay. What's your theory?"

"You're a criminal."

"Not a nice way to pass the morning."

"No," I said. "Let me finish. You're a criminal. You've done time and you're still involved in illegal activities, concerning antiques. You have a legit brother whom you can't stand, because he's always been straight as an arrow. But he's done his little thing with the Vikings and that's fine, what harm can that do to you, right?"

"If you say so."

I said, "Then, boom. Your brother does the impossible. He's reached his dream. He's found Viking artifacts, old items that will change the history of this area, that will put your brother in every newspaper and news magazine, and on most television programs in New England, if not the nation. Is this a good thing for your brother?

Absolutely. Is this a good thing for you, his criminal sibling? No. Absolutely not. Whatever bright light of publicity that shines on your now famous brother will slop over on you. You'll be mentioned in stories, in some of the write-ups. You'll start getting some unwanted attention about you, your background, and your current business. And that's intolerable."

Felix rubbed at his jaw, and I could make out the faint scrape-scrape of stubble against his palm. "Hate to say it, but I like your theory better than my theory. All right, then. Any idea what he's doing in this house in Sanford?"

"Waiting," I said.

"Obviously," Felix said. "But for what?"

I shook my head. "I don't know. But the Viking artifacts . . . they're the key, Felix. I think they're missing, and maybe that's why he's hiding out. Wait for the investigation to slow down some, and then pop up and start looking for where his brother hid them. I have a feeling that if Ray had the artifacts in hand, he'd be long gone. Not in the next state over."

"Okay. Then who was that mysterious man who whacked you one last week at Ray's antique store?"

I folded my arms, watched the passing landscape, as the Interstate now went through a series of flat salt marshes, stretching out to the horizon. "I had a theory about that, too."

"Oh. And what's the status of that theory?"

"About on par with the flat earth theory." And so I spent the next half hour telling Felix about my encounters with Professor Hendricks at UNH, Brian Mulligan up in North Conway, and, of course, William Bear Gagnon. Felix asked a few questions, and when I was done, he said, "You know, when I first met you, you were so straight and narrow that you had to put your underwear on with a ruler."

"That's a level of detail I don't think I've ever shared with you, Felix."

"Whatever." He laughed. "Man, either I've corrupted you or you've been corrupted through some other mysterious means. Holding a pistol on a guy, demanding that he drop his pants. That's pretty cold stuff."

"I wasn't really holding a pistol on him, and I didn't ask him to drop trou. I asked him to pull up a pants leg. Whole lot of difference."

"Not to ex-cons," he said. "They have such a low threshold for insults that ants can look over it without stretching themselves. Look, you've done well, and if we're lucky, we're about ready to pop this baby wide open. I just need to get a few things straight before we start barreling ass into Ray's little house o' paradise."

"Okay, talk away," I said.

He spared a glance at me. "What's the deal when we get there?"

"We determine he's there, and then we talk to him."

"We do, do we? And what are you going to ask him?"

I looked over at him this time. "Felix, get real."

"No, my friend," he said in a comfortable voice. "You get real. We go in there and you know what's going to happen. There's going to be a lot of bluff and bluster, and he's going to deny everything."

"Then it'll be my job to convince him to talk to us," I said, now looking out the window at the cold fall landscape.

Felix let that slide for a little bit and said, "You know what you're saying?"

"I do."

"We could find a pay phone, next exit, make a nice little anonymous phone call, give the Maine State Police a tip that he's hanging out there. That's attractive, isn't it?"

I let a breath out. "He's a suspect in the murder of my friend. I just want justice done, all right?"

"There's varying degrees of justice, Lewis."

I looked back at him. "Like the justice for three rapists of a young college girl in Rhode Island, am I right?"

There was a moment of silence, and Felix gave me a crisp nod. "Yes, you're right."

Oh, Felix being Felix and such, we soon passed over that little bump in our relationship, and after taking the Route 109 exit in Wells, we headed east, going through rural countryside, heading up to Sanford. Felix had handwritten directions in one hand, which he glanced at on occasion. He said to me, "You know who it was said life wasn't fair?"

"Whole lot of people have said that."

"You know what I mean. Somebody famous said that."

It took a second or two for my memory to kick in, and I said, "JFK. Don't know when, but yeah, he said that. Life's not fair."

"Wonder if he was thinking about that the day he took that trip to Dallas . . . Anyway, you know what's not fair?"

"What?"

He looked down at the directions again. "What's not fair is that most of the times I'm in with you on one of your noble causes, it always has to be out in East Whatever or West Overshoe. How come you never have me come along with you to someplace civilized? Like Boston? New York? Or New Orleans?"

"New Orleans?"

"Okay, some parts of it are civilized. Why is that, Lewis?"

"Maybe I lead an exciting life."

"Not likely."

The road was two-lane, twisty, and there were the usual New England decorations of stone walls, bare trees in orchards, and the usual car in disrepair on someone's front lawn. There was a panel truck that distributed water jugs for homes that was pulled over to the side, with the driver looking forlornly at a road atlas, and it looked like a young boy in jeans and windbreaker was trying to give him directions. Felix slowed and said, "Okay. Turner Road. Here we go."

We made a right onto a single lane, firm dirt and gravel, that went up a slight hill. Felix was going even slower, and it seemed with each reduction in speed, my heart rate increased. I remembered the words I had said earlier to Felix, about meeting up with Ray and what was to be done, and this close to where we had to be, that's what they had just been: only words.

"Okay. Right there. Sign that says COOPER, up on the left."

There was a dirt driveway to the left, and a wooden sign nailed to a pine tree that had COOPER in those black and gold stick-on letters that you can get from the hardware store. Felix drove by and said, "Ah, luck be a lady this morning. Here we go."

About a dozen yards up from the driveway was a wide stretch of gravel off to the right. He pulled in and switched off the engine, and we sat there in the silence and waited to see if any traffic was coming by. The road was empty. On both sides pine trees and saplings and brush crowded in toward the drainage ditches on both sides of the road. Besides the utility poles and the dirt driveway behind us, there were no other signs of what passed for civilization.

"Who's Cooper?" I asked.

"Some sort of distant relation to one of Ray's many girlfriends, from what I learned in St. Pete. I guess she was reluctant to let him stay there, but he was a way with words and his fists."

"That he does. He alone in there?"

"Yeah, just him and cable television and a freezer full of food. He wants to get out of here in the worst way, Lewis, and it's going to be our job to make him think that's what we're here for."

"Sounds good."

Felix swiveled in his seat one more time, and then looked in my direction. "You got a plan, then?"

"How about going up the driveway and knocking on the door, and politely asking him to get his ass on the floor with his hands up?"

"That's an approach, but I was thinking of something a bit more subtle."

"Go on."

"We go up the driveway, and then split. You take the rear of the house, I take the front. I knock on the door and try to appeal to his better nature, and take things from there."

"All while I'm standing in the backyard?"

"You got something better?"

"Yeah. The two of us go up to the front door and knock on it, and I'm there to back you up in case things go bad."

Felix shook his head. "This guy knows you, right? What happens if he's keeping an eye on the front yard and sees you waltzing up there? He may not know much about you, Lewis, but I'm pretty sure that he knows you're not in any way in hell involved with his antiques scam. I'd hate to start walking up there with you and have a lot of steel-jacketed rounds come zipping over my head."

"I still don't like the idea of you being up front there, all alone."

"Yeah, well, I still don't like the designated hitter rule for the American League, but you don't see me getting all choked up about it. Look, I know where you want to take this. Fine. But don't let your ego and your anger muddle things up. You've got to look at the whole picture, everything that's out there, and right now, that means doing it my way. *Capisce?*"

I nodded, opened the passenger door. "Yeah. What you said."

Outside, the air felt good but there was a tinge of something to it, of wheels set in motion, of plans coming together, about the approach of violence. I looked over at Felix, but he was now in work mode, single-minded, single-focused. He opened up a rear door of the car and reached for one of the duffel bags, unzipped it, and went to work. I went around to join him and was taken aback at what he was bringing out: a stubby-looking submachine gun, with a slightly curved magazine.

"Here," Felix said. "Hold this, will you?"

I did. He took off his long coat and dumped it on the roof of the rental car. I examined the weapon, a Heckler & Koch MP5, made in Germany. He took it from me and slung it over his shoulder, and then put the coat back on. Back into the duffel bag and back out with a spare magazine, and a pistol, which he stuck in his waistband. He noticed me looking at him and said, "What? Is there a problem, officer?"

"Some serious firepower you're packing there."

"Some serious guy we're going up against. Ex-con, right?"

"Yep."

"Well, they have a higher threshold for being convinced of the errors of their ways than normal civilians. One needs to focus their mind, and I find an MP5 will do that just fine."

"Aren't those illegal?"

"Oh, only if they're full automatic. This one is semiauto. Perfectly legal. Ready to go for a walk?"

"As ready as I'll ever be."

We went down the road—and still no traffic, not even the hint of a sound of traffic—and we started up the dirt driveway. I reached in under my coat, just to make sure my pistol was there—a brief bit of reassurance, that's all—and I said to Felix as we went up the driveway, "Don't you ever get tired of it?"

"Tired of what?"

"Walking into bad situations with firearms."

"You telling me you're scared?"

"Scared shitless, as the phrase goes," I said.

"Good. That will sharpen the senses, keep you up and running. If you told me you weren't scared, I'd have left you back in the car."

"But answer the question. Don't you get tired?"

He stopped, eyes flickering around, as he took in our surroundings. Dirt driveway ascending gently up to a rise, trees on both sides, still no sign of the house. "No, not yet, Lewis. I find . . . well, I find it comforting in an odd way. Comforting that I can still use my skills and what drives me, even at my increasing age. The time my knees start creaking or I need glasses, well, then it'll be time to retire and devote my life to more peaceful pursuits. In the meantime, no, I don't get tired." He spared me a quick grin. "Of course, with you as a neighbor, I sure as hell find myself getting into situations. C'mon, let's keep on keeping on."

We went another few score feet and Felix held up a hand. I saw what caused him to stop, which was the sight of a rooftop through the woods. "As much as this is sweet sorrow, chum, this is where we split up. You head through the woods, come out and around the rear of the house. I'll give you a ten minute head start. You wait, and when I come to the rear, it'll be all safe, and your buddy Ray will be there, ready and eager to talk to you."

"Sounds good."

"Then get going."

"Sure."

With Felix, of course, there were no words of encouragement, no whispered "good-lucks" or squeeze of the hands. There was just the calm assumption that you were a professional, were up to the task, and wouldn't let him down, and I found that more encouraging than anything he could have possibly said.

In a matter of moments Felix and the driveway had slipped from view, and I took my time, moving through the woods, keeping the roof of the small house in view. I didn't want to get too close, in case Ray was keeping watch on his surroundings. About ninety seconds into the walk my mouth was dry and my legs were tingly, like they were half anticipating that I was going to start tromping through a minefield, so I reached into my coat, slipped out the Beretta, pulled the hammer back. There was round in the chamber, and I suddenly felt better, knowing that I would be ready for whatever came my way.

The woods were sloppy with fallen leaves and muddy spots, but eventually I made it to the rear of the house. I was surprised at how good it looked. It was a typical two-story Cape Cod, in a cleared area of an acre or so, and the house was painted white. It looked in good repair, and there were no rusting washing machines, automobiles, or piles of tires in the rear. There was a window looking out toward the rear yard, and a door with short concrete steps, and a clothesline. That was it. The lawn, though covered with leaves, looked well maintained. I scratched at my ear as I stood behind a maple tree trunk, watching the rear of the house. I waited, thinking how nice it would be just to lean against the tree and let the morning pass along.

I strained to hear noises from the other side, of Felix walking up the driveway, of Felix knocking on the door, maybe a quick, hurried discussion and then . . . Felix emerging at the rear door, a smile on his face, a thumbs-up to indicate everything had gone well.

Nothing yet. Somewhere in the woods a chickadee announced her presence.

I shifted my weight, felt the leaves rustle under my feet. The Beretta was starting to feel heavy in my hand.

Still no sound. What was going on?

That's when the little train of thoughts started rumbling through my head, of how long would I stay out here by myself, had something bad happened to Felix, had he been ambushed coming up the driveway, was I now alone, what was going on, what was going to happen, what should I do—

Sounds. Shouting.

Movement by the rear window.

The rear door flew open.

And Ray Ericson ran down the steps, almost tripping over the last one, running by himself, wearing gray sweatpants and a white tanktop and black sneakers and—

I stepped out from behind the tree, went toward him. "Hey!" I yelled. "Hold it right there!"

Ray stopped and then looked up at me and grinned. "Out of the way, asshole."

I held my pistol out, both hands on the handgrip, pointing right at him. "On your knees, right now, Ray."

The grin was still there. "Man, who the fuck do you think you're dealing with?"

"I know," I said, moving toward him. "I know quite well. Now. On the ground."

Ray shook his head, came quick in my direction. "Man, I'm going to take that gun and shove it up your ass so far, there'll be—"

That was enough. I aimed and pulled the trigger, and the sound of the report was quite loud.

CHAPTER FIFTEEN

Ray Ericson dropped to the ground, just as a red-faced Felix came sprinting out the rear door, his coat bunched around him, his MP5 held out with one hand. Something was wrong, something was not right, for Felix's left arm was hanging in an odd way, but I had no time to ask him anything, as he came up and said, "He dead?"

"I don't think so."

"You hit him?"

"Only if my aim was off."

Felix's face was still red, a harsh scarlet that was frightening me, even though the focus of his anger was the man on the ground. Felix nudged him with his foot.

"You alive down there?"

Ray rolled over. "Fucker! That fucker shot me between the legs!"

Felix said, "Your unit still intact?"

"Shit, yes, but man, I could feel that slug pass right underneath my—"

And Felix drew back his foot and connected it with Ray's crotch, like he was trying to make the winning soccer goal in the World Cup with seconds remaining, and Ray rolled over and howled. Felix drew his leg back again and then stopped, and looked up at me, his eyes moist and reddened.

"Sorry," he said. "Emotions got away from me there for a second. You got this guy covered?"

"Yeah, I do. Felix, what in hell—"

Felix let his free hand drop the MP5, which hung on the sling, and then he gingerly examined his other hand, and I looked and felt nauseous. It was red and raw and blistered, and Felix looked up at me and said, "Guy was ready for me."

"He knew you were coming?"

"Well, maybe not me, but he was ready for a visitor. I knocked on the door and said I was here to pick him up, and he said great, and when I got in, he started acting hinky. He asked me if Curt had sent me, and I said, Curt who? That's when things went to the shits. Must have been a code word or something. So I followed him into the kitchen, and he made to go for a pistol on the kitchen table, and when he saw that I was carrying, he backed quick to the stove. Damn, he moved quick!"

"What did he get you with?"

Felix smiled, though it looked like he was also gritting his teeth. "Damn con had a pot of water on the stove, just boiling along. Nice, quick weapon, easy to use. Just picked it up and tossed it at me, nailed me good. Was out the door in seconds. Hey, by the way, great backup."

"Thanks," I said, the nausea still gurgling along in my gut as I kept my pistol aimed at the moaning Ray Ericson. "I think we need to move this party indoors."

"Why? I thought people in rural Maine don't mind hearing the occasional gunshot. Part of the surroundings."

I looked down at the man whose brother's murder had brought me here. "True, but they might get upset if they start hearing other things."

Felix nodded. "Good point. Yeah, let's get him inside."

"Are you sure you can—"

"Yeah, I'll take care of it. Still have one good hand and arm left." Felix reached down with his right hand, grabbed Ray's right ear, and twisted it. Ray howled again and Felix said, "Come along, little dogie, we're going in. You cooperate and I'll stop twisting your ear."

Ray got up and Felix said, "Lewis, anything funny, anything funny at all, shoot the fucker. And don't miss this time."

"I won't."

The three of us went into the house, Felix leading the way, Ray in the middle, and me following. Ray said, exasperated, "Damn it, you said you'd stop twisting my ear if I cooperated."

Felix gave his ear another twist. "I lied."

Inside Felix worked quickly and efficiently, even with one injured hand, and Ray was soon on the couch, his ankles bound together by thin dish towels, as well as his arms, tied behind him, not at the wrists, but at the elbows. Felix said, "I've got to get some things set up. You just sit here and keep an eye on our guest, okay?"

"Sure," I said, sitting in a kitchen chair, holding my pistol on Ray, only now smelling the scent of burnt gunpowder. From the rear of the house we had passed through a small kitchen and then into a living room that had the usual couch, two easy chairs, and a television set in one corner. There was a bookshelf full of romance and Harlequin paperbacks. I doubted that Ray had been perusing that bookshelf in the past several days, but I wasn't in the mood to start asking him questions about his literary interests. Ray sat there and watched us, breathing hard, not saying a word. His bald head was still bald, and his usual stubble had grown out some, so that he was about a week or so away from having a reasonable-looking beard. I thought that by my sitting with him, he'd start asking questions, start demanding answers as to why we were here and what we were after, but no, not a word. And that frightened me, his utter lack of concern for why we were here. I looked at his eyes and felt the chill deepen. Oh, he cared all right, but he didn't care about why we were here. His eyes were observing, evaluating, and I suddenly knew that this ex-con, the younger brother of my murdered friend, was going to be a tough one.

Felix came out of an adjacent bathroom, wiping some sort of ointment on his burnt hand and wrist. He grimaced but didn't say a word, and then he went out to the kitchen, where I heard running water. Felix came out and the redness in his face was fading, as he wrapped wet white towels around his damaged hand.

He said to me, "You doing okay?"

"Yeah. How about you?"

"For now I'm hanging in there, though we'll need to see somebody medical when we're . . . when we're done here. Hey, Ray, how are you doing?"

Ray just glowered, not saying a word. Felix said, "Well, take good stock of how you're feeling now, because it's going to change in a while."

And then Felix did something that spooked me even more. He went over to the television set and turned it on, and found MTV, which—for some strange reason—was actually playing music videos. Near the television was a small stereo system, built on a shelf, and Felix turned that on as well, finding an all-talk station. The noise level was loud—not deafening—but the mix of the music and the talk made it hard to hear what was going on in the room.

Which was the point, I'm sure.

Felix went over to Ray and said, "You still doing okay, Ray?"

And for the first time, even though he tried to hide it well, Ray was beginning to look nervous. His eyes blinked and his tongue just barely came out, touching what looked to be dry lips.

Then Felix leaned over and I thought maybe he was going to take a shot at Ray with a fist or an openhanded slap, but instead he just gently touched his cheek and said, "I'm going to get started in a little bit. You just hold on."

And that was it. Felix went into the kitchen, and while Ray was trying to look stoic, I was terrified. Seeing what Felix had done with the television and the stereo, and his gentle manner of dealing with Ray, made me think that if I had been in Ray's place, I would have been eager to confess to the JFK assassination before allowing Felix to proceed.

I swallowed. My mouth was dry. I suppose I should have done the civilized thing, to talk to Ray, to appeal to whatever better nature he had, but instead I listened to Felix whistling out in the kitchen, the clatter of some pots and pans, and I remembered Jon's office, his blood spatter over the desk and the lampshade. I remembered the first time I had met Ray, and how he had tried to punch me out. And I remembered the blisters on Felix's hand.

That made me feel better about what was going to happen. Not a hell of a whole lot, but enough.

Felix called out, "Almost ready, *mes enfants!*"

I tried to be cocky and said, "He's just back from Florida. St. Petersburg, in fact. And among the many things he came back with, was a talent for French."

No reply. Just the look of hate and the coldness in those eyes.

I smelled something cooking, heard the sizzle of something being stirred around, and then Felix came back out of the kitchen, whistling again. He carried a tall kitchen stool with him, another thick towel, and a frying pan. He set the stool down next to the couch, placed the towel down and put the hot frying pan on top of that. "Don't move, I'll be right back," Felix said. He grinned. "Hey, that was a joke. I liked that."

Felix came and went in a matter of seconds, and this time, he was carrying a wooden stirring spoon and a pair of kitchen scissors in his damaged hand, and another kitchen stool in his good hand. He put the stool down and sat on it, and then gently leaned forward with the scissors.

"Don't mind me, Ray," he said. "I've got some things to do here."

Ray didn't say a word, not a thing, as Felix pulled at the bottom of his tank top, and then, with the scissors, started cutting up. The shirt came apart easily enough, and then Ray was sitting there, the shirt in tatters on either side of him. His chest and belly were covered with black hair, and there was a thick scar off to the right, just above his belly. Maybe it was surgery. Maybe it was an old knife scar. I didn't know and didn't care to know.

Felix then went to the frying pan and picked up the spoon, and picked something up from inside the pan and flicked it in Ray's direction.

"Jesus!" Ray yelped, finally saying something over the sounds of the music and the talk radio. "Jesus, hold on, hold on . . . Christ . . . you fucker, that hurt."

Felix put the pan back down on the cloth-covered stool. "Oh, so you can talk."

"The fuck right I can talk, asshole."

"Glad to hear that. How does your chest feel?"

Ray glowered. "It hurts. You know it does."

"Sure," Felix said. "You nailed me with hot water. Fair enough, I guess. Now I'm returning the favor, but this time, I'm using olive oil.

Nice, hot, heated-up olive oil. Hot water can burn but hot oil . . . not only does it burn, Ray, it burrows into your skin. Burns you even deeper."

"You . . . you . . . you didn't even warn me."

Another chilly grin from Felix. "Ever hear the tale of the farmer and the mule? The farmer wanted the mule to do something, so he came out and whacked him in the head with a two-by-four. Somebody watching asked him why in hell did he do that without any warning. The farmer replied that he just wanted to get the mule's attention. Get the story, Ray?"

Ray nodded, eyes still filled with anger and fury. "Yeah, I got the goddam story. What the hell do you want?"

Felix nodded in my direction. "My friend here is going to ask you some questions. Answer them truthfully, honestly, and quickly, and the hot oil remains in the frying pan. Got it."

Now Ray looked at me. "You . . . fucking slug. You need this guy to back you up, huh? Not man enough to do this on your own?"

I waved the pistol back and forth a bit. "I was man enough our her to make you sing at a higher octave, right?"

Felix said, "Ray, the clock starts now. Lewis. Start asking the questions."

I looked into that angry and fearful face, and decided first to recheck something.

"You spend time up in Warren?"

"Yeah, so what?"

"You know a guy up there, serving time, name of William Gagnon?"

"Nope."

"Claimed to be an Indian. Sometimes went by the name of William Bear Gagnon. Hear or know of him?"

Ray said, "There are loons up there who claim to be Napoleon. No, I didn't know any friggin' Indian."

I nodded, trying to keep my concentration over the scent of oil and burnt flesh, and over the hammering noise from the television and the radio. "Your brother."

"Yeah?"

"Why did you kill him?"

He shook his head. "I didn't kill nobody."

"Anybody," I said.

"Hunh?"

"I didn't kill anybody," I said. "The way you said it, that's a double negative. The grammar police frown on that."

"The grammar . . . What the hell is going on?"

"What's going on," I said, "is I'm trying to find out who killed your brother. Story I hear from the cops is that you were over there just before he got killed."

Another violent shake of the head. "A goddam lie."

"There's witnesses that tell the cops you were there."

Ray looked over at Felix, and then me. "Maybe I was."

"But you didn't kill him."

Felix reached over to the spoon, just started gently stirring the hot olive oil. Ray started speaking faster. "No, shit, no. Okay, I was there, that night. But I didn't kill him. He was already dead when I got there. I was supposed to meet with him about some ship's brasswork he had found last week, I was going to sell it for him. I got there, let myself in. I yelled out for him but nobody was saying anything. Went into his office, saw him dead there. Blood everywhere."

Felix said, "How convenient."

"Shit, it's the truth!"

"And what did you do when you saw your dead brother?" I asked.

"What do you think?" he said. "I got the hell out of there."

"And didn't call the police?"

Ray smirked. "What, you think I'm stupid? Ex-con shows up at a murder scene. How long do you think the investigation will continue before I'm in Wentworth Superior Court, being tried for murder one? The hell with that. I got out and then I heard the news on the television, that I was a suspect. So I did the right thing. Which is how I got my ass here. Which reminds me, how in hell did you know where to find me?"

Felix took the wooden spoon out of the pan and gently tapped Ray on his nose with the dry handle "Tsk, tsk, Ray, you seem to forget who's asking the questions here. Lewis, any more?"

"Yeah, a few more," I said. "So you got there, right after your brother's dead. Any idea who did it?"

"Nope."

"Not one idea of who might have wanted your brother killed?"

"Shit, no, we didn't hang out together, you know? He had his life and I had mine."

"Laundering stolen antiques. Some life."

"Hey," Ray said. "It's a friggin' living."

"The artifacts," I asked.

"What artifacts?"

Felix interrupted. "I think the oil needs to be heated up, from all the bullshit that's getting flung our way."

"What bullshit?" Ray demanded. "He didn't say what kind of artifacts. Jesus!"

"The Viking artifacts," I said. "The ones your brother found."

He acted surprised. "You mean . . . he did it? Ray actually did it?"

I said, "Yes, he did. And now they're missing. Where are they?"

He shook his head again. "Man, I don't know anything about artifacts, I swear to God."

Felix said, "Lewis?"

"Yes?"

"I think he's lying," Felix said. "I'm sorry to say this, but I think he's lying."

Ray said, "I swear to God, I'm not. Honest!"

Felix sighed loudly, enough so he could be heard over the music and talk radio. "Lewis. I'm going to suggest we move to the next level. You've gotten too many crappy answers from this character."

"What do you suggest?"

Another sigh. "Guys like this, they can handle a lot of pain, a lot of punching and slapping and kicking and even a knife cut or two. But take off their pants and shorts, leave something soft of theirs exposed that they're very fond of, well, I find you can get to the heart of the matter rather quickly. What do you think?"

I looked over at Felix and then to Ray, whose eyes were starting to bulge out, and he started yammering that he was telling the truth, that everything he said was true, that he hadn't killed his brother, that he didn't know where the Viking artifacts were, even if they did exist, and I swear to God, I'm telling the truth, over and over again, and I made to open my mouth, to talk to Felix, when the window overlooking the front yard was suddenly smashed by a heavy object, flying through and thudding to a stop on the floor.

Felix yelled, "Lewis, cover your eyes!"

Which I tried to do, but I wasn't fast enough.

There was a bright flash of light that dazzled my eyes, and an ear-popping *boom!* that ripped through the living room. I fell off the chair and to the floor, and my ears hurt and suddenly felt like they were stuffed with cotton, and every sound that came my way was thick and muddy. My eyes were filled with after-flash dazzles, and the front door was heaved in, men tumbling in, wearing helmets, body armor, boots, and fatigues, yelling, over and over again, "Police! Hands up! On the floor! Hands up! On the floor!"

I rolled over and went *oomph,* as a cop knelt on my back, pressing one knee against the back of my neck. I went limp, allowed my arms to be snapped back, and there was a click-click as handcuffs were snapped around my wrists. Hands patted me down and a voice yelled, "Any weapons? Are you carrying any weapons?"

"No."

"Any weapons in the house?"

"I don't know," I said. "My pistol is on the floor over there."

Other voices, the scent of smoke, the cop still on my back, and a voice again: "Any weapons on you?"

"No."

Another patdown. "If you're lying, we'll strip you right here."

"I'm not lying."

"Good. I'm getting up. You move and you're fucked."

I closed my eyes, the carpeting rough against my cheek. There was movement in the room, lots of movement, and it was easy enough to see what had happened: Felix and I had discovered Ray Ericson's location about a half hour before the cops had arrived. Oh my. What a foul-up. This was going to be one for the books, depending on what kind of books ever got written about a disaster like this. My God. My stomach was rolling with thick waves of distress and nausea.

A boot nudged me. "You okay?"

"I've been better."

"Yeah, haven't we all. Time to get you up and out. Frank? Give me a hand with this character."

Strong hands grasped both my arms and I winced as pain shot through my shoulders. I got up and looked around. The room was a mess, filled with cops in SWAT gear, most of them now with their helmets off, their short hair matted with sweat. Ray and Felix were gone.

The stool holding up the hot oil had been turned over, and other cops were moving in and out of the other rooms. My legs were shaking, and then I was hustled out of the house by two cops, who weren't in SWAT gear, and who looked to be Maine State Police. The front yard was full of vehicles, including the panel truck we had seen earlier, parked to the side. The water delivery truck that I thought had pulled over for directions. Carrying the SWAT team, no doubt, and there was also no wonder why we hadn't heard anybody approaching. The loud noise inside the house had prevented that. I was taken out of the house and then put in the rear of a gray-colored Maine State Police cruiser.

"Watch your head," one of the cops said, and I almost started laughing at that. How many times I had heard that same phrase from watching one of those cop reality shows on television, sitting on my safe and comfortable couch, in my safe and comfortable house?

The door slammed shut and I tried to get comfy, which was damn near impossible, with the tight handcuffs around my wrists. I looked out at the circus taking shape in front of the house, at the different police cruisers from different police agencies. I thought I recognized Ray sitting in one of the cruisers, and Felix in another.

My fault. All my fault that this had happened. Damn, damn, damn.

The front door to the cruiser opened up and a Maine State Police trooper got in, picked up a clipboard, and turned around to look at me. He seemed tall and muscular and his black hair was streaked with gray.

"Name?"

"Lewis Cole."

"Date of birth?"

I told him.

"Address?"

I told him that, too.

"Mailing address?"

"Post office box nine-one-nine, Tyler, New Hampshire."

"Occupation?"

"Columnist for *Shoreline* magazine. Out of Boston."

The trooper scribbled some more and said, "You got anything you want to say about what just happened?"

I said, "I imagine I'm either under arrest, or will be shortly."

181

"You got that right, pal."

"Then no, I don't have anything to say."

The trooper gave me a dark look. "You're in a world of deep shit, Mr. Lewis Cole of Tyler, New Hampshire. We're going to nail you for trespassing, breaking and entering, criminal threatening, illegal discharge of a firearm near a residence, and maybe suspicion of tax evasion when we're done. So you might want to think that over again."

"Thanks, but I think all I'm going to say is that I want to call my lawyer."

"Gonna be a long wait."

I shifted in the seat, tried to ease the pain in my wrists. "No offense, trooper, but I don't think I'm going anywhere."

"You got that right again, pal."

He stepped out and slammed the door and I leaned my head back against the smooth upholstery, closed my eyes. What a mess. What an absolute mess.

I opened my eyes, took another look outside at all the cops and SWAT team members and cruisers, and there, standing by a York County sheriff's department cruiser, sipping from a cardboard cup of coffee, was Detective Diane Woods of the Tyler Police Department. She looked at me and I looked at her. Her face was impassive as she looked at me. I could not see what was going on behind those eyes of hers. The moment seemed to last a good long while. Then she turned away, to talk to a Maine State Police trooper, and after a bit, I turned away as well.

CHAPTER SIXTEEN

Eventually the trooper came back into his cruiser and started up the engine, and said something into the radio, and we went down the driveway. At the bottom of the driveway, I spotted a tow truck backing up to Felix's rental car. We made our way out onto the main road, and we didn't exchange a single word as we drove. Long minutes drifted by as I watched the landscape flow by, sometimes seeing people out walking or raking their yards and doing normal things. Once or twice somebody looked up and gazed in my direction, and I'm sure they felt a sense of peace and security, knowing that an evil criminal was now on his way to the justice he deserved. I half-listened to the chatter of the police radio and then, up ahead, I saw a two-story brick building, surrounded by a chain-link fence and razor wire on top. A sign outside announced YORK COUNTY HOUSE OF CORRECTIONS, and I was certain that I had just been introduced to my new home for the next day or so.

The trooper drove out to the rear, where a sliding metal garage door came up. We drove in and the door slid shut. The trooper got out, removed his pistol, and placed it in a lockbox bolted to the side of the garage door. Then he came around and opened the cruiser and said, "Swivel around, get your legs out."

"Sure."

He helped me get up and kept a strong grip on my upper arm as we passed through checkpoints and other doors. I stayed quiet and did what I was told, moved where I was directed to, and didn't complain as I was told to strip, and I was searched. My clothes were taken away, and I was presented with a stiff orange jumpsuit and paper slippers for my feet that were barely big enough. The standard fingerprinting and photo taking was completed, and then one of the deputy sheriffs asked me if I'd like to make a phone call.

"Yes. I would like that very much."

I made the phone call in a cubicle of a room, the phone fastened to the desk, the phone looking like it had been designed by the U.S. Air Force to survive a nuclear blast, way back in the 1950s. When my phone call was complete, I was brought down another series of corridors, another series of checkpoints, and was placed in a cell. The barred door made a terrific clanging noise as it was closed and the lock was set into place.

"Hungry?" the deputy sheriff asked. He seemed to be in his midfifties, thick mustache, heavyset. "Thirsty?"

"Yes to both," I said.

The deputy sheriff said, "Then take it easy. Lunch will be along in a while."

"Thanks."

"Nothing to thank me for," he said. "Them's the rules."

He walked away and I looked around at my new home. It seemed to be about eight feet to a side, the room made of concrete and steel. To the left was a plastic-enclosed mattress, with two wool blankets folded at the foot of the bed. A plastic-enclosed pillow was at the other end. A stainless steel toilet was in the corner, next to a stainless steel sink, set into the wall. I went over and saw there was no faucet, just a thick push button. I pushed the button and lukewarm water came out. I did that three times and washed my hands and face. No towel. Just a roll of toilet paper. I dried my hands on my jumpsuit and wiped my face with my upper arm. In the middle of the cell was a drain. I imagined inmates being placed in here, throwing around food, feces, vomit. What a job, to hose down and clean that place up. I lay down on the thick mattress, pulled a blanket up and over my cold feet. And thought a lot. And waited.

And waited.

Lunch came by, but at what time, I did not know. It was brought by a guy wearing an orange jumpsuit as well, and pushing a lunch cart, like the one used by flight attendants. He was tall, with a thin beard and stringy hair, and he wore clear plastic gloves. He slid the plastic tray under an opening at the base of the cell door, and said, "When you're done, slide the tray and all your trash out into the corridor."

"Okay."

He smiled, revealing a number of missing teeth. "Oh, and since you're new, here's a suggestion. Be nice and neat with your trash, or you might not like what gets dumped into your dinner later. Got it?"

"Gotten."

I sat on the bed and ate with the tray balanced on my knees. Lunch was a sandwich of bologna and American cheese, mustard and butter, on white bread. A carton of milk, a bag of Humpty Dumpty potato chips, and a chocolate chip cookie. The cookie was surprisingly good. I finished everything and washed my hands again, and then put the trash carefully and neatly on the tray, and slid the tray out onto the corridor floor. I heard a murmur of voices and the scrapes of other lunch trays, being placed out in the corridor, but I wasn't sure who my neighbors were, and I didn't think the so far polite deputy sheriffs would like it if I started yelling down the corridor to see if Felix was there.

So back on the bed I went, and continued the wait.

Which didn't last long.

The cell door clanged open and the same deputy sheriff was there. "Cole."

"Yes?"

"Some people to see you. Come along."

"Sure," I said.

"Turn around, put your wrists together."

It was the second time I had been handcuffed, and I didn't enjoy it anymore. Back along the corridor I went, and I glanced into the other cells, but no Felix, and no Ray. I was brought into a small conference room, with a nice shiny table and chairs. Three men were waiting for me on the other side of the table. The handcuffs were taken off and I sat down, and introductions were made, and I promptly forgot everyone's name. But there was a detective from the Maine State Police, a detective from the New Hampshire State Police, and a deputy attorney general from York County.

First things first. I was then quickly and efficiently and officially placed under arrest for a breathtaking series of crimes—just like the state police trooper had earlier predicted—and my Miranda rights were read to me. A form was slid across the table, asking me to check off and initial each right, so there was no misunderstanding that I did not fully and completely understand my rights. I nodded politely and made the little checkmarks and initialed with a firm "LC" at each proper place in the form.

"Now, Mr. Cole," the deputy attorney general said. "We're going to ask you if you would like to waive your rights and speak to us about what happened this morning with you, Mr. Tinios, and Mr. Ericson."

"How do I do that?" I asked.

"Do what?" he replied.

"Waive my rights?"

He said, "At the bottom of the form. Just put a check mark next to the box that says you fully and completely understand your rights, and that you're waiving your rights to speak to us without an attorney present."

I looked down and smiled nicely, and then slid the form back across the table.

"Thanks for asking," I said. "But the answer is no."

There were no harsh words, no pounding on the table. The deputy attorney general looked sorrowful, if anything. He said, "We don't know everything at the moment, but we'll find everything out, Mr. Cole. We know that Mr. Ericson is a suspect in his brother's death in New Hampshire. We also know that you and Mr. Tinios were at his house, and that a shot had been fired in the rear yard. You see, the house has been under surveillance for well over a day, before you two gentlemen showed up. And we also know that you and Mr. Tinios were engaged in . . . well, we'll say a rather brutal method of interrogation, before the police entered the home."

I nodded, said not a word.

The deputy attorney general said, "We've done a quick background check on you, Mr. Cole. Your record's pretty clean. Nothing like Mr. Tinios or Mr. Ericson. You cooperate with us, answer our questions, let us know exactly what was going on, and then I can make some recommendations on your behalf, recommendations that will be very helpful once you go to trial. Believe me, Mr. Cole, this is your window of opportunity, and the window is closing very quickly. Give us answers, work with us, cooperate with us, and it'll be to your benefit. You could be out of here and back home in Tyler Beach within a few hours. What do you say to that?"

I looked at the well-dressed and tough-looking men across from me, and there was that little yearning there, to roll over and cooperate, to be the good citizen. There I was, wrists still sore from the handcuffs, wearing an orange prison jumper and ridiculous paper slippers that kept falling off my feet, sitting in a room with men in suits, and I so wanted right then to do the good thing, so I could be a good guy and get out of this jumpsuit and back into my own clothes.

Instead, I said, "I'm sorry to disappoint you. I'm not going to waive my rights, and I'm not going to answer any of your questions."

The deputy attorney general gave me a crisp nod. "The window is now closed."

Back into the cell I went, and I laid back on the mattress and stared up at the thick green paint on the steel ceiling. The blanket went back onto my feet and I waited, thinking. If Jon had been alive and could see me right now, he'd be shaking his head in dismay. What a foul-up. What an incredible foul-up. To fail was one thing. But to fail in such a spectacular fashion, and to be arrested for what I had been doing, Jon would have ranked this disaster with other great disasters, like World War I and the Bay of Pigs invasion and the invention of loud car stereos. And more than anything else, of course, there was Diane.

Diane.

My very best friend in all of the world, and she had looked at me like I was a stranger with drool running down his chin, holding out a paper cup for a spare quarter. And who could blame her? She had warned me, days ago, that her plate was full, that there was too much at risk with Kara and her upcoming promotion, to clue me in on the investigation or to do anything else to hurt her and her career. That had made sense, perfect sense, and then I had gone out on my own to screw everything up for her. For what would happen once a smart detective from the New Hampshire or Maine State Police realized that one of the three men brought into custody this morning was a very good friend of the lead investigator?

I pulled the blanket up to my chin. Not good. Not to mention how things had been left, just before the police had broken in. Felix and I had been engaged in torture. Nothing could prettify that. As rotten as Ray Ericson was, and perhaps—despite all of his denials—he was still connected with his brother's death, did he deserve what Felix and I were doing to him this morning? Hot olive oil upon his skin? Tied and helpless in front of us? Was that the best I could do, the best I could be, to find justice for my dead friend?

Lots of questions. And I didn't want to consider any of the answers. So I lay there, blanket over me, and I only got up when the meal cart rattled by again for dinner. I rolled over and picked up the plastic tray. Dinner was a carton of milk, two lukewarm hot dogs in buns with mustard packets underneath, another bag of Humpty Dumpty potato chips, a salad in a plastic bowl with a plastic spoon, and another chocolate chip cookie. Even though I had been careful in following the meal deliverer's earlier instructions in keeping my trash neat and tidy, I picked up each hot dog from the roll and carefully examined the roll and the bun. Clean, it appeared, of any foreign debris.

I ate with the tray balanced on my knees, feeling out of sorts, for a number of good reasons. One was that when eating alone, I'm used to reading a newspaper or magazine. There's something about a well-written piece of news or commentary that goes well with a good meal. I can't explain. It just does. So eating a poor meal in a cold cell, it would have been nice to have reading material, but the only thing available was the back of the potato chip bag, where I learned that Humpty Dumpty—always a Maine icon of fine potato chip products—was now owned by a Canadian company.

Dinner and reading finished, I slid the tray out, washed my hands, and went back to my bunk. After a while I found that nature was calling, and was calling rather frantically. I looked at the cold steel toilet in the corner and saw how open it was to anybody walking by, and I waited and waited, until I couldn't wait anymore. I went over and got out of my jumpsuit and winced at the cold metal against my skin, and I closed my eyes and tried to pretend I was someplace else, and the pretending had to go on for a long, long while before I could relax and do what I had to do.

My humiliation continuing, I flushed the toilet, washed my hands, got dressed again, and went back to the hard, unyielding bunk.

Sleep came in bits and pieces during the long night. There were shouts and occasional yells from the other inmates—I couldn't yet bring myself to say "fellow inmates"—and there was the far-off chatter of radio traffic from some of the deputy sheriffs. Somebody at the end of the corridor was snoring so loud that I was certain seismographs from the Blue Hill Observatory in Massachusetts could detect the trembling of the building.

The lights were dimmed but not turned off, which made sleeping even more of a problem, and I tried to take care of that by rolling over and facing the wall, and draping the blanket over my head. But the smell of strong detergent from the blanket prevented that from working too well. As I lay there, I tried to keep my mind off my current problems by remembering great tales I had read in the past, from Solzhenitsyn and Koestler and Kafka, about those brave souls who survived the prison systems of the old Soviet Union and other totalitarian states, and thought about what strength, what values, enabled people to survive in such places, day after day. How many rose above their torture, their abuse, their imprisonment, to become poets, writers, and statesmen? From Mandela to Havel to Walesa, how many had survived and become stronger?

And me?

And what had I done? I had tortured another human, that is what I had done, and that had gotten me here. Nothing famous, nothing glorious, nothing uplifting in that.

I rolled over again, something bugging me, something different. It was the brief talk Felix and I had taken part in, while in his rental car and before walking up the dirt driveway to the cottage where Ray Ericson had been hiding out. Felix had been saying something, something that was niggling in the back of my mind, and I couldn't quite remember what it had been.

But it was important. Felix had said something important that was now resting in the dark and cluttered basement of my subconscious, and I couldn't get to it. My mind raced and poked and prodded, but what Felix had said still remained out of reach.

I was still trying to think it through again when I managed to fall asleep, and managed even to stay sleeping until the breakfast tray slid into my cell.

Later that morning one of the deputy sheriffs came by and said, "Time for a court appearance. Unless you'd like to spend some more time here."

"No," I said. "A court appearance sounds fine."

So the cell door opened and I was handcuffed again, and then taken down the corridor, through another checkpoint, and into a holding area. There were metal benches against each wall, and other prisoners were there as well, one hand chained to a metal loop against the wall. I was brusquely and efficiently sat down, and I looked around and there were seven of us. One of them was Ray Ericson, who stared quietly ahead, the quiet patience of a man who knew the ins and outs of the system, and who knew he wasn't going to be surprised that day.

The other face I recognized, of course, was Felix, who looked over at me and smiled and gave me a furtive wink, and I suddenly felt twenty pounds lighter from around the shoulders and the base of my neck. He was dressed in the same orange jumpsuit, but somehow he filled out the suit such that it looked good on him. Another trick of the trade, I suppose. I was also happy to see that his hand, the one burned by boiling water, had been professionally bandaged. We sat there for a while and then we were checked and rechecked against a listing, and, one by one, we were unshackled and stood up. And then, one by one, we were reshackled in a long line, and a deputy sheriff called out, "We're going outside to a van. Take your time and listen to directions. No talking. No spitting. Just move along."

A door to the outside was unlocked and opened up, and we went outside, shuffling along. Felix was first, maybe, I guess, because of his hand, and I was next to last. The man in front of me was pudgy and seemed ill, for his breathing was wheezy. The young man behind me looked like he had just started shaving, and he looked at me with contempt, like it was my fault he had gotten here. Outside the air was cold and sharp, but it was fresh air, the first fresh air I had tasted in more than a day, and I could forget for a moment that I wasn't wearing a coat. We were quickly and efficiently bundled into a large passenger van, colored brown and with YORK COUNTY SHERIFF'S DEPARTMENT emblazoned on the side, and up forward there was a mesh grill separating the passenger section from the driver and his partner. A sheriff's cruiser pulled in behind us as we went out into the light morning traffic, and I just stared ahead through the dirty windshield, as we made our way to another part of the criminal justice system.

The drive didn't seem long at all, and maybe that was because we were moving, or maybe because it had been so damn good to see Felix. We drove through Sanford—how appropriate, where this fouled-up adventure had begun—and then we were in the small town of Springvale, where the county superior court was located. We went around to the rear and the unbundling process began, as we were taken off the van and brought into another holding area in the basement of the courthouse. Same kind of benches, same kind of bolts in the walls where one hand was chained. All about us was the calm, efficient murmur of court and police officials, keeping us bad guys in check, and I had this funny little urge to speak up and say, "Hey, really, I don't belong here. I'm one of the good guys."

A funny little image, one I'm sure Ray Ericson wouldn't agree with.

Waiting. A lot more waiting, chained to the wall, and then a deputy sheriff came into the holding cell and called out, "Cole. Lewis Cole."

"Right here," I said.

"Hold on."

He came over and undid my wrist, and he said, "Come with me. And nothing funny, you understand?"

"I understand."

I was taken down another corridor and let into a room with a wooden desk bolted to the floor, and with the scent of stale tobacco smoke. Sitting on the other side of the wooden desk was an attorney from Massachusetts, one whom I had met only once before, and one who was a dear friend of Felix, and who I was hoping was going to get my butt out of here and on its way home.

"Lewis," Raymond Drake said, standing up. "Nice to see you, even though the circumstances aren't good, are they?"

"I hope I'm not paying for that understatement," I said.

Raymond allowed himself an embarrassed smile. "Knowing my history with Felix, you know exactly what this will cost you."

He was dressed in an expensive-looking two-piece suit, was tanned and fit, and was in his fifties. Gold bracelets were on both of his wrists, and as he sat down, I remembered how I had met him earlier, on another matter involving Felix. Some years ago, when both Felix and Drake had been younger, Drake had gotten caught up in a legal matter involving a relative of Felix's. Not quite knowing what he had gotten involved with, Drake had made a number of threats, which Felix's relative had countered with a late-night ride out into Boston Harbor in the rear of a cabin cruiser. Somehow Felix had learned of how this particular legal matter was going to be settled and managed to get a boat himself and secure Drake's release before he became lobster bait for the recovering Boston Harbor.

"Yes, you're right," I said. "Sorry to bring it up."

"No problem."

He opened up a folder and examined some papers. "Here's the deal. The goal right now is to get you out and home. Agreed?"

"Agreed."

"Okay. We'll be going in for a bail hearing shortly. I think we'll be able to succeed in taking care of business. You have a permanent address, standing in the community, and a relatively clean record. Bail will probably be set fairly high but I have resources. We can swing it. The thing is, Lewis, I need to know one thing."

"Sure."

Drake said, "If I'm going to get you out on bail, you're going to have to agree to a number of stipulations. Constant contact with either me or the Maine State Police. Surrendering your passport. Making each and every court appearance that will occur over the next several months. Is that going to be a problem?"

"Not at all."

"Good," he said. "I didn't think so."

"What about Felix?"

He put his folder back into a leather briefcase. "What about him?"

"Can you get him out as well?"

"I don't know," he said. "Felix's past history . . . well, let's just say

192

it's more detailed and colorful than yours. I don't rightly know. But I do know that I'm going to do my best for the both of you, all right? Don't worry about Felix. He'll be fine. Worry about yourself."

"I do worry," I said. "All the time."

Drake got up and went to the door, and a deputy sheriff came and brought me back to the holding area. Felix was next, and he gave me another smile as he went out, holding his bandaged hand carefully in front of him. I looked around and there was Ray Ericson, still sitting and staring straight ahead. There was a low murmur of the other prisoners talking among themselves, discussing who they were, what they had done, and how it was all a mistake, and I kept my mouth shut, for a number of reasons. There was still this odd sense of disbelief, that I really didn't belong here, that this had all been a terrible mistake, but that odd sense was outweighed by the magnitude of the trouble I was in, and the trouble I had no doubt caused Diane Woods. I wondered if she was in the courtroom. I wondered what she was thinking about me.

And so I sat, until my name was called, yet again, by another busy and efficient deputy sheriff. I got up and was taken to another doorway, and it was like I was going through some magical transportation device. Behind me was all concrete and steel and the smells of sweat and fear, and the processing of men who had gotten themselves into serious trouble, and by passing through the door, I was now in the world of calm and deliberative justice. I was now in a small courtroom with a female judge on the bench, looking down at us like some disapproving parochial school principal. Before me was Raymond Drake, standing behind a wooden table, motioning me over.

I joined him and stood still and tried to imagine what kind of contrite look would work for the judge, whose nameplate said ROSE ROBINSON. Her hair was thick and black and she had on reading glasses attached to a little gold chain that looped around her neck. She looked down at her papers, as a young man in a black suit passed other papers over to her. She gave them a glance and looked up and said, "Mr. Drake. From Boston. I take it you're representing Mr. Cole?"

"That's true, your honor," he said, in a firm, polite voice.

"Mmmm," she said, examining a few sheets of paper. "Seems like you've been a busy young man, Mr. Cole."

Drake nudged me sharply in the ribs, so I kept my mouth shut. At an identical wooden table just a few feet away, a woman about five feet tall, wearing a black skirt, black jacket, and ruffled white shirt was standing as well. Her long blond hair seemed to reach the top of her buttocks.

"Miss Harrison, what says the State?"

"Your honor," she said, in a loud voice that seemed out of place in such a tiny body. "Due to the severity and barbarity of the allegations against Mr. Cole and his confederate, we request bail in the amount of one hundred thousand dollars, cash or surety."

Sweet Jesus, I thought, feeling like the floor was trembling beneath me.

"Your honor, based on my client's firm ties with his community and his lack of a prior record, we feel the county's request is way out of line."

"Perhaps it is, Mr. Drake," the judge said, making a notation on a piece of paper. "But it's a line that's not too far off. Seventy thousand dollars, cash or surety. See the court officer to your right. Tom, who's next?"

The next several minutes was a confusing mix of papers being signed, documents being exchanged, and then Drake disappearing for a moment and reappearing with a plastic shopping bag. "Here," he said, handing the bag over to me. "The jumpsuit doesn't do anything for you at all."

My own clothes were probably still in a bag back at the York County jail. Whatever. I slipped into a nearby men's room and stripped off the jumpsuit and put on the fresh clothes. I don't know how he knew my size or where he found time this morning to do shopping, and I didn't particularly care. He had even included slip-on Topsiders that were soft and comfortable, and I looked at my face in the bathroom's mirror, just before I left. My eyes were red-rimmed and heavy, there was a day-old growth of beard on my face, and my hair was thick and greasy. But it wasn't the appearance that bothered me as much as it was the look in those eyes. They reminded me of pictures taken right after the end of World War II, when German war criminals were led into the dock. A look of what had they done. What they had done.

Outside Drake met me and I gave him the plastic bag, with the jail clothing inside. He passed over a small paper bag. Inside was my wallet, keys, and other pocket stuff. But no 9mm Beretta pistol. I'm sure that wouldn't be coming back to me any time soon.

Drake said, "Court appearance here in two weeks. I'll talk to you before then. Ready to go home?"

"Yes," I said. "But what about Felix?"

"I'm going to take care of Felix," he said, grabbing my upper arm. "Actually, Felix is going to take care of Felix. He always does. Let's get out of here before some member of the Fourth Estate makes our lives miserable."

We went out into the lobby of the courthouse, past groups of people here to either seek justice or to watch it in action. Outside, he led me to a parking area to a black BMW with Massachusetts license plates. There was a young woman standing by the shiny front fender who smiled at the two of us as we came closer.

"Mr. Cole, allow me to present Miss Wynn, my associate."

I gave her a quick shake of the hand. She had short, red, thick hair, a winning smile, and gray-blue eyes. She had on a short black leather jacket, short gray skirt, and black high heels. Drake went on, "She's here to take you home."

"And what about you?"

"I'm going to stay here and work with Felix for a while. See what we can work out."

"And what's that going to be?"

Drake smiled. "Sorry. Lawyer-client privilege."

"Mr. Cole?" Miss Wynn asked with smile still in place. "Ready?"

I held some of the paperwork in my hands. "I guess so."

Drake slapped me gently on the back and led me around to the passenger's side of the BMW, opening the door for me. I got in and leaned back in the soft leather seat.

"Well, you're a free man," Drake said, lowering his head to look at me.

I thought about everything I had done the past two days, and everything that had happened to me.

"No," I said. "No, I'm not."

CHAPTER SEVENTEEN

Miss Wynn got right to it as we left the courthouse parking lot.

"Mr. Cole, where would you like to go?"

"What do you mean?"

I liked watching the way her long-fingernailed hands worked the steering wheel and stick shift. I added, "I thought you were to take me home."

She flashed me a bright smile. "Raymond said I was to take you anywhere you wanted to go. If home is that place, fine. If it was Boston, fine."

"How about Los Angeles?"

She didn't miss a beat. "That would be fine, too. Though we'd have to go through a rather extensive and polite discussion over tolls, gas, and lodging arrangements."

"I'm sure," I said, suddenly feeling quite tired. "Any other day, Miss Wynn, that would be fun. But today, home will be fine. Tyler Beach."

Another nice smile. "Tyler Beach it shall be."

And so we headed south. If I was tired and felt soiled and didn't feel like talking, Miss Wynn took up the slack. She told me about her time growing up in Southern California, how she dropped out of college and worked for a hi-tech company, got burnt out, and how she ended up on the East Coast—"a long and boring story involving a married couple who had a very different idea of what an au pair should do"—and after a number of other misadventures, she was now a paralegal and working for Raymond Drake, and also taking night courses for a law degree from the New England School of Law.

"And how's law school?" I managed to ask as we passed over the Memorial Bridge into New Hampshire.

"Not bad, except for this law professor I have, claims to be a writer," she said. "He also claims to have a body of a nineteen-year-old paratrooper, but I keep my mouth shut and take good notes. And you, Mr. Cole—"

"Lewis."

"Sorry, Lewis. I understand you're a writer, too?"

"On a monthly basis."

"Excuse me?"

"I'm sorry," I said. "I write a column for a magazine out of Boston. Called *Shoreline*."

"Oh. Is it fun?"

"Most days."

She offered me another flash of a smile. "I guess this isn't one of those days, is it."

"Not hardly."

Miss Wynn talked some more as I gave her directions to my place on Tyler Beach, and I heard about a couple of times she had actually tried surfing on North Beach when she was dating some guy from Newburyport last summer—"claimed surfing was fine, just as long as you can ignore the wetsuit, and I tried it a few times and nearly froze my ass off"—and when she was getting to the part of the story where she and her guy were discovering ways of warming each other's butts, we were pulling into the Lafayette House parking lot. I said, "You can drop me off here, I'll walk down."

"Nope," she said, aiming the BMW to the rough dirt driveway. "Raymond said to drive you right up to the front door, and that's what I intend to do."

The plumbing and heating van was in its customary spot, and I gave a wave to whichever Duffy cousin was in there, keeping watch. I said, "Watch out, the undercarriage might get caught up."

"That's what tow trucks are for."

"And that sounds pretty cavalier."

I could sense the smile, since she was focusing on driving down to my house. "It's a leased vehicle, not mine, and I'm on the job. So there you go."

The drive down was bumpy but manageable, and she managed to pull in front of my house without catching the undercarriage on anything. Her long fingernailed hands rested on the steering wheel as she looked over at me. "Well. There you go, Mr.—oops, Lewis. Safely delivered."

"Thanks," I said.

"Is there anything else?"

"Anything what?"

She said, "Raymond told me that whatever you needed for today, that I'd take care of it. Which includes anything more you need besides delivery."

"Really?"

She stuck out her tongue. "I'm practically an officer of the court, Lewis. No fibbing is allowed."

"All right," I said. "Can I get you something to drink?"

"You have orange juice in that place?"

"I do."

"Then it's a deal."

She joined me as I went up to the front door, unlocked it, and went inside. She followed me in, and as I went to the kitchen, she paused and looked out my floor-to-ceiling sliding glass doors. "Damn, now that's a view."

"Thanks."

Inside my refrigerator I lucked out in finding a relatively fresh carton of orange juice, and after pouring her a small glass, I said, "If I heard you correctly, Raymond told you to do anything I asked. Right?"

"Yep," she said, sipping delicately at the orange juice. "Within reason, of course."

"Of course. Then you wouldn't mind running an errand for me?"

She turned and took another sip. "Not at all."

"If you could just wait for a moment."

"Sure."

I left her and then went upstairs, to my bedroom, where I stripped everything off and put on my terrycloth bathrobe. In the vanity in the bathroom, I grabbed a trash bag and stuffed the clothing and deck shoes Raymond Drake had purchased for me. I went back downstairs and Miss Wynn was leaning against the counter, finishing the orange juice, and if I was trying to get a rise out of her, I failed. She just looked at me with a bit of interest and I gently dropped the trash bag on the floor.

"If you don't mind, in your travels south, could you drop those clothes off at a Salvation Army or Goodwill location?"

"Not at all," she said, putting the empty glass down on my counter. I looked at her and she looked at me and she said, "Rough time?"

I thought about saying something witty but instead I said, "Yeah, pretty rough."

She shook her head. "Hope it improves."

"Me, too."

I looked at the smile and red hair, and I said, "You know, this is going to sound funny, but have you been up here lately?"

"To Tyler?"

"Yes."

"Nope. Except last year, for that surfing fiasco. Why?"

"I . . . I just have the oddest feeling you and I have met before."

She folded her arms. "Any other guy talking to me in his kitchen, wearing just a bathrobe, I'd think that was a pickup line. Nope. Must have been somebody else."

"Must have."

Miss Wynn picked up the trash bag with one hand and headed to the door. I walked with her and when she opened up the door, reached into a pocket of her short leather jacket and said, "Here. Take this."

"This" was a white business card, which had two phone numbers and where I learned that Miss Wynn's first name was Annie. "Thanks," I said.

"Office and home numbers are there," she said. "If you ever need any more help, or any more advice from a law student, give me a call."

I gave her my best smile. "So far, Miss Wynn, you're the best thing that's happened to me all day."

"Annie."

"All right, Annie."

I watched her as she went out to the BMW, and after she got in and tossed the trash bag next to her, she gave me a happy wave, which I returned as the BMW went back up the driveway.

The phone call I had been expecting all day came right at dusk, after I had spent the day lazing about, which had been preceded by a long shower that ended only when I had run out of hot water. I had also eaten three meals during the day, just enjoying the fact that I could eat anything and everything I wanted, whenever the mood struck me. The message was quick and to the point and sounded like it was being made from a phone booth, and I left and was out the door within five minutes.

I drove down to the Tyler Beach State Park, which is at the every end of Tyler Beach, next to the boat channel running out of Tyler Harbor and out to the Atlantic Ocean. It was dark by the time I got there, and a steady mist was falling. The park—which during summer is packed with RVs and campers, for it has good day rates for tourists at the beach—was practically deserted as I drove down the cracked asphalt into the parking lot. There were two open pavilions where picnickers did their meal duty in the summer, and my headlights caught somebody sitting on one of the picnic tables, at the south end of the pavilion.

Outside the cold mist was heavy enough to moisten my hair as I walked over to the pavilion, my hands in my coat pocket. There were no lights about, just the faint illumination coming from a streetlight, out in the far parking lot. I stepped up onto the concrete pad under the pavilion, as the person sitting there turned and looked at me.

"Hey," said Detective Diane Woods.

"Hey, yourself," I said, getting up and sitting down next to her on the wooden table. A breeze was coming in off the ocean, making me shiver, but I wasn't going to leave this place, not until everything was through.

"You okay?" she asked.

"Hanging in there."

"You know why I cut you off, up there in Sanford?"

"For a number of reasons," I said. "From the investigation to your career. And all good reasons."

"So you're not angry?" she asked.

I took my hands out of my coat, rubbed them on my pants legs. "I think I should be asking you that question."

She sighed. "So far, your participation in that little misadventure, and my connection to you, is either conveniently or fortunately being ignored. Detectives from the Maine staties and the New Hampshire staties are much more intrigued about your friend Felix's participation. They're looking into whether Felix has some connection with Ray Ericson, if Felix has been involved with Ray's criminal enterprises, if Felix was there on the orders of somebody from Boston or Providence. So that's where the focus of that little raid yesterday is being placed."

"I can imagine."

"They know the two of us have a relationship, but there's no discussion of anything improper going on. Lucky for the two of us."

"I guess."

And she turned to me, voice sharp, "And having said all of that, my friend, what in hell do you think you were doing, jeopardizing your life getting caught in crap like this, not to mention my career and my livelihood? What in hell were you thinking?"

I folded my arms. "You can figure it out, I'm sure."

"Oh, yes, I certainly can do that. Noble Lewis Cole, out commiting vengeance, seeking absolute truth and justice. Not depending on our boring little criminal justice system. No sir. Lewis has to do it on his own. And how does he do that? By hooking up with a local mobster, a guy with some serious actions on his head, and by finding the lead suspect in a homicide that I'm investigating. And what do the two of you do when you locate this lead suspect? Do you turn him in? Do you drop a dime? Do you?"

Out beyond the waters, I thought I could make out the lights of Cape Anne in Massachusetts. I burrowed my head some in my up-turned coat collar. "Nope. We did things on our own. That's what we did."

"'Things on our own,'" she quoted back to me. "That's a polite way of saying the two of you were torturing him. Am I right?"

I kept quiet. Diane went on. "That's what the SWAT guys told us when they cleared the room. That Ray Ericson was bound on the couch, and that you and Felix were there. And between the two of you was a frying pan with hot olive oil. That's what you were doing. Torturing him to find out whether he killed his brother, your buddy. True?"

"We were doing what we had to."

"You were, were you? And who the hell chose you?"

"My friendship with Jon chose me. That's what happened."

"Oh, come on, Lewis, that's so much bullshit. And you know it."

I paused, trying to think of how I could say it, and then I said, "Maybe it is. And I'm probably going to regret saying this, but in a state cemetery in Massachusetts lies the body of a man who raped and assaulted your Kara. And who died mysteriously in a prison in Massachusetts."

I wasn't sure how Diane was going to react, and she reacted by saying low and carefully, "That was different. And don't you dare try to make a comparison."

"No comparison," I said. "Each is different, and each of us did what we thought was right."

We sat there in the near darkness, both of us looking out of the wide and deep waters of the Atlantic, and Diane moved her legs about and said, "You feel bad about what happened?"

"Which part? The torture part or the getting arrested part, or the nearly ruining your life part?"

She gently nudged me with an elbow. "All of the above, I guess."

"Well, I'm doing all right."

Another pause, and I said, "Diane?"

"Yes?"

"What more is going on?"

She seemed to think about that, and then she said, "I think I'm going to make you feel worse, that's what."

"Oh. Well, go on then."

"You sure?"

"Yeah, I'm sure."

"Okay," she said, "and I don't need to remind you that this is confidential, all off the record. All right?"

"Understood."

"Good. Your man Ray. He's no longer a suspect in his brother's murder."

My hands went back into my coat pocket. "Go on."

"You see, we thought we had it nailed. A neighbor woman saw a guy that looked like Ray leave the house, right about the time the medical examiner said Jon had been killed. Pretty open and shut, right?"

"That's what I thought."

A long sigh. "Yeah, you and me and everybody else. Tell me, old Lewis, what are you going to be doing this weekend at your home?"

"Hunh?"

"Just before you go to sleep on Saturday night, are you going to be doing anything particular in your house?"

"I don't know, am I?"

"Sure you are. It's when we change the clocks to daylight savings time. You know, spring forward, fall back? We're all going to be moving our clocks ahead one hour. Everyone, of course, except for our witness. You see, the poor dear got confused and had already changed her clock. The time Ray was at the house was an hour later than she thought. And according to the medical examiner, poor Jon had already been dead for about that long. He claims he got there and went in and found his brother dead. It looks like he was telling the truth."

"Damn."

"Yeah, I said something like that, but a bit more forcefully. So sorry about that, Lewis, and I hope that lawyer who got you out of jail up in Maine gets ready for something else. I have an idea Ray Ericson might have a bone to pick with you and Felix before this is all over."

I couldn't think of what to say, so I said, "Damn."

Another soft nudge from Diane. "Look. I've got to get going. Kara is trying to unpack, one box at a time, and I promised to help. You be good, okay? And for Christ's sake, stay out of my business."

"You got it."

I was surprised, then, by the soft touch of her hand on my cheek. She said, "You want to go out and help somebody, stop trying to help the dead. Go help the living."

"In what way?"

"Paula Quinn. Your friend needs you right now."

"What's going on?"

Another soft touch of the hand. "You find out yourself, and you help her, okay? Good night, Lewis."

"Good night, Diane," I said, watching her walk around to the rear of the pavilion, where her car had been hidden, and I stayed on the cold picnic table as she drove away, heading back to her warm condo and her companion, and when I thought enough time had passed, I got off the table and made my own way home.

It turned out to be a restless night, filled with periods of half dozing, when random dreams and thoughts would go slouching through my mind, like the defeated troops of some great army, struggling to find its way home, struggling to find some semblance of order and peace. I thought about Jon and our meetings and our friendship, I thought about his brother Ray and what Felix and I had done to him, and I thought about all the miles driven to see a college professor, an Indian activist, and an angry old amateur historian. I thought, too, of that dark night in the antique shop and the man who attacked me, and of the time my Ford Explorer went off the road in Durham.

Lots of thoughts, lots of nagging. I turned over and over again in bed, trying to get comfortable, failing every time. There was a point when I read and reread a copy of *American Heritage* magazine, to try to get my mind focused on something else, but that didn't work either.

And for a few moments, here and there, I thought about the red-haired woman who had driven me home, and a red-haired woman, years ago, whom I loved dearly and who was now dead.

Was that why I had earlier thought I had met Miss Wynn before?

Didn't make sense.

And so I tried to sleep.

The next phone call came at seven a.m. sharp, and I rolled over in bed and grabbed the phone and grunted something into the receiver.

"Lewis?" came the slightly distorted voice.

"Yeah," I managed to say, rubbing at the sleep crusts in my eyes.

"Hey, it's Felix. How are you doing?"

I sat up in bed. "Where the hell are you?"

"In jail, where else?" Now I could see why his voice was distorted. There were voices in the background, the murmurs of other men, no doubt waiting in line to use the pay phone.

I said, "How's your hand?"

"It's been better. Look, this is charming and everything, but I don't have much time. I need to know how you're doing."

I rubbed at my eyes again. "I'm doing okay."

"No you're not," he said. "I know how the Lewis Cole mind works, and right now, it's filled with guilt. Am I right?"

"Felix, we were after the wrong guy," I said. "From a very good source, he didn't have anything to do with his brother's death. He was innocent."

"Then I guess he shouldn't have been acting guilty, right?"

"Felix . . ."

"Hey, don't get all mushy and sentimental over Ray Ericson, considering what he's done in his life. And what we were doing was trying to get information. Okay, so it turns out he was telling us the truth. We had to make sure. And besides, you weren't really going to have me take his pants down, right?"

I didn't say anything.

"Lewis, you're not answering me."

"Because I don't have much of an answer. I don't know what I would have done."

"Then you're an awfully poor judge of your own character, my friend. I don't care what you thought you were going to do, I'm positive about this. If those cops hadn't shown up when they did, you and I would have been out of that house within ten minutes, Ray Ericson would have been counting up some money for his troubles and cursing us for stopping by, and that would have been that. Damn cops. Always getting in the way."

"Speaking of getting in the way, what's your status?"

A brief laugh. "Still a prisoner, bail still up in the air, but don't worry, I'll be out of here soon enough. Okay? Look, the line behind me for this phone is getting pretty long and—"

"One more thing."

"Make it snappy."

"When we were in your rental car, just before walking up to the

205

house, you said something to me. Something important. But I can't remember it."

"Shit, Lewis, we were talking about a lot of things. About how we were going to approach the house. About what we had to do. About looking at the whole picture."

"There, right there."

"Hunh?"

"The last thing you mentioned," I said, now swinging my legs out of bed, sitting up, things clicking. "What did you say?"

"Cripes, I don't know. Something about having to look at the whole picture, everything that's out there. That's what I said."

Cissy Manning, my dear love, with her bright scarlet hair, dead all these years.

And Miss Wynn, who took me home and offered me so much.

And . . . damn it. There it was. Right there.

"Thanks," I said. "Thanks a lot, Felix. It's going to help a lot."

"Well, if you say so. You take care of yourself and don't fret about what we did to Ray. All right?"

"Sure."

"Good. Now, I've got to make another phone call, and see if these fine gentlemen behind me will grant me that boon."

Felix hung up, and so did I, and suddenly I felt better. Something had just snapped into place.

Time for a shower, breakfast, and to hit the road.

I got up and did just that.

CHAPTER EIGHTEEN

Just like the last time, I met up with Paula Quinn as she was sitting on the hood of her new Toyota Camry at the end of a driveway off of busy Route 1. And just like the last time, I got out of my Explorer and walked up to her, and she turned and gave me a look as I approached.

But everything else was different.

The fake Tudor English home of a New Hampshire poet named Donald Burnett was no longer there. At first I thought that Paula had pulled her plan off, but I saw how wrong I was when I got closer and saw the pile of timbers and wood and shingles and broken glass that had once been a house, and which Paula so desperately had wanted to turn into a home.

I sat on the cold hood of the car and put my arm around her, brought her close.

"Damn it to hell, I'm so sorry," I said.

"Not your fault," she said, voice quavering.

"Then whose fault is it?"

She wiped at her eyes and her voice got calmer, got stronger. "Oh, a whole number of people, I guess, starting with the greedheads who sit on the board of selectmen. You remember, there was this deal, right? Buy the house for one dollar, get it the hell off the property, and Sy Hartmann from Lawrence could built his convenience store or

QuickStop or whatever the hell they're calling it nowadays. That had been the deal." Then her voice lowered, to an anguished whisper. "Damn it, that had been the deal."

"What happened?"

"Sy sweetened the pot, though everybody denies it. He said he couldn't afford to wait for a buyer—namely me—to get the financing and get a moving company located and do everything else to get this house safely out of here. Claimed that bad weather would come and he didn't want to spend extra to have to build his place when the snows start up. So he offered a deal, making a donation to a local youth charity, in exchange for the selectmen changing the deadline as to when I could get the house out of here."

"A youth charity?"

"Yeah," she said, and I could see the tears trickling down her face, though her voice remained clear and calm. "A goddam youth charity, and guess whose wives serve on the board of directors for this little charitable effort? Nothing like a little pork slung their way to move government along."

I gave her shoulders another squeeze. "When did they start tearing it down?"

"Yesterday afternoon. The fuckers. I'm sorry . . . it's just, well, you know, they almost arrested me here, you know that? I was putting up a protest, I was about ready to throw myself in front of the bull-dozer, when a couple of Tyler's finest showed up and tried to calm me down."

She wiped at her eyes but the tears kept on rolling. "Then . . . I made a deal. Give me fifteen minutes inside the house and I'd stop fighting."

"What did you do with the fifteen minutes?"

"Oh, took a little last stand, I guess. I took my camera and went through the rooms and took all these photographs, thinking that one of these days, when Philistines aren't ruling the town, there would be a need or something for evidence of what was once here. When a poet with the heart of an Englishman lived here. Before progress came along and ripped this piece of history out of the town, and replaced it with a gas station."

I sat with her as the wind kicked up some leaves. A couple of shingles hanging loose from a piece of the destroyed roof flapped in the breeze. "Go on," she said. "You know you want to ask the question."

"None of my business," I said.

"Maybe so, but still, yeah, the first phone call and many subsequent calls I made were to my dear boy, one Mark Spencer, the town counsel. I won't bore you with the play-by-play except to say that there was nothing he could do. His hands were tied. He worked at the pleasure of the town and they were within their rights to do what they wanted with this property. Even if it meant screwing me over and destroying a part of our past. There was nothing he could do."

"Sorry again," I said.

"Men," she said, and that was a comment that was impossible to address. So I sat there and looked at the ruins of the house, and Paula patted me on the leg and said, "I need to get back to the paper. I'm going to try to do my best to write a calm, dispassionate story about how the selectmen—with the support of the town counsel, who supposedly represents the town—did something awful here yesterday."

"Your dear boy won't like that."

She smiled through the tears. "Then I'll tell him my hands are tied. That I work at the pleasure of my publisher, and they are within their rights to publish anything they damn please."

"Good for you."

Then she brushed away some of her fine blond hair and said, "And you, my friend. What have you been up to lately?"

"Stuff," I said.

"Stuff? That's one word that can mean a hell of a lot of things. Still on the quest?"

"Yes, I am," I said.

"Has it been a good one?"

I thought back to everything I had done these past several days, the people I had visited, the people I had hurt, from William Bear Gagnon to Ray Ericson.

"No, it's been a lousy one."

She smiled through her tears. "Then why keep it up?"

"Because . . . I owe somebody something."

"Jon Ericson?"

"Yeah," I said. "I owe it to him to get the facts straight, to get the story straight, to get the history straight."

She nodded and said, "Good for you. I just hope you wrap it up soon, Lewis. Sometimes, history . . . well, it grabs hold of you. Like this damn house. And if it doesn't work out, it has the potential to break you, break you in a very bad way."

Paula wiped at her eyes and said, "Enough of philosophy this morning. And I have a newspaper story to write. And you?"

"I have a quick question for you, if you don't mind."

"After listening to me here, you've got your question," she said. "Go ahead."

"Jon Ericson's funeral."

"Yes?"

I said, "I pretty much knew everybody there. You and Diane and Felix Tinios and a few members of town boards. Except there was this one couple, sitting in the front. Young couple. She had red hair, her friend had a beard. Do you know who they were?"

"No, but I bet I know who does."

"Who?"

"Carl Threadgold. Threadgold Funeral Home. I'm sure he'll be able to tell you everything you need to know."

"Why?"

She went around to the front of her car, opened up the door. "Because Carl loves to know the locals, loves to know who they are and where they live. Oh, he'll talk to you, Lewis, but be careful. He'll try to sell you a funeral package before you head out the door."

"Maybe someday, but not today."

"That's the spirit. Hold on." She leaned over and did something inside her car, and then came out, holding a dollar bill in her small hand. "Here. I won't be needing this."

I gently took her hand and clasped it tight. "Keep it. You never know when you might need it."

"A dollar?"

"Sometimes a dollar is just enough."

She smiled again and kept the dollar bill, and I leaned forward and kissed her on her forehead, and she said, "Thanks. Take care."

"You, too."

And I guess the noble thing would have been to stand there and watch her drive out, and mourn for a bit over the ruins of the house and Paula's dream, but I had things to do, so I got into my Ford and followed her out to Route 1.

210

Carl Threadgold was about ten years older than me, wearing a dark suit, white shirt, and blue necktie, and he had the cheerful persona of a man who knew that his line of business was recession-proof, depression-proof, and immune to almost every business cycle known to mankind. His hair was carefully groomed, as were his fingernails, and I had the sense he followed some internal guidebook on How to Look to Comfort the Grieved. He led me into his office and he said, "Sure, I remember you. You gave that nice reading at Jon Ericson's service."

"Thanks, but somebody else wrote it. I just read it."

"Well, we all certainly could sense the sincerity in your tone. How can I help you?"

I said, "During the services, I pretty much knew everybody who was there in attendance. But there was one couple, sitting up front. Man and woman. The woman had red hair, the man had a beard. Do you know who they were?"

His eyes narrowed a bit and he sat back in his chair and folded his hands together. "Is there a problem?"

"No, there isn't," I said. "Look. I write a column for a magazine called *Shoreline*. I'm thinking of maybe doing a memorial piece on Jon, his life, what he did here in Tyler. I thought I knew his friends, his acquaintances. But I didn't know that couple that sat up front. I thought maybe I'd talk to them."

His mood lightened and he unfolded his hands. "Well, I don't see the problem there. And besides, you could probably find out who they were just by asking them around. Mark and Jan Russell. They live up on Drakeside Road. Nice couple, just moved in last year."

"Really?"

"True."

"Do you have any idea why they were there?"

A gentle shrug of the shoulders. "Just to pay their respects, I suppose. Very nice couple, I've met Mark a few times at the chamber of commerce breakfasts. You're not a member of the chamber, are you?"

"Um, no," I said, now wanting to get out of there as fast as possible. "It's just that my business is being a writer and such, and—"

211

He held up his hand. "No need to go on. I understand."

"Mark Russell," I said. "What kind of business is he in?"

"Woodworking, I believe. Making toys. I'm sure you'll find him in today, if you go up there."

I got up and said, "Thanks, Mister Threadgold."

"Please, call me Carl. Not a problem. And Lewis . . ."

"Yes?"

"Not to be too forward, but before you leave, can you tell me, have you made any plans for your future, when your time comes?"

I tried to give him my best, most self-confident smile. "No."

"You really should, you know."

"I understand, but you see," I said, now walking out, still smiling, "I plan to live forever."

After a quick stop at a nearby service station to glance through the local phone book, I was now on Drakeside Road, a narrow two-lane country road that led out of the center of town, paralleled the busy lanes of the Interstate, and went out to the very edge of Tyler, before it met up with its thinner and poorer cousin of North Tyler. The Russells lived in an old farmhouse with an attached barn, and their land was bounded by two subdivisions, one called Drakeside Woods and the other Drakeside Arms. Next to the mailbox on their leaf-covered front lawn was a wooden sign, hanging from a pole: RUSSELL'S FINE WOODEN TOYS. I pulled into the driveway, parked near a rusting Subaru and a Ford pickup. When I got outside I could hear the whine of power tools coming from the barn, and I decided I'd try the house first. I walked across the lawn, actually smelling the salt of the ocean. Close but not close enough to see.

The door was answered after just one push of the doorbell. The woman with the red hair showed up, wiping her hand on a towel, wearing blue jeans and a bright blue sweater. I gave her another patented Lewis Cole, Interesting Magazine Writer smile, and I passed over my business card.

"My name's Lewis Cole, and I was wondering if I could talk to you and your husband for a few minutes."

She looked up from my business card. "Talk to the two of us. What for?"

I said, "I write a column for the magazine. Called 'Granite Shores.' I was a friend of Jon Ericson, and I was thinking about doing a memorial piece about him for a future issue. I noticed you and your husband at the church during his funeral service, and I was wondering if I could find out how you knew Jon Ericson."

Jan Russell opened the door wider and I stepped in, making sure to wipe my feet. She was smiling and tossed her towel over her shoulder. "Oh, you can talk to us if you'd like, but I'm afraid it'll be a very short talk. You see, we weren't friends with him at all. Hardly even knew him."

Oh. Damn, there goes another theory, I thought. She went on, "Let's go into the kitchen, and I'll see if I can't drag Mark away from his work."

From the doorway I followed her through a dining room and I immediately noticed the floorboards: they were highly polished and they were wide, quite wide. From the outside this farmhouse looked like any of a half dozen or so within a mile of downtown Tyler, but the wide floorboards told me right off that this house was old. The first settlers here had their choice of timber, and the oldest houses always had the floorboards from the oldest, and widest, trees.

From the dining room we went right into the kitchen, which was red-tiled, and I sat down at a square oak table while she went up to a massive black cast iron stove and said, "How about a cup of coffee?"

"That would be great."

She poured me a cup and rustled around in the refrigerator for a moment, and came back and passed over the cup and a little tray with cream and sugar. I dropped a spoonful of sugar in my cup and looked around. The kitchen was comfortable and cluttered, and on a shelf near a window that looked out to the wide rear yard, I noted little wooden toys, from a train set to a group of dinosaurs on wheels. Jan said, "Let me see if I can tear Mark away from his latest project."

By the refrigerator there was a door that looked like it led outside, but she surprised me by standing by the door, and flipping a series of light switches, up and down, up and down. Jan noticed my look and laughed. "He gets to working so long, with the saws and vacuums running, wearing ear protection, the only way I can get his attention is by blinking the lights on and off a few times."

And sure enough, a minute or so later, there was a clumping

sound, of boots treading upon flooring, and the door opened and Mark Russell came in. I stood up and his wife made the introductions, and I shook his hand, feeling the rough calluses on his palms. He seemed to be in his early forties, with black hair and a thick beard that was liberally sprinkled with sawdust. His jeans were dirty as well, and he had on a black shopkeeper's apron that went up to his chest.

"Ah, coffee," he said, sliding into a seat across from me. "Jan, will you pour me a cup and join us?"

She briefly stuck her tongue out at him. "Sawdust must be getting in your brain cells again, 'cause I didn't hear that magic word."

"Oh, all right, hon, will you please give your poor working man a cup of joe? Pretty please?"

I smiled at the give-and-take, and soon enough, the three of us were sipping cups of coffee, and before I got into the business of the moment, I said, "Have the two of you lived here long?"

Mark scratched at an ear. "Depends on what you mean by long. I grew up here as a kid, and then left when I was eighteen. Joined the navy. Spent twenty-five years in nuclear boats before retiring and coming back to the family farm."

"When was that?" I asked.

"Last year. My parents moved to Florida years ago, and they had a bunch of renters here, year after year. But when I got out, well, I always wanted to have a little woodworking business. No money, of course, but with my pension, well, we do all right."

His wife said, "Mr. Cole is thinking of writing a magazine article about Jon Ericson, and I told him I wasn't sure if we could help him or not."

"Really? Jon Ericson? Why do you think we knew him?"

"Well, I saw the two of you at his funeral last week."

Mark slapped a hand on the table. "Damn it, dear, you're right, the sawdust is starting to clog up my brain cells. I thought I recognized you, the moment I came in the house. Something about the face. Sure, you said some words at the funeral. Now I remember."

"All right," I said. "If you didn't know him, why were you at the funeral?"

Jan said, "We just thought it'd be the polite thing to do. You see, we did meet him, the day before he got murdered. Terrible thing. We had a nice chat with him and all, and then, when we found out that he got killed, Mark and I thought we should go there, to show our respect."

I gingerly touched the rim of the coffee cup. "How did you come to meet Jon Ericson?"

Mark took a noisy slurp from his own cup. "Mutual friends . . . well, maybe, mutual acquaintances. You see, when we moved back here, we went through some stuff that's been in the family for generations, and—"

"Excuse me," I said, my hands now in my lap, where they were firmly grasping each other.

"Yes?" Mark said.

"I . . . I'm sorry to interrupt you, but I was wondering. How long has your family owned this land?"

Jan said proudly, "Since the beginning. Just like my family."

"The beginning of what?" I asked.

"Since the beginning of Tyler," Mark said. "One of my ancestors was one of the original settlers, came over with the Reverend Donus Tyler. Got a land grant here from King Charles the First. A Russell family has been here ever since. Of course, most of the original land's been sold off, cut up for subdivisions."

I grasped my hands tighter. "All right, then. What did you mean, some stuff that's been with the family?"

"Oh, hell, there's stuff in the barn in boxes that have been kept here, years and years. Old books. Parchment. Even some clothes. So I moved some of the stuff around for the woodworking tools and tables, and we found some old Indian stuff in a wooden box. Well, we thought it was Indian stuff. I wanted to get it checked out and I made a couple of phone calls, and Jon came down and said he wasn't sure if it was Indian artifacts, but he was certain it was old."

I cleared my throat. "The day before he got killed, right?"

"Yep," Mark said.

"Where are the artifacts now?" I asked.

"Oh, we let him take them," Jan said. "I mean, they didn't look like much, and Jon promised he'd give them back to us when he was through investigating them. I guess they're still in his house. He said not to worry, they'd be in a safe place."

I said, "Did you let the police know about what happened?"

Mark said, "We talked to a state police detective. Very nice fellow.

215

He said the artifacts appeared to be missing or misplaced from the house. He said they would probably show up eventually, and he asked us if we knew anybody who might want to harm Jon. We told him no, that we hardly knew Jon at all."

Mark smiled and picked up his cup of coffee again. "He even asked me where I had been, the day he got killed. Just following procedures, he said. Hell, I knew what he was doing. Just checking to see if I might have had something to do with it. Lucky me, I was at the Marston School, doing a presentation to some kids on my toys."

I looked at them both, the smiling faces of the descendants of Tyler's very first European settlers, and I said, "These artifacts. What did they look like?"

Peter rubbed at his beard. "Well. Let's see, there was a rounded stone with a hole in the center. A couple of stone carvings, showing guys with cloaks on or something. Even a couple of coins, rubbed pretty bare. Couldn't make out if they were English or Spanish or French. And this was strange, there was a piece of metal. Looked like an axhead or something."

I could only nod. After all this time, all this searching, after all these years.

Jan said, "I mean, it had to have been a colonial axhead that the Indians managed to get through trade. Like the coins. Right?"

"Sure," I said, wondering just how faint my voice really sounded to them. "You're right. How did Jon act when he saw them?"

"Oh, he seemed pretty happy. Like he knew what they were when he first spotted them. And then he asked me this strange question. Well, maybe it wasn't that strange."

"Mounds of earth," I said.

He smiled. "Hey, that's pretty spooky. How did you know that?"

"Jon told me earlier he'd been looking for a farm in Tyler that once had these earth mounds on them."

Mark nodded. "Yeah, that's exactly what he said. He asked me if there had ever been these earth mounds on our land, and I said, well, I wasn't too sure, but it sounded familiar. So I went to Ezekial's diary."

"Ezekial?"

"Yep," Peter said. "Ezekial Russell. Great-great grandson of Jonah Russell, who came over in 1623. He kept a regular diary about the farm when he was living here. Pretty boring stuff, actually. I did a high school term paper on it one year, and mostly it talked about the weather. Rain and snow. Drought. How much corn was planted. Stuff like that. And one spring, he had bought another piece of land, adjacent to the original land grant. This piece had these long earth mounds on it that he broke up with plows and shovels, in 1781, I think."

"And when the mounds got broken up, is that when the artifacts were found?"

Jan said, "That's right. It was mentioned in the diary as well. Something about ruins of the old noble savage, and that was that."

I looked around the kitchen, thinking that just over a week ago, Jon had been here, Jon had finally found it. Finally found the dream he had followed for years and years. How good he must have felt, how triumphant. After years of doubt and work and searching, he had come here, had come to this old farm and—

"Oh," I said. "One more thing. You said you met Jon through a mutual acquaintance. Who was that?"

Mark said, "Not really a mutual acquaintance of ours, but an acquaintance of my parents. You see, I called down to dad and asked him who I should go to to get the Indian stuff checked out. You know, I just wanted to see what it was all about. Dad wasn't too sure, but he told me, and I called him, and that guy said I should give Jon a call."

Although I knew the answer, I had to hear it from them.

"Brian," Mark said. "Brian Mulligan. He used to run the Tyler Town Museum. I gave him a call and he said we should call Jon Ericson. So we did."

Jan said in a helpful tone, "He lives in North Conway."

I smiled at them both. "Yes, I know."

I was back home and started working the phones. It took a while but I got ahold of the cable company that had the franchise for North Conway and found out that, indeed, they had a community affairs program called Valley Vision. After being bounced around a bit, I talked to a young and enthusiastic man named Charlie.

Charlie said, "Okay, could you repeat that again, please?"

"Sure," I said. "I write a column for a magazine called *Shoreline*. I'm doing a piece on what goes on at local planning board meetings, about the type of items that get discussed. I want to contrast what

217

goes on in the seacoast with what goes on up in the White Mountains. I thought I could purchase a copy of a tape you have of a North Conway planning board meeting."

"Heck, that'll be a first, to have someone out of town buy a tape copy of those folks," he said, chuckling. "Which meeting would you like?"

"The most recent one," I said. "From last Wednesday."

Charile's voice changed. "Ah, sorry, can't do that. Can do about any month before that, up to last year. But not last Wednesday's."

I turned around in my office chair, looked out at the bleak landscape of rocks and dirt and scrub grass. "Really? Why's that? Wasn't there a meeting last Wednesday?"

"Sure was," he said, "but we don't have a tape of it."

"You mean, it wasn't recorded?"

"Oh, it was recorded," Charlie explained. "But the damnedest thing, somebody came in when I wasn't around and erased the tape. The whole damn thing. Can you believe that?"

Brian Mulligan, who said his presence in North Conway was backed up by that tape.

"Sorry to say," I said. "I sure can."

CHAPTER NINETEEN

After getting off the phone with the cable television guy from up north, I forced myself to sit in my office and think for a while. Everything that had gone wrong these past several days had come from my assuming a lot and forcing my way into situations before getting the facts straight, before getting all the questions answered. So far, that had led to some awkward encounters and an arrest record, for the first time in my life.

But not tonight. I was going to do it right. I was going to have my facts and information nailed tight before I proceeded, before I charged anybody with doing anything, and that meant the artifacts.

They were missing, but something the Russells had told me had given me another place to go, another place to think about.

But I wanted to make sure. I needed to make sure.

So I made another phone call, lucked out, and with appointment firmly in hand, I left my house and got in my Ford Explorer and gave one of the Duffy cousins a thankful wave as I went out toward Atlantic Avenue, thinking that if I was lucky, the Duffy cousins would be back at their home this time tomorrow, ready to do something else for their patron, Felix.

I spent the next twenty minutes driving to Exonia, a small town next to Tyler in the west that boasts a number of authors in residence, along with the famous Phillips Exonia Academy, a prep school to the rich and famous years ago, and now prep school to the rich, famous, and smart who are fortunate enough to get loans or scholarships. The house I was looking for was in a rural part of town, down a narrow one-lane country road, but the directions I had been provided were excellent. I made a left at a mailbox designed to look like a lighthouse and went up the dirt driveway, parked behind a light blue Subaru station wagon. The house was a simple two-story colonial, painted light red with black shutters, and I got out of the Explorer and walked to the front door. The lawn was free of dead leaves, and there were rhodenendron and lilac bushes around the front of the house.

The door was answered at the first ring, opening to reveal the smiling face of Professor Olivia Hendricks, and then a flash of white and black between my feet, racing out the door.

"Oreo!" Hendricks called out, almost laughing. "You get back in here!"

"Hold on, I'll get him," I said, turning around and going back to the lawn. The cat looked at me with a look of disgust—like a prisoner escaping to find a guard on his back—but he let me pick him up and bring him back inside. Hendricks was in the living room, right off to the left, sitting down on a couch. I came in with the cat squirming in my hands and Hendricks laughed and said, "You can put that bum down wherever you want, Lewis. I just don't like him going out by himself. There are dogs out there, foxes, and, at night, coyotes. I don't want him going out and not coming back. I'd miss the poor fella too much, and I think a lot of students would as well."

I gently let him down on the Oriental rug and sat down on a couch on the other side of the room. It was a cozy place, filled with books and warmed by a fireplace that was actually burning a few chunks of wood. Between us was a thick coffee table with books and magazines on top—*Newsweek, Time, The Nation*—and books also overflowed from bookshelves along three walls. Classical music from the local NPR station played from speakers in the corner. A window overlooked the front lawn and our vehicles, and I settled into the couch as Hendricks looked over at me. She had on jeans and a UNH sweatshirt, and she said, "All right, I must admit, your call was intriguing. Tell me again what's going on?"

I said, "I think I might have a lead on where those Viking artifacts are located."

She nodded. "The ones supposedly discovered by your friend Jon Ericson. Okay. Go on. I'm listening."

"And I think I also know who might have murdered Jon. But I want to be sure about the artifacts before I go to the police."

Hendricks clasped her hands together. "How can I help?"

"These artifacts. The people who owned them, they thought they were Native American. They met with Jon the day before his death. Jon obviously thought they belonged to his Viking friends. And in your position, I was hoping, well, I was thinking that . . ."

She nodded crisply. "You'd like me to evaluate them, correct? Ensure their authenticity?"

"That's right," I said. "I don't want to go to the police and have wrong information. I want to make sure I'm right."

"Who doesn't?" Hendricks said. "Look. I have a pot of water on, I was making myself a late afternoon cup of tea. Care to join me? And then you can tell me more about the artifacts and what they supposedly represent."

I really wanted to get a move on, but I also wanted to be polite. "Sure. Tea would be fine."

She got up off the couch, just as something sharp bit at my ankle. I looked down and snapped my leg away, and I heard Hendricks say as she went by me, "That damn Oreo. Sometimes he's just not friendly to strangers. Just push him away and he'll be fine."

I kept my eyes down on the cat, who looked up at me with the scorn that only a cat can display, when you're disrupting their routine or their territory or their life. I said in a low voice, so the good professor wouldn't hear me, "Tell you what, pal. You go your way, I'll go mine, and nobody gets hurt."

He seemed to ponder that for a moment, licked a paw and rubbed his face, and then wandered over to the fireplace, where he plopped himself down and rolled over on his side. From the kitchen I could make out the sounds of dishes rattling and silverware clattering, as Hendricks hummed a little tune to herself. My hands felt twitchy, like they needed to have something in them, and I leaned over a bit to the coffee table, looking at some of the magazines, and the books they were covering.

Three of the books were identical, and they had a cheap paper cover and block lettering. I recognized them as bound galleys, one of the last stages of publishing a book. Just before a book gets published, a hundred or so quick copies are printed up—without the last typos and corrections being taken care of—with a cheap cover slapped on it. The books are sent to chain store buyers and independent bookstores and reviewers, and the one I now held in my hand bore the title *They Lived by the Shore: New England's Original Peoples*.

And the author was none other than Olivia Hendricks.

I caught her out of the corner of my eye as she came in, bearing a tray, which she put down on the table between us. The tray had two cups of tea and a plate of Pepperidge Farm Milano cookies. "Oh, I see you've noticed my latest opus."

"It looks interesting," I said. "What's it about?"

I looked up as she sat down on the far couch. "It's a book I've been working on for almost a decade. A real look at the Native Americans who resided on the coasts, and how their lives were disrupted when the Europeans first arrived. It took so much time because I wanted to tell the story from their point of view and not the Europeans'. We've all grown up with the tales of the Pilgrims and their first Thanksgiving. Well, my book tries to tell the tale from the Indians' perspective, about what it was like to have their lives so violently interrupted, and all because they lived by the shore. The shore that was their home, the shore that was the new home for the peoples leaving Europe."

I put the book back down on the table. "A lot of work."

"Yes, quite a lot of work, and my editor and I are very excited about it. It's going to have quite a respectable first printing for a historical work of its kind, and there's a good chance that it might have some major national reviews." The smile that came next didn't seem to bear much humor. "You know the phrase, publish or perish? That's so true in my field, and especially when you publish, your work disappears, and you still perish. But this one . . . ah, this one, this might secure my future. It might make everything right, finally, for all those years doing fieldwork and teaching."

"I look forward to reading it," I said.

She shrugged, got up from the couch. "You can have one of those galleys, if you'd like."

"That's very kind of you," I said, but I was no longer thinking of the cheap paperback book in front of me. I was watching Hendricks as she approached the coffee table and the tray, for she was limping.

She was limping.

At her office at school, she was always behind her desk.

And now, I had not seen her move, being distracted by that damn cat.

But she was limping.

I looked at the book again. A book that was going to make everything right, secure her future.

Hendricks picked up a cup of tea, put some milk in hers, and then limped back to the couch. She sat down and nibbled delicately on a cookie. "These artifacts. What can you tell me about them?"

The room was warm, was comfortable, and I felt like I could spend an evening here, just browsing through the bookshelves and enjoying the music and the warmth of the fire. If I stayed out of the way of the neurotic cat on the floor nearby—but I needed to get the hell out of here, and fast.

I tried a smile. I don't think I succeeded. "Look. I've imposed upon you already, professor. Why don't I leave and get the artifacts and bring them back to you?"

She said, "Why don't you take me to them? Are they in your car?"

"No, they're not," I said, my feet urging me to get the hell up and out. "Really, I shouldn't impose upon you. Why don't I—"

And she smiled and leaned forward, putting her teacup down on the tray, and a hand went down and there was the noise of a drawer sliding open, and her hand came up holding a pistol, which was pointing right at me.

"All right," she said. "This is how it's going to be. Lean back, be quiet, and put your hands behind your head."

"Professor," I said, trying to put a shocked tone in my voice. "What's this all about?"

Her eyes and gaze were now icy. "You can put away the shocked tone, Mr. Cole. I don't care to hear it. So listen to me. Lean back on the couch, put your hands behind your head."

"Is this some kind of joke?" I asked, seeing if I could possibly defuse the situation, get her comfortable, get her—

"No, no joke," she said sharply. "And if you don't do as I say, I'll shoot you right here, just like I did your friend. Jon Ericson. Got it?"

Oh, yes, I thought, my feet and hands growing chilled. I certainly got it, for Professor Hendricks had just confessed to me that she had committed murder last week, but the confession didn't seem part of her seeking any kind of forgiveness. She certainly didn't seem to be in a mood to ask for forgiveness, no, sir. I leaned back as she told me, put my hands behind my head, elbows straight up. The cat looked over at me, looked bored, and went back to work, cleaning his face with his paw.

"You know, the surprise on your face is wonderful to see," Hendricks said.

"I thought most college professors were against firearms in the home," I said in reply.

She managed a thin smile at that. "You thought correctly. I'm just a minority, that's all. In fact . . . that's what I've been, right from the start. A minority. You read about the enlightment of the college campuses, how wonderful and equal it all was, and that's so much nonsense, Mr. Cole. And you want to know something? Want to know when I first started carrying firearms? When I was a grad student, that's when. When I came back from Tunisia."

Hendricks took a deep, shuddering breath, and I thought she was going to cry or collapse, but she said, "You see, in Tunisia, I was doing fieldwork. All part of getting that anthropology crown. You have to go out and prove something, write something, do some original research. Which is what I did. I went into a remote mountain village, on the counsel of my advisor, who had worked there before. I was doing a piece on marriage rituals. Pretty funny, correct? And while wandering around one night, I ran into three men. Three men who wanted to pass on their own rituals, with what they do with a college-educated American woman whom they find out alone at night, unarmed, defenseless."

Another deep breath. "My advisor was no help. The school was no help. They didn't want a scandal, they didn't want to impact the school's relationship with certain government officials in Tunisia. So my thesis was approved, I got my doctorate, and here I am. And ever since then, I've never depended on anyone else—especially men—to provide me with safety and security. Never."

I looked down at the coffee table and said, "Your book. Am I right?"

She smiled, but her eyes were still like ice. "Oh, yes, the blessed book. You know, you tell someone of the hours and days and weeks and months and years that go into writing a book, and they nod at you politely and they change the subject. They don't realize the time, the slow-moving time, that goes into visiting libraries and historical societies and people's living rooms, begging and scratching for that one piece of information, the one scrap that will connect to another. No realization at all. And then you get all that information together, and you try to write your tale. Try to make sense of something, try to interpret it differently from other historians, and my God, you have to be careful, because every nut or grad student with a grudge out there is ready to pounce on you for plagiarism. Oh, yes, ready to jump on you in an instant. And then you try to write, all the while teaching blockheads and football players, going to faculty sessions, trying to kiss the right bottom, and finding minutes and hours, here and there, to get some writing in."

There was a soft thunk, as a piece of log fell in the fireplace, releasing a shower of sparks. Near the fireplace was a poker set, with a nice, long, heavy poker. I was gauging the distance between me and the fireplace as Professor Hendricks went on. "And then, after the writing, comes the rewrite. And then the rewrite again. All the while organizing your notes, your footnotes, your source materials. And when the book is sent out, the waiting begins. Days to weeks to months. Waiting to see if your years of labor are worthy of the time of some editor in New York, who is working for a corporate master that doesn't give a hoot about good history, only about making quarterly profits. And then . . . Mr. Cole, the lightning strikes. Not only will your book be published, it's going to be a big deal. A very big deal. Oh, we're not talking interviews on *Good Morning America* or *Today*, but we are talking about a good print run, good national reviews, a way to finally make my name. All coming together . . . the galleys are out, the publicity plan is devised, your future as a serious historian is secure . . . and then . . ."

I said, "A barefoot doctor, an amateur historian, comes forward and ruins everything."

Her eyes flashed at me. "Exactly! Vikings! My God, Vikings, on my shore, with my Indians, ruining everything! Can you imagine what I felt like, when that bumpkin idiot called me up from a pay phone? He said he had the proof, the proof he had been looking for, all these years, and he laughed at me. Actually laughed at me. You see, the meeting we had in my office wasn't that polite, and I practically had to throw him out. And now that he claimed he had the artifacts, he tossed it back in my face. Said something about, who was the real scientist now, hunh? Who was going to change history now, hunh?"

"So you killed him," I said.

"Oh, very good, Mr. Cole. Of course I did. I went over to his house and tried to be polite, tried to be interested, tried to get him to tell me where the artifacts were. We started out in his living room, then went into his office, all the while he was laughing and laughing at me. Finally I couldn't take it any longer, and I took care of him in his office."

"But the artifacts weren't there."

She still seemed angry. "You're so right they weren't there. I figured a clown like him would have them right at his fingertips, right there in his office. But they weren't. I searched his place, his garage, even his dirty car, and then I left, before some other local idiot showed up. But I remembered something he had told me, about his brother the antique dealer. So I went up there, figuring that part of his family might have the artifacts. No such luck."

I kept quiet, which she picked up on rather quickly. "It was you, wasn't it. You and some friend of yours, who jumped me at the antique store. Am I right?"

I nodded slowly. "I'm afraid so."

"Thought I'd recognize your voice, the minute you called me to make the appointment to see me at school. What? You think I'm a moron?"

Something came back to me and I said, "How in the hell did you get my Explorer wrecked, while I was there talking to you?"

She wiggled the pistol a bit in my direction. "Nothing finer in the world than a dumb male who needs something, Mr. Cole. This particular dumb male was a football student on a scholarship who needed a good grade. It didn't take much on my part to convince him to play with your tire. A prank, I told him, on an old school chum. I think the fool actually believed it. And I knew all about you, before you showed up. That barefoot doctor, when he called me, said that you'd be doing a story about his discovery, no doubt about it."

"You wanted me hurt, in the hospital, so you could search my house."

"Of course. But you see, it all now comes back to you, yet again. Mr. Cole, the artifacts. Are they in your car?"

"No."

"Are they in your possession?"

"No."

"But you know where they are, don't you?"

I kept silent. The cat was now stretched on its side, apparently purring.

"Mr. Cole," she said in her best professor voice. "I'm talking to you."

"Yes, you are."

"Where are the Viking artifacts?"

"I can't tell you," I said.

"You can't," she said slowly, "or you won't?"

I kept silent again. Waiting for God knows what.

She sighed. "Mr. Cole, I'm going to give you five seconds to tell me where those artifacts are. Right now."

"All right," I said. "I'll tell you."

"That's better."

"They're in a safety deposit box. In Tyler. Rented by Jon. And I've got the key."

"Where's the key?" she asked.

"In Tyler," I said. "At my home."

She smiled, nodded at me. "That's a very good answer."

And then she held the pistol with two hands.

"But," she said, "I'm afraid that's the wrong one."

And then she shot me.

CHAPTER TWENTY

My good friend Felix had been shot once, years ago, when he was much younger, and he told me of the surprise and the fear and the shock to the system, but he never told me about how damn cold he got, which happened to me after the pistol went off.

I found myself on the floor, both hands clasped tight against my lower left shin. Something wet was oozing between my fingers. There was a smell of burnt gunpowder in the air. My ears rang a bit from the sound of the gunshot. My view was of the rug and the fireplace and the legs of the coffee table. I'm sure I made some sort of noise. A groan, a whimper, something. I don't know. All I did know is that I had been shot. Something had torn at my flesh, had violated me, had caused me to bleed. Even though my fingers were warm with whatever was sliding through them, I started shivering from the cold.

The coffee table moved. Somebody knelt down next to me.

"Don't worry for now," came the soothing voice of Professor Hendricks. "That was a Ruger twenty-two I used on you. Not the nine-millimeter I used on your friend. So the damage shouldn't be that bad. I'm quite a good shot. Every week at the range, either outdoors or indoors. And the thing is, I was planning to replace the couch and the rug anyway. This will just give me more incentive. Still, I didn't like scaring the cat like that. Poor Oreo won't talk to me for a month."

My voice was weak. "Why?"

"Why? A number of ways of interpreting that question, I suppose. Why are you here? Why am I armed? Why did the fates conspire so that when I finally get my moment in the sun, some retired accountant with dirt under his fingernails and in his shoes decides it's his right to crowd me out? But I guess you want to know why I shot you. Correct?"

"Yes." I was surprised that the only thing that hurt was my shoulder, when I hit the floor. It must have hit first, though I didn't remember ending up on the floor from the couch.

Professor Hendricks came into view, staring down at me. "First, because you stabbed me, back in Porter. I figured I owed you one. But I could have overlooked that if you had brought the artifacts with you, but you didn't. So I shot you. Because you told me a damn clumsy lie, that's why. And I will not tolerate that."

Still no pain in my leg, though the shivering continued. Hendricks said, "When you first called, to ask if you could see me, you said that you were going to show me the Viking artifacts tonight. My dear boy, it's well after six p.m. Is there any bank in this entire state that is open at that hour? Is there?"

"I guess not," I said, hating how weak my voice sounded.

"True," she said. "So you started off by telling me a damn clumsy lie, and I wanted to show you that there was going to be a consequence to that lie. I will not tolerate fabrications, Mr. Cole, not at all."

She moved around and something started poking at my other leg. She said, "So this is going to be the arrangement. In the next few seconds, you're going to tell me where those artifacts are. And if I think you're lying, I'm going to shoot you in your right knee. That will shatter your kneecap, crippling you permanently. So keep that right in front of your mind as we proceed. Mr. Cole, where are the Viking artifacts?"

I tried to keep my voice even, without quivering or shaking. "You're going to kill me anyway, aren't you. So why should I tell you?"

"Tsk, tsk, that decision lies in the future. You need to focus on the present, Mr. Cole. And the present will shortly involve some additional agonizing pain for you. So." There was a poking sensation against my right knee. "Tell me where the artifacts are or you lose your right knee. Forever."

I closed my eyes and just gave up. "Tyler. They're in Tyler."

Hendricks actually laughed. "Well, with more than a hundred communities in New Hampshire, that certainly narrows it down, doesn't it? But I'm going to need better information than that, Mr. Cole. So where in the name of God are they in Tyler?"

I kept my eyes closed. My fingers were still tight against my lower shin. My shoulder still hurt and the shivering was increasing.

"At the Tyler Town Museum."

I felt something, as the pistol barrel raised itself up from my knee. "Have you seen them?"

"No."

The pistol barrel was back on my knee again. "Then how do you know that they are there?"

Eyes stayed closed. "Because . . . because the day Jon found them, he found them at a family farm in Tyler. Said he was going to put them someplace safe. Not in his house. Not in his garage. Not with his brother. Seems like the only reasonable place left . . ."

"Damn," she said, admiration in her voice. "I do believe you might be right. Tell me, Cole, where is this museum?"

"It's in Tyler . . . I don't know the name of the street . . ."

Something grabbed at my throat and I opened my eyes. Her strong left hand was grasping me. I looked up into Hendricks's face. "The address, Cole. Where the is the museum?"

"It's . . . it's near the Meetinghouse Green . . . I don't know what the street is called . . ."

Hendricks seemed to ponder that. I looked at her, pistol in her other hand. I suppose if I had been Felix, I would have done something strong, something magnificent. I would have kneed her with my good leg, snapped the pistol out of her hand, and called the police. Or something. But I was afraid to move my now-wet hands. Afraid that if I moved my hands, the bleeding would get worse. And that the real pain would soon begin.

She shook her head. "Damn it, I haven't been to Tyler since I was a student. Hated the damn place. Too much sand, too much sun. Damn."

Then she moved out of view. I heard her in the kitchen. I rolled over some, my leg still drawn up to my chest. She came back in, pistol and towels in her hands. She dropped the towels on me.

"This is what's going to happen," she said. "It's not open to negotiation. You're going to take those towels, bandage up your leg as best you can, and then we're going for a drive. Your vehicle is an automatic, correct?"

"Yes."

"Good. Mine's a standard. We're going to take a nice, leisurely drive to Tyler and that museum. And you're going to drive. Even with one bad leg. Now." She walked over and gently tapped her foot against my head. "Get to work. Now."

No choice. Stay and get shot. Or bandage my leg, get a move on, and get shot later.

Later meant opportunities.

There was no opportunity here.

I gritted my teeth and removed my hands, dripping red with my own blood, the red a striking, bright, and evil color, even though it was coming out of my own body. My lower leg felt warm, tingling, and I sat up and wiped my hands as well as I could, the hands shaking. One towel was quickly soaked and I tossed it aside, and she said, "Damn it, Cole, not on the good rug. Put it on the floor."

I said nothing, picked up the soiled towel, dropped it on the exposed hardwood floor. My hands were still shaking, and I still was cold, as I took the other towel and wrapped my leg as best I could. I took a longer, thinner towel, with bright roses and vines decorating it, and tied off the first towel. Then the throbbing started, the deep, pulsating throb which was probably the first signal from my body that something was severely wrong.

No kidding.

I wiped my hands again. She tossed over another towel, this one soaked in cold water. I wiped my hands one more time, and she nodded in satisfaction.

"Looks like you did a good job," she said. "Were you a Boy Scout when you were younger?"

"Yes," I said.

"Figures," she said. "Fascist organization. Uniforms and paramilitary and all that nonsense. All right. Get up."

I sat up against the couch, where I had been sitting peacefully a century or so ago, and levered myself up on my good leg. The throbbing was now matched with a burning sensation, running up and down my leg. Hendricks maneuvered in front of me, backing out, opening the door. She looked distressed and looked over at me and said, "Oreo."

"What?"

"The cat. It's his dinnertime. Well, he can wait. I don't think we'll be gone long. Come on."

I walked slowly, holding on to the wall for balance, trying to keep as much weight as possible on my right leg. She kept her eyes on me, the pistol firm in her grasp, and I was hating myself for being so damn weak, so damn cowed. But that pistol in her hands was magic, a piece of fabricated metal and plastic and springs that could end everything for me, with one gentle tug of the trigger.

My mouth was dry. I tried to swallow. Nothing. We were now on the outside steps. A small outside light was on, illuminating a portion of the front lawn and driveway. Otherwise it was dark, the air was sharp with the promise of winter approaching and lots of dead things piling up in the woods and along the shore, and I said, "Not too late, you know."

"How's that?" she said, now on the lawn, as if she was leading me along, which in a way she was.

"Not too late for it to end it well," I said, holding the railing tight as I went down the concrete steps.

She shook her head. "It's going to end just fine, thank you."

"But the murder and the betrayal and the—"

Hendricks snapped. "Be quiet, all right? Just hush. Now. Where are your keys?"

"Pants pocket."

"Toss them over."

I reached the bottom of the stops and I gasped out loud as my left leg took more of the weight than I anticipated. I clenched my teeth and closed my eyes, as tears welled right up, and then I tried to shake it off, taking my right hand, putting it in my right pants pocket, and pulling out my key chain. I tossed it over and it landed short, and before I could do anything, she swooped down and picked them up, with a smile on her face.

"Not bad," she said. "I figured you were trying something right there. Make me go for the keys, perhaps catch me off guard. What did you think you were going to do? Run to the woods?"

She laughed at me as she went over and opened the front door of my Explorer. She climbed in and started the engine, and then went around and sat in the passenger's seat. The passenger's door was open and the pistol was still aimed at me.

"The life of a teacher," she said. "Explaining the obvious to the clueless. Come around and climb in, and then we'll be off. All right? And you walk over here in a straight line and nothing unusual, nothing funny. Just get into your seat."

I tried to see what was going on behind those eyes and I failed. For a moment I thought about Ray Ericson, tied and bound on the couch, facing me and Felix. Did he feel like this? Did he feel as vulnerable, like a staked goat, waiting to become a meal for some ravenous lion? Was that what I did to Ray, sitting there, waiting for the hot oil to be flung on his exposed skin?

"Cole!" she shouted. "Get a move on!"

I moved as reasonably as I could, leaning in on my good leg, now reaching out and holding on to the smooth and shiny hood of the Explorer for balance. I gave a quick glance around the neighborhood, wondered if anyone would report a shooting, if I suddenly ducked down and tried to make my way to the rear of the house. Where at least it was dark, there was cover. It could work. It might work.

My left pants leg got hung up on the front license plate, and the pain nearly caused me to screech like an owl swooping in for the kill. I paused again as the burning and throbbing spiraled right up my leg and into my belly and my head, and I took some deep breaths and worked my way around to the driver's seat. No, that wasn't going to happen. No quick escape to the rear of the house. And the surrounding woods were so dark, I doubted any neighbors nearby would hear anything, even if it was the pistol shot to the back of the head that would spatter what was Lewis Cole onto the lawn and dead leaves of the surrounding trees.

Somehow I got to the front seat. I backed my way in and I yelped again as I dragged my wounded leg in and tried to ease it under the steering wheel. When Hendricks saw that I had made it inside, she closed her door and said, "All right, close the door. And I'll give you a minute to catch your breath. But only a minute. Don't take advantage of my generosity."

I tried to think of something to say and I just gave up. I closed the door and grasped the steering wheel, tried to ease my breathing. The pistol was now in my ribs. I said quietly, "I'm freezing. I need to turn on the heat."

"Go ahead."

I worked the controls and the heat started flowing about my legs and face, and even then the shivering wouldn't stop. Hendricks said, "Turn on the headlights."

I did just that.

She swiveled around and said, "All right. You can back it up, nice and slow. I'll tell you if anything's coming. Oh, and one more thing."

The pistol moved again, and I winced as she jammed it between my legs, right up to my crotch. She leaned into me and said softly, "I know how your mind works. I know how all men's minds work. Being hurt or cut or injured doesn't scare you, not at all. But this"—and she jammed in the barrel again—"losing these few miserable inches of flesh and tubing, this scares you more than anything. So this is going to be the arrangement for our delightful drive to the museum. If you flash your lights, or try to exceed the speed limit, or decide to take your chance by running us into a stone wall, just remember where my finger is. One deep pothole and if I think anything untoward is going to happen, you're going to lose something intimate of yours. I might be injured, I might go to jail, and you might survive, but imagine the rest of your life without a major piece of your plumbing. Well, you do understand, don't you?"

The engine was idling nice and even. I stared at the garage and her parked Subaru. She jabbed me again with her pistol. "Well? You do understand, don't you?"

"I do. What I don't understand is how you've gotten this far without a piece of plumbing. Something called a conscience."

She laughed in my ear. "Why, Mr. Cole. Haven't you kept up with the latest in higher education? There is no such thing as a conscience. It's just a social construct, like everything else. Who's to say nowadays what's right or what's wrong? Now. Put this vehicle in reverse, and let's get going. Back her up, nice and slow."

I shivered some more, reached up to the stick shift, and within a second or two, we were slowly moving backward. I kept view in the rearview mirror and Hendricks said, "Very nice. Dead on. Dead on. Okay. Stop. Very good. No traffic. Ease on out now."

I pulled out onto the street, stopped, and then shifted into drive. Another poke. "All right. Next stop Tyler."

For some reason the drive to Tyler brought back little bits of memories, like an incoherent slide show, flipping through my mind, with no sense of order or place. I recalled the times I had driven somewhere —to the dentist, to a job interview, to a first date—when I wanted to make the drive drag out, where I would actually pray for traffic lights or traffic jams or tree branches across the road, anything to slow my progress to whatever doom awaited me. And then I would snap back to reality, as Hendricks moved some in the seat, as the metal barrel with the potential of so much bloody destruction was pressed against me.

The road we were on passed through the campus of Phillips Exonia Academy, where signs in the middle of the road warn one to stop for pedestrians. A group of prep school students—mostly female— were striding along the crosswalk, not even bothering to see if traffic would stop for them. It was a nice demonstration either of self-confidence or assurance that nothing would hurt them, not ever, and I slowed to a stop to allow them to pass. At the end of the procession, tagging along, was a young girl, maybe sixteen or seventeen. She looked at me and gave me a quick wave of thanks, and then I think she noticed the look on my face. For she then sped up, walked quicker, as if afraid that I would step out of my Ford and go over and harm her.

The procession ended. Another jab of the pistol. "All right," Hendricks said. "The next generation is gone. Get a move on."

I sped up and within a few minutes, we were through the downtown of Exonia, and we were then on the Tyler road, about twelve or so minutes away from the museum. And as I drove, I also remembered snippets of conversation with Jon, talking about the past, talking about the future. "Look around you," he would say. "Everything around you has been trod by the feet of people who lived and loved and breathed here hundreds of years ago. You're a part of history as well, my friend. People will be thinking of you and what you did, and how you lived, years from now."

Sure, I thought. And maybe they'll be thinking of the way I'll die, and I winced as I recalled the snappy comment I had made to the funeral home director the day before. I plan to live forever. Sure. Who doesn't? But was I now getting punished for that flip comment? Truly?

A signpost. We were in Tyler, passing through farmland. Amazing that a place so close to the metropolitan colossus that was Boston could still have open land, even scant yards away from the Interstate. Amazing. And amazing, too, what my leg was doing. The throbbing had slowed to a dull ache, maybe helped along by the bandage. I don't know. I just tried to keep my left leg still and keep on driving, and try to think through what I could possibly do when we arrived at the Tyler town museum.

Now we were in a chunk of Tyler suburbia. Farmland divvied up into house lots, everyone with their American dream, their American pleasure, and I wondered if any sensitive souls in those comfortable and warm and safe homes, if they trembled a bit as we drove by, me bleeding from a bullet wound, a madwoman at my side, a pistol held against me, if they could detect just a scent of what was going on, just outside their safety zone.

The speed limit was thirty-five. I was keeping it at thirty-four, and when we went through a curve in the road, a Tyler police cruiser was parked there at the side of the road, running radar.

"Don't you dare do a thing," she said.

"Right," I said.

I drove by the police cruiser, my speed still below the limit, and Hendricks glanced back and I looked to the mirror, and damn me if that green and white police cruiser didn't pull out of its hiding spot and come out in the road, following us.

"What did you do?" she demanded, turning back to me.

"Nothing," I said. "I drove by. You saw that. I'm doing the speed limit and I didn't flash the lights or anything."

Hendricks's gaze was strong upon me, and she said, "If those blue lights come on and we get pulled over, it's over for you. You got it?"

"Got it a long time ago," I said. "And shut up, will you? I'm trying to focus on my driving."

Much to my surprise, she did shut up. The road went over a little bridge that spanned the old Boston & Maine railroad tracks, and we came to a four-way intersection and a set of lights. I looked up to the rearview mirror again. The police cruiser was still there. It had two choices. My lane, which meant it was going straight or taking a right. If that was going to be the case, then I had a quick plan. I'd slowly pump the brake lights, flashing back toward them. I'd try for an SOS if I had enough time, maybe the cop back there wouldn't recognize the Morse code, but hopefully, he'd recognize something was wrong, something was going on. And I knew what Hendricks was threatening me with but I couldn't believe she would actually open fire with a cop coming up during a traffic stop. Cops hate traffic stops, and the sound of a firearm being discharged would throw them into an automatic response, and even Hendricks should know that there would be a good chance that some police-issued bullets might be flying in her direction if she fired at me first.

The cruiser came close, my left foot was firm on the brake pedal, and—

Like I said. The cop had two choices. The lane behind me, or the lane next to me, which meant a left-hand turn to the uptown sec tion of Tyler. He took that lane and came to a full and complete stop next to me. Hendricks said, "Keep your eyes straight, Cole."

And I was thinking of what I could say, what I could do, when the light turned green and the Tyler police cruiser made a left. Hendricks laughed as I slowly made the right turn. "I guess this just isn't your day."

"Yeah," I said. "I guess so."

In the space of the next three minutes, we passed through another traffic light, made a left-hand turn by the same church where the services were held for Jon Ericson, all those days ago, and my memory came back as I made another series of turns, and came up on Meetinghouse Green. There. The Tyler town museum, lights off and quiet.

"Pull in the back," she said. "I don't want anybody to see us."

I turned in and drove around to the back. There were three windows in the painted green clapboards, a rear door leading inside, and two trash barrels. I pulled up and put the Explorer in park.

"Kill the engine," she said, "and the lights."

I did just that, and with the heater off, I quickly started getting cold again. Hendricks looked around us. Trees and high shrubbery hid us from most of the surroundings, and a utility pole at the other end of the small parking lot offered some illumination.

"This place have an alarm system?"

"Nope."

"You sure?" she asked.

"Christ, yes," I snapped. "The place pretty much is run on donations and volunteer help. Damn place will probably be shut down because you killed the best guy they had to run the place."

"When I sell the movie rights to my book," she said, and her voice sounded quite serious, "then I'll make an endowment or some damn thing. Time to get out. You first."

I undid the seat belt and opened the door, and I was able to get my injured leg outside without passing out. I leaned against the front left fender and Hendricks came around to me, pistol still in her hand. I thought the damn thing was so heavy she'd holster it or something, but she must have been operating on some crazed energy this evening.

"Let's go," she said. "Rear door."

I walked to the door, Hendricks behind me, and I tried the doorknob. Locked, of course.

"Key?" she asked.

"Not a clue."

"Hold on. Keep looking ahead. Don't move."

I kept still, my mind still racing, evaluating, thinking. What could I do once we got inside the building? Where could I hide? How could I get help?

She came up behind me, thrust a rock in my hand. "Break one of the windowpanes, and make it snappy. I want to get in there, and now."

I took the rock and, without hesitating, rapped it sharply against one of the lower windowpanes. The window snapped quickly and I reached in and undid the deadbolt and the lock. Without seeing if she wanted me to do it, I opened the door and stepped in, and Hendricks was behind me once again. Her breathing quickened, and I wondered if it was excitement, or nervousness, or both. Our feet crunched on the broken glass as we entered the museum.

She shut the door and said, "What's the layout?"

"Office and storage to the left. Display cases in the main room. That's about it."

"We'll start with the office."

She pushed me ahead, and I went into the small office—about

the size of a large closet—and she seemed to like the fact that there were no windows. We went in and she closed the door behind me and turned on a desk lamp. "Stand in the corner," she said. "And be still."

I leaned back against the door as she went through the drawers of the desk, and it was like she was talking to herself. "Four coins. Three statuettes. A grinding wheel. And an axhead. Small enough to hide but not too small to hide that well. Damn it, where did you put it?"

All of the desk drawers were opened and closed. There was a closet that she rummaged through, going through cardboard boxes and brown shopping bags. Nothing. My leg throbbed and my head hurt and my hands and feet were cold, and I was still thinking hard, still looking ahead.

She turned to me. "Nothing."

"Not my fault."

"Of course. Exhibit area next. Get a move on."

I opened the door and she turned off the light, and we made the short walk to the exhibit area. The shades were open and there was light coming in from the utility pole out by the parking lot, and Hendricks walked over —still limping, and that's when I wished I had severed an artery in her damn leg—and fussed with the shades, and then closed them. On the walls were framed proclamations, old prints, and a couple of Civil War swords. Then she switched on one bank of lights, and the glass cases and the framed works on the walls came into sharper view. There was still that musty odor of old things brought into the present, and Hendricks went around and said to me, "There's no place for them to be."

"Excuse me?"

She raised up the pistol. "This was a damn waste of time, you fool. There's nothing here."

I closed my eyes and actually laughed, which I think angered her severely. I laughed and laughed and she said, "Damn you, what's so funny?"

"You," I said. "You haven't even looked yet. And for a college professor, you know crap about hiding things. You forget your Poe."

"My what?"

"Your Edgar Allan Poe. 'The Case of the Purloined Letter.' How best to hide something?"

"You . . . oh. Oh, my."

And she went up and down the glass cases, like a dog sniffing for a hidden treat, and then she gasped and held a hand to her face. "Oh, there they are. Just like that fool said. Right here. Oh, look at that, will you."

Hendricks looked over at me. "Here they are. In a display case for Native American artifacts. Like he was making one last joke. Hunh. I guess the laugh is on him again, right?"

I said nothing.

She raised her pistol. "Well, time to use this again."

CHAPTER TWENTY-ONE

She turned the pistol around in her hand, and brought the base of the grip down on the glass case. The case shuddered. She brought the pistol up again, and down again, harder, and the glass top shattered.

I said, "Is that the approved way of excavating a site? Breaking your way through?"

She peered into the display case. "Why? Were you hiding a key or something?"

"No, I wasn't."

Hendricks reached in with her free hand and then said, "Ouch!" and drew her hand out. "Cut myself on the glass. Damn it!"

She shook her hand and said, "Come on. Make yourself useful. Get over here and get this stuff out of the case."

I looked around me, at the paltry little collection of display cases, of the history that they were preserving for the future, and I thought I was in the presence of an ancient Goth or Vandal, working her way through the streets of Rome, shattering and destroying anything she didn't want or need. I limped over and she backed away, pistol still in my direction, and then I had my first glance at what Jon had been fighting to find, all these years, and which caused his death and so much heartache.

Among the broken glass and a leather belt with beadwork and a collection of stone arrowheads and some pottery shards were four coins, lined right up in a neat row. Behind the coins were three little statues, maybe three or four inches tall, carved from stone and showing faces that were bearded and definitely not Indian. To one side of the statuettes was a round stone that I remembered was used as a grinding stone, and to the other side was a rusty triangle of metal. Despite all that had gone on and what was about to go on, I felt so proud of Jon. Good job, my friend, I thought. You really did it. Good job.

"Stop wasting my time," she said. "Get in there and get them out."

I gingerly reached into the top of the broken display case, picked up each metal coin and laid them down on an adjacent glass case with its top still unbroken. Hendricks looked down and examined each one of them with a close eye, looking through her glasses. "Hmmm. Without a doubt. Norse coins, at least a thousand years old."

Next came each little statue, which I stood up next to the coins. Hendricks tone softened a bit, as she said, "See these statues? Probably a religious significance. Perhaps a saint, perhaps an old god, like Odin or Thor. The Norse at that time were Christian, but they still held on to their old beliefs, their old rituals. The church at the time just grafted on their own set of beliefs onto the old ones."

"What are you going to do with this?"

"Do? Young man, I intend to take them home and take a blowtorch to the coins, break up the statues, and drop the grinding stone and axehead in the middle of the ocean. Do you think I'm going to allow these . . . these pieces of pollution to ruin everything?"

"Some professor," I said. "Joining the ranks of the fools who burned down the library at Alexandria, blew up the Parthenon, and destroyed those statues of Buddha because they were an affront to Islam."

"Yes," she said sharply in return. "Some professor, ensuring that the right history gets noticed, the correct history gets the attention it deserves. Now, come along. You're almost done."

Sure, I thought. Almost done.

I reached in with both hands and winced as I scraped one wrist against a piece of broken glass, and then picked up the grinding stone. It was heavy and I let it drop some on the top of the glass case. The vibration caused the three statues to topple over, Hendricks looking at them for a moment, and that's when I went back into the case, grabbed the axehead and took it out and slammed it against her face.

I think I broke her nose. I wasn't sure.

But I was sure as she howled and fell back that I broke her glasses.

And I wasn't going to stick around to find out any more than that. I dropped to the floor and rolled under the display cases, coming up against the near wall. Hendricks whipped around, looked for me, just as I crawled along the base of the wall, gritting my teeth against the pain in my left leg, and I reached up and switched off the lights.

And waited. Breathing in the darkness, trying to keep my mouth up against a coat sleeve, to muffle the noise.

"Cole? You little piece of nothing. I'm going to put a whole clip into you. Just you wait."

No glasses, I thought. She has no glasses. And she told me before she had bad eyesight. I moved again and there was an ear-splitting bang as she shot at the wall, about five feet away from me. Voices inside of me were screaming to get up and make a run for it, and I told those voices to shut up. I had two choices. Front door or rear door. Which way?

"Cole . . . damn it, you broke my nose, Shit! It's bleeding. If you think you're getting away . . ."

Back door was open. But it was on the other side of the building, and I'd have to pass close to her. And even if she was half blind with her glasses gone, I was sure she'd see me making my way over there.

And the front door was right here.

But it was locked. And trying to undo the locks would make noise. A lot of noise in this quiet building.

I reached up with my hands, against the wall, trying to remember what was there, and my hand grabbed onto something metallic. I felt the curved shape and lifted it off the wall and sat back down again.

A sword. Sure. What could be said about a writer who brought a sword to a gunfight? "Cole, it's just a matter of time."

Another explosion of a gunshot, and in the reveberations of that report, I drew the sword out of scabbard.

There.

In the dim illumination from the outside, I could see Hendricks moving down the line of display cases. It looked like she was heading in the direction of the short corridor that led to the office and to the rear parking lot.

Now.

243

I tossed the scabbard in that direction, and Hendricks turned to the sound of the noise as it fell on the floor and fired again, and I got up, sword in hand, and made the three or four steps to the door. Hendricks was shouting something, was moving back there, and the hysterical voice inside my head said, work the locks, work the locks, ignore what was going on out there, and I undid a deadbolt, an interior lock, and all praise to the gods of history, I got the door unlocked.

I threw the door open and was immediately rewarded by more light than I needed, and damn it, I was now silhouetted. I ducked and moved through the door, followed by another snappy gunshot from Hendricks, and I saw the lawn back there, and a distant line of trees, and I started moving as fast as I could, using the sword as a cane, to relieve the thumping pain in my left leg, the treeline calling to me as a place of sanctuary.

How long could it take to get to the treeline before the half-blind and fully mad professor behind me could shoot again?

Pretty damn long.

I hadn't gone more than a half-dozen feet when I heard the screech of her voice behind me, another gunshot, and I turned and tripped and fell right on my ass.

Hendricks was there, running at me.

Running right straight at me.

Still shouting.

But she was looking over me. She was looking across the field.

No eyeglasses. Not much vision.

She kept running right at me, and when she got close enough, I came up, the sword held tight and firm in both hands, and caught her in the belly.

There was no yell. No scream. Just a muffled groan as her headlong run continued, the sword torn from my grasp, and she faltered, turned, weaved back and forth, and then fell to the ground, hands clasped to her front. And a quick thought came to me: this was the second time I had struck this woman with a cutting instrument, and I certainly wished I had done a more thorough job the first time. I was also pretty sure the sword was out of her by then, but I had a more important thing to think about. I started crawling over to the grass, and then she said something to me, a fierce whisper I couldn't make out. There. Just barely visible in the glare from the streetlight.

The pistol, nestled in the grass.

And about a foot away from her hand.

"You," she said. "Damn you."

Her hand flailed about, just barely missing the pistol, and I slid forward over the grass, grimacing at the pain in my leg. There. Right there. In the cool and damp grass, the pistol was in my hands, and as I started picking it up, a voice called out, "You there, drop it!"

A light came on, and then another, and I dropped the pistol and sat up. Some harsh breathing behind me from Professor Hendricks. Two men approached, the lights from a parked vehicle illuminating them both, and they got closer and a familiar voice said, "Mr. Cole?"

I held up a hand against the bright lights. "Frank Duffy? Is that you?"

"Um, no, it's Tom, but yeah, it's me and my cousin."

They came forward, almost at a crouch, holding their own pistols out in a two-handed combat stance, and Tom said, "You okay?"

"Considering, yeah, I'm fine."

"That woman dead?"

"I don't know. I—Guys, what in the hell are you doing here?"

Tom said, "Frank, go check on the broad." He knelt down and said, "We talked to Felix this morning. He was trying to get himself out of jail, up in Maine, he said we should take a more active role in your protection. Said we should follow you, make sure you didn't get in any trouble."

"Any trouble . . . Shit, Tom, no offense, but that crazy woman over there shot me in the leg a while ago, and was trying to do the same to my head. Where in the hell have you been?"

Tom said sheepishly, "Sorry. We got lost following you out of Exonia, after you went to her house. It was Frank's fault, he was driving. And man, we didn't hear anything coming from the house. How were we supposed to know what happened?"

Frank called out, "She's still breathing, but man, she's bleeding something awful. Did you get her with that sword, Mr. Cole?"

"Yeah, I did."

"Jesus," Frank said. "And besides, it was your fault we got lost, you were distracting me."

I rubbed at my face with both hands. "Got lost . . . Okay, you guys should get lost again. And quick. Get the hell out of here and call the cops. Use a phone booth or something, say you heard gunshots at the Tyler town museum. Okay?"

Frank came back to join his cousin. "Sure, Mr. Cole, sorry we screwed up. Look, can I ask you a question?"

"A quick one."

Frank turned to his cousin and then looked at me. "You're not going to tell Felix what we did, are you?"

"Guys, get moving. All right? Get the hell out of here, and make that call."

They did just that, returning to their van, and then pulling away. It was quiet again. I heard Hendricks moaning and breathing behind me, and I thought about what she had said earlier, about sneering about my time as a Boy Scout. I guess a true and honorable Boy Scout would go over there and provide first aid, but I hadn't been a Boy Scout in quite a long, long time. So I sat there and listened to her sounds, thought about Jon and what had happened, and I lowered my head and tears came to my eyes, and they wouldn't stop, until I heard the far-off and quite welcome wail of the sirens.

About a half hour later, I was back in Exonia again, at their fine hospital, on a padded examining table in their emergency room. The brisk and efficient firefighter-EMTs from the Tyler Fire Department had transported me here a while ago, and it was a great comfort to be safe and secure in the rear of the ambulance as we made our way west. In this part of the emergency room, curtains had been drawn around, to offer some privacy, and an ER doctor and nurse worked on my leg, murmuring to each other. A painkiller of sorts had been injected into my leg and it felt like a wooden log from the knee down, and I could sense things being cleaned, moved about, and stitched.

Joining the medical team working on my leg but ignoring what they were doing was Diane Woods, who had a metal clipboard in her hands, taking notes, keeping her face impassive.

I said, "Look. I had no idea the crazy professor was involved in Jon Ericson's murder. All right? I thought it was Brian Mulligan, the previous head of the museum. I just went to the professor's place to ask for her help in verifying the Viking artifacts that Jon discovered.

That's all. And if the artifacts were the real deal, then I was going to go to you and give it all up. Honest."

"Unh-hunh," Diane said, in a tone she usually reserves for drunken suspects who claim that the voices in their heads made them rob the convenience store. "Really?"

"Really."

"All right, then tell me again what happened."

And I did that, while the work went on on my leg, as there was the sound of objects being moved around on a tray, the gentle snip of thread being cut. There were now tugging sensations at the bottom of my leg, and I still had no interest in seeing what was going on.

Diane said, "Okay. So you saw her limping. And that caught your attention because of another little adventure you didn't tell me about, when you and Felix broke into that antique store. I think there's a detective in Porter who might want to talk to you when I'm finished."

"He can take a number then. Yeah, that's what happened. I saw the professor limping and looked at her book, and decided I wanted to get the hell out of there. She had other plans, and that's when she took out her Ruger .22."

Diane stopped writing and looked at me, her face no longer impassive, her eyes filling up with tears. "Enough questions for now. How are you doing?"

"I'm doing okay. I'm alive."

She reached over and brushed some hair off my forehead. "You're alive, but you're also in shock. The next few weeks will be rugged ones, Lewis. My interview with you is going to be followed by an interview with a New Hampshire State Police detective, a detective from the Maine State Police, and somebody from the attorney general's office. And speaking of attorneys, you might want to think about getting that Massachusetts attorney lined up. Professor Hendricks isn't very happy with you."

"A sentiment I share with her," I said. "Where is she?"

"On the other side of the ER, handcuffed, and I think she's going up to surgery in a few minutes. She's claiming a lot of wild stuff, that you had kidnapped her, brought her to the museum against her will, that she shot you in self-defense, and that you viciously stabbed her without any reason whatsoever."

"You've got to be kidding me."

"Nope." She slapped shut the metal cover to the clipboard and then bent down to kiss my forehead. "Don't worry, friend, it won't stick. She shot you with a twenty-two and we recovered a nine-millimeter pistol from the lawn outside the town museum. Two separate firearms, both belonging to her. And I have a very good feeling that when we run ballistics on the nine-millimeter, we're going to find out it matches the one used on your buddy."

"Thanks."

She shook her head. "Want me to hang out for a while?"

"If you'd like."

"I would like that," she said, now holding my hand. "Oh, one more thing."

"What's that?"

She suddenly squeezed my hand so hard it hurt and leaned into me, so I guess the doctor and the nurse on the other end of the bed couldn't hear so well.

"Don't you ever pull a series of stunts like that ever again," Diane whispered. "You understand? Besides whatever nonsense came my way during this little fiasco, I . . . I don't like seeing you get hurt. Okay? So leave it to the professionals. Do I make myself clear?"

I tried to squeeze back with my hand, but Diane was too strong. So instead I said, "Yes, perfectly clear, detective."

Then she smiled. "Wrong."

"What do you mean . . . oh." I smiled up at my dear friend. "I get it. Yes, perfectly clear, detective sergeant."

She let my hand loose. "There. That's better."

After a while of poking and prodding, the ER doctor—who had an Italian name of about twenty syllables, which I instantly forgot—said, "Your leg will be fine, Mr. Cole. It'll be weak for a while and we'll give you some exercise suggestions before you're discharged. We're going to keep you overnight, just to make sure the wound drains properly. You were very lucky. The bullet went through-and-through, and the damage to the muscle and the tissue was minimal."

Then Diane gave me another kiss on the forehead and left. I was then wheeled out of the ER, and I was thankful that I didn't have to go past the curtained area where Professor Hendricks was being worked on, and was loudly proclaiming her innocence to all concerned.

Later, in my room, I got two visitors. The first was Paula Quinn, who came in, bearing flowers and a balloon, and big kiss to my lips. Tears were in her eyes as well, and she pulled up a chair and said, "You . . . damn it, Lewis, what in hell were you doing?"

I smiled at her, my leg stretched out before me, it still feeling like a wooden log. "You really want to know?"

"Yes, I do," she said. "And don't worry, my notebook is in my purse. When and if Rollie wants to know what happened from your point of view, I'll tell him you're in a coma or something."

"Every day?"

Paula said, "Every day, until Rollie forgets all about it. Look, tell me, will you?"

So I told her, from start to finish, keeping it simple and to the point, not going into much detail. She wiggled her nose at me a couple of times and said, "A college professor . . . holy Christ, Lewis, a college professor."

"Sure," I said. "And if you poke around a few more rooms in this joint, you might just find her. Get the story from her point of view."

Paula folded her arms and put her feet up on the edge of the bed. "Why?"

"Why?" I scratched at the back of my hand, where an IV tube was running in. "You know . . . right now, I'm not sure. I guess I started out trying to find out why Jon was killed, and who did it. And toward the end . . . well, it just spun out of control. Strange, right?"

She shook her head. "No, not knowing you. You have some wonderful traits, Lewis, loyalty being one of them. I'm just surprised it took this long for you to get shot."

"Thanks," I said. "I think."

She reached over and rubbed me on my shoulder. "How long will you be here?"

"Just the night."

She said, "That's good. You belong home."

"That I do."

So we talked for a while, about politics in Tyler, about how the story she wrote about the destruction of the Donald Burnett house had ticked off most of the selectmen, and how she didn't care one way or the other. We laughed a few times and then she got up and kissed me on the cheek.

"Time for me to head out," she said.

"Sure you don't want to stay for whatever they serve for dinner here?"

Paula shook her head, a bit too quick. "No, I'm sorry, I'm going to—"

"Have dinner with the town counsel. Correct?"

"That's right."

"I guess the two of you are doing okay," I said. "Even with your dream house being turned into scrap lumber."

"It happened," she said. "And . . . you know, after it happened, I remembered something your friend Jon said, months ago."

"Jon? About what?"

She stood up, put her purse over her shoulder. "He was giving a talk at the Rotary Club. Nothing about Vikings this time, just a straight talk about the early history of Tyler. And at the end, I don't know, he seemed to be in an odd mood, he said something about not letting history have a death grip on your throat. Or your soul. He said history should be honored and should be respected, but when you let the past rule your life, then you end up with places like the Balkans, or Northern Ireland, or the Middle East. Where ancient feuds and deeds still rule the ground. I thought about that some, the day the house came down. I had to make a choice, whether to let that old house ruin what might be between me and Mark."

She fiddled a bit with the flowers on the windowsill. "There're possibilities there, Lewis. Possibilities I want to explore. And we're working through things and I don't want to let the past control me. Okay?"

"That's fine. You go on, now. Before he wonders where you are."

She smiled and left the room, gave me a wave, which I returned, IV-attached hand and all.

Dinner was a chicken dish that was actually fairly good, and I settled back into the routine of being in the hospital. The stiff bed, the clean sheets and blankets, the constant mutter of voices and people walking by. The nursing staff was cheerful and efficient, and I half-watched the television, my leg starting to throb, and I refused to think of any-thing that had happened last hour, last day, last week.

There was an announcement that visiting hours were coming to a close, and I shifted my leg, trying to find a place that didn't hurt as much, when somebody came in with a smile and said, "Hey, welcome to the club."

I couldn't believe what I saw. Felix Tinios, well dressed and grinning, was shaking my hand, his other hand still bandaged from the burn he had received when we had gone a-visiting to Ray Ericson. "Club?" I asked. "What club is that?"

He took the chair vacated by Paula and said, "The club of those on the receiving end of speeding bullets. That's when it comes to you, that you're not quite Superman. That you're not as fast as a speeding bullet, nor as strong. Where were you hit?"

"Lower shin."

"With what?"

"Twenty-two long rifle, I think. Went in the front and right out the back. Doc says I'll be out tomorrow."

Felix nodded. "I'll pick you up then, get your ass home. What happened?"

So I told the story for the third time that evening—Diane, Paula, and now Felix—and when I was through, I said, "And excuse me for changing the subject, but what in hell are you doing here?"

He looked hurt. "That's not a very nice thing to say."

"You know what I mean. When I got out of court yesterday, your lawyer wasn't sure how many days it would take for you to get out. I didn't think it would take just one."

He leaned back in the chair, one big hand behind his head, the bandaged one in his lap. "Thing is, Lewis, I went to the bank."

"What bank is that?"

"First National Bank of Felix Tinios," he said. "Best bank there is."

I thought for a second and said, "I guess this bank doesn't have much in the way of funds but has a lot in the way of information."

"Exactly, my injured friend. You see, in all my years of work, here and there, I've come across interesting bits of information about certain events. I suppose I should have done my good civic duty and reported them to the proper authorities but . . . see, I never got around to it. And when I was in serious discussions with the attorney general's offices of both Maine and New Hampshire, I decided it was time. I offered them some very interesting information which led to certain arrangements. I won't bore you with the details. Let's just say any and all charges against you have been dropped. I might have a couple of court dates ahead of me, but nothing to worry about. Oh. And I decided to clean up one more loose item."

I don't know if it was the painkillers or just the soothing tone of Felix's voice, but I was definitely beginning to feel better. "Seems like you've already had a busy day. What else, then?"

"Ray Ericson."

"Oh."

"C'mon, don't get all mushy about it, Lewis. I came to him and worked out a deal. He'll stay out of your way, he forgets about doing anything to you in return, and I've set him up someplace where he can get suntanned and meet interesting women."

"St. Pete?"

"The same." The smile on his face was quite wide and said, "Yeah, a hell of a day. Anything else you need?"

I said, "Hate to do this to you, Felix, but yeah, there's one more thing you can do for me."

"Not to worry. You're an injured lad, and I take pity on injured lads. Go ahead. What else do you want?"

I told him. He pondered it for a moment and said, "Yeah. Doable. Tomorrow morning okay?"

"That will be fine."

He let his chair fall forward with a bang. "I've got to get going on it. And then, Lewis, let's stop worrying about favors for friends and deceased friends. All right?"

"I'll try."

The last thing he said as he left was "The hell you will."

The night went all right, fitful and passing with naps and long dozes, and after a breakfast of a cheese omelet and coffee and toast, Felix came back, looking tired, and bringing along a very unhappy Brian Mulligan. Felix said to me, "He was a reluctant cuss at first, but here he is. As promised."

Brian stood there, glowering like a student brought before his high school principal. Both hands were in the pockets of his coat.

I said, "How did you convince him to come along?"

Felix just smiled. "I made him an offer he couldn't refuse." He laughed and headed out the door, and said, "Jesus, I love saying that line. Look, I'll be outside, in case you need anything."

Felix stepped out and I said to Brian, "This won't take long."

"Good."

"You weren't straight with me up in North Conway."

He shrugged. "So?"

"So why didn't you tell me that the Russells had contacted you about their artifacts? And that you had given them Jon's name?"

Brian said, "You're a smart fella. I'm sure you can figure it out."

"That's what I've been doing, all night. I guess maybe you gave the Russells the name of Jon as a joke. All the grief and heartache he caused you, maybe you thought you'd get a little bit of revenge, get Jon all spun up about possible artifacts, and then see him get disappointed again. A good guess?"

He said, "Yeah. Not a bad guess at all. Only thing I got wrong was that the artifacts were real. That's what the papers said today."

I moved some and winced as a bolt of pain rippled up my leg. "But after he was killed? What was the difference then? Why keep it a secret? Why not tell me? Or the cops?"

The glowering look in his face returned, and he spat out the words. "Why? I'll tell you why. That damn fool chased me out of town and my home because of his dreams about those damn Vikings. That's why! And do you think I was going to give him the satisfaction of being right? Even from the grave? To have the people in Tyler talk about him, years from now, as being a guy who eventually was right about the history of Tyler? Him and not me? The hell I would." His face was red and his lips trembled. "The hell I would."

I lay there and suddenly wanted him gone. "You can leave, now."

He looked defiant. "Suppose I don't? Suppose I want to stay here and give you a piece of my mind?"

"Then I'll ask the large gentleman standing outside to come in and assist you."

He stared at me, called me a variety of names, and then left. After a bit, Felix came in, sat next to me.

"So," he said. "Got what you needed?"

"I suppose I did. Where's Brian?"

"Gave him cab fare, bus fare. I imagine he'll be home by tonight." Felix looked at my leg. "You ready to head home?"

"In a few hours, I'm told."

"Good, I'll stick around."

"That would be nice," I said.

He pulled his chair closer to me and said, "How are you doing?"

"Me? I'm doing all right."

He shook his head, patted me on the shoulder, an usual gesture from someone like Felix. "Maybe so, but listen to your Uncle Felix. You're still high on survival and painkillers. You'll go home today and you'll be so happy and energetic, you think you'll have enough energy to run the Boston Marathon. But soon enough, you're going to crash, and you're going to crash hard. You've been shot, my friend, you've been violated in a very obscene way. And when you realize that, that old black dog of depression is going to jump on your back and sink its claws into you. Remember that."

"I will."

Felix sighed, sat back in the chair. "No, you won't. But when that black dog comes visiting, give me a call. I'll get you out."

"You will?"

"I will."

"Thanks," I said.

"Don't mention it," Felix said.

"I'll try not to," I said, and then we both changed the subject, and talked about the World Series and Halloween and what kind of winter we might have, all the time up to when the nice people from the hospital came to my room and sent me on my way.

CHAPTER TWENTY-TWO

The day of the accident, I found myself thinking not only of what Felix had told me, but one of the stories Jon had passed along during the short time I had known him. "History doesn't just live in books and old documents," he had said one night over beers. "It lives around us. Just look at what's about you, and look at it through their eyes. Not your eyes."

Sure. I had thought about that during the nights I had been home alone, in my old house. I thought of all the ghosts that had lived in these timbers, wondered about their lives and their deaths, and I guess I was focused on the death aspect, for as Felix had predicted, the dark dog was now square on my back, jaws and paws firmly clenched. I was still limping some, the stitches pulling and tugging, and the days were long and dark, filled with reading books I didn't care to read, and watching television I didn't want to see. The nights had been restless ones, filled with dreams where an old determined lady with a pistol was a better or a quicker shot. Those usually woke me up, breathing hard, the sheets soaked through with sweat. There had been phone calls here and there from my friends, checking up on me, but no visitors came, none at all. For the past several days it had been just me, alone, wounded and in my old house.

The accident wasn't much. I was washing the dishes from a

meager lunch, and a slippery drinking glass flew out of my hand and to the floor. The glass shattered into pieces that seemed to fly into every corner of the kitchen, and in cleaning up the mess, I twice banged my wounded leg on a table—leading to some quite colorful and profane language—and once got a shard of glass stuck in my skin, a shard the size of a rice grain, and it hurt like hell. And when the broken glass had been swept up and put into a paper bag, I opened up the counter under the sink, noted that the trash can there was overflowing. Time for a dump run today, and if I was lucky, I'd get rained on while unloading my car. I looked out my kitchen window, at the gathering storm clouds, and wished it was summer. If it was summer, I could open the window and in a very non-PC way, just toss the damn bag out there.

Why not? I was sure that the people who had lived here once had—

Once had done what?

Well.

I'll be damned.

I carefully put the broken glass on top of the trash, and then hobbled out to the front door, where my homemade archaeological gear was waiting. I picked up the bucket and spoon and colander, and went outside, not even bothering with a coat, though I started shivering by the time I had rounded the house and was on the rocky shoreline. Near the support timbers of my outside deck, I stretched out on the rocks and dirt, gauged the distance underneath my kitchen window, and started to dig.

And it didn't take long. By God and by Jon, it didn't take long.

After just a handful of minutes, I uncovered a brown piece of glass. And another. And then the neck to an old bottle, a light, translucent green. I lined all of the pieces up on a large flat stone, and continued to dig, ignoring the pain in my leg, ignoring the shivering in my arms and legs. Then pieces of pottery came up, some of them glazed white and with blue flowers on them. Then two old clay pipes, their stems broken, and my hands were shaking and I was breathing with excitement. Was this it, I thought, as I widened the hole, was this how it was like, Jon, just over a week ago, when you finally held those Viking treasures in your hands? After all those years of dreaming and waiting and digging? This sweet taste of joy and victory in your mouth, the weight of the old treasure in your hands? Was this what it was like?

The digging went on for a while longer, until raindrops started splattering the back of my hand, and then there was an odd scrape as my spoon struck metal. I dug around and at first thought I had found a coin, but the object didn't seem to be the right size or shape. I made careful scrapings around the round piece of metal, and then popped it out. I held it my hands and gently rubbed the dirt free, using some of my own saliva, and then it was exposed. A metal button, with an eagle and U.S. inscribed in the center.

An old army uniform button, from when this place had been home to a coastal artillery unit.

I carefully put the button in my pocket, winced again as I stood up, and I got into the house before the heavy rain started.

But I didn't let the rain hold me back. I had a place to go.

Back at the High Street Cemetery I went, driving slow through the narrow lanes, and it was easy to spot the fresh grave. The dirt still looked fresh and the headstone looked new and shiny. I got out of my Explorer and slowly limped across the slick grass to Jon's final resting place, and I stood there in the cold and the rain, just looking at the simple headstone, with his name and his birth and death dates inscribed.

I wondered what to say over the grave and over the dirt, and all I could say was, "Good job, Jon. You did it. You really did it."

And then I took the old army button, placed it gently on top of his headstone, and went home.

At home the October rains were coming down, even heavier than before, and I was in my office, staring at the computer screen, knowing I had exactly twelve hours to put together a column for *Shoreline* magazine, and knowing I had exactly squat. My fingers seemed fat and numb over the keyboard, and as I wrote, erased, and wrote again, for some reason, the telephone next to my computer seemed to be beckoning to me.

And I remembered the earlier invitation. Call. Anytime.

And I remembered, too, what Paula had said. About sometimes leaving the past behind.

I picked up the phone, looked at something on my cluttered desk, and dialed the number. It was answered on the third ring.

"Hello?"

I cleared my throat. "Annie Wynn, ex-au pair and law student?"

The laughter in her voice was nice. "That's right. Who's this?"

"Lewis Cole, from Tyler Beach."

"Oh, of course. How are you, Lewis?"

"I'm hanging in there. And you?"

"The same."

I looked outside at the rain and said, "This may sound forward, Annie, but would you like to have dinner with me tonight?"

Not a hesitation. "That would be lovely."

"Great," I said. "Now this is the part where I'm going to get myself into trouble, because I have a request."

"A request? Sure."

"Would you mind driving up to Tyler to meet me?"

She laughed again. "You better have a good excuse."

I looked down at my leg, stretched out to one side. "Does a bullet wound to one's leg count as a good excuse?"

"Sure does," she said. "Just so long as you're not lying."

"I'm not."

Annie said, "I might demand an on-site inspection, when I get there."

"And you'll get it."

And after a few more cheerful moments of conversation, I hung up the phone and looked around my office, and the old timbers holding up my house, and then outside, at the cloudy day.

I had a good feeling the rain wasn't going to last long.